D1557082

Trust
Finding Anna Book 4

By
Sherri Hayes

TWCS
PUBLISHING HOUSE

First published by The Writer's Coffee Shop, 2014

The Writer's Coffee Shop
(Australia) PO Box 447 Cherrybrook NSW 2126
(USA) PO Box 2116 Waxahachie TX 75168

Paperback ISBN- 978-1-61213-222-8
E-book ISBN- 978-1-61213-223-5

A CIP catalogue record for this book is available from the US Congress Library.

Cover image by: © depositphotos.com / George Mayer
Cover design by: Jennifer McGuire

www.thewriterscoffeeshop.com/shayes

About the Author

Sherri spent most of her childhood detesting English class. It was one of her least favorite subjects because she never seemed to fit into the standard mold. She wasn't good at spelling, or following grammar rules, and outlines made her head spin. For that reason, Sherri never imagined becoming an author.

At the age of thirty, all of that changed. After getting frustrated with the direction a television show was taking two of its characters, Sherri decided to try her hand at writing an alternate ending, and give the characters their happily ever after. By the time the story finished, it was one of the top ten read stories on the site, and her readers were encouraging her to write more.

Seven years later, Sherri is the author of seven full-length novels, and one short story. Writing has become a creative outlet for Sherri that allows her to explore a wide range of emotions, while having fun taking her characters through all the twists and turns she can create.

Dedication

I'm dedicating this book to my street team. They share their love for this series almost daily. Thank you all.

Acknowledgments

A huge thank you goes out to my readers. I was having difficulty coming up with a title for this book, and they came through for me. I ran a contest on my blog asking for title suggestions and after receiving over one hundred entries, the title of *Trust* was chosen. It was submitted by Betti Gefecht of Germany. Thank you to all that participated and a special thank you to Betti.

I can't forget to thank my beta reader. I don't know how I would have gotten through writing this story without her. *Trust* is my longest book to date and it was a challenge to write. She pushed, and pulled, and nudged me through. Thank you!

Another huge thank you goes out to Mack. He has been my Dom advisor for the last two books, but on this one he ended up being a lot more than that. In addition to being a Dom, he is also an ex-cop. We went back and forth on several things throughout this story to make sure they were accurate and believable. Thank you, Mack.

Also, I need to thank my editors: Wyndy, Michele, and Andrea. They have all been huge fans of this series, and have supported me throughout. Like everyone else, they were waiting with bated breath to get their hands on this book. Thank you for everything you do ladies.

This book contains conversations, flashbacks, and various other items regarding abuse that may be disturbing to some readers.

Chapter 1

Cal

If I kept this up, I was going to need to replace the flooring in my living room before the year was out. I stopped my pacing and glanced up at the closed bedroom door, then out the large window that framed my backyard. To say I was worried was an understatement. I wanted to punch something. Or maybe *someone* was more accurate. Unfortunately, I didn't know who to focus my anger on at the moment.

The first person to come to mind was Stephan Coleman. He'd made Anna depend on him, need him, and now she was completely lost. She was worse now than that first time I'd seen her. For the last two months, she'd barely left her room. At first, even getting her to eat had been a challenge, but with Jade's help, we'd gotten her to eat something, even if only a bowl of soup or some toast. She was wasting away in that room without him, and there didn't appear to be a damn thing I could do about it.

So much had changed about Anna. She was no longer the girl I'd known when I was a kid—when we were both kids. Anna rarely smiled anymore. She was never playful or teasing. I missed that. I missed the girl I used to know.

"Aaaah!" Anna screeched as she tried to run away from the frog I had in my hand. Worms she had no problem with, but for some reason frogs scared her to death. "Stop it, Cal, or I'm going to tell."

I laughed and continued to chase her down toward the creek. We'd been heading there anyway, but I'd gotten sidetracked when I noticed a frog right off the path.

Our fun came to an abrupt stop when we came to the clearing and realized someone else was already there. Jesse was my age, and for some reason, he'd taken to picking on Anna. My dad said it was because he liked her, but I didn't like it, and neither did she.

Taking hold of Anna's arm and pulling her behind me, I stepped forward, protective.

Slamming my fist down on a large wooden beam alongside the window, I took a deep breath and let it out slowly. If only things were as simple now as they had been then. As much as I wanted to blame Coleman, what was going on with Anna wasn't entirely his fault. No. There was plenty of blame to go around there, starting with her father, John. It was hard for me to believe after knowing him all my life, but there it was.

I'd seen John twice since he'd been arrested after trying to kidnap Anna. Both times he had tried to plead his case to me. He wanted to see Anna, and he wanted my help to make that happen. For some reason, he was still under the delusion that I was on his side. I wasn't. If there was one thing Coleman and I agreed on, it was that Anna needed to be kept as far away from her father as possible. Jonathan Reeves had done enough damage. He didn't need the opportunity to do any more.

The door to Brianna's bedroom opened, and Jade stepped out. She glanced up at me and turned to take the dishes into the kitchen. I noticed they were empty. That was good. At least Brianna had eaten something this morning.

Following her, I stayed off to the side, leaning against the counter. Jade had been great. Better than I could have ever asked her to be. She'd practically moved in since Anna arrived. It wasn't something we'd ever discussed. Jade had her place, and I had mine. We were both busy, and that worked for both of us. After my first attempt to console Anna, however, her presence had become a necessity. Jade could interact with Anna in a way I couldn't. Touching Anna in any way was off-limits when it came to me. Every time I tried to hug her or hold her hand, she would cringe away as if I'd touched her with a hot branding iron. It nearly killed me to know she'd been abused and to see how badly it had affected her even in regards to a simple gesture. That didn't happen with Jade. Anna accepted her comfort, even though she typically remained rigid during the exchange. I wanted to do more for Anna. I just had to figure out how best to help her, and in a way that she would accept.

"I'm worried about her."

My gaze found Jade's as she turned to face me. How she put up with all of this boggled my mind, but it made me love her even more. "I am, too. I don't know how to fix it, though. She won't let me near her."

Jade crossed the short distance and wrapped her arms around my waist. I pulled her closer so that her breasts were pressed up against my chest. "She misses him."

I sighed. "I know."

This was one of the few places where Jade and I disagreed. She was firmly in Coleman's corner. I, however, was not, and she knew it.

"Maybe we could—"

"No." I stepped back and released her. The last thing I wanted was to fight over this again.

"Cal, you don't understand."

"What is it I don't understand, Jade?" Trying to keep my voice down so

Anna couldn't hear it, I moved closer until there were only a few feet between us.

"She loves him."

"That's not love. That's dependence. There's a difference."

Jade shook her head. "How can you say that?"

"Easy." Pointing to the closed bedroom door, I drove my point home. I knew a thing or two about dependence. Feeling like there was no choice. Anna had a choice, and I was going to make sure, one way or another, that she knew it. "Look at her. She can barely function now that he's not around. I don't think it gets any clearer than that."

"You are so stubborn. What is it you have against Stephan that you can't see that, on top of everything else, Anna is suffering from a broken heart? Maybe it's different for guys. Maybe you don't deal with it the same way. But it's not uncommon for a female to lock herself away from the world for a week and bury herself in a tub of ice cream."

"A week?" I turned away from her again, marching back to the window, wishing the twisting in my gut would stop. "I could've handled a week. She's been like this since she got here."

"It's different."

I glanced over my shoulder, meeting her gaze. "Of course it is. And it's his fault."

She tilted her head back, looking up at the ceiling, and sighed. I got the feeling I'd be sleeping on the couch again after this conversation. "Usually when you break up with someone, it's because it isn't working anymore or the other person wronged you. That didn't happen in this case. She's intentionally keeping herself away from him in order to protect him. She didn't stop loving him. He didn't stop loving her."

I started to open my mouth to contradict her, but she cut me off.

"I don't care what you say. I believe he loves her. Why would he go to all that trouble with her if he didn't?"

"Easy. He wanted a compliant sex toy he could have his way with."

"Cal Ross. That is one of the most callous things I've ever heard you say."

I hated fighting with Jade, but as she'd said, I was stubborn. The problem was she was just as pigheaded as I was when she thought she was right. "It's the truth."

"No. It isn't. That's not how it works."

"How would you know?" I lowered my voice an octave. "He's screwed up, Jade. The things he likes to do to women . . . I can't let him do that to Anna. I can't."

"And if it's what she wants?"

"It's not."

She took a step toward me. "If it is?"

"Jade . . ."

Before I could say thing more, she was standing directly in front of me, her nose just inches away from mine. "If you want to be Anna's friend—a true friend—you will want her to be happy." I opened my mouth to speak, but she placed her hand against my lips, silencing me. "Stephan Coleman makes her happy. You need to accept that and deal with it. Stop thinking about yourself for once and think about Anna. The man she loves is having his life dragged through the mud right now because of her. Think about how you would feel if something happened to me and you couldn't do anything to stop it or help me."

She raised her eyebrow, questioning. As much as I didn't want to admit it, she had a point. If Jade were in trouble and I wasn't allowed to help her, I would probably slowly drive myself crazy.

Closing my eyes, I nodded, and she removed her hand from over my mouth. "I still don't like it."

Jade chuckled and circled her arms around my neck. "No one said you had to like it, but this isn't about you. It's about Anna, and right now she needs us—both of us—to be on her side."

I nodded.

She smiled and brushed her lips across mine in that sensual way she did that drove me insane and made me putty in her hands. I grabbed hold of her ass and pulled her hips against my growing erection.

Jade laughed.

"Not so fast. Emma's going to be here soon."

I groaned and let my head fall to Jade's shoulder. "I forgot."

Jade reached between us and rubbed her hand up and down my semi-erect cock. "I promise to make it up to you later."

Closing my eyes, I stopped the movement of her hand. "Not helping."

This only made her laugh harder. Jade and I had to adjust our sex lives after Anna had moved in with me. Given her history, we didn't think it would be good for her to see or hear anything of a sexual nature. That meant most of our recent escapades had occurred either as quietly as possible late at night or in my office. We'd snuck away to her apartment a couple of times when we were desperate, but I didn't like to leave Anna alone more than I had to.

As it was, Jade and I had adjusted our schedules so Anna was only in the house by herself a handful of hours during the week. I started my workday at six in the morning, rather than the eight or eight thirty I used to, so I could be home no later than three. Jade didn't leave the house until ten or eleven, depending on her class schedule. That meant sometimes she didn't get back until late. I had to admit it had taken its toll on our relationship, and not just the sexual part of it either. Taking care of Anna meant she was the focus of our lives more often than not.

"What are you thinking about?"

I gave Jade a chaste kiss before stepping back. "I was thinking about how much our lives have changed since Anna moved in, and how much you've had to put up with."

"They have changed, haven't they?"

I reached in the cabinet for a mug before pouring myself some coffee. "Yes."

We stared at each other for several minutes, not speaking but saying plenty. Jade stepped closer and reached out to brush her fingers along the back of my hand.

Turning my hand over, I laced our fingers and squeezed. We stayed like that, trapped in the bubble we'd created, until there was a knock on the door.

"I'll get it. Why don't you let Anna know Emma's here."

Jade nodded.

Once she was inside Anna's room, I opened the door and invited Emma in. "Morning, Emma."

"Good morning, Cal. How are you?"

"As well as can be expected at eight thirty on a Saturday morning."

She stepped inside, tucking her long blond hair behind her ear while adjusting the strap on her briefcase over her shoulder. "You're used to getting up earlier than this now, aren't you? I'd expect you to be ready for anything at this point."

I took a sip of my coffee, shrugged, and closed the front door. "Can I get you some coffee?"

"Yes, please," she said, walking over to set her briefcase down on the kitchen table.

I could hear her opening her case and the sound of papers being shuffled around as I worked in the kitchen. For her age, Emma was already a prominent attorney. She'd been named as one of the best in Minnesota, which was a huge accomplishment for someone in her early thirties. Anna was lucky to have her. Then again, Anna had Emma because of Stephan and his money. At least he was good for something.

The door to Anna's room was still closed, but I knew it wouldn't be for long. There was only one person who was guaranteed these days to get Anna to come out of her room, and that was Emma. Two weeks after Anna moved in, I'd gotten a phone call at my office from Oscar Davis, Coleman's lawyer. We'd talked for over an hour while he filled me in on what was happening. Apparently Coleman had thought it might go over better coming from Mr. Davis than from him. He was probably right.

Things were getting complicated. The feds were now involved, and they were insisting on going through not only all of Coleman's personal financials but also those of The Coleman Foundation. A team of lawyers had been brought in, hand selected by Mr. Davis. The media, of course, was all over it given Coleman's position in the city. It was swiftly becoming a circus.

That was where Emma came into the picture. Both Coleman and his lawyer felt Brianna needed to have legal counsel in order to protect herself from whatever fallout there might be. They were going to try to keep her out of it as much as possible, but with her father telling anyone who would listen that Stephan Coleman had kidnapped and brainwashed his daughter, the chances she'd not have to get involved were slim.

It had taken only one meeting between Emma and Anna for them to form a bond, which given Anna's aversion to people in general was strange. She was a woman, so that helped. There was also the fact that she was there to help Anna in any way she could. Part of that was keeping Anna up to date on all things Stephan Coleman.

I placed Emma's coffee on the table far enough away from her papers so nothing would get damaged. "Here you go."

"Thanks." She took a sip and then placed the mug back down on the table. "How's Anna doing this morning?"

"She ate. That's all I know. She hasn't—"

I was just about to comment on how she hadn't come out of her room yet, when the door opened and Anna took a step out into the room. She had a faraway look in her eyes, and I could tell she'd been crying. Her demeanor changed instantly, however, when she spotted Emma.

Anna's steps were measured, as they always seemed to be, as she crossed to where Emma waited at the table. Jade appeared in the doorway but remained unmoving as Anna approached. This was always iffy. Anna had a fight or flight response that always leaned toward flight. If something startled her, she would be across the room faster than seemed humanly possible.

Once she'd taken a seat, we all relaxed some. "Would you like some coffee, Anna?"

She shook her head and focused on Emma. "How . . . how is he?"

I closed my eyes, trying not to let my temper get the best of me, and walked back into the kitchen. Jade joined me and wrapped her arms around my waist, trying to comfort me. It didn't work, but I appreciated the effort.

"It's not great, Anna. I'm sorry. The feds aren't backing off. They seem to want to make an example out of him."

"They can't!"

Her scream pierced through my heart almost as much as her tears did.

"I'm sorry, Anna. I really am."

"There . . . there has to be something. Something I can do."

Emma became motionless, and for the longest time, the only sound in the room was Anna's near silent sobs.

"There is . . . something. Maybe."

This got Anna's attention, as well as mine and Jade's.

"You hold a lot of power here, Anna. More so than Stephan, really."

Emma leaned back in her chair and folded her arms. I knew by her posture I wasn't going to like what she was going to suggest.

"You lived with Ian Pierce for ten months. You have firsthand knowledge of what he did. What he's capable of. All Stephan has is hearsay and observations, outside of the evidence of him purchasing you, which doesn't help his credibility. You could offer to testify against Ian in exchange for Stephan's freedom."

"No!"

Everyone, including Jade, jumped at my intrusion.

"There is no way you can make her stand up in front of the man who tortured her for ten months and talk about the things he did to her. No."

I looked over at Anna and saw a determination in her eyes that had been missing since that evening in Coleman's condo.

"No one is making me. It's my choice."

"Please, Anna. Don't do this. It will destroy you."

She turned away from me and faced Emma again. "I want to do it. I have to."

"Anna, you understand this will most likely mean that the media will find out who you are. Not just your name but what you look like, and maybe even where you live. People are going to have a lot of questions. They're going to want details of your time with Pierce. Are you sure you're ready for that?"

"Stephan saved me. I won't let him go to prison for it."

Everyone was silent. I don't think any of us could quite believe this was happening.

"Okay. I'll approach the federal prosecutor with your proposal and get back to you."

Emma didn't stay long after that. She did bring Anna a stack of papers to look over as she always did. I had no idea what they were—Anna never shared that with either of us.

As soon as Emma drove away, Anna retreated into her room, and I was left to stew over what had just happened.

"Are you all right?" Jade asked.

"Not really," I admitted.

"She's right. It is her decision."

"I wish it wasn't."

"It'll work out. It has to."

As much as I wanted to believe Jade, I'd seen enough of the world to know that wasn't always the case. "I have to do something."

"Like what?"

"I don't know. I need to think."

An hour later, it came to me. I wasn't sure why I hadn't thought of it before, but I immediately picked up the phone and called Emma. Thankfully, being the weekend, she hadn't spoken with the other lawyers yet and agreed to meet me for lunch.

We sat across from each other outside a little café with our food, when she decided I'd been quiet long enough. "I know you aren't pleased with Anna's decision, but I hope you know that as her attorney, I have to abide by her wishes."

"I'm aware of that."

"So what is it you wanted to talk to me about, then?"

"What about a compromise?"

"I'm listening."

"Anna is scared to death of people. You know that. Getting in front of an entire court room . . . I'm not even sure if she *could* do it. No matter how much she wanted to. What if . . . what if she made a statement instead. Couldn't they use that just as easily?"

"They could. It's not as effective with a jury, though, if it goes to trial."

"What if Jade and I added statements about our observations of Anna? That combined with Coleman's and Anna's has to be worth something, doesn't it?"

"It's possible. Let me feel out the prosecution and see what kind of a deal they are willing to make. As I told Anna, I think it's more that they want to go after Stephan. Make an example out of him. I'm not sure why, though. He's done a lot for people in this city."

"He's a rich boy born with a silver spoon in his mouth who thought he was above the law."

She smirked. "Something like that."

"Look. As much as I don't like Coleman, I don't really think he deserves to go to prison. He saved Anna. That has to count for something."

"Are you willing to make a public statement to that affect?"

I nodded.

"I'll do whatever it takes to keep Anna off that witness stand."

Chapter 2

Brianna

I sat on my bed hugging my knees to my chest as I stared blankly out the window. It was sunny today. Probably warm since it was the third Monday in August. That was only a guess, though, since I hadn't been outside for almost a month. Other than to see Emma, my lawyer, I'd only left my room a handful of times, when Cal's or Jade's pleading did me in. I didn't want to be around anyone. It had nothing to do with them. I felt . . . lost and . . . hollow inside.

Reaching up, I skimmed the edge of Stephan's collar with my index finger. About a week after I'd moved in with Cal, he'd tried to get me to take it off. Jade had to come in between us, begging him to let it be, after I'd locked myself in my bathroom for most of the day. I knew Cal still didn't like Stephan—just thinking his name caused me to whimper and my chest to constrict—but I wouldn't let go of the one part of Stephan I had left. The only part that was still mine.

My gaze drifted to the nightstand beside my bed where I kept the papers Emma had brought. From the very beginning, she'd seemed to understand my need to know what was going on with Stephan, and this was her way of doing that. Anytime Stephan was in the papers or on the news, she would catalog it for me. She would never know how grateful I was to her for that.

Moisture pooled in my eyes as I let the sadness I felt engulf me. I missed him. I missed him so much. It hurt every day.

Jade kept telling me it would get better—this horrible feeling I had in my chest—but it hadn't. It had been over two months since I'd seen him, touched him. Oscar said it had to be this way, and I understood. I would do what was best for Stephan. I had to. He'd done so much for me. Risked everything. I would be strong for him now. I would do what needed to be done . . . even if it killed me.

Oscar had arranged for me to have Emma. He'd come to see me himself a week after my birthday and brought with him the car Stephan had bought for me—the one I'd never gotten up the nerve to try and drive yet—along with the birthday gifts I'd left behind at Stephan's condo. "Stephan says they're yours, and you should have them with you."

I hadn't argued with him, although I didn't completely agree. Stephan had bought me those things when I'd been his, and I wasn't any longer.

Gripping the silver band of metal around my neck, I began to rock back and forth. I wanted his arms around me. I wanted to hear him whispering in my ear, telling me that everything would be okay. I just didn't know if that was true in this case.

Emma said things weren't looking good for Stephan. She and I had a long talk the first time she'd come over to see me. We'd sat in Cal's living room for most of the day, me huddled in a chair in the corner, her on Cal's couch. It had been sunny that day as well, the sun streaming in through the large windows, giving the illusion of warmth. All I'd felt was cold—cold and empty. Emma had explained, as Oscar had, that he and Stephan had felt it best for me to have my own legal counsel . . . just in case. Emma did most of the talking that day, until she'd asked me what I wanted. My answer had been simple—I wanted whatever was best for Stephan.

Since then, she had stopped by every Saturday morning and updated me on what was going on with the FBI investigation. The man in charge, Agent Rick Marco, seemed to want to see Stephan punished. Agent Marco didn't appear to care what the truth was. He only cared that Stephan had given Ian a large sum of money without any explanation. With John's ranting, it seemed at the very least Agent Marco was trying to pin kidnapping on Stephan. I'd only met Agent Marco once, and I didn't like him.

The only thing that had kept Stephan from being charged up to this point was that, other than the money exchange, they couldn't find any connection between Stephan and Ian. We'd thought that Oscar and Michael James, The Coleman Foundation's new CFO, turning in the evidence they'd put together against Ian and a man named Jean Dumas, along with about twenty others, would change Agent Marco's focus. According to Emma, what they'd accumulated could not only put Ian away for a long time, it also had the potential of dismantling a large underground black market. Instead of keeping Agent Marco at bay, though, it had done the exact opposite. I knew I had to do something.

A knock on my bedroom door caused me to jump. I turned my head toward the door, watching . . . waiting. It was most likely Jade . . . or Cal. Either way, they'd let themselves in eventually. They always did.

Sure enough, the door slowly opened, and Cal poked his head inside the room. "Hey."

I didn't answer. Cal meant well, and he was nice enough to let me stay in his house, but we didn't talk much. He wanted me to be normal, and that wasn't something I would ever be again. I also knew he blamed Stephan, at least in part, for the way I was. I wish he could understand, but it wasn't something I could explain. I loved Stephan. I missed him. But he wasn't the reason I was messed up.

"Can I come in?"

"Okay."

He hesitated and then walked into the room. Cal kept the door open behind him, having learned from experience that closing it would cause me to feel trapped. He crossed to the chair in the corner by the window, and I sat back against the headboard, tapping my fingers absentmindedly against my leg.

As soon as I began the rhythmic motion, I could hear Stephan's voice in my head telling me to stop fidgeting. I immediately sat on my hands to stop the mindless action.

Movement at the door drew my attention away from Cal. Jade appeared and stood in the doorway. They were both here. In my room. Had something happened?

I quickly turned my gaze back on Cal. "What . . . what's happened? Is Stephan—"

"Coleman's fine." The sharp edge in Cal's tone reminded me, yet again, of his feelings regarding Stephan.

No one spoke for several minutes while I tried to calm myself. If Cal said Stephan was fine, I had to believe him. I didn't think he would lie to me. Not about that.

"Anna, I wanted to talk to you about something."

"Okay."

When Cal didn't continue, I started to worry. What if something had happened and he wasn't sure *how* to tell me?

Just as I felt the air in my lungs constrict with anxiety, Cal leaned forward, his elbows on his knees. I tried to brace myself as best I could, but I could already feel the pressure in my chest increasing, tightening.

"I asked Emma to have lunch with me today."

"Wha-wh-why?"

"Anna, I want you to hear me out, okay?"

I didn't respond, and after a minute he continued.

"I don't like the idea of you testifying against that man." I opened my mouth to say something, but he cut me off. "No. He . . . Anna, you have trouble talking to regular people. You have trouble talking to me—someone you've known nearly all your life. How do you think it's going to be for you to sit up there in a room full of strangers and confront the man who *owned* you for ten months? I don't want to see you go through that, Anna. I don't."

To be honest, I didn't want that either. I didn't know if I could do it. If it prevented Stephan from being put in prison because of me, then I would have to. He'd saved me. He'd given me my freedom, my life. I'd been told about that girl—the one Ian had before me. That could have been me. It probably would have, if not for Stephan. I would do anything for him. Even stand up in front of a room full of strangers and face the man who had not only raped and tortured me for ten months but who'd also made me think I was no longer a person, only a thing to be used and abused in any way he or his friends saw fit. A chill settled in my bones, and I hugged myself tighter.

Cal appeared oblivious to the war being waged inside me. He was too focused on what he wanted to say. Sighing, he stood and walked to stand in front of the window. "I want to offer you a deal."

I looked over at Jade. Her face wasn't giving anything away, which made me think she wasn't thrilled with whatever this deal was.

"Emma's going to talk to Oscar and see if they can come up with a solution to get Coleman off the hook without requiring you to testify. You'd still have to give an official statement against Ian Pierce but hopefully not have to make an appearance in court. As a family friend, and as an upstanding member of the community, I'd publicly go on record that what Coleman did to get you away from Ian Pierce should be commended, not punished. I have friends in the media. So does my dad. I can use them if I have to. And it's not a secret that I'm not a big fan of Coleman's personally. My coming out in support of what he did would make an impression. Especially if I emphasize that fact in any statements I make to the press."

"I don't . . . understand." He'd said a deal, and he didn't like Stephan. Why would he do this?

He took a deep breath and met my gaze. His eyes were almost pleading. It was so unlike him that it had me concerned about what would come out of his mouth next.

"In exchange for me doing this, defending Coleman, doing what I can to keep him out of prison, I want you to get counseling, Anna. I want you to talk to someone who can help you . . . help you get through what . . . whatever it is you went through." He clenched his teeth when he spoke his next words. "Someone who doesn't have a hidden agenda to try and get you into his bed."

Before I could say anything—defend Stephan—Jade was across the room and standing between Cal and me. She didn't say anything. At least, not anything I could hear. She just laid her hand flat on his chest, until he closed his eyes and stepped away.

Cal walked toward the door, leaving Jade standing on the far side of the room alone. He reached the door and stopped. Without turning around, he lifted his head as if he were looking at something in the other room. "Think about it, Anna. Please."

Before I could even consider answering him, he was gone.

I could feel Jade watching me, but all I wanted to do was hide in my bed, so that's what I did. Burrowing under the covers, I rolled over and closed my eyes. Several minutes later, I heard her leave the room, closing the door behind her. It was only then that I let myself think about what Cal had said. He wanted me to talk to someone. Talk to them about what had happened to me.

A shiver ran through my body from head to foot, and I curled up into a tight ball, clutching the sheets around me. I just wanted the world to go away.

Somewhere along the line I must have fallen asleep, because when I opened my eyes, it was dark outside. Pushing the sheets aside, I walked into the small bathroom connected to my room. My bathroom at Cal's was nothing like the one I'd had at Stephan's. This one was nice, but it was less than half the size. I turned on the light and got a drink of water using the cup I kept next to the sink.

A part of me registered that my hair was sticking out in various places and that I was wearing the same clothes I'd put on two days ago. Usually I didn't change unless Jade or Cal said something. Most of the time it was Jade. She would come in with food or under the pretense of wanting to talk to me and mention that maybe a nice shower would make me feel better. It didn't, but both of them seemed to be happier after I emerged showered and in clean clothes.

I don't know how long I was in the bathroom, but when I walked back into my room, Jade was sitting on the end of my bed. "Hi."

"Hi."

She had a serious expression on her face, so I knew she had something to say. "Cal went into town to get a pizza for dinner. He should be back soon."

I nodded, climbing back into my bed.

"I talked to Cal about this afternoon. I know you don't like what he had to say, but I think his heart is in the right place." She reached out and touched the tips of my fingers before retracting her hand. "He's worried about you."

"I'm fine." It was the same phrase I repeated almost daily. I was fine. Or as fine as I was going to ever be. There was no magic cure. Nothing that would make my past go away. This was my life now. I would survive, just as I had before.

"I know you're doing the best you can. After what you've been through, I can't imagine it's easy." She paused. "I also know leaving Stephan was really hard for you to do."

Jade was the only one who understood about Stephan. "I miss him."

She reached out again. This time, her fingers lingered over mine. "Of course you do. You love him."

We both sat in silence for a long time. I could hear the crickets outside playing their mating song. When I'd first moved in, the sound had kept me up at night. Now it was a reminder that there was a world outside my small room.

"Jade?" She glanced up at me and waited. It was one of the things I liked about her. She wasn't impatient. "Do you think Cal speaking up for Stephan . . . would help him?"

"Honestly? I have no idea. Cal said Emma was going to talk to Oscar and see what he thinks. I can't see where it would hurt, though. Your man needs all the people in his corner he can get right now, and Cal's right about one thing. With him being an old family friend, his endorsement could turn the media to Stephan's side. That might put some pressure on Agent Marco and get him to back off." She gave my hand a small squeeze before releasing it.

I looked down, picking at the fabric of my pants. "He's not . . ." I took a deep breath and tried once more. "He's not my . . . man anymore."

"Of course he is. You still love him, right?"

I glanced up, meeting her gaze. "Always."

She smiled. "That's what I thought."

The sound of a car pulling up outside caused us both to look toward the door.

"Cal's back with the pizza. You gonna come join us in the living room? We can put in a movie."

The mention of pizza and a movie instantly reminded me of Stephan. My hand went to my neck, and I pressed back more firmly against the headboard. "I'm not hungry."

"You sure? I can bring some pizza in here for you if you want?"

"I'm sure."

Jade stared at me for a long minute before getting up and going to the door. She stopped and turned, her hand on the doorknob. "We'll be out here if you change your mind."

I didn't respond. Instead, I rolled over on my side and stared out into the darkness, allowing the pain in my chest to grow until tears welled up in my eyes. Just as every other night since I'd left Stephan's home, I cried myself to sleep.

Chapter 3

Stephan

I unlocked the bottom right-hand drawer of my desk and retrieved the picture I had hidden away under a stack of financial reports. It was the one of Brianna I used to keep on my desk. That first week after Brianna left was one of the hardest of my life. Every reminder I found of her around my house caused me some level of pain. It was hard to believe so much time had already gone by. August was drawing to a close. She'd been gone for sixty-five days. It felt like years, and since neither the press nor Agent Marco appeared to be letting up, it was hard to tell how long we would have to be apart.

To be safe, and completely without Oscar's prompting or knowledge, I'd enlisted Logan's, Lily's, and even Daren's help in dismantling my playroom and removing all my toys. If a warrant was issued to search my home, discovering my kinky side would only work against me. Logan arranged to store everything with a fellow Dom he trusted, someone I had no connection with. It was better that way.

When I'd sat down at my desk on my first day back to work after Brianna left, my gaze had fallen on the picture of her in her beautiful gown. I'd known I would have to remove it, had known I should give it to Lily to put with the rest of my things, but I couldn't do it. I needed to have something of her, so I kept it tucked out of sight. It was the only way I had hope of getting any work done. At least I knew it was nearby if I needed it, like I did today.

No one but me had a key to my desk, and it would be harder for the authorities to get a warrant to go through my office than it would be my home. Brianna had only been inside this building twice, and both of those times had been brief. I was hoping that was enough to keep Agent Marco and his minions away from the foundation—and my desk. Besides, it wasn't as if I could deny I knew her. She'd accompanied me to a charity event and had been photographed with me by her side.

I leaned back in my chair, holding her picture. She was beautiful in the purple dress Lily had picked out for her to wear. Her hair was pulled back away from her face, showcasing my collar around her neck.

A lot had changed that night. Karl Walker had shown his true colors and given me a reason to fire him. Ross had reentered her life, something I had never viewed as a positive thing—however, I was glad with everything that had happened in the last two months that she'd had somewhere she felt safe enough to go. I'd also learned the details of what had happened between her and Daren that night he'd first met her—details that still haunted my relationship with Daren. Although, since everything started hitting the fan, he'd proved himself a true friend and stuck by my side.

It hadn't taken long for my name to be leaked to the media. Jamie had called my cell phone a little after nine on Tuesday morning to say the phone lines were being flooded with calls from various news outlets. There were also reporters in the lobby, wanting to interview anyone who had something to say about me.

Tom had called from downstairs a few hours later saying he'd had to kick a few reporters out of the building, but that they were camped out on the sidewalk with cameras. I'd called Oscar and let him know what was going on. He wasn't all that surprised. Apparently John hadn't stopped talking since he'd been arrested, and people, at least the local police and media, were listening. They'd already subpoenaed my bank records along with some preliminaries for the foundation. They knew I had paid Ian a large sum of money. At this point, that was all they knew for certain.

With only one more week left in August, not much had changed since that first week. John was still in custody and not likely to see freedom for a very long time, if ever. In his eagerness to point the finger at me, he'd also said enough about his own involvement to seal his fate. The state of Minnesota didn't look kindly on men who sold their daughters into slavery to pay for their gambling debts. As soon as the story broke, his hometown of Two Harbors had organized a special election to remove him as sheriff. He was now rotting in a jail cell while he awaited trail, and I hoped he stayed there for the rest of his miserable life.

Ian Pierce was also in custody. Oscar had turned over the information Michael had found regarding the missing girl. With the money trail we'd provided, and the timing, they'd had enough to hold him. He was a flight risk, and they weren't taking the chance on him leaving the country.

The intercom on my phone buzzed, and I reluctantly put away the picture of Brianna before answering Jamie. "Yes, Jamie?"

"There's a woman here to see you. She says she's a friend of yours. Sarah Evans." Jamie's voice came through the phone with a cold professionalism. She'd never said anything to me directly, but I knew her view of me had changed. She wasn't alone. Most of the people I worked with now looked at me with uncertainty. They didn't know what to believe, and I couldn't exactly blame them.

Hearing Sarah was here, though, brightened my day considerably. "Thank you, Jamie. You can send her in." Sarah had sent me an e-mail a few days ago saying she was coming to town. I'd expected her tomorrow or maybe Saturday. Her showing up in the middle of the week piqued my curiosity. She hadn't said *why* she was coming, just that she was.

Three light taps sounded against my door before it opened. Sarah smiled when she saw me and stepped inside my office, closing the door behind her. Her long brown hair was swept up in some sort of high ponytail. She was pretty, but then again, she always had been.

She took two long strides toward me before stopping and placing her hands on her hips. "You've gotten yourself in quite a mess, haven't you?"

I gave a half laugh. It was just like Sarah not to beat around the bush. Most people who met her would never guess she was a submissive. Outside the bedroom, Sarah tended to radiate confidence and control.

I stood and walked around my desk to stand in front of her. "Did you come all this way to tell me how stupid I am?"

Sarah placed her hands on my shoulders. "Hardly. I know you, Stephan, and I figured you could use all the friends you could get right now."

Taking a deep breath, I sighed and pulled her in for a hug. "How long are you in town?"

She pulled back and looked me in the eye. "As long as you need me."

"You don't—"

"You'd do it for me."

She was right. I would.

"See. That wasn't so hard."

This time, I did laugh.

Sarah glanced over at the couch and then pulled me over to sit down. "So tell me. How are you doing? Really."

I sighed. "As well as can be expected, considering."

She looked toward the door, then back at me. "Your assistant didn't seem too crazy about my being here."

"It's not you. This whole thing with the media has been trying on her. She's the one who has to field all those calls and say 'no comment' all day long. I'm sure you passed through the maze of reporters on your way into the building."

Sarah sat back on the couch and folded her arms. "They're vultures. As soon as I stepped inside, they were surrounding me, wanting to know who I was." She glanced down at her designer clothing, then back up at me, smirking. "I guess maybe I shouldn't have dressed so nice to come see you today. Perhaps a burlap sack would have been better."

"I'm not sure even that would have been enough."

Neither one of us said anything for several minutes. "You look tired."

I leaned my head against the back of the couch and closed my eyes. "I haven't been sleeping very well lately. I'm fine, though."

"How long has it been since you slept through an entire night?"

I opened one eye to look at her. What was this, an inquisition?

"Don't give me that look. You're not my Dom anymore."

"I don't need a babysitter."

"Apparently you do. How long?"

Leveling my gaze at her, I took in her posture. She held her shoulders back and had that look on her face as if she were about to go to battle. Maybe she was.

I sat forward, running a hand quickly through my hair. What difference did it make if she knew or not? "A couple months."

"Is it because of that girl? The one they say you kidnapped?"

I didn't respond, and apparently, that was answer enough for Sarah. She cocked her head to the side and watched me for what felt like a very long time. "You care about her."

It wasn't a question, so again I didn't bother with an answer. Sarah knew me well. She'd been my submissive for a little more than a year. We'd shared a lot of things together, but one thing we'd never shared was love. Our arrangement had been one of friendship and mutual gratification. Neither of us had been under any illusion that it was more than that. When she'd graduated and moved away, there had been no hard feelings. We'd known the relationship was temporary, and that had suited us both at the time.

"Do you love her?"

I opened my mouth to reply, but no sound came out. The answer was simple. Yes, I loved Brianna. I always would. Things were complicated now, however. And even though my feelings for Brianna weren't in question—at least for me—I didn't know if I should share them with anyone. It didn't have anything to do with trust. I trusted Sarah. The reality, however, was that if worst came to worst and I was charged, Sarah and anyone else who knew me could be called to testify. For their own safety, I had to keep things to myself.

Luckily, my cell phone started ringing, giving me an excuse not to answer her. I looked at the caller ID. It was Oscar. "Hello?"

"Are you able to come by my office today?"

I glanced over at Sarah, who was waiting not so patiently beside me. "Sure. When do you need me there?"

"As soon as possible. Emma called. She wants to talk to the two of us."

Before I knew it, I was on my feet. Sarah followed after me, a look of concern on her face.

I ignored her as my sole focus was on Oscar. "Is something wrong? Is Brianna all right?"

"Calm down, Stephan. As far as I know, Brianna's fine. Still living with Cal Ross. I didn't get the impression something was awry, more that she wants a discussion. "

I took a deep breath, feeling the tension ease. "I'll be there within the hour. Will that work?"

"That should be perfect. I'll call Emma and let her know."

Pocketing my cell, I walked behind my desk and began closing everything down. I would go see Oscar and then work from home for the rest of the day. There wasn't anything here that needed my immediate attention.

Once I had powered down my computer and had the papers I was taking with me in my briefcase, I looked up to find Sarah staring at me with a smug look on her face. "What?" I asked, not understanding her expression.

"Well I guess that answers one of my questions, at least."

"What question is that?"

"Stephan Coleman has finally fallen in love."

Sarah rode down with me in the elevator to the parking garage. It was secured, which meant it was safe from reporters. They'd be waiting at the entrance, however. I wasn't sure exactly what they were waiting for considering most days all I did was come to work and then go home. My life wasn't that exciting, especially since Brianna was not currently a part of it.

"Do you want to get dinner later?"

I opened the door to my car and tossed my briefcase onto the passenger seat. "Thanks, but I think I'll just throw something together at home. Maybe some other time."

"Stephan Coleman. Don't you dare try and give me the brush off. If you want to stay in, I understand, but the last thing you need is to be cooped up in your condo all alone moping." Sarah adjusted the strap of her purse as she headed back toward the elevator. "I'll pick up some Chinese on the way. Six good for you?"

I shook my head and smiled. Ever the brat. "Sure. Six is fine."

The elevator doors opened, and she stepped inside. "Good. And make sure your doorman knows I'm coming. I'd hate to be mistaken for a reporter."

Sighing, I climbed behind the wheel of my car and drove to Oscar's office. I noticed a few cars following me, but that was the norm. It seemed I couldn't go anywhere anymore without being followed by at least one reporter trying to catch me doing something newsworthy. Last week, Richard and Diane had stopped by my condo to see how I was doing—they'd been amazingly supportive, all things considered—and the next day a picture of them leaving was on the front page of almost every newspaper in the Twin Cities area saying our family was being ripped apart by the scandal. The entire experience gave me a new perspective on what celebrities went through on a regular basis.

I pulled into the parking garage adjacent to Oscar's building, which, unfortunately, wasn't private. As soon as I stepped out of the vehicle, cameras started flashing, and one reporter yelled, "Why are you going to see your lawyer today, Mr. Coleman? Are there charges pending against you? Do you have any information on Brianna Reeves's current whereabouts?"

Because Brianna was living with Ross, where she was staying was not public knowledge. That was good. I had no doubt that if the press knew where she was, they'd be staking out Ross's house as well, and that was the last thing she needed. This had to be difficult enough for her. I knew how hard being separated was for me.

The reporters faded into the background as I walked past the reception desk, and security, which I'm sure Oscar called in advance to warn of my arrival, prevented the vultures from following me any farther. I slipped inside the elevator and went to the fifth floor where Oscar's office was. Before that night two months ago in my condo, I'd only been to Oscar's office a handful of times. Most of those were shortly after my parents' death, and then once to finalize the transfer of my trust after I'd graduated college and took over control of The Coleman Foundation.

In the last two months, though, I'd been making regular appearances. It was usually easier for me to come to Oscar's office than for him to come to me. Plus, if we needed to meet with Emma, Brianna's legal counsel, it had to be at Oscar's office. We were trying to keep her out of the public eye as much as we were Brianna. Once the media connected her to the situation, they would start digging to find out who she was and how she was involved. After that, it would be only a matter of time before they found Brianna.

Oscar's receptionist greeted me the moment I left the elevator. "You can go on in, Mr. Coleman. Mr. Davis is expecting you."

"Thanks, Phyllis."

When I walked into Oscar's office, Emma was already sitting in one of the large wing-backed chairs across from his desk. Beside her was a man I didn't recognize, but by the suit he was wearing, he was probably another lawyer. "Stephan. Perfect timing."

I spared Oscar a brief smile before turning my focus on Emma. "Is something wrong with Brianna?"

Oscar sighed. He sounded slightly irritated. "I told you Brianna was fine over the phone."

"I understand that, but I'd like to hear that from Emma."

She looked up, meeting my gaze. "Nothing major has happened to change Ms. Reeves's well-being."

For the first time since receiving Oscar's phone call, I felt I could breathe a little easier. "Thank you."

Oscar motioned to the empty chair in front of him. "Stephan, if you'll have a seat we can get started."

I took my seat, eager to find out what had prompted this impromptu meeting.

They didn't make me wait long. To my surprise, however, it was Emma who began speaking. "Ms. Reeves wants me to offer a deal to the FBI."

That got my attention. "What do you mean? What kind of a deal?"

"In exchange for giving you immunity from any and all charges surrounding your involvement with Ian Pierce and the purchase of Ms. Reeves from him, she would agree to testify against him."

"What! Absolutely not," I shouted, surging out of my chair.

"Stephan, sit down. She's not finished."

I looked down at Emma, panic causing every muscle in my body to tense. Brianna couldn't do this. I wouldn't let her. She was to worry about herself. Take care of *herself*. Not me. That was Oscar's job.

Emma raised one eyebrow, clearly waiting for me to sit back down before she continued with whatever other nonsense she had to share. Taking a deep breath, I eased myself back into my chair.

"Apparently you're not the only one who feels the way you do about her suggestion. Cal Ross had a similar reaction."

For once, Ross and I seemed to be on the same page. I wasn't sure how I felt about that.

"He's offered a countersuggestion. I ran it by Vince here." She motioned to the man I didn't know. "He's a criminal attorney in my firm and knows a lot more about that side of the law than I, or even Oscar. I'm also going to run it by Ms. Reeves, because ultimately it's her decision. She's my client, not you and not Mr. Ross."

She paused, and it took everything I had in me not to demand she get on with it already.

"Cal Ross has offered to speak on your behalf, Mr. Coleman. He would go on record, publicly, in support of you and what you did for Ms. Reeves. He agrees, as I do, that Ms. Reeves will have to make an official statement regarding what happened to her during her time with Mr. Pierce, but he is hoping that his statement, along with Ms. Reeves's, will be enough to force the FBI's hand and get them to stop pursuing you in this matter."

Although I still didn't like the idea of Brianna being involved at all, I'd known keeping her out of it would be nearly impossible once Jonathan Reeves confessed. The FBI knew her name, and they were going to want to know everything else about her as well. Sooner or later, the story was going to come out. It was only a matter of how.

"What do you think, Oscar?"

"Actually, I think you need to hear what Vince has to say first."

Refocusing my attention on the other man, I waited for him to begin speaking.

Vince shifted his weight and crossed his arms as if settling in for the long haul. "I think it's a bad idea. Right now, all the FBI has on you is a monetary transaction, correct?"

"Yes," I confirmed.

Vince nodded. "Then my advice is to leave it at that. Unless Ian or Brianna or someone else who knows what that money was for starts talking, then all they are going to be able to do is guess. They can't prove anything."

"So what you're saying is you think we should do nothing."

"That's exactly what I'm saying. This Agent Marco is trying to spook you into doing something that will give him the ammunition he needs to go after you. I say we don't give it to him."

"But what about Ian?"

"My guess is he won't say anything either. It's not really in his best interest."

That made sense, and it would keep Brianna out of things as much as possible. "So what now?"

"We wait. We wait and let Ian make the next move."

I didn't like that. "And if he decides that since he's going down he wants to take me with him?"

"Given your position in the community, I think we could discredit anything he said. Worst-case scenario, we can always fall back on Ms. Reeves and Mr. Ross's suggestion. I just wouldn't recommend it at this point. While Agent Marco is fishing, he doesn't have anything solid against you. If he did, we'd be having this conversation in an interrogation room rather than an office. Besides, approaching the FBI with a deal before an arrest makes it look like you have something to hide. While technically you do, we don't want it to look that way."

I closed my eyes and ran through my options. There weren't many, so it didn't take that long to decide.

"All right." I paused. "If something happens, though, I'm going to need you to arrange for me to see Brianna. Press or not, we'll figure something out."

"Stephan, you know that wouldn't be a good—"

"I don't care if it's a good idea or not, Oscar. There's no way I'm letting her sacrifice herself for me." I turned to level a hard look at Emma. "Do you understand that? Under no circumstances am I allowing Brianna to throw herself under the bus to save me. I'll spend the rest of my life in prison before I let that happen."

Chapter 4

Stephan

I spent another hour in Oscar's office going over the plan, which basically amounted to everyone involved going about their business and keeping their mouths shut. It also meant I was no closer to seeing Brianna. Oscar felt it was still in everyone's best interest to keep us apart. He didn't think I'd be able to keep my hands off her if we were in the same room together, and he was probably right, especially if I thought she was hurting in any way. I was constantly hounded by the press nowadays. Suggestive pictures of us wouldn't help the situation if the worst happened. We needed the public to be on my side, and the press had the power to influence that for better or worse. Right now, they were only curious. We were trying to keep it that way.

The parking garage seemed unusually cavernous as I pulled into my parking space. I turned off the engine and rested my head against the steering wheel. I missed Brianna. I missed coming home to her. Talking to her. Sharing my day with her. The last thing I wanted to do was go up to my condo and her not be there.

Closing my eyes, I remembered the feeling of her in my arms. How she used to sit in my lap and play with the buttons on my shirt. I reached up and touched the button to the right of my heart, the one she always went to first. It had been so long since I'd heard her voice or felt her breath against my neck as she told me about her day. More than anything, I wanted to hold her and know she was all right.

The sound of my cell phone ringing caused me to open my eyes. I dug the phone out of my pocket, looked at the caller ID, and cursed. It was Sarah. Glancing at my watch, I realized I'd been sitting in my car, hunched over the steering wheel, for almost two hours.

"Hello." My voice sounded as if I had sandpaper in my throat.

"Stephan, where are you? I'm here with dinner, and your doorman says he's not heard from you and I'm not on the *approved* list."

I could see her rolling her eyes in my head, and I couldn't help but smile.

"I got . . . caught up in something that took longer than I expected. Let me talk to Tom."

"Always so bossy."

"Always so bratty."

She laughed, and I knew I was forgiven.

I heard movement in the background, then Tom's voice. "Mr. Coleman?"

After exiting my vehicle, I hit the locks as I walked toward the elevator. "Hi, Tom. You can add Ms. Evans to the approved list."

"Of course, Mr. Coleman. Did you want me to go ahead and send her up, or shall I have her wait a few minutes?"

I should have known Tom was watching my entrance from the security monitors. "You can go ahead and send her up, thanks."

There were a few more words exchanged between Tom and Sarah I didn't quite make out before Sarah came back on the phone. "I'll see you in a minute."

The phone cut off, and I shook my head. That woman was badly in need of a spanking. It made me wonder if she currently had a Dom, and if so, how he was dealing with her behavior. Then again, she might have been acting this way because it was me and we had a history. Sarah was extremely intelligent and rather good at reading people. There had been many times when she'd gone out of her way to act out in order to get a reaction out of me. Was that what she was doing now? And if so, why?

Letting myself into my condo, I went straight to my bedroom and removed my jacket and tie. I was on my way to the kitchen when the monitor lit up to let me know Sarah had arrived.

I paused to take a deep breath before opening the door. Sarah stood on the other side, hand on her hip, carrying a large plastic bag. I could already smell the sweet and sour chicken, her favorite. She swept into the room, and I had a moment of déjà vu. Lily had done something similar in the past. It made me wonder why I'd originally thought Lily would make a good play partner. Was it because in some ways she reminded me of Sarah? It was certainly something to consider.

"Thank goodness for the Internet. You left your office in such a hurry earlier I didn't have a chance to ask you where you typically get your Chinese food around here." I opened my mouth to speak, but she continued talking, not paying any attention to me. "I didn't ask you what you wanted earlier, so I just got your usual and a double order of sweet and sour chicken. I figured if your tastes had changed, you could always share mine. You always did like to steal some of my chicken anyway."

Although I didn't typically order beef and broccoli anymore, I could still eat it. She was also right that I'd most likely steal some of her chicken as well. It was one of the many reasons I tended to order multiple dishes now. I liked to have a variety.

Without my saying a word, Sarah began laying everything out on the dining room table. I walked to the kitchen to get us some drinks.

Once she had all the food out of the bag and arranged how she wanted it, she pulled out a chair and sat down. I'd barely reached for my own food before Sarah started in. "What's she like?"

I paused for a second before resuming opening the carton containing my beef and broccoli. "Why do you want to know?"

"Come on. I've known you almost six years now, and never once have you ever fancied yourself in love with anyone. Plus . . ." She hesitated, and I looked up to find her with an expression on her face that told me she was thinking hard about her next words. "You're different."

"How so?"

"You're going to make me work for this, aren't you?"

"You don't have to work for anything, Sarah, but I'd like to know why you think I'm somehow different than I used to be."

She pursed her lips. "Well first of all, you seem depressed. Granted, I didn't see you after you broke it off with Tami, but I never got the impression when we talked or e-mailed that you were anything other than your normal self, if maybe slightly ticked off. You also used to be very . . . controlled. Even when we'd let loose in college, I could always tell you were in complete control of yourself. Today, though, I saw you go into a near panic when your lawyer called. You've changed, and that's not a bad thing, but it makes me want to know the reason for that change."

I started eating and thought about what she'd said. Sarah wasn't wrong. I'd never come close to falling in love before Brianna, but was I different? Based on what she was telling me, I was. Brianna was the most important thing in my life. Her happiness, her safety, trumped everything else. Looking at it that way, I guessed I was different.

My throat clenched tight with emotion as I opened my mouth to speak. I took a drink of water and tried again. "She's . . ." Closing my eyes, I tried not to let my emotions overwhelm me. "She's beautiful. Inside and out."

Sarah didn't respond, which was strange for her. Keeping quiet had never been one of her strengths.

When I looked over at her, her eyes were glassy, and I could tell she was on the verge of tears. Another oddity for her.

We sat in silence for several minutes until I couldn't take it anymore. "Sarah?"

She jerked, picked up her napkin, and turned to the side, dabbing the corner of her eyes. I could tell she was somewhat embarrassed by her display of emotion, although I didn't know why. Again, it was unusual for her, but I'd seen her cry in the past. I wondered if it was the cause of her tears that had her feeling self-conscious or something else.

I was about to ask her about it when she turned back around, laid her napkin on the table with a flourish, and stood. "May I use your bathroom?"

It took me a few seconds longer to answer than it should have. "Of course. There's a bathroom up the stairs and to your right."

"Thank you."

She was up the stairs before I could gather my thoughts on her weird behavior. Although Sarah and I hadn't seen each other in nearly two years, we did keep in touch, and this wasn't like her. She wasn't prone to sudden outbursts of crying. In the year we'd been together, I'd seen her cry twice outside of play—once when her grandfather died, and the other when her mom had called to tell her she was leaving Sarah's father and filing for divorce. Both times her tears had made sense.

While she was upstairs, I cleaned up what was left of my food and the extra she'd brought. My appetite was next to nonexistent these days. The only reason I ate most of the time was because I forced myself. It wasn't as if the food had much taste. I ate because I needed the energy to keep myself going, to do what I needed to do for myself and Brianna. I could only hope Brianna was doing the same, and that Cal and Jade were encouraging her to eat. The thought that she might not be taking care of herself caused the food I'd just eaten to churn in my stomach.

Hearing Sarah coming down the stairs, I pushed my discomfort aside and walked back into the dining room to meet her. She had a somewhat serious expression on her face.

"What's wrong?" I asked.

Sarah turned away from me and headed into the living room. I followed. She reached the couch, paused as if she were going to sit down, then walked to the large window overlooking the city, and started pacing. After several moments, I took a seat in my chair and decided to wait her out. It wasn't as if I had anything better to do with my evening.

Even so, I was grateful she didn't make me wait long. She didn't look at me when she spoke, which made me uneasy. Sarah didn't have trouble looking people in the eye. Ever.

"I wasn't completely honest with you about why I'm here."

Instead of acknowledging her comment, I remained silent.

"I mean, I did come here because I want to be here for you. That wasn't a lie, but . . ." She took a deep breath and wrapped her arms around her middle, hugging herself. "That wasn't the only reason."

Pain was etched across her face, and I debated whether to go comfort her.

I was about to cross the room when she continued. "I met a guy. We were together for about six months. He . . . he wasn't a Dom, but I liked him. I thought. I thought maybe in time I could introduce him to the lifestyle."

It didn't take a genius to see where this was going. To many, BDSM was taboo. Some people felt that in order to be involved in the lifestyle, one had to be sick or twisted in some way. It was far from the truth, but to some that didn't matter.

"One night, I pulled out some of my toys and asked him to use them on me. At first, he just looked at me with this blank stare. I thought he didn't understand what I was asking, so I explained."

She held herself tighter, and I couldn't stay seated any longer. I knew what it was like to be rejected because of what I enjoyed, to have someone you cared about treat you as if you were a freak of nature for your desires. Taking hold of her shoulders, I pulled her against me, and she buried her face in my neck.

"He said I was disgusting. Tha-that he never wanted to see me again."

"I'm sorry, Sarah." I felt moisture seep through my shirt and knew she was crying.

We stood there as the sun began to set over the city. "There's something else I have to tell you."

Leaning back so that I could look at her face, I watched as she brushed the tears from her cheeks and tried to compose herself. "You can tell me anything. You know that."

She glanced down, her dark brown hair obstructing her face. A flash of Brianna standing before me, head bowed and about to confess something, caused me to suck in a deep breath. My chest clenched painfully.

I almost welcomed it when Sarah looked back up and I could see her face. It didn't make the ache go away, nothing ever did, but I would take what small reprieve I could get.

"Two weeks later, I realized I was late."

Blinking, I stared into her eyes. I wanted to make sure I understood. "You're pregnant?"

She nodded.

"Does he know?"

She shook her head. "I don't know how to tell him. Not after what he said. What if he . . . tries to take the baby away from me?"

Tears returned, and I held her close. "We'll figure it out."

"Stephan, you don't have to. You have enough to deal with right now. I wasn't even going tell you."

"I'm glad you did."

When her tears began to ebb, Sarah laughed, but there was little humor in it. "I cry at the drop of a hat now."

I laughed. "I think that's normal."

She nodded.

"Do you know how far along you are?"

"About eight weeks."

It was my turn to nod. Even though she couldn't see me, I knew she felt the movement.

"Where are you staying while you're here?"

"At a hotel not far from downtown."

"You're going to be here a while?"

"Yeah. I need some time to figure out what I'm going to do." She paused. "Plus, I really do want to be here for you, Stephan. I don't know about this woman, but I know you."

I hugged her, grateful for her friendship. "I'm going to call Lily. She can go back to the hotel with you and get your things." She glanced up at me, confused. "You're here to see me, right?"

"Yes."

"Then you're staying here. I have a guest room upstairs now. It might as well be used for something useful."

"Stephan, I can't—"

"I don't recall asking."

Sarah opened and shut her mouth several times. "Thank you."

"You're welcome. Let me call Lily and see if she's free. If not, I'll take you, but considering the number of reporters following me around, it would be better if they didn't see me going into a hotel with you."

I took out my phone, and she shifted nervously from one foot to the other. "I don't want my staying here to cause problems for you."

"You're staying."

She didn't argue, and after selecting Lily's number, I placed the phone to my ear. Lily answered on the third ring. "If you're not busy tonight, I need a favor."

Chapter 5

Brianna

I nervously glanced at the clock for the twelfth time in less than ten minutes. It was almost four. Cal was normally home before four, especially on Fridays, which was why when Emma had called, saying she needed to talk to both of us, I'd told her four o'clock.

Looking again, I realized the clock hadn't changed. Why wasn't he home yet?

At the sound of a car in the driveway, I whipped my head in that direction, even though I couldn't see the front of the house from my room. Glancing down, I noticed that I'd pulled several threads loose from my jeans. When I heard someone open the door to the house, I dismissed my observation completely. I held my breath as I waited.

"Anna, I'm home," Cal called out from the main room.

I released the breath I'd been holding.

That first week I'd moved in, Cal took off work. It was awkward, but knowing he'd been in the house had helped. Cal had installed a security system, as well as setting up what he called a panic button. There were several of them around the house, and he said if anyone tried to break in and hurt me, I could hit one of those buttons and it would send a signal directly to him and to the police. Even with all the added security, I tensed and waited for Cal or Jade to call out to me when they came home, letting me know it was them.

Knowing Cal was here, and that Emma would be coming any minute, I knew I needed to force myself to get up from my bed. My legs didn't want to cooperate. It felt as if I had metal rods in them as I moved. What seemed like several minutes had passed before I reached the door that separated my bedroom from the main house, and once I got there, I paused with my hand on the knob.

You can do this. It's just Cal.

Turning the knob, I slowly opened the door. It made no sound, but as I stepped into the kitchen Cal must have seen movement out of the corner of his eye, because he turned around abruptly and knocked a bread roll he had lying on the counter to the floor.

When he realized what he'd done, he sighed and bent down to pick it up. I plastered myself against the wall next to my door.

He glanced in my direction as he tossed the dirty roll in the trash. "Is everything okay, Anna?"

I nodded.

Cal frowned but went back to making his sandwich. He used to try and approach me at times like this, but he didn't anymore, especially when Jade wasn't around. I didn't mean to freak out on him, but too often he would get frustrated with me and raise his voice or move his body a certain way, and I'd hit an eight or a nine within seconds.

The first time it happened, I'd screamed *yellow* at him as I'd backed myself up into the far corner of my bedroom. He'd looked at me as if I were speaking a foreign language. Luckily Jade was there and had understood. *"I think it's something Stephan taught her to say when things are getting to be too much. I think it means she needs space, Cal. You need to give her some space."* She'd been right, and he'd reluctantly backed off.

After a similar thing happened two other times, Cal had taken to keeping his distance from me. He never came within three feet of me unless he asked first. If we were standing, it was more like five. I know the whole situation upset him, but I was grateful he was being such a good friend to me. He was letting me live here after all. I doubted I could ever repay him for everything he was doing.

"Did you want a sandwich? I've got ham and turkey."

"No. Thank you."

He glanced in my direction once more and went back to what he was doing.

"Emma called."

That got his attention, and he abandoned his sandwich to face me. "What did she say?"

His voice was commanding, and I could see the muscles under his shirt flexing. My gaze fixated on his arms, his posture, and I swallowed, feeling my heart rate increase.

"Anna. What did Emma say?"

My gaze snapped to his, my eyes wide.

He sighed. "I'm sorry. I shouldn't have said it like that. I'm just . . . I guess I'm anxious to hear what she had to say."

I closed my eyes and took in a slow, deep breath, trying to calm down. I spread my hands wide behind me, feeling the texture of the wall, allowing it to ground me just as Stephan had taught me. "She's . . . coming over."

Cal didn't speak for several long seconds. "When?"

Before I could answer, we heard another car.

"I guess that answers my question." He abandoned his food and went to get the door. I stayed where I was.

Muffled sounds from the front entry floated into the back of the house. I couldn't hear what they were saying, but I could tell by Cal's tone that he was questioning Emma. She'd said on the phone that she wanted to talk to us both together, so I doubted she would say anything to him without me in the room.

Sure enough, less than a minute later, Cal came marching into the kitchen with Emma in tow. He didn't look all that happy, but when he saw me, he made an effort to soften his features. I knew he was trying not to scare me, and he was probably as anxious to hear what Emma had to say as I was.

"Hi, Anna."

"Hi."

"Can we get started?" Cal took a deep breath, causing his shoulders to rise and fall dramatically.

"Of course."

Emma sat at the kitchen table with Cal. They both looked over at me, obviously wanting me to join them.

I pushed myself away from the wall and walked slowly across the room. Once I was seated, Emma didn't waste any time getting to the point of her visit. She looked to Cal first, then to me. "Did Cal tell you he came to see me, Anna?"

"Yes."

"Good." She seemed relieved. "I met with Stephan's lawyer, as well as a criminal attorney from my firm. We've discussed the situation in detail and have concluded that the best thing for you to do, Anna, is nothing."

"What?"

Emma's focus turned to Cal, briefly acknowledging his outburst. "We still think it's a good idea for you to publicly show support for Mr. Coleman, if you're willing, but there should be no mention of what happened to Anna or his part in it."

"I don't understand. Why not?"

"Right now all the FBI has is a single transaction made to Ian Pierce by Mr. Coleman. They don't have any evidence as to what it's for, other than a small notation that is Anna's name. And unless one of the parties involved speaks up, that's all they have. We don't want to give them reason to think there's anything else there by coming forward and offering a deal. It wouldn't look good."

"Wait a minute. Does that mean the *monster* that did this to her will get off free and clear?"

"For what he did to Anna . . . yes, I'm afraid so." Cal opened his mouth to interrupt, but Emma was faster. "Anna has indicated to me on numerous occasions that her first priority is protecting Stephan. This is the best way to do that."

Cal stood abruptly, causing his chair to crash to the floor, and I jumped, poised on the edge of my chair, ready to run.

He didn't notice, but Emma did. She frowned at his retreating back.

No one said a word for several minutes, and the air around us seemed to be charged. I debated. I wanted to go, but I needed to stay and hear what Emma had to say about Stephan.

When Emma finally spoke again, her voice was soft. "The FBI has plenty of other evidence against Mr. Pierce. I don't think he'll ever be getting out of prison. They found another body."

I went cold. It felt as if I'd suddenly been plunged into an ice bath.

After that, I only heard bits and pieces of the conversation. They'd found a girl, about my age. Another one. I didn't hear where or how they'd found her. My guess, given Emma's tone, was that she'd been discovered much like the other girl—Juliet.

Juliet. It could have been me. It would have been me if—

Someone touched my arm, jarring me out of my thoughts.

I didn't acknowledge who had touched me, or why. The only thing I knew was that I needed to get away, to escape. I scrambled from my chair and ran full speed to my room. Looking around frantically, I tried to decide where to go. The corner? No, too exposed. The closet? No. There was no door on the closet here.

Within seconds, I zeroed in on the bathroom and took off in that direction. Once inside, I climbed into the bathtub and curled into a ball behind the curtain.

At some point, I heard someone moving around in my bedroom, but eventually they went away. Tears streamed down my face as I rocked back and forth, surrounded by the cold harshness of the bathtub. I wanted Stephan. I needed him so much.

I pulled at his collar around my neck. The metal dug into my skin, causing more tears to form in my eyes. I didn't care. It was the only part of him I had left, and I needed to feel something . . . anything of him.

Slowly, the pain began to overtake the fear, and I eased my grip on the collar. As I did, a body-racking sob shook my entire body. Memories of Stephan . . . his touch . . . his lips . . . I wanted him to wrap his arms around me and tell me it was going to be okay.

Harsh light filled the room, and I looked up, panicked. Who'd found me?

The shower curtain was gently pushed aside. Jade glanced down at me, her eyes sad. "I sent Cal into town for some food."

I didn't respond.

Jade sat on the edge of the tub and looked down at her hands. She seemed nervous, and it increased my anxiety even more.

"Cal told me what happened—what Emma told you." Wiping her hands on her legs, she met my gaze. "Are you all right? I can't imagine what you're going through after hearing—" She paused and sighed.

The sound of our breathing seemed to echo in the small space.

"It would have been me," I whispered.

She nodded, not attempting to sugarcoat the situation.

"I should be dead."

"But you're not." Jade reached out and touched my arm. I flinched, and she dropped her hand. "You're not dead, Anna. You're here. Alive. And you have your whole life in front of you."

I shook my head but didn't comment.

Jade stood. "Do you think maybe we could go out into the living room? The couch has to be a lot more comfortable than the bathtub." I didn't answer. "Cal will be gone for a while. I told him I wanted Greek, so he's driving across town to get my favorite. Come on. It'll just be us." She extended her arm, offering me her hand.

For several seconds, I stared. I didn't want to move. All I wanted to do was stay hidden forever.

Looking up, I debated my options. I could stay where I was. When Cal came home, however, he wouldn't let me stay in here. I knew he wouldn't. The last time something like this happened, he'd threatened to pick me up out of the tub and carry me back into my bedroom if I didn't get out on my own. He'd meant it, too, so I'd pushed myself up from the cold, hard surface and ran to my bed where I'd hidden under the covers for the rest of the night. He hadn't been happy with my new place of refuge, but he'd let me be. I didn't want that to happen this time.

Taking Jade's hand, I stood. She helped me out of the bathtub before releasing me.

Following her, I cautiously made my way back into the main part of the house and into the living room. Jade took a seat on the couch.

I looked at the space next to her—even the opposite end of the couch— but it felt too exposed, so I chose the chair on the far side of the room. It was close to the wall and faced the door.

Curling my legs under me, I turned toward Jade. She frowned slightly and then smoothed out her features. I'd disappointed her by not sitting next to her, but I wasn't ready for that. Even now, the living room felt too big. I wanted to be back in my space. Alone.

"Anna, I'm going to be honest with you. Cal's worried, and so am I." Jade paused and leaned her head back against the couch. She closed her eyes briefly before turning her head to the side and meeting my gaze. "Cal told me that Emma still thinks having him publicly support Stephan is a good idea. He's willing to do it—for you—but . . . Anna, he still wants you to go talk to someone. And after today, I'm thinking that's not a bad idea."

I started shaking my head. I didn't want to talk to anyone.

Before I knew it, Jade was kneeling down in front of me. "Hear me out, okay? Anna, you've closed yourself off so much since you've been here with us. When I first met you, you were scared, yes, but you were able to interact with us. Smile. Laugh. I know you miss Stephan, and I'm guessing you used to talk to him about things . . . what happened to you. You don't have that now, and I think . . . I think you need someone to talk to."

"I can't . . . ." The words died in my throat.

Jade reached out, took my hand, and squeezed. "I don't like how Cal did it—making it a condition of him showing support for Stephan—but he doesn't know what else to do. He sees you suffering, and he wants to help you in the only way he knows how."

Before I could stop them, tears were streaming down my face, blurring my vision.

"I'll go with you if you want, so you don't have to go alone. I can talk to some of the professors . . . get a recommendation. Say you'll at least try, Anna. Please?"

The sound of the clock ticking on the mantel measured the seconds passing as Jade waited for my answer. "You-you'll go?"

"If you want me to, I will. Cal will, too, if that's what you want. We just want you to get better, Anna." She was pleading with me.

"Cal will help Stephan?"

She nodded and squeezed my hand once more.

"Okay. I-I'll talk . . . to someone."

Jade smiled and cautiously leaned in to give me a hug. "Thank you, Anna. I know this is hard, but we'll make it through it. I promise."

I returned her hug with little enthusiasm, closing my eyes and allowing a mixture of dread and hope to seep into my body. Dread—because whoever this person was I was going to talk to would want me to relive my time with Ian. Hope—because maybe all this pain would be worth it and I could save Stephan . . . just as he had saved me.

Chapter 6

Brianna

Cal pulled up in front of a small brown building. It had been two weeks since Jade had gotten me to agree to talk to someone. She'd spoken with the head of the university's psychology department—she'd taken a psych class during her sophomore year as an elective thinking it would help her relate to her future clients better. They'd given her a handful of names, but only two were women.

Jade had spent three hours with me as we searched the Internet for anything we could find on the two psychiatrists. They were both known for their work with trauma patients. The one we'd settled on, however, had written her dissertation on the effects of human trafficking on its victims.

Her name was Candice Perkins. She was forty-six years old, according to her profile, married, with two children. The picture on her website showed a woman with a big smile and kind eyes. I only hoped that once I met her, I would like her.

Opening the back door, Jade waited for me to step out onto the sidewalk. I did so reluctantly. Even though I'd agreed to this, I wanted to beg Cal to take me back to the house. The only thing keeping me from doing just that was the bargain Cal and I had made. I would meet with this woman, or someone like her, for at least the rest of the year, and in return, Cal would make a public showing of his support for Stephan.

Jade felt four months of therapy was a lot to ask me to commit to considering we didn't know how I would react. I understood. If I said I wasn't scared, I'd be lying. What Jade didn't understand, however, was that I doubted this woman could hurt me any more than Ian had. I'd survived that, and I'd survive this, too.

Taking a deep breath, I edged closer to Jade. She took my hand and squeezed it.

"I'll meet you guys inside once I find a place to park." Jade nodded to Cal, and he pulled away from the curb.

"Come on. Let's get inside. Maybe that will make you feel more comfortable."

I walked beside Jade into the building, but nothing would take away the nauseous feeling in my stomach.

The lobby was generic, much like any other waiting area I'd seen when I was younger. It reminded me most of Dr. Chandler's office. He'd been my mom's oncologist, and she'd seen him every month. The only difference was that his office had a painting along one wall of a girl playing in a field of wild flowers. This office had paintings, but they were more abstract. I preferred the wildflowers.

When the door behind me opened, I jerked away from Jade and backed up several steps before realizing it was Cal. He'd been trying to be better about not scaring me, but most of the time it wasn't his fault. Cal was a big guy. He was taller than Stephan. His arms were also twice the size of Stephan's. I knew it was because of Cal's job—it was a lot more physically demanding than Stephan's—but fear was fear. One thing Stephan had taught me was that while I couldn't control *what* I was afraid of, I could control how I reacted to it. I was trying to be better, but it was difficult when all my instincts told me to run in the opposite direction.

Cal stopped several feet in front of me, his brow furrowed. "You ready, Anna?"

"Yes."

He nodded and led us down a short hallway until we came to a door at the very end marked *Dr. Candice Perkins* in fancy lettering. Without pausing, Cal opened it and stepped inside.

This room was different from the lobby we were in moments before. The walls here had color, and the furniture looked newer and more welcoming. It reminded me of a beach, for some reason.

Jade led me over to a set of chairs in the corner, while Cal went to talk to the lady behind the desk. "Brianna Reeves here to see Dr. Perkins."

"Has she been here before?"

"No. This is her first visit."

"Okay, then. I'm going to need her to fill out some paperwork."

She handed him a clipboard and a pen. He took it and walked back toward us.

Instead of handing the paperwork to me, he thumbed through it himself. "Most of this is insurance stuff." He seemed to be talking to himself and not expecting Jade or me to answer.

Placing several sheets of papers off to the side, he handed the clipboard to me. I took the pen he offered and looked down at the forms. There were only two left after he'd sifted through them. One wanted general information—my name, age, address. The other asked about my medical history.

I filled the papers out as best I could and then gave them back to Cal. He walked them back to the receptionist and returned to sit beside me. For some reason, the fact that Jade and Cal were flanking me allowed me to breathe easier. I knew, despite all the ways he made me nervous, Cal would protect me if anyone tried to hurt me.

Less than five minutes later, a door to our left opened, and Dr. Candice Perkins appeared. She was shorter than I'd thought she would be, maybe five two, and her hair was lighter than what it had seemed in her picture. It almost had a reddish tint to it.

"Brianna?" She looked straight at me.

I glanced at the door, then back at her.

"Would you like your friends to come back with you? I don't mind. I want you to be comfortable."

Jade squeezed my hand to get my attention. I looked over at her. "It's up to you, Anna."

"Please."

Cal and Jade stood, and so did I.

Dr. Perkins's office was much as the waiting room outside had been. It was full of soft colors that reminded me of water and sand. She motioned for us to take a seat on a large couch along the wall.

"Hello." She smiled as she took a seat across from us.

Jade and Cal remained silent on either side of me, and it made me feel self-conscious. I knew I was here to talk to Dr. Perkins, but I didn't like having everyone focused solely on me. Glancing down, I started picking at the fabric on my jeans. "Hello."

"I heard your friend call you Anna. Do you prefer Anna or Brianna?"

"Anna's fine."

Another smile. "Anna it is, then. It's nice to meet you. You can call me Candice."

I nodded but didn't comment.

"Maybe we should start by having you introducing your friends."

"This is Cal." I motioned toward my left first, then my right. "And this is his girlfriend, Jade."

"Have you known Cal and Jade for a while?"

"Cal and I . . . we grew up together."

"Sounds like you've been friends for a while, then."

"O-our fa—"

Jade gripped my hand, trying to comfort me. I saw Cal open and close his fist reflexively. He wanted to comfort me, too, but he knew how I'd react if he tried to touch me.

"Our fathers were friends." Cal's voice had a clipped tone to it. I knew he was angry with John. He'd told me about going to see him at the jail. I also knew that Cal wasn't all that happy with his own father. When Cal had told Neil what happened with John, he'd defended my father, insisting that the Jonathan Reeves he knew would never do such a thing. Since then, Cal had had little contact with his dad. It was yet another thing for me to feel guilty about.

Dr. Perkins tilted her head to the side. "It doesn't sound like you're happy

Talking to Dr. Perkins today, although it hadn't been as horrible as I'd thought it would be, had reminded me of yet another thing I missed about being with Stephan. I could talk to him. He *made* me talk to him. Even though I didn't like it, I trusted him. I knew I could tell him anything, and he would always be honest with me.

As much as I appreciated Cal and Jade's friendship, there were times I knew they weren't telling me the whole truth. I didn't think they were trying to withhold information from me. It was more that they were trying to protect me. Cal would sometimes push, but only about Stephan. He never pressed me to talk about how I was feeling or what I'd gone through with Ian. Jade would ask me if there was anything I wanted to talk about . . . that or she would just come into my room and lie down beside me.

I knew this was the main reason why they wanted me to see Dr. Perkins. They wanted me to talk, but they didn't know how to get me to open up to them. I understood. They cared about me and didn't like seeing my breakdowns. I didn't blame them. My panic attacks were scary. Even to me.

Curling into a ball, I reached for Stephan's collar and pulled tight, feeling the bite of it as it pressed into the skin of my neck. I would go and talk to Dr. Perkins, and Cal would help Stephan. That was all that mattered.

Chapter 7

Stephan

"I still can't believe you didn't own a coffeemaker. How do you function in the mornings?" Sarah stood leaning against the kitchen counter sipping a cup of coffee as I walked toward her. She'd been living with me for over two weeks, and it was almost like old times. Almost.

"Easy." I went to the refrigerator and removed the cream cheese before putting a bagel in the toaster.

"You're strange."

I glanced over my shoulder at her. She was wearing a huge grin. "Maybe you don't need that coffee as much as you think you do. You're awfully chipper this morning."

"That has nothing to do with the coffee."

My bagel popped out of the toaster, but before I could grab it, Sarah leaned around me and stole it, cursing at the heat burning her fingers.

I stared at her, raising my eyebrow.

"What? I was hungry. I'm eating for two now, remember?"

Shaking my head, I took another bagel and started again. Part of me wanted to give her a hard time about what she'd done and the coffee she was downing in large gulps, but I couldn't seem to muster the energy. I wasn't in the mood to fight with her or anyone else. It had been another rough night for me, and all I wanted to do was go through the motions.

Once my breakfast was ready, I took a seat beside Sarah at the island. She'd finished her bagel and coffee and was now sipping on some juice as she eyed the coffeepot with longing.

"Aren't you going to ask me why I'm so energized this morning?"

It appeared she wasn't going to allow me to eat in peace—not that she had since she'd arrived—but she usually allowed me a few hours in the morning to put on my game face. "Why are you so perky this morning?"

She frowned at my less than heartfelt question. "Well, if you really want to know . . . I got a job."

I paused, turning to look at her. Sarah was a certified public accountant.

She loved crunching numbers. It was a game to her. The only reason I hadn't considered her when I was looking for a new CFO was that she preferred to work with small businesses. The size of the foundation's books made the job undesirable to her.

"Where?" I asked, going back to my breakfast.

"I was talking to Daren the other day. He has a friend who got in over his head and needs some help getting his business finances in order. I said I'd help."

"What about your other clients?" I knew she worked while I was at the office. Most of her client work could be done on the computer, which allowed her to travel—that and Sarah having a business partner who didn't mind manning the office while she was gone. After she'd told me about Clint, I doubted his accommodating demeanor was of a purely platonic nature. Sarah seemed oblivious, though.

"It's not tax season, so I have time. Besides, you're gone all day. It will give me something to do and get me out of the house for a while."

I nodded and finished the last of my food. "Barring any unexpected meetings, I should be home by six."

"I'll order something for dinner."

The morning dragged even with a visit from Lily around nine thirty. She was acting a little strange—even for Lily—but I dismissed it. Given my mood, I could be reading into things that weren't really there. Since Brianna's departure, she'd made it a point to check on me at least once a day. I wasn't sure what she expected to find. It wasn't as if I couldn't function. I could, and I did.

"Mr. James is here to see you, Mr. Coleman." Jamie's voice came through the phone cool and detached, pulling me back into the present.

I saved the file I'd been working on before answering. "Send him in."

Seconds later, our CFO strolled into my office. He closed the door behind him. "I won't take up much of your time, Mr. Coleman, but I wanted to give you an update."

Michael's appearance in my office was a surprise. It wasn't as if he'd avoided me these last three months. We attended meetings together, and I would pass him in the hall, but he'd tried to keep things as professional as possible. I couldn't blame him for that. He'd been on the job less than two weeks before I'd gotten him involved in a massive scandal. Honestly, I was surprised he hadn't turned in his resignation yet.

I nodded, waiting to see what had brought him to my office this morning.

He leaned back in his chair and met my gaze. "We're finally making some progress on the money that was taken. As you know, I had to enlist the help of a decoding expert. Whoever it was, they covered their tracks well, and I don't think they did it alone."

"What did your expert find?"

"The information was inputted into the system from a remote site."

That got my attention. We may not be a bank, but there was a lot of money that passed through these walls. Our computer security was good—very good. For someone to get through our firewalls took skill. The money had been extracted without tripping any alarms, and that meant we had a huge problem on our hands.

"Whoever did this had access to the company, which means he or she had someone on the inside."

That made sense. Whoever pulled this off knew when Lily made her purchases. That wasn't information just anyone would have access to. "What happens now?"

"I've had security pull video of Ms. Adams's floor for the days in question. It's going to take a while, but I'm going to go through the tapes and see if anything suspicious turns up."

"You think it was someone close to Ms. Adams?"

"It had to be. How else would they know when the transactions were taking place?"

It was hard to believe that one of Lily's staff was embezzling money. There were only a handful of individuals who'd joined us in the last two years. Most had been here since my father ran the foundation ten years ago.

After Michael left, I tried to get back to my work, but I couldn't concentrate. Saturday was my twenty-fifth birthday, and my life was far from what I'd thought it would be. In two days, it would be ten years since my parents' death. I wasn't prepared for that—although, I'm not sure one ever could be. It seemed like only last week they had both been here smiling and laughing. You would think after ten years the hurt would have gone away, or at least lessened.

My next thought was of Brianna. She was the one person I'd been able to share my parents with. She—more than anyone—understood.

I pushed away from my desk and stood, forcing the tears that beckoned back where they belonged. Crying wouldn't help anything. It wouldn't bring Brianna or my parents back. I had to be strong, do what needed to be done, and stop worrying about what I couldn't change.

At five minutes before twelve, Jamie informed me that Ross had arrived. I'd gotten myself back under control from earlier, but hearing his name sent mixed feelings rushing through me—excitement, dread, fear . . . and something close to joy. No matter how much the man irritated me, he would have news of Brianna. If nothing else, he could give me something no one else could.

Ross strolled into my office looking less cocky than usual. "Coleman."

"Ross."

He walked to the center of the room and glanced around the office as if taking it in for the first time.

As much as I wanted to demand to know why he was here, I bit my tongue. For now, at least, I would wait him out.

"I was wondering if you'd join me for lunch."

It was a good thing I didn't have anything in my mouth, because I would have choked. "Excuse me?"

He sighed, clearly frustrated. "Lunch. You know, the meal one typically has in the middle of the day."

"I'm aware of what lunch is, Ross. What I don't understand is why you want me to join you."

"I've . . . made a deal with Anna."

"What kind of a deal?"

He waved me off. "That's not important."

"I assure you, it is. Now what 'deal' did you make with Brianna that has you wanting to have lunch with me?"

He stared at me, the anger burning behind his eyes. Ross didn't like that I'd questioned him.

"I told her I'd show my . . . support. For you. Publicly," he said through gritted teeth.

I didn't answer right away, trying to digest what he'd said. "You're trying to help me?"

"Yes." Ross almost spat the word.

"And what does this entail exactly?"

He threw up his hands. "For goodness sake, Coleman. I'm trying to do you a favor here."

I was still skeptical. "All right. We'll go to lunch."

"Good." Ross turned toward the door while I picked up my suit jacket. He didn't wait for me, and that was just as well. I was still trying to wrap my head around this turn of events and why, all of a sudden, Cal Ross wanted to help me. Brianna was no longer testifying against Ian, so what exactly did he have to gain from it? One way or another, I was going to find out.

As soon as Ross and I emerged from the building, we were surrounded by the local media. To my surprise, Ross planted a smile on his face and continued walking. I quickly realized what he was doing and followed suit. Cameras were flashing everywhere. Ross wasn't as well-known as I was, but he wasn't a hermit either. It wouldn't take long for the reporters to realize who he was, and then not long after that to make the connection between him and Jonathan Reeves.

I followed Ross, allowing him to take the lead. Lunch was going to be uncomfortable at best. We didn't get along, and I wasn't sure we ever would. This was just for show, and we both knew it.

He turned the corner and slipped inside an upscale seafood restaurant. The place was filled with businessmen and women, all in suits. A few of them glanced up briefly at our entrance before going back to whatever they had been discussing prior to our arrival.

Ross gave his name, apparently having planned ahead and made a reservation. We were immediately taken to a table.

Taking a seat, I glanced around and realized instantly what he'd arranged. We were seated at a corner table by a large window. The placement of the table gave us some privacy, while the window allowed the photographers outside a clear and unobstructed view. It was the perfect photo opportunity. I had to hand it to him. He'd put a lot of thought into this.

Our server approached our table, and we both placed our orders. Once he was out of earshot, I planted a smile on my face and asked what I'd been dying to know since he'd walked into my office. "How is she?"

Ross dragged his gaze away from whatever he'd been looking at across the room. "She's as well as can be expected under the circumstances."

I nodded and let out a lungful of air. "Is she eating?"

He paused before answering. "Most of the time."

The server came back with our drinks. I thanked him and returned my attention to Ross, ready to ask my next question. He beat me to it, though.

"I know you want to know about Anna. And since she knows I'm with you today, she's probably going to have a million questions for me when I get home. The problem is I'm not sure how much I want to tell you. I don't trust you. Not with her. But you already know that."

"Yes. You've made that quite clear."

He was getting agitated, but I saw him trying to school his features so that his irritation wouldn't show to anyone observing our conversation. "You've made her dependent on you. I can't support that."

"Why are you here, then? Isn't showing your support for me to the press contradictory?"

"No. As much as it pains me to say this, you don't deserve to have your life ruined. You got her out, got her away from that . . . that . . . monstrous bastard. For that, I will play nice—at least as far as the public is concerned. You and I both know, and I want to be clear, I don't approve of this . . . relationship—if that's what you want to call it—you have with her. It's messed up, and it's not what she needs."

Our food arrived, preventing me from responding. After thanking our server, I took a few minutes to consider my words carefully. "I suppose since we are being honest here—laying our cards on the table—I should reiterate that I couldn't care less what you think of my relationship with Brianna. With that said, however, I also concede that at the moment you are able to give her something I can't. But that doesn't mean my feelings for her have lessened. And whether you believe it or not—whether you understand it or not—I *do* love her."

"You love to hurt her, you mean." Although his words were said pleasantly enough, there was no disguising the animosity behind them.

"I would never hurt her. Ever."

He took a deep breath and smiled. "You'd better hope you can keep that promise, Coleman."

Very little was said for the remainder of our meal. We fixed pleasant looks on our faces and pretended to be enjoying each other's company. Although I wasn't looking at it from the outside, I thought we were pretty convincing.

The server arrived with our checks, and I got an idea. "Would you come back up to my office with me?"

"I don't do after-lunch rendezvous, Coleman."

I snorted. "Not exactly what I had in mind, Ross, but thank you for the clarification. I'd like to write a letter for you to take to Brianna."

"Why?"

"It's been three months."

For a moment, I thought he was going to refuse.

"Fine. I don't like being your messenger boy, but maybe it will put a smile on Anna's face."

"Thank you."

"I'm not doing it for you, Coleman."

"I know. You're doing it for Brianna. I'm still grateful."

Ross stood, tossing his napkin and some money down on the table. I did the same. "Come on. Let's get this over with."

Chapter 8

Brianna

"What if they got into a fight? What if they hurt each other? It would be all my fault." I knew my voice held a hint of hysteria, but I couldn't help it.

Jade took hold of my hand and laced our fingers together. She'd skipped her classes today, knowing how nervous I'd be about Stephan and Cal's meeting. "I'm sure it was fine. They're both grown men. I'm positive they can control themselves."

"Cal doesn't like Stephan. He doesn't understand."

She continued to try and soothe me. "He made you a promise, Anna. He'll keep it."

I looked up at her and saw she earnestly believed what she was saying. In her view, the goal would outweigh any perceived obstacles. I only hoped she was right.

The afternoon dragged on as Jade tried to distract me. Cal had said he would be home early, but it was getting close to three and there'd been no sign of him. Jade had even tried to call his cell, but it went straight to his voice mail. With every passing minute, my anxiety increased. If Jade hadn't been with me, I probably would have retreated into myself.

As it was, when we finally heard him arrive, I was shaking due to nerves. They were supposed to have met for lunch. No one had lunch this late, did they? Where had Cal been? What had he been doing? What had taken so long?

Jade held tight to my hand while we waited for Cal to make his way to my bedroom.

He caught sight of us on the bed and stopped. "Everything okay?"

"I don't know." Jade's tone made Cal raise his eyebrows. She didn't raise her voice, but it had that "I'm not happy" inflection I remembered my mom had used with my stepdad sometimes. "Is there a reason you didn't come home right after your lunch or, at the very least, pick up your phone to let us know how everything went?"

"Oh." For the first time in . . . well, ever . . . I saw Cal look somewhat guilty.

"Oh?"

"Sorry about that. I-I needed to clear my head and think about a few things."

"And your phone?"

He sighed. "I turned it off. Like I said, I needed time to think, and I didn't want the office calling me."

Instead of responding to Cal, she rubbed my arm and spoke to me. "I don't see any marks on him, do you?"

Cal stood at the end of my bed, and I took a long minute to look him over from head to foot.

"No."

"What are you two talking about?"

"Anna was afraid you and Stephan would get into a fight. She's been a nervous wreck all day." The look Jade sent him gave me chills. "Which you would have known had you *called*."

Cal stood motionless, staring at me, before pulling up a chair beside my bed. He reached out but didn't touch me. "I'm sorry, Anna. I didn't think, and I should have."

"It's okay," I whispered. My reaction probably wasn't normal. I didn't want him to feel bad because I wasn't strong enough to deal with things. It wasn't his fault.

"No. It's not. Jade's right—I should have called." He paused. "I have something for you."

Cal reached into his back pocket and handed me what looked to be a folded piece of paper, careful not to let our fingers touch.

"What is it?"

When he remained silent, I looked up at him. "It's a letter from Coleman. He asked me to give it to you."

My eyes opened wide, and my hands began to tremble. Stephan had written me a letter?

I started to open it and then stopped, noticing my audience.

"Let's give her some privacy," Jade said, standing. Cal was reluctant to go. Eventually Jade grew tired of his stalling and reached for his hand, dragging him with her out of the room.

Alone, I glanced back down at the letter. For a split second, fear raced through me. What if this was it? What if he'd finally realized I was too much to deal with? We'd been apart for three months—the same amount of time I'd lived with him. What if this time apart had convinced him—had shown him how much he'd given up for me?

I let the paper drop from my hands and watched as it landed on top of my thighs. As I continued to stare at it, the fear lessened and was replaced by a mixture of joy and sadness. What if he missed me even half as much as I missed him? It was difficult for me to accept, but I couldn't deny how much I wanted it to be the truth.

Reaching out, I skimmed my fingers along the folded edges. I had to know. No matter what he said—even if it was that he didn't feel for me as I did for him—I had to find out.

Before I could stop myself, I picked up the letter and opened it. Stephan's handwriting filled the page, and as I began reading his words, my eyes filled with tears. I had to start over twice before I was able to get through it.

> Brianna,
> I hope this letter finds you well.
> Ross came to see me today—he's sitting on the couch in my office as I write this, bouncing his leg impatiently. I was surprised he agreed to deliver this letter to you, but grateful. He says you're doing as well as can be expected. I'm not sure what to take from that, and he isn't elaborating. I asked him if you were eating, and I wasn't encouraged by his answer. You need to eat, Brianna. Do you understand?
> He says you've made some sort of deal with him. This worries me. I don't want you doing something you don't want to do just to make things easier for me. I knew the risks, and I chose to take them. If I had to do it again, I would. You're worth it. Remember that.
> There is so much I want to say, yet I know I shouldn't. Please take care of yourself.
> Yours,
> Stephan

Flipping over the letter, I hoped to find more of his writing on the back, but there was nothing. I wanted more. Then again, I wanted Stephan. I wasn't picky about which parts. I'd take anything he was willing to give me.

I sat there clinging to Stephan's letter. I had no concept of how much time had passed, but eventually I heard someone enter the room and felt the mattress give as the person sat down. No one spoke, so I knew it must be Jade. Cal would've said something after a few minutes. He hated prolonged silence.

Jade shifted, propping herself up against the headboard beside me. After a few minutes, I leaned my head against her shoulder. Her only response was to wrap her arm around my shoulders and hold me.

At some point in the middle of the night, I woke up alone. The letter was still in my grasp. Even in my sleep, I'd been unable to let it go.

Sitting up, I reached over and turned on the lamp beside my bed. Light illuminated the room, revealing a figure in the corner. Instinct kicked in, and I screamed.

Jade ran into the room seconds later. "Anna?"

She followed my horrified gaze to Cal, who was now standing frozen halfway between the corner chair and my bed.

"Cal, what are you doing in here sneaking about?" she asked as she gently made her way across the room to my side. Jade silently asked permission to touch me, and I nodded. It wasn't the same as having Stephan comforting me, but I accepted it just the same.

"I didn't think she'd turn on the light. I only wanted to make sure she didn't have a nightmare like in the beginning."

"Well, you nearly gave her—and me—a heart attack."

Cal sighed. "I'm sorry, Anna. I'll just . . . I'll be right back."

Once he left the room, Jade leaned back and searched my face. "I don't know what I'm going to do with him. I know he means well, but . . ."

"It's okay. I shouldn't . . . I shouldn't have reacted—"

"He was hiding in the corner of your room while you were asleep. You had every right to react the way you did. He's lucky you didn't throw something at his sorry ass."

That made me giggle.

Jade smiled.

She brushed the hair away from my face. "He's worried about you. I think he was hoping that Stephan's letter would get a different response."

We both looked up when Cal strolled back in the room with a glass of water. He handed it to Jade, who gave it to me. "I thought hearing from Coleman would make you happy. Instead, it's caused you more pain. I shouldn't have agreed to give it to you. I'm—"

"No!"

Both Cal and Jade jerked at my violent response. The water in my hand spilled onto the bed, as well as on Jade and me. Luckily Stephan's letter was far enough away and was spared any damage from my outburst.

Without comment, Jade went to the bathroom and retrieved a towel to clean up the water. While she was dabbing at the wetness, Cal let out a frustrated groan and stomped over to the window. It was dark, so I doubted he could see much of anything, but he stared intently out into the night as if it held some vital answer.

Jade shook her head. "I think we're going to need to change the sheets. This towel isn't doing much, I'm afraid."

I heard her, but I was focused on Cal. "If . . . if I give you a letter, will you give it to Stephan for me?"

Cal spun around, a look of bewilderment etched on his features. "What?"

Although I was trembling, I muttered the words again. "Will you give Stephan a letter for me?"

He took several steps forward and then stopped himself. "You can't be serious."

"Cal." Jade's tone had a note of warning in it.

Cal ignored her. "No. You can't be serious, Anna. Here I was thinking getting a message from him would put a smile on your face. Instead, it made you cry. No. I won't let you do that to yourself. I won't."

I opened my mouth to yell at him, but nothing came out.

My chest constricted, and it felt as if walls were closing in around me. Closing my eyes, I begged. "Please." The word came out in a broken whisper.

When I opened my eyes again, Cal was kneeling on the floor next to my bed, looking up at me. He seemed to be in pain. "Don't ask me to do this. I'd do anything for you, Anna, but don't ask this of me."

Trembling, I reached out and touched his face. It was the first time I'd willingly touched Cal since he'd come back into my life.

He closed his eyes. "If he hurts you . . ."

I slowly removed my hand and placed it back in my lap. "Thank you."

Without a word, Cal stood and left the room. I heard cabinets open and close and then the sound of a bottle being opened. Cal had gotten into the liquor cabinet. I felt bad that I'd caused him so much grief—he didn't deserve it, but I needed this.

"We should change the sheets before the water soaks in any more."

Jade's voice pulled my attention back to the woman now standing at the foot of my bed holding a fresh set of linens. I scurried off the bed, tucked Stephan's letter in my pants pocket, and began removing the wet sheets.

On Friday afternoon, once again, Cal and Jade took me to see Dr. Perkins. Cal wasn't really speaking to me. I knew he wasn't happy about the note I'd written Stephan, but he'd taken it and begrudgingly promised to deliver it next week.

Unlike last week, when Dr. Perkins had opened her door inviting me into her office, Cal and Jade didn't accompany me. This time I went in alone.

"How are you feeling today, Anna?"

I glanced around the office. Dr. Perkins had left the door ajar like last time, so I wouldn't feel trapped. I appreciated that. "I'm okay."

"I see your friends came with you again today."

I nodded.

"Does it make you feel more comfortable knowing they're here with you?"

Glancing down, I picked at my jeans. I was torn. Cal and Jade said I needed to talk to someone. Stephan told me not to do anything I didn't want to do. I didn't *want* to talk to Dr. Perkins, but after reading Stephan's letter many times over the last two days, I'd realized that maybe, if I talked to her, she might be able to help me get better. That was her job, right? And if I could get better, then maybe I could be what Stephan needed me to be. It was a long shot, but I had to try, didn't I?

"Cal isn't talking to me."

"Why isn't he talking to you?"

I looked nervously around the room. This would be so much easier if Stephan was with me, but he wasn't. I was on my own. "It's complicated."

Dr. Perkins jotted something down on the pad of paper she was holding and then redirected her attention to me. "Does this have anything to do with this Stephan?"

I nodded.

"I noticed tension between you and Cal last week when his name came up. Why don't you tell me about Stephan?"

Without thinking about it, I drew my legs up, hugging them to my chest.

"Is there a reason you changed positions, Anna? Do you feel as if you have to protect yourself?"

I didn't know how to answer her question. "Cal doesn't like him."

"Why doesn't Cal like him?" She leaned forward slightly in her chair, waiting on my answer.

"He thinks . . ." I took a deep breath. "He thinks Stephan has made me too dependent on him."

"And has he?"

I looked Dr. Perkins straight in the eye for the first time. It was a struggle to keep my voice from shaking. Everyone was against Stephan. I didn't understand it. He didn't deserve their ridicule. He'd done nothing to deserve it. "No."

"I see." She picked her pen back up and scribbled something in her notes.

Clenching my fists, I prepared for the battle I knew would come. I'd had it out several times with Cal in the last two days. He kept trying to get me to change my mind about responding to Stephan. I hated fighting with him —I hated fighting with anyone—but I wouldn't let him say bad things about Stephan. I wouldn't.

Suddenly, I wondered if Cal had talked to Dr. Perkins without me. What if he'd told her things about Stephan that weren't true? What if he'd filled her head with lies and she believed them? I would have to fight against her, too. She wouldn't see how much he'd helped me. She wouldn't understand. She wouldn't listen.

My heart began to pound in my chest. I felt hot and cold at the same time. The voices were back, but this time I couldn't understand what they were saying. Why were they yelling? Why wouldn't they leave me alone?

Something touched me.

I had to get away.

Without hesitation, I located a spot at the far side of the room where there was a large plant and took off toward it. There was a small space between it and the wall that I squeezed between, and I curled up into a ball. They would go away. They had to.

Chapter 9

Stephan
Agent Marco slammed the folder down onto the desk inches away from my hands. The urge to pull them back was there, but I resisted. I wasn't willing to show weakness in front of this man. It was exactly what he wanted.

"Cut the bullshit, Coleman. I know you know more than you're saying. Jonathan Reeves has been more than forthcoming with information. I know how you tied him up in your dining room and interrogated him. According to him, you were very protective of his daughter—more protective than just a *friend* would be. Why is that, Mr. Coleman? You've not given me one good reason as to why Ms. Reeves was living with you for three months. And I don't buy this knight-in-shining-armor story you're trying to sell."

I opened my mouth, ready to give him the standard answer Oscar and I had rehearsed, but my lawyer was faster. "My client has already provided you with an explanation, Agent Marco. It's not his problem, nor mine, that you don't accept it. Now, do you have any *new* questions for my client, or are we done here?"

Agent Marco stood to his full height and crossed his arms. He leveled a hard stare in my direction. "That's all. For now. I still don't want you leaving town, Coleman."

The moment we stepped outside, we were surrounded by the media. Cameras flashed, and reporters were shouting questions. I had little doubt that Agent Marco had tipped them off that I would be here. He was trying to rattle me.

Because of the crowd, it took us longer than it should have to reach our vehicles. Oscar paused when we reached my car. "I'll call you tomorrow. Until then, keep your head down. I'm fairly sure Agent Marco's only attempting to push your buttons, but I want to be positive."

I nodded and got into my car. "You know me—always careful."

My lawyer snorted and shook his head before turning on his heel. He walked two steps and then paused to look back over his shoulder at me.

"Oh, and Stephan?"

"Yes?"

The stern expression Oscar typically wore softened momentarily. "Happy birthday."

Before I could respond, he was halfway to his car and too far away for me to reply without drawing attention. Although my birthday *was* tomorrow, it wasn't something I usually spent a lot of time celebrating—at least not since my parents had died. During the time I spent with my aunt and uncle, Diane had attempted to mark the day with a small celebration, even if it was just her, my uncle, and Logan eating my favorite cake. She seemed to understand that, given the timing, I didn't want anything elaborate.

Today was the ten-year anniversary of my parents' death. It wasn't a day I went out of my way to remember. It was also a day I would never forget.

This time of year was always difficult for me. I'd hoped after so long that it would get easier. In some ways, it had. Or maybe I only got better at masking the effects. This year was different. I felt their loss more so than I had in years. A lot of that had to do with Brianna. I wished they could have met her, and she them. They would have loved her as much as I did.

Instead of heading directly for home, I took a detour out of town. It wasn't a route I took often. That was perhaps a good thing given a brief glance in my rearview mirror. I only noted one reporter still following me. The others must have assumed I was going back to my condo. That was good.

Taking a few unnecessary turns, I successfully lost the single car following me and drove the final five miles to the cemetery.

I drove through the large iron gate at the entrance and followed the winding road that led back to where my parents were buried. Parking my car, I stepped out into the sun.

The walk to the twin graves was short, and unlike when I'd gone with Brianna to visit her mother, the clearly marked tombstone was easy to spot. Stopping directly in front of the large granite marker, I folded my hands in front of me and bowed my head. Any words that came to my mind died in my throat. There was nothing to say that hadn't already been said. Ten years ago, on the eve of my fifteenth birthday, their plane had crashed, killing them both instantly. That day, my life had forever changed.

A gust of wind blew through the cemetery, drawing attention to the single tear that had slipped down my cheek. Taking a deep breath to steady myself, I returned to my vehicle and headed back into the city.

The elevator ride up to my condo seemed to take longer than normal, although that was undoubtedly only my perception. All I wanted to do was get home and hole up in my room with what had become my most prized possession—Brianna's journal.

The ease of executing that plan, however, would largely depend on Sarah. She refused to let me mope. It was only at night after she'd retired to her room for the evening that I was able to allow the overwhelming loss I felt to completely consume me.

Before I was able to get my key into the door, it was opened from the inside. Instead of Sarah, however, I came face-to-face with Logan. "You're late."

"If I knew I was expecting company, I would've tried to get here sooner."

I took another three steps inside before I noticed it wasn't just Logan. There in my living room sat all of my friends. Sarah and Lily were at one end of the couch with their heads together. That sight alone caused me to worry. Those two on their own could be forces of nature. Together . . . I didn't want to begin to imagine the trouble they could get themselves into. Daren was sitting in one of the chairs, his girl, Gina, on the floor at his feet.

"What's going on?"

Sarah stood and walked toward me, a sly smile on her face. She was up to something. "You're late. I thought you'd be home almost an hour ago."

"So I've heard." I let my gaze fall on each of my friends' faces before returning my attention to Sarah.

Grabbing hold of both my hands, Sarah pulled me farther into the room.

The door closed behind me seconds before Logan appeared at my side. "You didn't think we'd let you celebrate your birthday alone, did you?"

I was beginning to get a bad feeling about this. "I appreciate you guys coming over, but I would rather be left alone tonight."

Logan clasped my shoulder and squeezed. "Not a chance, my friend. We're not letting you celebrate alone. Not this year."

I looked around the room again and realized, unless I wanted a fight, I was going to have to go along with whatever they had planned. It wasn't as if it mattered. The one thing I truly wanted for my birthday, I couldn't have. "Fine. What did you have in mind? I'm sure we can order takeout or something, and I think I have a few board games around here."

Daren stood and ran his hands down the front legs of his slacks to smooth out any creases. It was then I realized they were all much too dressed up for a night in.

"I know what you're going to say, Stephan," Daren said, "and we've already thought of the entourage of reporters following you around."

While I wasn't at all interested in going out, my curiosity was piqued. I raised my eyebrow in question and waited for him to continue with whatever this brilliant plan of theirs was.

"It's a private party. Logan and Lily are friends of the couple hosting. It's a small gathering—no more than twenty people, including us. And most importantly, no press allowed."

I didn't need for him to spell it out for me, but I wanted to make sure we were all on the same page. "You want to take me to a lifestyle party?"

Lily stepped in front of me. The look on her face was pure innocence. I didn't buy it for a second.

I narrowed my eyes at her. "This is why you've been acting strange the last few days, isn't it?"

A guilty expression crossed her face for a moment, but it was soon replaced with determination. "I knew if we told you ahead of time that you would come up with some excuse not to go."

"I don't need an excuse, Lily. I can simply refuse."

"Come on, man. You need to get out of here for a while. All you've done for the last three months is go to work and come home. I understood the need not to go to social events while Brianna was here—she needed you— but now what's your excuse? Sure, she's not here anymore, but your life's not over. Tomorrow is your birthday, and as your friends, we are taking you out."

I stared at Daren in disbelief. They were all ganging up on me. Did they really think I needed some sort of an intervention?

Sarah tugged on my left hand. "Come on. Please? It's just a casual dinner party with maybe a little play afterward. It'll be fine. I promise. You don't have to do anything you don't want to. We just want you to come with us."

Tilting my head toward the ceiling, I closed my eyes. All I wanted to do was shut myself in my bedroom and get lost in Brianna's words. However, I knew better than to think that was going to happen anytime soon. Even if I refused to go with them, I was in serious doubt that they would leave me in peace for the rest of the evening.

Opening my eyes, I briefly looked at each one of them before settling on Logan. "What if someone there goes to the press? It wouldn't be unheard of, you know."

"We've got you covered. Lily and I know everyone coming tonight. No one will say anything."

I sighed. "If I do this, you all are going to promise me that I'll never come home to an ambush like this again. Agreed?"

Logan slapped me on the back, while the rest of them smiled at me. Although he didn't say anything, I knew he was worried about me. He, more than anyone, understood the impact of today's anniversary. If I had to guess, he'd been the mastermind of the entire evening—his way of making sure I wasn't dealing with my grief alone.

"What time do we have to be there?"

Daren checked his watch. "About an hour, but we should leave soon. It's outside the city, and it's about a forty-minute drive."

Nodding, I loosened my tie and headed toward my bedroom. "Give me ten minutes."

I didn't wait for a response before closing the door. If I was going to be forced to socialize tonight, I needed a few moments to put on my game face. I had a feeling tonight was going to be more difficult for me than any of them would understand.

Logan parked the car along the driveway, and we walked up a winding path to the front door. The house was modern in design with lots of windows, all of which were covered with thick curtains—the only telltale sign of what kind of party this was.

I'd debated the entire ride whether or not I should demand they take me home and call off this charade. The only thing that had stopped me was when I saw how happy my acceptance had made my friends. They cared about me and were attempting to help. I couldn't fault them for that, even if I didn't exactly agree with their methods.

A man who looked to be in his forties greeted us at the door. He looked vaguely familiar, but I couldn't place him. "Logan. Lily. Welcome."

"Hi, Daniel. Sorry we're late."

He waved his hand in dismissal. "We were just sitting down to dinner. Your timing is perfect."

After quick introductions, Daniel led us into a large dining room where all the other guests were already situated. I took note of how everyone was arranged around the table. Unless I was mistaken, everyone was in couples.

That assumption was cemented once the meal began. While every guest was seated at the table, each couple's dynamic began to show. Even Logan and Lily, and Daren and Gina, slipped into their Dominant and submissive roles with ease. It might not be obvious to everyone, but for those who knew what to look for, it was easy to spot.

Sarah and I were the only exception. She sat at my left, eating her food and chatting happily with a woman I heard introduce herself as Missy. For my part, I focused on my meal and let the conversation flow around me. If someone spoke to me directly, I would answer, but for most of dinner everyone let me be.

After dinner, the group moved into a large, well-lit room. Most of the space was filled with various seating areas clearly meant to encourage conversation. Along the one wall was a buffet of desserts and bottles of water. Daren immediately gravitated in the direction of the food, taking Gina with him, while the rest of us moved to one of the larger seating areas.

For the first half hour, most of the couples talked with one another—a few even wandered over and introduced themselves. Logan and Lily said they knew everyone in attendance, but to my surprise, Daren and Gina knew most of them as well. They'd been living in the area for less than a year. Apparently they got around more than I'd realized. Then again, I hadn't been active in the local scene since Tami.

Thoughts of Tami led me back to the two hours I'd spent being questioned by Agent Marco that afternoon. One of the many topics of conversation had included my ex. He'd spoken with her, and of course, she'd been more than happy to leave him with the impression that I was an abuser and a manipulator. Agent Marco had eaten it up and used it to try and goad me into admitting some sort of wrongdoing. Oscar hadn't allowed that to go on long, however, before he brought up the fact that Tami had never pressed any sort of charges against me.

That simple fact had only redirected his line of questioning. He'd wanted to know why I had ropes in my condo and how I'd learned to tie them so well. He'd made it sound like Jonathan Reeves had intently inspected my handiwork while bound, which wasn't the case. His being unconscious while I'd trussed him up made that feat impossible.

Thinking about Brianna's father inevitably led me to wonder about the woman herself—not that she was ever far from my thoughts. She would never have been able to come with me to a party like this. Not only were there too many people she didn't know, but there would eventually be play taking place on the far side of the room. This wasn't what those in the lifestyle called a sex positive event. Any play that occurred would be done without penetration. That wouldn't matter to Brianna, though. She and I had never ventured into my playroom. For all I knew, just the sight of the equipment would send her into one of her panic attacks. Add to that her reaction to the simple scene we'd watch Logan and Lily perform . . . it wasn't something I would ever chance again.

That was if I ever got the chance to do anything with Brianna in the future. I was still worried about this deal she'd agreed to with Ross, but there wasn't much I could do about it. The letter I'd sent was risky enough. Contact was supposed to be off-limits for the time being. If I wrote something that could be taken out of context and Ross decided his hatred of me was more important, I could easily find myself dealing with a whole new set of problems. If I thought the media was bad now, they would be ten times worse given access to private communication like that. I was only hoping that Ross's loyalty to Brianna overrode everything else.

Movement on my right drew my attention back to my friends. Daren was leading Gina to the far side of the room where the small play area was set up. It wasn't anything fancy—a Saint Andrew's cross hung against the wall, and there was a spanking bench off to the side. I also took note of a short table with various impact toys: several floggers, canes, and paddles. It was a tiny sampling, all things considered.

"Hey." Sarah sat on the edge of her seat, frowning at me. "You're not enjoying yourself at all, are you?"

I smiled at her, even though I knew it was weak. "It's not your fault."

Sarah reached for my hand and squeezed. "Is there anything we can do?" She paused. "I'll even let you spank me if you want."

If she'd not winked at me, I might have reacted differently, but her teasing made me chuckle. The sound was enough to garner the attention of Logan and Lily who were sitting on her other side.

"Thanks, but I think I'll pass."

"What did we miss?" Lily asked.

I shook my head, but Sarah felt the need to fill her in. "I offered to let him spank me."

"Oh. And?" The expression on Lily's face was far too eager in my opinion.

Sarah released an exaggerated sigh. "He turned me down."

"Too bad. I would have let you spank Lily, too, if you wanted. It is your birthday after all."

Although Logan and Lily were monogamous, I knew Logan's offer was sincere. I was his best friend, and Lily and I had a history. Plus, they all seemed to be grasping at straws to try and turn my mood around. Unfortunately, there was only one person who could make what I was feeling disappear, and she wasn't here. I would have given anything to spend the evening with Brianna—just the two of us. Knowing my one birthday wish would never be granted, and not wanting to ruin my friends' evening, I made an effort to at least play the part they needed me to play. I could do that for one night.

Chapter 10

Brianna

I didn't want to go in there.

The last two days were awful. After my "episode" in Dr. Perkins office on Friday, she'd given me a sedative and sent me home with Cal and Jade to "rest." They'd both hovered over me like mother hens, trying to get me to take another dose of the sedative anytime they thought I was getting worked up about something. Taking it once had been enough, though. I didn't like the way it made me feel—as if I weren't connected to my body. It reminded me too much of how I'd been when I first came to live with Stephan. I didn't want that again.

Because our session had been cut short on Friday, Dr. Perkins had insisted I come see her on Monday. That was how I found myself standing outside her office with what felt like a swarm of bees buzzing around in my stomach.

"It'll be okay, Anna. I promise."

Jade's reassurance did little to help the chaos in my stomach. If anything, it made it worse.

Before Jade could attempt any more encouragement, Dr. Perkins's door opened, drawing our attention. "Good morning, Anna."

I swallowed, trying to push down the fear.

When I stepped forward, Jade touched my arm. "Are you sure you don't want me to go in with you?"

I shook my head. No. If I was going to find out what Cal had told Dr. Perkins about Stephan, I had to do it on my own. Didn't I?

Dr. Perkins smiled as I walked past her into her office. I took a seat on the couch, the same as I'd done the last two times I'd been there.

"How are you feeling this morning?"

I looked up at her and then back down. "Fine."

She was quiet for too long, so I glanced up. The frown on her face told me she hadn't liked my answer. I wasn't sure what she wanted from me, though. I *was* fine—for me at least. There was nothing wrong with me physically, and although I was nervous about this meeting, I wasn't in so much of a panic that I couldn't think clearly.

"How about the weekend—did you do anything fun?"

I shook my head. "No."

Dr. Perkins set her notepad aside and leaned forward, resting her elbows on her knees. "Anna, I feel like something happened last time that I'm not understanding. Can you explain it to me?"

This was it. I needed to ask what Cal had told her about Stephan.

I opened my mouth to ask, but no sound came out. My throat was dry, as if I hadn't had anything to quench my thirst in days.

"Take your time."

Closing my eyes, I fought back the tears that threatened to fall. I reached up and took hold of Stephan's collar, trying to find the strength I needed. The sound of his voice filled my head as I replayed his letter in my mind. I'd read it so many times over the last five days that I had it memorized. The simple letter might not have meant much to someone else, but it did to me.

After several minutes, I took a deep breath and opened my eyes to look at Dr. Perkins. She hadn't moved. "What did . . ." The words sounded gravelly, so I cleared my throat. "What did Cal tell you?"

She tilted her head to the side, and her brow furrowed in confusion. "What did Cal tell me about what?"

Holding tighter to the collar around my neck, I felt it dig into my skin. "Stephan."

"The only thing I know about Stephan is what you've told me and your friend Cal's reaction to him the first day you were here. Were you concerned he'd spoken to me independently about him?"

I nodded.

"And that upsets you."

I nodded again.

"Anna, even if your friends had told me something about Stephan, it wouldn't matter. This is about you, and whoever Stephan is, he's obviously important to you."

We sat in silence for a long time. She appeared to be waiting for me to say something. I decided to take a chance. That was what I was here for after all. "He saved me."

Dr. Perkins sat back in her chair. "What do you mean when you say *he saved you?*"

I didn't answer right away. Even though she said everything we talked about would remain between us, I couldn't risk putting Stephan in danger by admitting anything that could hurt him. "He took me into his home . . . after. He helped me."

"Ah. So you feel grateful to him. Protective of him since he helped you."

"Yes." I wasn't sure I should tell her that I loved him. That felt like a betrayal somehow.

behind them.

His posture was stiff as he strolled across the room before stopping several feet away from me. I felt myself react to his nearness and had to remind myself to breathe.

He crossed his arms and leaned one hip against Emma's desk. "I know you don't like me, Miss Reeves, but avoiding me is not in your best interest."

Jade snorted. "After the last time, can you blame her? You weren't exactly the epitome of warmth and helpfulness."

Agent Marco shifted his attention to her briefly and then back to me. "My apologies if I came across a little . . . aggressively. This is a serious matter I'm dealing with, and I need your help since you appear to be at the center of it."

"What exactly do you want from Miss Reeves, Agent Marco?" Emma asked.

Instead of answering her, he looked at me when he spoke. "I have a proposition for you. Your father has given us a statement regarding his relationship with Jean Dumas, and his part in your apparent kidnapping. He knows as well as anyone how unfavorably a jury would look at a father who turned a blind eye knowing his daughter had been taken. I'm confident the information we garnered from him coupled with the bank records provided by Coleman and his lawyer will be sufficient to put both your father and Dumas away for the rest of their natural lives."

He paused before continuing. "Perhaps you should know that, given your father's cooperation, his attorney has negotiated for him to be kept separate from the general prison population. Because of his law enforcement background, he wouldn't last that long in gen pop. He should be going before a judge within the next few weeks, and after that, he'll be transferred to one of the state prisons to serve out his sentence."

I wasn't sure why he was telling me this, and apparently neither did Emma. "Is there a point to all this, Agent?"

Agent Marco shrugged. "I just figured Miss Reeves would like to know her father's fate."

"Well, now she does. Can we move on, please?"

One side of Agent Marco's mouth lifted slightly at Emma's admonishment before he resumed his speech. "My case against Ian Pierce isn't as solid as I would like it to be, which is where you come in. Although I'm confident I can nail him on several counts of theft and money laundering, a good team of lawyers, which he has, will probably be able to talk down the charges so that with good behavior he won't spend more than a decade or two behind bars. I, for one, don't want to see that happen. I'm assuming you don't either."

"What about the other women?" Jade questioned.

Again his gaze shifted to Jade and then back to me. "There isn't enough evidence to get him for the murders. According to him, the other two women stayed with him for a few months and then left on their own. He claims never to have seen either of them after that. While I don't believe one word of it, I can't prove otherwise, and his girlfriend, Alex, is backing up his story."

Of course Alex was backing up his story. He was her Master. She would never contradict him.

"That, once again, brings us back to you. I know you didn't escape, Miss Reeves. I think I'm pretty good at my job, and I know when things add up and when they don't, even if I can't prove it."

I didn't say anything. How was I supposed to respond to that?

"So let me tell you what I do know. Your father owed Dumas a large sum of money. Dumas owed Pierce, so Dumas sold you to Pierce to pay off a debt—kill two birds with one stone. Then about ten months later, Stephan Coleman comes into the picture. I haven't quite figured out the how or why of it, but he bought you from Pierce. For three months after that, you lived with him. Then, suddenly, the day your father shows up trying to snatch you from Coleman's building, you move out—disappear—except you now have a lawyer to represent you. A lawyer who seems to be close friends with Coleman's attorney."

The air was thick—the only sound was our breathing. Agent Marco stared at me but remained where he was.

Eventually, Emma broke the silence. "That's a riveting story, Agent, but I still don't see the point."

He never once took his eyes off me. "I'll tell you what I want. I want to see that arrogant bastard pay for what he did to those two women and what I know he would have done to you as well, if given the chance. What I want is for you to help me put him away and keep him there."

Agent Marco didn't give any of us time to answer before he pushed off the desk and stood to his full height. "For whatever reason, you're protecting Coleman. I don't like it, but in order to get what I want, which is Pierce, I'm willing to make you a deal. You help me put Pierce away, and I'll stop pursuing Coleman. At best, he's small potatoes in all of this anyway. Although his arrest would make for a good headline, I want Pierce more."

For the first time since entering Emma's office, he turned to face her. "Think about it. Talk it over. Keep in mind that if I find something solid on Coleman between now and the time you make your decision, I'll run with it. The man's hiding something. I just haven't found out what it is yet." With that parting comment, he marched out the door and disappeared.

Emma held up her hand to hush Jade when she opened her mouth to comment. Going to the door, Emma checked to make sure Agent Marco was nowhere in sight and then locked it.

She returned to her desk, folding her hands in front of her. "I'd want everything in writing, but it's a good offer, Anna. Stephan would be protected, and Ian Pierce would get what he deserves."

The first thing to cross my mind was that I wanted to talk to Stephan, but I knew that was impossible. It was too risky. I had to make this decision on my own. No one could make it for me.

"What would it mean for Anna, though? I mean, would she have to testify?"

I hadn't thought of that, but it was a good question. Jade had been a good friend to me. I didn't know how I'd ever repay her.

"It's possible," Emma said, "although we could include that in the conditions of the agreement—specify that only as a last resort would you be required to testify, Anna. I'd like to hope that once Pierce's lawyer sees your statement, he won't want to pursue the charges in court. I don't think a jury would react well to your story. They'd want to burn him at the stake. Any lawyer worth his salt in this town would know that. "

"Okay," I whispered.

The two women looked at me with concern. "Are you sure?"

I took a deep breath, reached up to touch the one part of Stephan I had with me, and gave her my answer. "As long as you can protect Stephan, then I want to do it."

"Anna . . ."

Turning to the side, I met Jade's worried gaze. "Even if it means I have to testify in front of all those people."

Jade's shoulders lowered, defeated.

"Very well, then. I'll get something on paper and have one of our criminal attorneys look over it. Once I have everything put together, I'll give you a call."

Walking out of Emma's office, I felt a pressure I hadn't realized was there lift from my shoulders. Stephan was going to be okay. I was going to make sure of it.

Chapter 11

Stephan

It was hard to believe a week had gone by since my last meeting with Ross. Our lunch this week wasn't as tense as the last one. He gave me a rather brief update on Brianna, which included him insisting that reading my letter had upset her, the opposite of what he'd expected. Ross did comment, however, that whatever I'd said had made a difference in her eating habits. I'd known he hadn't been completely truthful when I'd inquired about how she was eating. Brianna internalized when she was upset. I knew that would more than likely spill over into her not eating as she should.

Once he shared all the information he was willing to regarding Brianna, we moved on to the less emotionally charged topic of the fall gala. It was just over three weeks away, and given his company donated a significant amount of money to the foundation, someone from his family typically attended. I wasn't sure how that was going to work this year with Brianna living under his roof. Would he bring his girlfriend and leave Brianna by herself, or would he choose to come alone? I hadn't seen his RSVP, but I would guess he'd marked it as plus one. That would make sense given he and Jade had been dating for over a year.

I tried to pay attention to the conversation as much as possible, but my mind kept slipping back to Brianna. What was she doing while we were sitting here eating lunch, trying to act as if we were friends instead of two people who merely tolerated each other? She'd been upset with my letter, although I had no idea why. I couldn't think of anything I'd written that would have garnered such a response.

The walk back to my office was relatively uneventful. There'd been breaking news of some sort of political scandal this morning. Most of the reporters had left their post for something juicier than the mundane activities outside an office building. The few remaining reporters kept a respectable distance.

Jamie glanced up as we stepped off the elevator. She'd been less hostile this week. I had a feeling Lily had said something. My assistant even managed a small smile as we passed by her desk.

The door to my office closed behind us. I strolled over to my desk and took a seat. We both knew he wouldn't stay long—this was all for show after all.

When Cal began to pace, it drew my attention away from my computer monitor. He was clearly agitated about something. It was on the tip of my tongue to ask him what his problem was, when he turned abruptly to face me. "I have something for you."

When he didn't elaborate, I said, "Okay. What is it?"

He sighed and reached into his back pocket.

When he handed the item to me, I realized it was an envelope. It was sealed and had no markings on the outside. I raised my eyebrow in question.

"It's from Anna. She wanted to write you back. I'm not happy about it, but I promised her I'd give it to you." Before I could reply to his rushed explanation, he turned on his heel and rushed toward the door as if someone were chasing him. "I'll see you next week."

As soon as he was out of sight, I stood and made my way over to the door to shut and lock it. I didn't want anyone to disturb me. Brianna had written me back. I took a deep breath—the first real one since the day she walked out my door—and sat on the couch.

Maybe I should have savored the moment, but I didn't have it in me. Ripping the envelope open, I then removed the folded paper inside. Seeing Brianna's handwriting made me smile. She'd always been better at putting her feelings down on paper, and I couldn't wait another moment to see what she'd written.

> Stephan,
> When Cal told me he had a letter for me from you, I was excited. Thank you. I know you didn't have to write me, but I'm glad you did. Cal isn't happy I'm writing you back. He doesn't understand why I cried reading your letter, but I think you will.
> At least, I hope you do.
> I've been trying to eat better the last couple of days. You're right. I need to eat. Cal and Jade seem to be happy about that at least—that I'm eating more. I don't know what it is, but nothing tastes the same, even the premade stuff. It's probably just me.
> Cal wanted me to talk to someone—that was the deal he told you about. It's not something I want to do, but maybe he's right. I used to talk to you, and now I can't, so maybe this is a good thing. I've only had two meetings with Dr. Perkins so far. The first one didn't go too bad, but I had a panic attack

during the second. She gave me a sedative and sent me home with Cal and Jade. I'm supposed to go back Monday. You probably won't get this until Wednesday when you see Cal, so I will have already seen Dr. Perkins.
Hopefully I don't panic this time. I want to get better.
Maybe this will help.
Yours,
Brianna

I read over the letter twice more before I let it fall to my lap. She was going to therapy. He was making her *talk* to someone.

Anger, followed by fear, surged through me. Within moments, I was on my feet marching toward the door. I wasn't sure what I was going to do exactly, but I needed to do something.

As I reached for the doorknob, the sound of voices outside halted me. What was I doing? I wasn't supposed to have any contact with Brianna. She'd chosen to leave in an effort to protect me. No matter how much my instinct to protect her was screaming at me to do something, I had to respect her wishes. Didn't I?

Taking what I hoped would be a deep calming breath, I walked back across the room to retrieve Brianna's letter from where I'd let it fall to the floor in my haste, before going back to my desk. I refolded the letter and tucked it into the pocket of my jacket.

It took me a while to calm down. No matter how frustrated I was with the whole situation, I couldn't react without thinking it through first. For the rest of the day, I contemplated my options. There weren't many. I could do nothing, call Cal and give him a piece of my mind, hoping that he'd let Brianna out of this ridiculous deal she'd made with him, or since Brianna had given me the therapist's name, I could do some digging on her myself.

The first truly wasn't an option. There was no way I could sit by and do nothing with the information I'd been given. Calling Cal, while tempting, wasn't likely to produce positive results. The only real option, then, was to find out all I could about this Dr. Perkins.

Picking up the phone, I dialed Oscar's number. As much as I would have loved to do the research myself, the last thing I needed was the press or even Agent Marco getting wind of what I was doing and put two and two together. I was sure both of them would find some way to spin the information to their advantage.

"Davis and Associates."

"This is Stephan Coleman. I need to speak to Oscar, please."

"One moment, Mr. Coleman."

She put me on hold for roughly thirty seconds before Oscar picked up the line. "Stephan. I wasn't expecting to hear from you today."

I hadn't been expecting to call. "Could you stop by my condo on your way home tonight? There's something I'd like to discuss with you."

"Sure. I can do that. Everything all right?"

"That's what I intend to find out."

"Sounds ominous. I have some things to finish up here if it's not urgent."

"That's fine."

"Okay, then. I'll see you . . . say around six?"

"I'll see you then."

After hanging up with Oscar, I glanced down at my desk and realized how little work I'd gotten done since reading Brianna's letter. The clock on my computer read three fifty. I hadn't left the office early by choice since Brianna left, but today I felt it necessary. I wasn't getting any work accomplished, and I'd snapped at Jamie the one time she'd knocked on my door. Since I didn't want to end up apologizing to everyone on my staff that I came in contact with, I figured going home was the best option.

I walked into my condo and was greeted with blissful silence. Sarah had been spending more and more hours working with that business owner Daren had set her up with, which meant she was gone most of the day. That was good, because I needed time to think about my upcoming conversation with Oscar. The Dom in me wanted to take action. Of course, that was warring with the logical part that said even though Brianna still wore my collar—at least as far as I knew—she wasn't my responsibility right now. Circumstances dictated that she couldn't be. I had to trust her. The problem, however, wasn't that I didn't trust Brianna—I did. Who I didn't trust was this Dr. Perkins. I knew nothing about her, and after what I went through after the death of my parents, I inherently didn't trust psychiatrists.

While I waited for Oscar, I read over Brianna's letter again, this time taking note of the small things. She said she thought I would understand why she'd cried over my letter, and reading her words again, I did. Our separation was hurting her. She missed me as much as I missed her. I had to find a way to end this, or at least make it safe for us to see one another. Being apart wasn't good for either of us.

The monitor coming to life drew me out of my reverie. Seconds later, the door opened, and Sarah came breezing into the condo with a grocery bag on her hip. "Oh. You're home."

"I came home early."

She frowned. "Everything okay? Nothing happened did it?"

I knew what she was asking. Agent Marco had made the rounds with my friends as well. "No."

Sarah sighed and ambled into the kitchen to put the food she'd bought away. "That's good. I can honestly say that if I ever have to talk to that Agent Marco again, it will be too soon. He's a class-A jerk, if you ask me."

There wasn't any point in responding since I agreed wholeheartedly. The man was like a dog with a bone that wouldn't let go. I couldn't worry about him right now, though. Oscar would be here soon, and I still hadn't figured out how I was going to get him to do what I wanted. Sure, I could remind him that he worked for me, and if push came to shove, I'd do just that.

"How was work?" Sarah plopped down on the couch across from me with a soda in her hand.

"You shouldn't be drinking that, you know."

She took a drink of the beverage anyway and rolled her eyes. "I only had one cup of coffee today, *Doctor Coleman*."

"Fine. Do what you want." I got up and went to the kitchen for some water. Most of the time I didn't mind having Sarah here, but right now I didn't want to deal with her brattiness.

A hand touched my left arm as I reached into the refrigerator. Sarah stood there, worry creasing her brow. "I'm sorry. I know you're only trying to help."

I didn't comment as I removed the pitcher of chilled water and poured myself a glass.

"Hey. Talk to me."

Taking a sip of my water, I met her concerned gaze before setting my glass back down on the counter. "Oscar will be here in a few minutes. I'm going to go change."

Not giving her time to respond, I marched across the living area and into my bedroom, firmly closing the door behind me.

True to his word, Oscar showed up a few minutes after six. Sarah let him in and then reluctantly retreated up to her room. I knew she was curious, but after talking it over shortly after her moving in, we'd both agreed it was best if she made herself scarce when my attorney made an appearance. There were some things she was better off not knowing.

We settled ourselves in the living room. I didn't waste any time with pleasantries. Oscar had known me all my life, and we both preferred the direct approach. "I need you to look into someone for me."

He cocked his head to the side, and his face became guarded. "Who?"

"All I know is that her name is Dr. Perkins and that she's a therapist somewhere in town."

Oscar frowned. "And who is this woman? Why is she important?"

This is where things had the potential to get dicey. Oscar didn't know about the letter I'd sent Brianna. I decided to keep it simple and hope he didn't ask questions. "I found out Brianna is seeing her."

He quirked an eyebrow and hardened his stare. "How did you find out this information?"

I considered lying, but as with my uncle, Oscar could usually see right through me if I wasn't being completely truthful. "Brianna wrote me a letter. She told me. She and Ross have some sort of deal going on."

"I see. I'd heard the two of you were acting unusually chummy lately. That explains why." He adjusted his position on the couch, resting his arm along the back. His posture was casual, but I knew what was coming. "I am curious, however . . . if Brianna left in order to protect you, why is she now writing you letters?"

"One letter."

The look he shot me said he was not thrilled with my defensiveness.

Sighing, I stood and walked over to the window. Perhaps it was cowardly, but I didn't want to see his reaction. "She wrote me a letter because I wrote her one first."

"I see."

I turned around, leaning against the window ledge. "I was careful. I didn't say anything I shouldn't. It's not a secret we know each other."

"You're walking a very fine line, Stephan. If that letter got into the wrong hands . . ."

"I know."

Neither of us spoke for several minutes. Oscar was not one to be rushed into making decisions, and I was under no misconception that he could turn down my request.

"What do you hope to accomplish by digging up information on this doctor?"

"I only want to make sure Brianna is safe. You know I don't trust psychiatrists."

He studied me for a long moment. "All right. I'll do some research, make sure she has a good reputation—but that's it. You don't need the complications this could bring if it gets out."

"Thank you."

Oscar snorted as he rose from the couch.

I followed him to the door to let him out.

He paused in the entryway, turning to face me, his hand on the doorknob. "Oh, and Stephan? No more private parties. You want to go out with your friends to a public restaurant, fine, but nothing secretive. Got it?"

"It—"

Oscar held up his hand, cutting me off. "I don't want details. Just don't let it happen again."

Chapter 12

Brianna

It was Thursday, and I hadn't heard anything back from Emma yet. I was getting nervous. Why hadn't she called?

The last few days had been tense. Jade wanted to tell Cal what was going on, but I begged her not to. I knew what he'd say. He'd made it clear that he didn't want me testifying under any circumstances. If he knew what was going on, he'd be furious.

Cal strolled into the house around three thirty as he usually did. He'd met with Stephan yesterday, but he hadn't said much about the meeting except that he'd given Stephan my letter. One other good thing had come from his meeting with Stephan—Cal had started talking to me again.

"Anna!" He's eyes went wide when he saw me.

I stepped farther into the kitchen. He very slowly started digging into the refrigerator to find a snack, never taking his eyes off me for long. "Hey."

Little by little, he put food onto the counter. Once he seemed to have everything he wanted, he paused. "Are you hungry?"

I started to say no, but then I remembered Stephan's words that I needed to eat. Breakfast had been more than five hours ago, and I hadn't had anything since. "Okay."

Cal froze. He looked at me, shocked. "You want a sandwich?"

Swallowing, I nodded.

To my surprise, he responded with a huge grin. "Okay then. One sandwich coming up."

We ate together at the kitchen table. I didn't finish mine, but I thought I did pretty well.

He did, too, apparently, because he was all smiles as he cleaned everything up. "Did you want to watch some TV? Jade won't be home for another hour or two."

I glanced toward my bedroom and pressed my lips together.

"I promise I'll sit on the couch, and you can have the chair. How about that?"

Not waiting for me to respond, Cal ambled across the room and took a seat on the couch just as he'd said he would. I stayed where I was for several minutes and debated whether or not to join him in the living room or retreat into my bedroom. The pull toward my room was great, but there was a little voice inside reminding me that I wanted to get better. If I was going to stand up to Ian—and help Stephan—I needed to get better. Cal wasn't going to hurt me. I could do something normal like watch television with him, right?

Forcing my legs to move, I walked timidly over to the chair and sat down. To his credit, Cal's only reaction to my decision was a small smile that tugged at one side of his mouth. Other than that, he remained motionless.

We stayed like that until Jade arrived around five thirty. She took one look at the scene in the living room and stopped in her tracks. "Hi."

Cal looked over his shoulder at her. "How was class?"

Jade laid her backpack on the table and headed toward us. "Good." She nodded in the direction of the television. "What ya watching?"

He shrugged. "Anna and I were catching up on some talk shows."

"I see. Anything good?"

"Not really." Cal stood and wrapped his arm around Jade's waist, pulling her closer to him. He placed a chaste kiss on her lips, but it lingered just a little too long.

It dawned on me at that moment that they'd been holding themselves— their relationship—back because of me. Scurrying out of the chair, I mumbled an excuse and ducked into my bedroom.

I should have known my rapid escape wouldn't have gone unnoticed. Less than five minutes had passed before Jade was knocking on my bedroom door and letting herself in.

"Everything all right?"

Nodding, I went back to plucking at the fabric of my jeans.

She sat down on the edge of the mattress, facing me. "I'm sorry if seeing Cal and I kiss bothered you, Anna. We'll try to be more careful next time."

"No!"

My exclamation made her jump.

I took a deep breath and tried again. "No. I don't want you . . . I don't want you to *not* do things because of me."

She reached out and touched the back of my hand lightly with her fingertips. "What don't you think we do?"

Closing my eyes, I tried to find the right words to explain. "Cal wanted to kiss you more, but he didn't—because of me."

She chuckled, and I opened my eyes to find her with an amused expression on her face. "Trust me, Cal can survive not getting every little thing he wants all the time. Besides, it's not like he never gets to kiss me the way he wants."

"But he would have kissed you more if I weren't there."

"Probably."

"So my being here changes your relationship. I don't want that."

Jade sighed and squeezed my hand. "Cal and I can survive showing a bit of restraint. It won't hurt us. And we didn't know if you'd be okay seeing us be affectionate."

"But you shouldn't have to."

She sat up and slapped her palms against her thighs. "Tell you what. We promise not to hold back any more than we would if we were in front of our other friends, but only if you'll let us know if it's making you uncomfortable."

That I could live with. I didn't want to be any more of a burden than I already was to them. "I promise."

Later that night, I joined them at the kitchen table for dinner. No one said much beyond the normal pleasantries, but I did notice that Jade was attempting to keep her word. Every now and then, one of them would glance at the other with a sly smile—as if they shared a secret no one was in on but them. It made me miss Stephan even more, but that was okay. They were happy. That was what mattered.

Just after noon on Friday, Emma finally called. "Hi, Anna. I was wondering if I could stop by today. I finished putting the paperwork together, and I want to go over it with you before I present it to the federal prosecutor."

"Sure. But . . ." I paused. "Could you come soon? I-I don't want Cal or Jade here. I want it to just be us."

Emma didn't response right away. "Are you sure, Anna?"

This was the one thing I was sure of. "Yes. I need to do this on my own."

"Okay. I'll get everything together and head over there within the next half hour."

I waited anxiously for Emma. Cal lived roughly twenty minutes from her office, so I knew it would take her at least that long to arrive. Unfortunately, that didn't help the butterflies in my stomach.

Almost thirty minutes after her phone call, Emma pulled into the driveway. I watched from the window. She parked her car and strolled briskly toward the front door. Cautiously, I went to let her in. I'd never answered the door at Cal's before, and the last time I'd done so at Stephan's, I'd mistakenly granted my father access to the one place I'd felt safe. Even though I knew it was Emma, I still looked through the peephole before reaching for the doorknob.

Emma smiled when she saw me. "Hi, Anna."

"Hi." I glanced down and then shifted from left to right, unsure.

"Can I come in?"

"Oh. Yeah. Sure." Quickly stepping out of her way, I waited until she was clear of the door and then made certain to shut and lock it.

She automatically sat down at the kitchen table, and I joined her as soon as I could get my feet to move.

"I know you're nervous, so I'll cut to the chase. After consulting with

Vince, the criminal attorney in our office I told you about, we put together what I'm hoping will be an agreeable proposal for all parties involved."

Emma handed me a stack of papers on her law firm's letterhead.

"What it says is that you agree to give a full statement against Ian Pierce regarding any criminal activity of which you're aware, and that you will aid in the prosecution of Mr. Pierce up to and including testifying should that become necessary. In exchange for your full cooperation, both you and Stephan Coleman are granted immunity from any and all charges related to the crimes and prosecution of Mr. Pierce."

"So I'd have to testify?" Just thinking about it caused me to tremble.

"Not unless the prosecution feels it's the only way to win their case. We've put a provision in there that says you only agree to testify in front of a jury after all other avenues have been exhausted." Emma reached out and touched the tips of my fingers. "I'll be honest with you, Anna. I don't know if they'll agree to that or not, but it's worth putting it in there to get the ball rolling. Considering your history and how you are around people, putting you up in front of a jury and having you be cross-examined would be an unknown that I'm hoping their attorney doesn't want to chance."

I stared blankly at the document in front of me. This was it—Stephan's freedom lay in my hands.

"Did you have any questions for me?"

"No."

She waited, but after several minutes, I still hadn't said anything. I wasn't sure what I was supposed to say . . . or do for that matter.

Emma reached across the table and began flipping through the papers I still held loosely in my grasp. "If you agree, I need you to sign your name there at the bottom."

I swallowed but otherwise didn't move.

"You don't have to do this, you know. We can try to find another way or just wait out Agent Marco's investigation."

I looked up and met her gaze. "This will protect Stephan, right?"

She nodded. "Yes. If they accept the deal, they can't charge either of you with any crime related to their case against Pierce."

Taking a deep breath, I picked up the pen lying on the table in front of her and pressed it firmly against the white paper. Even though he'd taken the time to write me a letter, that didn't mean anything. I was still broken, and the press haunted Stephan's every move. As I put the finishing touches on my signature, though, I knew this was right. I was going to make sure Stephan had a future that didn't involve the inside of a prison—even if that future didn't include me.

Chapter 13

Stephan

Two sharp knocks sounded on my office door, pulling my attention away from the e-mail I'd been in the process of typing. Since Jamie hadn't called to announce that I had a visitor, I was fairly confident it was Lily. She was the only person able to get around Jamie without my assistant making a fuss. On more than one occasion, Jamie had given an earful to someone for trying to bypass her to get to me. Even with Jamie's cooler attitude toward me, that hadn't changed.

"Come in, Lily."

With a huge smile plastered on her face, Lily sashayed into my office. She let the door close behind her and, without prompting, took a seat across from my desk. "The final menu came in this morning."

Lily handed me a printout of the e-mail she'd received. I glanced over it, not really caring about the food that would be served.

Handing the paper back to her, I leaned forward, resting my forearms on my desk. "And you couldn't have just forwarded that to me in an e-mail?"

"I could have, but I was coming to see you anyway, so I figured I'd bring it along. Two birds with one stone kind of thing."

"I see. And what else was bringing you to my office this morning?"

Lily shifted in her chair and looked out the window.

I didn't have the patience for this right now. To be honest, I didn't have patience for much of anything anymore. "Lily."

She sighed and once again met my gaze. "I need to know if you're bringing Sarah with you to the gala or if you're . . . bringing someone else?"

Taking a deep breath, I tried to steady myself before answering her. As the gala got closer and closer, the weight of knowing Brianna wouldn't be accompanying me became heavier. This was the foundation's big night. I wanted her there by my side. Unfortunately, that wasn't an option. While the political scandal last week had taken some of the vultures away, there were still a handful who didn't want to move on—too afraid they'd miss something. An appearance from Brianna would only kick up the frenzy once more. I wouldn't do that to her. "I haven't asked Sarah, but I will. When do you need to know?"

Lily looked disappointed. Believe me, so was I. "I have to get a final count to the hotel and the caterers by the end of the week."

I nodded.

"I'll ask her tonight." Thinking that was all, I turned my attention back to my computer. Lily didn't move, though. "Was there something else?"

She looked down at her hands before glancing up again. "I miss her." Lily paused. "Have you heard anything recently? Anything since the letter?"

Although I hadn't shown Lily the letter Brianna had sent back to me, I'd shared bits of it with her. The two women had struck up a friendship, and when Brianna cut ties with me, Logan had thought it a good idea for Lily to keep her distance as well—at least for a while. I wasn't sure I agreed with him, but it was ultimately their decision, not mine.

"No. Nothing new."

Lily frowned and nodded solemnly. Even so, she seemed reluctant to leave.

"I'll let you know if I hear something, but I doubt there will be any news before Wednesday."

"You're having lunch with Cal Ross again, right?"

"Yes." I'd told Lily and Logan about the lunches and explained the purpose behind them. Although they were all for anything that protected Brianna, like me, they were still guarded when it came to Ross. I wasn't sure I could ever fully trust the man. It was bad enough I was being forced to trust him with Brianna's care. Having to trust him with helping to preserve my public image was a blow to my pride.

Lily didn't stay long after that, and I attempted to push everything out of my mind but work. It was already the last week in September, and there was a lot to be done in the weeks leading up to the gala that had nothing to do with the event itself. Every year at the gala, the foundation revealed their new marketing campaign for the upcoming year. Although the marketing department handled most of the grunt work, everything had to be finalized by the board, which was why I was trying to write the agenda for tomorrow's board meeting.

I was putting the finishing touches on the agenda when my cell phone rang. When I saw the caller was Oscar, I abandoned what I was doing and answered the phone. "Oscar?"

"Hello, Stephan. Is this a good time?"

"Of course. What's going on?"

"I have some papers I want you to take a look at, and I was wondering if you could stop by my office this afternoon?"

"What papers?"

He paused, which was unlike Oscar. "I'd rather go over them with you in person."

"What's going on, Oscar?" I couldn't hide my frustration.

"There have been some . . . developments. And before you ask, that's all I'm going to say for now. I'll wait for you to get here." Before I could argue my point further, I heard a click on the other line letting me know he'd hung up.

Stunned, I stared at my phone. I couldn't believe Oscar had hung up on me.

With a quick look at the time, I realized it was already after four. Saving everything, I e-mailed the file to myself so I could work on it later at home. I would never be able to concentrate on anything but the mysterious papers in Oscar's possession, so I didn't even try. Shutting everything down, I grabbed my jacket and was on my way to my car in less than five minutes.

It was close enough to rush hour that getting to Oscar's office took longer than it should have. Every time I tried to take a shortcut to bypass traffic, it backfired on me and I was moving slower than I had been before. I finally gave up trying to hurry and decided to use the extra time to try and figure out what sort of developments there'd been that required me to stop by his office to go over some papers. Unfortunately, every scenario I came up with didn't make sense with how things had been left. As far as I knew, Agent Marco was still chomping at the bit attempting to put together something against me while Brianna and I kept our silence. Unless something major had changed, I didn't understand Oscar's urgency.

I exited my vehicle quickly once I parked my car outside Oscar's office building. Two cars had followed me, and I didn't want to give them time to get into position. The pictures they managed to get from a distance were bad enough.

When I stepped off the elevator, Phyllis greeted me as always. "Good afternoon, Mr. Coleman. You can go on back. Mr. Davis is expecting you."

I nodded and thanked her before headed down the hall to Oscar's office. His door was open, so I didn't bother knocking. Just like the last time, he wasn't alone—Emma sat perched on the edge of one of his high-backed chairs.

As soon as I saw her, I halted my movement. "Brianna?"

"Is fine," Oscar answered.

Emma, however, looked nervous. Something was wrong.

Oscar walked past me to close the door and motioned to the chair beside Emma. "Why don't you take a seat? We have a few things to discuss."

I didn't sit down, and my gaze never left Emma. "What do we have to discuss?"

My lawyer took his seat and sighed. "The federal prosecutor wants to offer you a deal."

I was still watching Emma. "What deal?"

"In exchange for your testimony against Ian Pierce, they are willing to grant you immunity."

Whipping my head around to look at Oscar, I asked the obvious question.

"Why? And why now?"

Both of them remained silent.

"I'll ask again. Why?" I was trying very hard to stay calm, but the little sanity I had left was slipping. What had happened? What had prompted this?

"Agent Marco and the federal prosecutor think your testimony would help drive a nail in Pierce's coffin."

I shifted my gaze to Oscar. "You and I both know I don't have enough firsthand knowledge of what he did to Brianna to convict him of holding her against her will. If I did, we would have had this conversation three months ago."

"You're right. Alone, you don't."

It didn't take a genius to put the missing piece of the puzzle together, and before I knew it, I was flying across the room toward Emma. Her eyes widened at my sudden advance. "You were supposed to protect her! How dare you throw her to the wolves like that? You had one job. One!"

Oscar suddenly appeared between us, pushing against my chest, which was probably a good thing. I wanted to get my hands on Emma. I wanted to hurt her for doing this to Brianna. She was supposed to look out for her! Take care of her when I couldn't. How could she do this?

"Stephan, calm down. You aren't helping anyone this way."

I didn't budge, my nostrils flared with my anger. If looks could kill, Emma would be a dead woman.

"Stephan, please. Calm yourself." Oscar's voice was forceful as he tried to get me to see past the red in my vision.

Flexing my fingers, I attempted to get a grip on my emotions. It wasn't easy, but finally I was in control enough that I ripped myself out of Oscar's hold and marched across the room away from Emma. Truth be told, I couldn't look at her. She'd betrayed Brianna. She'd betrayed me.

The only sound I could hear was my ragged breathing. The rise and fall of my chest gave testament to how upset I was. I wanted to punch something, break something—anything.

Leaning forward, I rested my fists on the window ledge and gazed out at the city. I'd done everything I could to keep this from happening. Obviously it wasn't enough. I'd failed her.

Someone approached me on my left. I closed my eyes, willing myself not to do something I would regret.

"I know you're upset, Stephan, but I think this is a good thing. It might not be a perfect solution, but we knew going into this that something was probably going to have to give somewhere along the line."

I listened to Oscar's words, but they sounded hollow.

"What if I confess to buying her? Will it change anything—keep her from having to testify?" I sounded desperate, and I was.

This time Emma spoke—brave of her, all things considered. "No."

I whipped around. "What do you mean 'no'? Why wouldn't it?"

"Anna's already signed her part of the deal. To be truthful, you don't have to agree to what is being offered to you in exchange for your testimony. Anna already secured your immunity by agreeing to give the federal prosecutor her full cooperation. The only thing this will do is help put Pierce securely behind bars where he belongs and would decrease the likelihood of Anna having to actually testify. The more evidence they have against Pierce, the less likely the case will go to trial, and he will likely make a deal."

"So you're saying if I agree to this, Brianna *won't* have to testify?"

I had to give Emma credit, she looked me square in the eye and didn't back down. "It would be unlikely. There are no guarantees, however."

Swallowing, I asked the one thing I had to know. "What all does she have to do?"

"Don't you want to know what *you* have to do, Mr. Coleman?"

"No." Once again, I marched across the room, closing the distance between the two of us. I felt Oscar's presence close by, but I ignored him. This was between me and Emma. "I couldn't care less what happens to me. Brianna is always my first concern. Always. Are we clear?"

She surprised me by laughing.

I, however, was not amused. "What, may I ask, is so funny?"

"You two sound exactly alike." I must have looked as confused as I felt, because she continued to explain. "I can't tell you how many times Anna has told me that keeping you safe is the only thing she wants."

Frowning, I turned my attention away from Emma to Oscar. He looked as if he were lying in wait, ready to jump in and break Emma and I up again if need be. While I still wasn't happy with her at the moment, or Brianna for that matter, it appeared there wasn't much I could change on that front. The only thing left to do was ensure that Brianna didn't have to testify. In order to accomplish that, I needed to be involved. "Where do I sign?"

"Don't you want to know the details?"

"I agree to give my statement and testify against Ian Pierce in exchange for immunity. What else is there I need to know?"

Oscar stared at me for a long minute before he sighed, reached for a pen, and pushed the papers in front of me.

Without waiting, I flipped to the last page and signed my name.

Pushing the documents back across the desk toward Oscar, I faced Emma again. "I want to see Brianna."

Although I was addressing Emma, it was Oscar who spoke. "I don't think that's a good idea, Stephan. At least not yet."

I lifted my eyebrow in question. I could go see her on my own, or even call Cal or Jade to arrange something, but it would be easier with Emma's and Oscar's help. The press was still an issue.

"As soon as Agent Marco and the federal prosecutor announce this. And believe me, I have no doubt they will make an announcement—this case has already drawn enough media attention. With this new ammunition, they will be doing everything they can to put pressure on Pierce."

"I won't continue to stay away from her, Oscar. Not if there is no longer a danger. She left to protect me. That's no longer an issue."

"Do you want her to be hounded by the press?"

The look I gave him must have been answer enough.

"That's what I thought. Just let things cool down for a few weeks, and then we'll see about setting up a meeting between the two of you." He paused. "But Stephan, it's going to take some time for things to cool down. This is a huge deal. It's not every day a man like Ian Pierce is prosecuted for human trafficking. If you want to be with her—long-term—then you're going to have to have patience."

Patience. That was one thing I had in short supply. I had no idea if I could make it through another day without seeing Brianna, let alone weeks.

Chapter 14

Brianna
"You did what?" Cal's irate voice echoed off the walls.

I cowered behind the couch where I'd been sitting, watching television with Cal and Jade, when the news anchor had interrupted for a special report. They'd cut to a scene outside Agent Marco's office and announced that an official indictment had just been made against Ian Pierce. As soon as his name was mentioned, Cal had been all ears, turning up the volume.

They hadn't said much, really. At least, nothing we didn't already know. Not about Ian anyway. What had set Cal off, however, was the mention of a witness who'd come forward.

"Sources say this witness was not only aware of Pierce's alleged illegal activities but was one of his victims. A name hasn't been release, however many in the media have speculated that it may be the mysterious Brianna Reeves, who disappeared from the public eye shortly after her father, Jonathan Reeves, was arrested."

After that, they'd shown the picture of my father and proceeded to go into detail about his arrest. Even though the reporter kept saying "we're told" and "sources say," his information was accurate. Toward the end, a picture of Stephan and me from the hospital ball was put up on the screen.

"As many in the Twin Cities are aware, Mr. Coleman has come under scrutiny recently regarding his connection with Pierce and possibly Brianna Reeves herself. In the press conference held just moments ago, the FBI confirmed that Coleman is no longer a person of interest in their investigation."

The television was blaring in the background, but no one was paying attention to it anymore. Cal's gaze darted back and forth between me and Jade, his face red, his chest heaving with every breath he took. I'd never seen him so mad before—not even that time at Stephan's when I'd thought they were going to fight. I was shaking. The only thing holding me to reality was my death grip on the back of the couch.

"Cal, you need to calm down. You're scaring Anna."

"I'm scaring Anna? *I'm* scaring Anna?"

"Yes. And if you'd just take a deep breath and sit down for a minute, we can explain."

Instead of sitting back down, Cal turned on his heel and marched toward the front door.

"Where are you going?" Jade yelled.

"I need some air."

The door slammed shut behind him, leaving a deafening silence in his wake.

After a few minutes had passed, Jade turned down the volume on the television and came to kneel beside me. I hated causing problems, but I'd had to do it. I had to.

"He'll be okay, Anna. He just needs some time to cool off, absorb the information, that's all."

I didn't know if she was right or not, but I hoped she was.

She stayed by my side, holding tight to my hand, until I was no longer shaking. "Are you hungry? I'm thinking ice cream sounds really good right about now."

"No." I didn't want ice cream. What I wanted was for Cal not to be mad at me. I had done what had to be done. Why couldn't he understand that?

Eventually Jade stood, encouraging me to go back to where I had been sitting on the couch. Once I was settled, she disappeared into the kitchen for a few minutes and returned with a glass of water.

I accepted it and took a small sip. The cool liquid coated my parched throat. It felt good, so I took another drink.

Jade sat on the floor and leaned back against the couch, her knees bent as she held a glass of amber liquid in one hand. Jade didn't drink often—in fact, I hadn't seen her drink anything harder than soda since that night at the club. It was only now, seeing how her shoulders slumped and her head bowed, that I realized what I'd done by asking her to keep this from Cal. I'd put a wedge between them—I'd made her choose between us.

"Do you want me to leave?"

Her head snapped up. "What?"

"Do you want me to leave?"

Jade looked confused. "Why in the world would I want you to do that?"

"Because Cal's upset, and it's all my fault. I shouldn't have asked you not to say anything to him. I shouldn't have—"

"Stop right there. I could have told you no, but I didn't. I understood your reasoning for not wanting Cal to know ahead of time, and you were right. He would have tried to stop you."

"But I've caused problems between you."

"Cal has a temper sometimes. He'll get over it."

Jade crossed her legs in front of her and leaned forward, holding her glass in both hands.

"I never told you this, but I had a friend my freshman year of college who was raped on her way across campus one night."

I gasped. Was this why Jade was so nice to me?

"She had a rough time of it afterward. I was there for her as much as I could be, but in the end, she was the one who had to fight through her fear and stand up to the guy who attacked her."

Jade took a drink, and I watched the muscles in her throat move as she swallowed.

"She said it was the hardest thing she's ever had to do but that she was glad she did it. He'd taken her power away from her, and standing up to him gave her some of it back."

She paused again and looked down. I waited, not knowing what to say.

"I understand why Cal doesn't want you to get involved, I do. But that doesn't mean that I agree with him." Jade looked up, meeting my gaze. "This has to be your choice, Anna, and yours alone. If standing up to this guy means you get your life back, then I'll support you one hundred percent."

Jade downed the rest of her drink, stood, and strolled back into the kitchen. When she returned, it was with a large bowl of rocky road ice cream, two spoons, and a dining room chair. She set the chair down to my right and sat down.

Without a word, she handed me a spoon and dug into the ice cream. After a minute, I did the same. We sat there, staring at the television, eating ice cream while we waited for Cal to return.

It was dark by the time I heard the front door open and close. I'd retreated to my bedroom, but I could hear the hushed but heated voices coming from the main part of the house. It was my fault he was upset, and I'd struggled with how to fix it all evening. So far, I hadn't come up with anything solid. Jade insisted he'd get over it, but I wasn't so sure.

Eventually their mumbled voices faded, and I heard the door to their room close. Sighing, I leaned back against the headboard of my bed and looked out the window at the night sky. Surely Stephan knew what I'd done by now. Was he mad at me, too?

Before I could second-guess myself, I reached into the drawer and dug out a piece of paper and a pen.

Stephan,
Please don't be mad at me.
Brianna

Tomorrow was Wednesday, and I was hoping Cal would be having lunch with Stephan like he had for the last two weeks. Folding the note, I laid it reverently on the pillow beside me as I slid down under the covers.

I didn't sleep, just stared at the paper on my pillow and waited until morning. As the first signs of the sun began to appear against the trees, I heard movement in the main part of the house. I crawled out of bed, grabbing the note, and inched toward the door.

Gathering my courage, I opened my bedroom door. Cal stood with his back to me. He was dumping cereal into a large bowl. I waited until he was finished pouring his milk before I interrupted him. "Cal?"

He jumped, sending milk and cereal across the counter and down on the floor. His loud curse filled the otherwise silent space, causing me to backpedal. Maybe this wasn't such a good idea.

"Shit, Anna. You scared me. What are you doing up this early?" Cal snatched a towel from one of the drawers and started to clean up the mess he'd made.

I didn't move.

He stopped halfway through his cleanup, looked over at me, and frowned.

Throwing down the towel, he walked to the table, cutting the distance between us in half. He pulled out a chair and sat down. "I'm sorry I yelled, but you scared the crap out of me."

Before I could lose my nerve, I thrust the paper I was clutching in my right hand out to him.

Cal stared at it before he arose and took it from me. Flipping it over, he examined it. "What's this?"

"A-a note. I-I want you to give it to Stephan."

He tightened his hold on the note, and for a moment, I thought he was going to rip it up. "Did he know about what happened yesterday?" Cal scoffed. "Of course he knew. He had to."

"H-he didn't." Cal looked skeptical, and I knew I had to explain. "It was my decision. Just mine."

"Yours and Jade's, you mean."

I shook my head. "Please don't be mad at her. She only did what I asked her to do."

"You asked her to lie to me?"

Lowering my gaze to the floor, I took a deep breath and finished my confession. "I asked her not to tell you. I knew you'd try to stop me, and I couldn't let you do that."

"Why, Anna? Why would you do this after everything Coleman and I have done to try and protect you?"

Looked up through my eyelashes, I met his frustrated gaze. "Stephan saved me. He saved my life. Agent Marco offered me the opportunity to save him. I had to."

He didn't respond.

"Will you please take Stephan the note?" I paused, but when he still didn't say anything, I added, "For me?"

After another very long and tense moment, Cal nodded.

I'd nearly torn a hole in the leg of my jeans by the time Cal returned home. It was completely out of character for me, but when I heard him come in the door, I ran from my room and into the main part of the house.

He stopped when he saw me. "I gave Coleman your message."

"Did he say anything?" I probably shouldn't have asked since he hadn't wanted to deliver the note in the first place, but I had to know.

"What is this, high school?" Cal muttered as he strolled into the kitchen and began his afternoon routine of making himself a sandwich. "I didn't give him a chance to."

I wanted to ask why, but I didn't. It didn't matter as long as Stephan had gotten my message. That was what I'd asked Cal to do for me, and that was what he'd done.

While Cal was busy slathering mayonnaise on two pieces of bread, I slunk back into my room. Maybe one day both Cal and Stephan would forgive me.

I must have fallen asleep, because the next thing I knew I was waking up to yelling, and the sound was getting louder. I heard my name and knew that once again I'd caused a rift between them. I had to fix it.

Seconds later, I opened my bedroom door, following the voices. They weren't difficult to find—they were in their bedroom. The door was open, and they were both glaring at each other.

"You can't be serious?" he huffed.

Jade stood with her hands on her hips. "I'm completely serious. This has gone on long enough."

"The whole point was to keep her out of the public eye. So what, you just plan to throw caution to the wind now?"

I halted my movement at the door. I'd never been inside their bedroom before.

"Don't be ridiculous. Of course not."

It was then they finally seemed to notice me.

Jade lowered her arms and walked to where I was huddled by the door. "Oh, Anna, I'm sorry. We didn't mean to frighten you."

I didn't move. Whatever they were fighting about had to do with me, that much I knew.

Cal let out a defeated sigh and ambled over to the window. "You might as well tell her."

That got a reaction out of me. "Tell me what?"

Jade smiled, and I could see excitement in her eyes. "Would you like to see Stephan?"

My eyes went wide. Stephan? "Yes! How?"

"Well, I have an idea." I was listening. "Cal and I are going to The Coleman Foundation's big fall gala in two weeks. What if we could arrange for you two to meet privately? No press, and no one would know but us."

Was she serious?

"So what do you think?"

I opened my mouth to give a resounding "yes, please," when reality slapped me in the face. What if he didn't want to see me?

Jade must have noticed the change in my mood. "What's wrong?"

"What if he doesn't want to see me?"

Cal snorted.

Jade scowled at him over her shoulder and then turned her attention back to me. "Of course he wants to see you. Why wouldn't he?"

"I don't know," I whispered, looking down.

She tilted my chin up with her fingers until I was looking at her again. "Well I do, and we're going to find you the perfect dress. You're going to knock his socks off."

Jade was practically beaming, and it was impossible not to get caught up in her emotion.

"Okay."

"Perfect!" Jade took hold of my hand and led me back to my room.

She went directly to my laptop and plopped down on my bed, patting the space beside her. Cal had followed us but lingered at the door. I could see the worry lines etching his face.

"Cal you might want to find something else to occupy your time. Anna and I have some dress shopping to do."

Chapter 15

Stephan

I glanced in the mirror, making sure my bowtie wasn't crooked. Tonight was The Coleman Foundation's big night, and something I usually looked forward to. That wasn't the case this year. Too much was going on in my life, and I didn't have the one person I wanted beside me.

Tugging on my jacket, I realized the man in the reflection looked tired and years older than his twenty-five years. The last two weeks had been hell. I'd spent two days the week before going over the details of my statement with Agent Marco and one this week with the federal prosecutor. I didn't understand the need for repetition, but they insisted it was necessary to make sure nothing was left out—that and people tended to remember specifics the more they talked through an incident.

Agent Marco had done a complete one-eighty when it came to me. He was no longer in my face, trying to weasel a confession out of me. With this immunity agreement, I was suddenly his new best friend. He'd even let it slip at our last meeting that he'd seen Brianna the day before. I'd come to find out after grilling Oscar that Brianna had been required to officially acknowledge that Ian Pierce had held her against her will in the agreement she'd signed, but that they were slowly working with her to rehash the details of her captivity.

Knowing that she was suffering and I couldn't do anything to stop it—to help her—was killing me. Not to mention the note Ross had given me the day after the indictment had been announced. I'd wanted to respond, but how? I wouldn't lie to her. I was upset, and part of that was directed at her. Everything I'd done to protect her had been in vain.

"Knock, knock."

I looked over my left shoulder. Sarah stood, framed by the open doorway. She'd chosen a dark blue gown with short, sheer sleeves and a high waist to disguise her growing baby bump. The dress had a slit up the front, showing off her long legs, and she'd pinned up her hair off her neck. She looked beautiful. Once upon a time, the sight of her like this would have caused a physical reaction in me. The only thought running through my head at that moment, however, was how Brianna would look in the dress. Brianna had taken my breath away in the purple gown she'd worn to the hospital ball, and I'd hoped to get to see her all dressed up again as she accompanied me to tonight's event. Fate had dealt us different cards.

Knowing how protective I'd been recently of my personal space, namely my bedroom, Sarah remained at the door while I slipped my wallet, keys, and phone into my pocket. "You look handsome."

I shrugged. "You've seen me in a tux before."

She stepped back into the main room as I came closer. "True, but that doesn't make you any less handsome."

Ignoring her attempt to bait me into casual conversation, I checked to make sure I wasn't forgetting anything before heading for the closet to get our coats. "Ready?"

Sarah sighed. I helped her with her coat and held the door open for her before locking up.

"You know, it wouldn't hurt for you to try to have a good time tonight. People are going to notice your sour mood if you don't at least make an effort."

I waited until we were in the elevator on our way down to the parking garage before answering her. "Once we get there I'll do what I have to and play the gracious host." I looked her square in the eye. "I didn't think I had to pretend with you, Sarah."

She frowned. "That's not what I meant, Stephan. I know you miss her. I see the effect being away from her has on you every day."

"Then what exactly do you want from me?"

"I don't know. I guess I was just hoping that my being here would somehow cheer you up, make it better—easier—somehow."

The elevator doors opened, and I motioned for her to exit first. I followed her to my car and held the door open while she got in.

It didn't take long to reach the hotel. Sarah hadn't attempted to restart the conversation. Instead, she kept glancing over at me with a worried look on her face.

Finally, as we pulled up to the front of the hotel, I addressed the elephant in the car. "There are no words to describe how much I miss her. It's not something I can explain to you or anyone else. I know you're trying to help, and I'm grateful, but please let me do this my way."

Before she could respond, the valet was there. I handed over my keys and hurried around the car to join Sarah. As we walked inside, I noticed a few photographers off to the side snapping pictures, but nothing outside the norm. I knew that wouldn't last, though. We were early. I wanted to check in with Lily before people started to arrive to make sure everything was as it should be. Given who would be attending tonight, there would be plenty of press both inside and outside the main ballroom. My only hope was that they would pay more attention to the local celebrities than to me. With recent events, I knew it was a longshot, but I was holding out hope.

Once inside the grand ballroom, I found Lily near the caterer's entrance talking to one of the servers. She took me through the basic setup for the night, including a mock run-through of the PowerPoint presentation on the marketing strategy I was introducing. This wasn't our first time at this, but it never hurt to double check everything before doing it in front of over five hundred people.

The main feature of the evening was along the back wall where several hundred items, all donated, were awaiting tonight's silent auction. Assured everything was in place, I went to check on Sarah. While I had been conversing with Lily over details, she'd retreated to the silent auction table.

"See anything you'd like to bid on?"

She laughed. "Sure. Tons. I seriously doubt I'd bid high enough to win any of them, though. I mean, a week at a luxury spa? Season tickets in a Twins box? These are some serious donations."

"Lily and her team are relentless. Before she came on board, we'd have one or two big ticket items—the rest were things like dinner for two at a fancy restaurant."

"Wow. I'm impressed."

"Lily is pretty impressive."

Sarah leaned in to whisper in my ear, her voice laced with amusement. To the outside observer, I was sure it looked a lot more intimate than what it was. "I was talking about you. I think that's the most I've heard you say about something that wasn't Brianna since I've been here."

Before I could say anything in return, Sarah grabbed my arm and began pulling me toward the bar. "You still don't drink, right?"

"Right," I mumbled, allowing myself to be manhandled.

"Well, right now neither do I, but I need something, so I guess I'll have to see what the bartender can come up with that doesn't have any alcohol. Hopefully I can survive the night without the added help."

"You didn't have to come, you know."

She stopped and turned to face me. "Yes I did. I may not always know the right thing to say or do, but I wasn't about to let you come alone tonight. You know as well as I do there will be reporters all over the place. You need someone to watch your back. That's what I'm here for."

Sarah smiled, triumphant.

"You're here to watch my back?"

"That's right." She slipped her arm around mine and resumed moving toward the bar. "Now, let's find the bartender."

Sarah hadn't been wrong. We always invited the press to this event because . . . well, it was good press. Most of the reporters present weren't looking for gossip, thankfully. They were here to cover one of the biggest charity events in Minneapolis and to support a good cause.

True to her word, Sarah stayed by my side as I mingled through the crowd while the hors d'oeuvres and cocktails were served. Anytime she thought someone—a reporter or otherwise—was being too nosy about my personal life, she'd do something to distract them. One time she even went as far as spilling some of her drink. It missed everything important except the carpet beneath our feet, but it was enough to deflect and give us an excuse to get away. I had to admit, she was good at this. Sarah would have made a good wife in that regard. Too bad neither of us felt that way toward each other.

Halfway through cocktails, my aunt and uncle made their way through the crowd to say hi. "It's a great turnout tonight." My aunt leaned in to kiss my cheek.

"It is." I made sure to keep the smile I'd been wearing all evening plastered on my face. The last thing I needed was the press to get a shot of me scowling at my aunt and turn it into some sort of family feud regarding Sarah.

"It's good to see you again, Sarah."

"Likewise, Diane. I'm glad I was able to come with Stephan tonight. The event has grown since the last time I attended."

"That's right. You did come with him that one year. How did I forget that?" A slight blush covered Diane's cheeks.

Sarah chuckled. "Don't worry about it. That was five years ago. A lot has changed since then."

My aunt glanced down at Sarah's growing stomach. "Yes, it has. How have you been feeling?"

Richard wrapped his arm around Diane's waist and pulled her against his side. "Sweetheart, I'm sure Sarah doesn't want to talk about that here."

Diane glanced around and noticed all the potential eavesdroppers. "Oh. I guess you're right. Maybe I can stop by sometime and we can have lunch?"

Sarah smiled. "Sure. I'd like that."

A few minutes later, I saw Lily heading in my direction. It was time. "You ready?"

"As ready as I'll ever be."

I said a quick good-bye to my aunt and uncle and turned to Sarah. She was smiling.

"Just do your thing," she said. "You've got this."

Sarah took her time walking across the room to our table while I turned toward the stage. I wished I had Sarah's confidence. Lately I was feeling as if I were missing an appendage. It left me unbalanced and lacking the surefire decisiveness I always had.

Squaring my shoulders, I ascended the stairs to the small platform that had been erected, and strolled over to the podium. "Good evening, everyone. I'd like to thank you for coming to The Coleman Foundation's Fall Gala. If you'd please take your seats, we'll get through the business part of the evening, and then you can relax and enjoy dinner."

The rest of my speech was given with as much animation as I could muster. I felt like an actor on a huge stage hoping that no one started throwing rotten tomatoes at me.

When I finished spouting all the figures and statistics I'd memorized, I stepped off to the side of the stage and hit the remote I'd been given earlier by Lily. As if by magic, the lights dimmed and the screen behind the stage illuminated.

Our marketing department had done a wonderful job putting together this year's presentation. There were pictures of some of the people we'd help over the last year, along with snippets of their story. Everything was set to music. It was very moving.

As the slideshow began winding down, I glanced over at my table where Sarah was sitting. She knew what the foundation did, but I was curious as to her reaction to the video. Before my gaze could zero in on Sarah, however, it was drawn to the opposite side of the stage and to the left. Lily was talking with someone, and she looked rather excited about whatever it was.

At first, I was going to dismiss it, but then I realized the other woman looked familiar. I took a closer look. My eyes widened as I realized it was Jade.

I searched for Cal somewhere nearby, but he was nowhere to be found. During the cocktail hour, I'd scanned the room for them to no avail. Eventually I'd given up, thinking that they'd decided to forego the gala. I had been mistaken.

The two glanced over at me. With the lights off, I couldn't see their expressions very well, but I could tell they were both smiling. I had no idea what was going on.

When the presentation ended, I briefly took the stage once more. "Thank you all again for coming. Your support and generosity helps to make thousands of lives better. Please enjoy your dinners and the silent auction. Ms. Adams will announce the winners just before midnight."

Jogging down the steps with purpose, I made a beeline for Lily. Jade had conveniently disappeared.

"Was that Jade?"

"Well hello to you, too."

"Don't toy with me, Lily. I'm not in the mood."

Lily released an exasperated sigh, but the joyous expression never left her face. "She wanted to deliver a message."

"What message? Why didn't she just give it to me herself?"

She looked over my shoulder, then back at me. "Not here. Follow me."

Without a second thought, I followed her.

I figured once we exited the ballroom, away from the noise and interested ears, she would relay the message. To my surprise, she didn't stop once we were in the foyer. She was also moving fast. So fast that I had to work in order to keep up. "Lily, where are you—"

"You'll find out in a minute."

Although I wasn't in the mood for games, I decided to play along. At least for the moment. The only thing I could think of was that Cal, since I hadn't seen him in the ballroom, needed to speak to me in private. It was the only thing that made sense.

The elevator doors reopened, and the first thing I saw was Cal and Jade standing at the far end of the hall. "What—"

"Patience."

It was my turn to sigh. I was trying very hard not to lose my temper.

"It's about time, Coleman."

Jade elbowed Cal. "Stop it."

"What's going on?"

Cal didn't move, but Jade did. She slipped a key card into the door and opened it.

Not knowing what was going on, but figuring the sooner I got inside the sooner I would get my answers, I stepped over the threshold and into the room. Three seconds later, I stopped breathing.

Chapter 16

Brianna

"You're not going to stand there all night, are you?" Lily pushed her way
around Stephan and enveloped me in a hug.

It took me less than a second to react and return her show of affection. I'd
missed Lily, too. She'd been my only friend, my only lifeline besides
Stephan. We'd talked almost every day before I moved in with Cal. It had
been difficult not to pick up the phone and call her these past few months,
but I'd had no idea what she thought of me after I left.

She pulled back, and I noticed her wiping moisture from her eyes.

"Hi, Lily."

Lily smiled and then glanced over at Stephan. I followed her gaze. He
hadn't moved from his position near the door. The look on his face
confused me. Did he not want to see me?

"I guess I should get back to the party," Lily said, sounding slightly
disappointed. "Will you call me?"

I nodded and watched out of the corner of my eye as she swept back out
of the room, only pausing to whisper something to Stephan. He bobbed his
head up and down minutely but never took his eyes off me.

Jade stepped forward, and behind her, I saw Cal looked uncertain. "We're
gonna go downstairs, Anna. I'll be back to get you around noon tomorrow.
If you need anything, you just call, okay? We're only one floor down."

"Room 304." Cal appeared to be attempting to burn the words into
Stephan with his mind rather than relaying the room number.

Again, I nodded.

The two of them left, closing the door firmly behind them and leaving
Stephan and I alone. He still hadn't moved, and I was getting nervous. The
muscles in my throat constricted, and my heart raced. Maybe this hadn't
been the best idea.

As if some sort of switch had been flipped, Stephan took a step forward.
Then another. Before I knew it, he was standing directly in front of me,
only inches separating us. I looked up into his eyes and gasped. They held

an intensity I'd never seen before from him. It both excited and frightened me. If it had been anyone else but Stephan looking at me like that, I would have been running for the nearest hiding place I could find. Because it was Stephan, I remained frozen, waiting.

Slowly, he lifted his right hand to my face. I closed my eyes and leaned in. His touch sent tingles down my spine. Warmth spread from his fingers down my neck to the pit of my stomach where the butterflies circled furiously.

He stepped closer, bringing our bodies in line with one another. His right hand never left my face as his left slid around my waist, holding me against him.

I itched to touch him, too. It had been so long. Lifting my arms, I wrapped them around his waist.

Stephan took this as a sign and pulled me against his chest. As he encircled me in his arms for the first time in four months, his chest heaved beneath my cheek before he released a ragged breath.

We stood there holding each other for a long time. I had no idea how many minutes passed—it didn't matter. All that mattered was that he was here. With me. Holding me. I didn't ever want him to let go.

A strange sound caused me to glance up at him. He looked down, meeting my gaze, and I realized he was crying.

Reaching up with both hands, I used my thumbs to wipe the moisture from his cheeks. He'd gotten choked up that time he told me about his parents, but this was more than that. Fresh tears were streaming freely down his cheeks.

My gut twisted in response to his pain. I'd done this to him. My leaving had done this to him.

Before I could lower my hand, he captured my wrist, trapping me.

A split second later, he lowered his head, and his lips brushed against mine. I couldn't help the noise that escaped—something between a sigh and a sob. I'd missed this . . . him.

Taking my reaction as encouragement, he released my wrist and cupped his hands around my head. He threaded his fingers through my hair as his mouth increased its pressure on mine. As if they had a mind of their own, my fingers sought out his hair and held tight.

He moaned and increased his grip on my hair, pulling slightly. I opened my mouth in reaction, and he took full advantage, sliding his tongue inside. I kissed him back with all the emotion I'd been storing . . . saving just for him.

Tears streamed down my face as we continued to kiss. When he realized I was crying, he placed soft kisses along my cheeks, wiping away the tears. I breathed deep, feeling the calm of being in his arms once more.

Satisfied my tears had stopped, Stephan rested his forehead against mine. I closed my eyes briefly, leaning into his touch as he caressed my face. When I opened my eyes again, I saw how concerned he was. "I missed you.

So much."

Stephan smiled, but it didn't reach his eyes. "I've missed you, too." He paused, his fingers continuing to work their magic against my skin. "You know I'm not going to let you go again, don't you? It nearly killed me. I can't do it a second time."

I nodded. There was still so much going on in our lives, but he was right about one thing—staying apart was no longer an option. I didn't think my heart could take it. Not again.

He looked down and took a deep breath. "Where did you get that dress? It looks absolutely amazing on you." As if to solidify his words, Stephan took hold of my waist with both hands and squeezed.

Even to such a simple gesture, my body reacted. I was still his. He still wanted me.

"Jade helped me pick it out."

As soon as I'd seen the dress online, I knew it was the one I wanted. It was gray, not a color I normally wore, but I loved how it hugged my torso and flowed from my waist to the floor. I'd also remembered what Lily had said about Stephan liking strapless dresses. If the look in his eyes was any indication, he liked the dress a lot.

"You look stunning in it."

I felt my cheeks heat in response to his compliment.

He chuckled and stepped back. Taking hold of my hands, he led me across the room to the sofa beside the bed. He sat down and pulled me into his lap. I folded my body into his, laying my head on his shoulder and reaching for the buttons on his shirt. As soon as I realized what I was doing —that I'd ruin his shirt, and he needed to be presentable to go back to the party later—I snatched my hands away.

To my surprise, he stopped me. "You can play with my buttons, love." I looked up at him, confused. "I don't care if you ruin my shirt. I can always get another one."

"But the party—"

He kissed my forehead. "I'm not going back to the party tonight."

"But you have to."

Stephan raised an eyebrow. "I do?"

I looked down at my lap sheepishly before glancing back up at him. "Don't you?"

He brushed his fingers up my arm until he reached my face and tilted my head to look at him. "No. I've done my part. Lily can take care of the rest." He placed a chaste kiss on my lips. "I'm all yours for the rest of the night."

Smiling, I hugged him.

He laughed and hugged me back.

This felt so good. I hadn't been this happy since the day I'd left his condo.

Settling back into my favorite position, I began playing with the buttons on his shirt again, this time not caring about the potential damage.

Time slipped away as we sat there holding each other. He never stopped touching me. It was as if he had to remind himself that I was real, that this was real. In many ways, I was feeling the same way. Being with him again after so long apart felt more like dream.

A rumbling in my stomach broke our quiet moment. He tilted my chin up and looked me in the eye. "You're hungry. When was the last time you ate something?"

"About one o'clock."

He scowled. "Lunch? Why didn't you eat dinner?"

I tried to look down, but he held tight to my face. "I was too nervous. About seeing you again. I didn't know . . ."

"Continue."

"I didn't know if you'd be mad at me."

His scowl became a frown.

Stephan released my chin, reached into his jacket pocket, and removed his cell phone. After punching in several numbers, he held it up to his ear. "Are you able to get away for a few minutes?"

He paused.

"Brianna hasn't eaten dinner. Can you get something from the kitchen and bring it up to the room for her?" He nodded, although whoever he was talking to couldn't see. "We'll see you in a few minutes, then."

Placing his cell phone back in his jacket pocket, he patted my leg, indicating he wanted me to stand. I had some difficulty in the dress, and he helped so I wouldn't rip the beautiful garment.

Once he knew I was safely on my feet, he strolled into the bathroom and returned with a glass of water. He handed it to me. "Drink. My guess is that if you haven't eaten anything since lunch, you haven't drunk anything either. Am I right?"

Feeling guilty, I looked down as I took a sip of the water. "Yes, Sir."

Stephan sighed and brushed a strand of hair away from my face. "I thought I told you to take care of yourself."

"I've been trying to eat better, but today . . ."

"You were nervous."

"Yes."

"That I would be upset with you." It wasn't a question.

"Yes."

Before he could respond, there was a knock on the door. "We'll address that in a minute."

I didn't have to look to see the scowl had returned to his face.

Staying where I was, I waited for him to come back. I heard Lily's voice in the hallway, and I realized she must have been the one Stephan had called to bring me food. He thanked her and closed the door, making sure it was locked. In his hands, he held a tray with what I assumed was food.

Without a word, he laid the tray down on the coffee table and helped me to sit back down on the couch. I loved this dress, and Stephan seemed to as well, but I wasn't used to wearing clothes like this, and I felt as if one wrong move would destroy it.

He removed the lid covering the food, and my mouth began to water. Chicken, in what looked to be a rich cream sauce, along with asparagus and mashed potatoes filled one plate. Beside it were a salad and a slice of cheesecake. It was more food than I'd eaten in months at one time.

When I didn't immediately start eating, Stephan picked up the utensils and handed them to me. "Eat your dinner, Brianna."

To my amazement, I ate more of the food than I'd thought I would, even devouring over half the delicious cheesecake. Stephan sat beside me as I ate, not commenting. When I was finished, he replaced the cover and carried it over to the desk out of the way before returning to sit beside me on the couch.

He draped his arm over my shoulder and held me against his side. "Thank you," he whispered.

I burrowed my head on his shoulder, pressing my nose against the column of his neck, inhaling his scent. It was one more thing I'd missed about him.

His chest vibrated with amusement, and he squeezed my shoulder. "Stop trying to distract me, Brianna. As much as I'd love to skip to more pleasant things, we have something we need to talk about."

A lead weight formed in my stomach, and I stopped my movement. Was he going to yell at me? Should I apologize even though I'm not sorry?

"Tell me why you thought I'd be upset about you coming tonight."

Swallowing, I reached for the buttons on his shirt. They were my comfort. They grounded me. I'd missed them, too. I'd missed everything about him. "Not about me coming. I thought . . ." I paused. "I thought you'd be mad about my agreeing to testify."

He tensed. "Ah. That."

Stephan didn't say any more, and neither did I. There was a tension that filled the room, though—tension I'd never felt before when I was with him. My anxiety level rose again, and the air coursing through my lungs felt heavier.

"Breathe, Brianna."

He increased his hold on me, lifting me onto his lap. I clung to him.

Sighing, he brushed his lips across my forehead. "I wasn't happy about the agreement you made. I'm still not happy. However, there isn't anything I can do about it. What's done is done. My only fear is what it will mean for you. I would've rather spent the rest of my life in prison than see you hurt, and I know reliving that nightmare will cause you pain. It kills me that I can't protect you from it."

I reached up and cupped his cheek. He looked down, the pain he was feeling etched on his face. "I'll be okay."

His only response was to cover my mouth with his. The kiss began slow and gentle but soon increased in intensity. I gripped the lapels of his jacket, and his fingers dug into my waist. It was as if we couldn't get close enough to each other.

After several minutes, to my disappointment, he pulled away. We were both breathing heavily, our chests rising and falling rapidly. "Maybe you being on my lap isn't such a good idea. I seem to be having trouble controlling myself. We've been apart too long."

It was my turn to frown. I wanted to be here, on his lap. It was my favorite place in the world.

He leaned back, bringing my head down to rest on his shoulder. I relaxed a little when he began running his fingers through my hair. "Who am I kidding?" It almost sounded as if he were talking to himself and not to me. "There's no way I can let you go."

Chapter 17

Stephan

I felt as if I were dreaming. Brianna was really wrapped in my arms, resting against my shoulder. I could smell her coconut shampoo as I laid my cheek on top of her head. There was so much I wanted to ask her, but I didn't want to break the spell. For the first time in four months, my world didn't feel as if it were tilted off its axis.

Brianna's appearance had rocked me so much that I'd completely forgotten about Sarah. My date for the evening hadn't crossed my mind until Lily whispered on her way out the door earlier that she and Logan would make sure Sarah got home safely. I should have felt guilty, but I was so overcome with joy at having the woman I loved here with me that I couldn't muster a single ounce of regret.

We must have fallen asleep at some point, because when I woke up, I had a crick in my neck, and Brianna was snoring softly against my chest. She looked so peaceful, but I knew I needed to move us to the bed, or our bodies would be protesting in the morning. I shifted in an attempt to get my arms under her enough to be able to lift us both from the couch, trying to be gentle. My movement, however, woke Brianna.

She gazed up at me, confused for a moment, and then she smiled. "Hi."

I chuckled. "Hi." After pressing a soft kiss to her forehead, I helped her sit up. "It seems we fell asleep."

Brianna blushed.

"What?"

"I missed sleeping with you."

This time, I kissed her on the lips, letting my mouth linger. "I missed sleeping with you, too. We should move to the bed, though."

Without waiting for me to help her, Brianna started to get up. Her dress, however, had other ideas. She must have stepped on the hem, because before either of us knew what was happening, she tumbled headfirst back into my lap.

Brianna looked up at me in horror.

I laughed. "Are you all right, sweetheart?"

She nodded, her expression softening. Even after all this time, she worried I'd be upset over a silly accident.

I helped her up before standing and stretching myself. Although the couch was comfortable enough for sitting, it wasn't designed for sleeping.

Taking her hand, I led her around the coffee table and into the center of the room. I skimmed the tops of her bare shoulders and ghosted down her arms until I was holding her hands in mine. Goose bumps peppered her skin in the wake of my touch. "We should get you out of this dress. As much as I love how you look in it, you'll be much more comfortable sleeping with it off."

Her breath hitched, and I saw her swallow, but she nodded.

Using my grip on her hands, I pulled her toward me until our chests were touching and placed her arms around my waist. She gazed up at me, her eyes showing her apprehension. From the way she'd fisted my shirt around her fingers, I didn't think it was because she didn't want me to undress her. It had been four months since we'd been together. Four very *long* months.

Reaching behind her, I found the zipper and began lowering it, inch by inch. Her eyes never left mine as the zipper descended, revealing more and more of her flesh to my hands. I felt lace. More than anything, I wanted to see what she had on under her dress, but I knew I needed to go slowly. This had to happen at her pace.

The bodice loosened, and I gripped her waist with my hands, pulling the dress down slightly—just enough to see the edge of the black bra she was wearing. It was covered in lace, just as I'd suspected.

Brianna's gaze followed my own as I stared down at her newly revealed undergarment. Color crept up her neck. "Jade found it in my things."

"Look at me." I waited until she looked up, her face filled with shy embarrassment. While I held her gaze, I shimmied the dress down her torso until it pooled at her waist. Lace scratched my fingers as I traced a path back up her sides until my thumbs rested just beneath her breasts. "Beautiful," I whispered.

Her chest rose and fell rapidly as I continued to caress the undersides of her breasts. My gaze was still locked on Brianna's, but I could feel the movement of every breath she took, and I knew what I was doing was affecting her. Without removing my hands, I took a slight step back— enough to allow the remains of her dress to slide off her hips and down to the floor.

Finally looking down, I took in the full effect. Brianna was wearing a black lace corset that hugged her body in the most delicious way and a pair of matching panties. Unable to resist, I reached down and palmed her ass, lifting her off the ground. She responded by grabbing hold of my shoulders to steady herself.

Without stopping to think, I left the dress lying in a pile on the floor and carried her over to the bed. Laying her down, I removed my tuxedo jacket and bowtie, along with releasing the top few buttons on my shirt, before crawling on top of her. She looked nervous. "Do you want me to stop, Brianna? I will if that's what you want. We can lie here in each other's arms and go to sleep."

She pressed her lips together, and I could see the wheels turning in her head.

Cupping her face, I forced her to look at me. "Tell me what you're thinking."

"I'm scared."

"Of?"

"I'm still not sure I can be what you need me to be."

I cocked my head to the side, looking at her. What was she talking about? "What exactly do you think I need you to be, Brianna?"

"You want someone . . ." She must have seen the look I was giving her and corrected herself. "You want me to be your submissive."

"Yes."

"What if I can't?"

I was utterly confused. "What makes you think you can't be?"

She tried to look away, but I held tight to her face not letting her. "At Logan and Lily's, I—" Moisture pooled in her eyes. "I—"

"Love, what happened at Logan and Lily's was my fault, not yours." She started to shake her head, but I stopped her by resting my forehead against hers. "No. I will not let you blame yourself, Brianna. I pushed you too far. It was my mistake."

"But I should have been able to—"

"You should have been able to what? Not be scared? Not have a flashback? Those aren't things you can control. You feel how you feel."

She was crying in earnest now, and although I hated seeing her tears, I knew we needed to have this conversation.

"But it's what you want."

"Who says it's what I want? I never said that."

"I don't understand."

I kissed both of her cheeks before I answered her. "Brianna, I don't like to play in public. I never have. That afternoon at Logan and Lily's was meant as a demonstration only. I wanted you to see a loving couple engaging in play since you've had so much negative experience with BDSM." Massaging her temples with my thumbs, I found her gaze again. "It's not something I need. What I need is you, trusting me. If you can do that, we can figure the rest out. Just the two of us."

"But what if in the future you want something I can't give you? I'm broken, and I might always be broken."

Anger bubbled up from my chest. "Don't say that. You are *not* broken. Look at how far you've come in the months since I met you." Glancing down between us, I let my eyes linger over her form. "Look at where we are now." I pressed myself firmly against her center, letting her feel my erection. Her eyes went wide, but there was no fear in them. "Six months ago we would never have been able to do this."

Brianna reached up and ran her fingers lightly over my face. "I don't want to disappoint you."

"That's impossible. You are the bravest person I know, and I love you. You could never disappoint me."

The tears were back, but this time I knew they were because she was happy. "I love you, too."

"That's good," I said, bending down to kiss her neck. "Because I'm not planning to let you go anytime soon."

"What about—"

I placed a finger over her lips and asked her the one thing above all else that I needed to know. "Do you want to be with me, Brianna? Not just for now, but for always?"

She nodded. "Always."

I smiled. "Then that's all I need to know. We'll figure out the rest of it together."

Without another word, I kissed her with all the passion I'd been stifling since walking into the hotel room. Brianna threaded her fingers through my hair and met my enthusiasm with equal fervor. After only a few minutes, my desire to remove the clothing that was still between us became my number one priority. It had been four months since I'd felt her bare flesh against mine. The need to feel her again took complete control over my thoughts and actions.

Using one hand, I unbuttoned my shirt until it was hanging open, revealing my naked chest. Already I could feel a difference, and apparently so could Brianna. She sucked in a lungful of air and tugged at the strands of my hair. Even with her lingerie between us, I could feel the heat radiating from her body, as I was sure she could feel coming from mine.

Resting my weight on my elbows, I unbuttoned my cufflinks and quickly removed my shirt, tossing it somewhere across the room. At the moment, I didn't much care where it landed. I had the one person I'd been dying to have in my arms lying beneath me, kissing me, moaning as I ran my hands up and down her body. I couldn't wait to be inside her again.

The moment that thought crossed my mind, I stopped. Brianna lay panting under me. She opened her eyes.

Why did I start something I couldn't finish? Sure we could still pleasure each other, but that wasn't what I wanted. I wanted her. All of her. There was only one problem with that—no condom.

"Did I do something wrong?"

I buried my head in her shoulder and released a humorless laugh. "No, you didn't do anything wrong."

"Okay." Her voice held a hint of uncertainty.

I sighed. Bringing my face level with hers, I met her gaze. "I just realized I don't have any condoms on me." To lighten the mood, I flashed her a cheesy smile. "I wasn't expecting to run into a beautiful woman I wanted to have my way with tonight."

"Oh." She was silent for a long moment, and then she glanced down between us. Given our positions, I knew she couldn't see anything, but I was sure she could still feel my arousal pressed against her. "Jade . . ." She swallowed, nervous.

"What about Jade?"

"I think she . . ." Brianna's blush was back. "I think she put some in my bag."

At that moment, the look on my face was probably priceless. Just when I'd thought sex with Brianna was off the table for the night, hope dawned on the horizon. "Where's your bag?"

"In the dresser."

I hopped up off the bed, hating to leave her warmth, but knowing it would be worth it in the end, and rushed the few feet to the single dresser in the room. There were only three drawers, so it wasn't difficult to locate the one that contained Brianna's overnight bag. It did, however, take me a minute or two to locate the foil squares tucked away in one of the side pockets. There were four. I couldn't help but smile, and I wondered if Brianna and I could burn through all of them before we had to say good-bye tomorrow. It was worth a shot.

Turning back toward the bed, I stopped and took a few moments to admire the woman sprawled out on it wearing some of the sexiest lingerie known to man. I grew harder, knowing that in a short amount of time I'd be claiming her once again as mine.

She gazed up at me, her eyes filled with the same desire echoed in mine. Brianna wanted this as much as I did. It was hard to believe this same woman had been terrified of sex. The only trembling she would be doing tonight was in ecstasy. Once I had her in my arms, in my bed, I'd be hard pressed to let her go.

I helped her to stand. She looked confused but followed my lead.

Running my hands along her bare arms, I took a deep breath, trying to maintain what little control I still had. "Do you need to use the bathroom? If you do, tell me now, because once I get you into that bed, I have no plans to let you out of it until morning."

She took what looked to be a steadying breath of her own. "Yes, please."

"Go do what you need to do."

Brianna scurried off toward the bathroom while I waited impatiently. I tossed the condoms on the nightstand where they'd be easily accessible, then quickly picked up our discarded clothes. It wasn't that I cared about the items being on the floor. It was more having something to do so I wouldn't go insane while I waited.

The bathroom door opened, and Brianna emerged. She was still wearing the black corset and panties, and I was itching to take them off her. I motioned for her to stand in front of me by the bed. Once she was within arm's reach, I twisted her around and swiftly unhooked the eyelets holding her corset together. It released from her body, freeing her breasts, and I threw it over to join her dress.

Taking her by the shoulders, I pulled her back against my chest and kissed her shoulder. Looking down, I admired the view of her bare breasts exposed to me for the first time since she'd left. My dreams had not done her justice.

Brianna sighed as I snaked my hands down her torso and hooked my fingers into the sides of her panties before lowering them to the ground. She stepped free of them without any prompting.

Turning her around, I wrapped one arm around her waist and the other around her neck as I gave her a long hard kiss. "Get into bed. I'll join you in a minute." Without waiting for her to respond, I strolled into the bathroom.

When I returned, she was in bed waiting for me. I removed the rest of my clothing and slipped into bed naked beside her.

She was warm, and I let that warmth seep into my bones, having missed it for far too long. Wrapping my arms around her, I brought our bodies in line with each other once more. Brianna smiled up at me.

Brianna whimpered as I palmed her breast with my right hand. She closed her eyes, and her mouth opened slightly. I took advantage and kissed her, plunging my tongue between her parted lips.

As much as I would have loved to go slow, take my time, and show her how much I loved her—all of her—that would have to wait for the next round. I needed to be inside her.

Continuing my assault on her mouth, I flipped us over so that I was on top. Spreading her legs to bracket my hips, I removed my hand from her breast and slid it down her stomach until I reached the junction between her legs. Her breath hitched as my fingers made contact with her pussy. She was wet, and her heat radiated against my palm.

Not wasting any time, I slipped first one finger and then two inside her. Her interior muscles flexed against the intrusion before relaxing.

Releasing her lips, I worked my way down her neck, kissing and sucking a path to her left breast. I took it into my mouth and began sucking and nibbling. I needed her primed and writhing in my arms by the time I thrust my cock into her. She was almost there, but she needed just a little more.

Leaning up, I gave her a quick kiss before reaching over to grab a condom. I made quick work of rolling it down my length and retaking my position on top of her. I lined myself up with her entrance, pressing only the tip of my cock inside her.

I watched her facial expression, looking for any sign that she needed me to stop, but there was nothing but complete bliss on her features. Lowering myself on top of her, I resumed my attention to her breast while placing one hand on her waist to hold her steady. With my other hand, I reached up and gathered her hair in my fist.

The moment she realized what I was doing, Brianna opened her heavily lidded eyes and moaned. I'd learned my girl liked to have her hair pulled. It was good to know that hadn't changed in our months apart.

Pressing my cock the remaining inches inside her, I began to move, using both my hand on her hip, as well as the one in her hair, to provide a counter motion. I increased my attention to her breasts, switching to the other one, needing to mark it the same as I had its mate.

The closer I came to my climax, the more aggressive my movements. If Brianna's reactions were any indication, she didn't mind. Her muscles clenched around my cock with every thrust, and her chest heaved with labored breaths as I drove both of us closer to orgasm.

When I knew I wasn't going to be able to hold out any longer, I adjusted, centering my thumb over her clit. "Come for me, sweetheart. Let me feel you."

As if a dam broke, Brianna began shaking. Her mouth opened wide, and her back arched. The sight alone was enough to trigger my release. She screamed out, and so did I.

Chapter 18

Brianna

I woke up for the first time in four months with a smile on my face.
Stephan lay beside me, his arm draped possessively over my stomach, and
his head resting on a pillow near my shoulder. I never wanted to leave this
bed.

The sun was already shining strong through the curtains, so I knew it had
to be at least midmorning. We didn't get much sleep last night. After we
had sex that first time, Stephan had insisted on the two of us taking a
shower to clean up. I'm not sure we got all that clean, though, since he'd
given me two more orgasms, one with his hands and the other with his
mouth, while we were in there.

Afterward, we'd climbed back in the large bed, and he'd gathered me to
his chest, constantly kissing and touching me. It was as if he needed to
reassure himself that I was there. I couldn't blame him. It felt surreal to me
as well.

Sometime before dawn, he woke me again. This time, it was with barely
there kisses all over my body that had my skin tingling. As he slid his penis
inside me the second time, he held my hands over my head, pinning to me
to the mattress, and murmured he loved me over and over again in my ear.
It was almost magical, that feeling of being surrounded by him—loved by
him—protected by him. It sent me into a spiral of sensations that ended in
another intense orgasm.

When we finally fell asleep for the second time, I was wrapped tightly in
his embrace. The position didn't allow me much movement, but I didn't
care. He was here, and I would be in whatever position he needed me to be
in. After I'd left, I'd worried he would realize he didn't really feel the same
way about me that I did for him. It seemed I was wrong. Being apart had
affected him immensely. Even though I knew I'd done what I had to, there
was guilt there. What if there had been another way that wouldn't have
meant us being separated all this time?

"What are you thinking so hard about, sweetheart?"

I looked over to find him staring at me. His expression was curious, but there was concern there, too, and I knew I had to be honest. "I'm sorry I hurt you."

"Hurt me?"

I tried to avert my eyes, but he held my face with his hand so I couldn't look away.

"By leaving. I hurt you."

Scooting closer to me, he propped himself up on his elbow so that he was hovering over me. He studied my face for several minutes. "Brianna, as much as I hate the decision you made to leave, I do understand why you did it, just as I understand the reason you agreed to testify if need be against that bastard who tortured you. I'm not your owner. You will always have free will with me. And yes, I was hurt when you left. My heart broke because the woman I loved was walking away from me."

Tears flowed down my cheeks, and he wiped them away. "I never wanted to hurt you."

"I know."

He lowered his lips to mine and kissed me. It was soft, his mouth barely touching, yet it caused my body to heat just the same.

Stephan continued to kiss me for several minutes, and his erection slowly grew against my hip. "Hmm. It seems as if my body hasn't had its fill of you yet." When he looked down at me, his eyes had already dilated with arousal. "We still have two condoms left."

I nodded, not sure what to say. He could take me as many times as he wanted. I wouldn't object. Stephan may not own me in the way that Ian had, but he owned my heart and, with it, my body and soul.

Surprising me, he rolled onto his back, threw the covers off both of us, and pulled his knees toward his body. "Come sit."

Sitting up, I lifted my leg and placed it on the other side of his waist. I'd only been on top once before, so I was a little nervous.

Almost instantly I remembered I shouldn't have been. Stephan was in charge. He'd take care of me—tell me what I needed to do.

Gripping my hips with his hands, he instructed me to lie back. This was new. Different, but I did what I was told. My back lay flat against his legs, and my knees were bent. I didn't understand the meaning of this new position until he started touching me. He ran his hands up and down my inner thighs. Every time he'd get close to my center, he'd head back down.

The motion continued until I was aching for him to touch me. Moments away from begging, he grazed his thumbs over the edges of my folds. "Do you like that?"

"Yes." My voice sounded breathy even to me.

"How about this?" Without warning, he began tracing the opening of my entrance, and then traveled up to circle my clit. I wanted so badly for him to touch that spot that gave me so much pleasure, but instead he retreated back down to where he'd begun.

As he continued, my hips began to lift of their own accord—my body silently begging for what it wanted. He halted his movement altogether, and I nearly screamed out in frustration.

I glanced down the length of my body and found him smirking at me. "Keep those hips still, Brianna. We do this on my timetable, not yours."

Another wave of guilt crept up, but I tried to suppress it, to remember all he'd said in the past. I wanted to please him so badly. Taking a deep, calming breath, I closed my eyes and concentrated on trying to remain as still as I could.

After another minute had passed, he began touching me again. At one point, when he inserted two fingers inside me and began moving them in and out at a rapid pace while rubbing circles right above my clit, I gritted my teeth in an attempt not to move.

"Good girl. Now I want you to count to ten for me, and when you reach ten, you may come."

Sweat dripped down my forehead as I started to count. "One." As soon as the word left my lips, the speed of his fingers increased, and his thumb that had been teasing my clit pressed in firm circles sending a jolt of heat throughout my body.

By the time I reached six, I was shaking. Concentrating on the number I was on, and on not coming, was taking every ounce of energy I had. Even then, I wasn't sure I hadn't missed a number—or said one twice.

"Ten." The last number was spoken without sound as a dam broke inside me and my climax over took my entire body.

When I opened my eyes again, Stephan was sitting up, and I was in his arms. "Are you all right?"

I nodded, not sure if I could speak.

"Was that good? Did you enjoy it?"

I nodded again.

This time he chuckled. "Did I leave you speechless?"

Smiling, I gave talking a try. "Maybe."

"I guess not." He was clearly amused. "That's good, because I'm not done with you yet."

My eyes widened at his statement, but he didn't give me much time to register what was happening before he lifted my hips and positioned his penis right where he wanted it to be. Pulling me against his chest, he kissed me as he lowered me onto his erection. I was still sensitive from my orgasm, and I could feel every inch of him as he slid inside me.

His fingers dug into my flesh as he lifted and lowered my hips to meet his thrusts. I circled my arms around his neck to ground myself as he moved. His gaze never left mine, and he appeared to be completely focused on what he was doing. For some reason, that made the heat between my legs increase even more.

I knew he was getting close when his movements were less fluid and more abrupt. His brow was furrowed, and he was sweating. I brushed my fingers along his forehead, tracing the crease.

"I love you, Brianna. Don't you ever forget that." His breath was hot against my cheek as he continued to thrust.

Reaching between us, he took hold of my breasts and began pulling on my nipples. Every tug sent a spark of energy from my breasts down to where we were joined. I closed my eyes, letting the sensations overtake me.

"Touch yourself."

I opened my eyes, not sure I'd heard him correctly.

Apparently I had. He released one of my nipples, wrapped his fingers around my right wrist, and guided my hand down between my legs. I could feel where we were connected. "Rub your clit. Make yourself come."

I didn't move.

"Do it," he ordered as he went back to my nipples.

Tentatively, I attempted to mimic what I'd felt him do in the past. It took a couple of tries, but once I found what worked—that pleasure—I was climbing faster and faster toward that peak.

"There you go. Rub faster, Brianna. I want to feel you come around me. Come for me, sweetheart."

Just as I fell over the cliff—my orgasm claiming me—Stephan wrapped his hand around the back of my neck and covered my mouth with his own. I felt him jerk twice, moaning against my lips as he found his own climax.

He brought us back down onto the bed, panting and smiling. "I missed you. I missed this. I missed everything."

"Me, too."

We lay there, coming down from our high, until his gaze landed on the clock on the nightstand. He sighed. "It's already eleven thirty. Ross and Jade will be here in a half hour to get you."

In response to our impending separation, Stephan held me tighter, burying his head in my shoulder.

I hugged him back. "I wish I could go home with you."

"I know. So do I. Hopefully it won't be much longer. Once the press finds something else to sink their teeth into, we won't have to worry about them."

As much as I didn't like it, I knew he was right. Cal said a few reporters had tried to follow him home two weeks ago. "When can we see each other again?"

He kissed my neck, sliding his thumb back and forth over my collarbone. "Soon. I'll think of something."

"Okay."

Kissing my lips, he reluctantly pulled away. "We should shower. As much as I'd love for you to leave here with the smell of sex on you, we don't need to draw attention to either of us."

Without a word, he helped me out of bed, and we strolled hand in hand into the bathroom. This shower was worlds away from the one last night. The looming good-bye was weighing heavily on both of us, and it filled the small shower enclosure as we washed the evidence of our night together from our bodies.

Dressed with only minutes to spare, we sat together on the couch, holding each other. "You still have your laptop, right?"

I looked up at him. "Yes."

"Good, because I have an idea."

I waited, anxious to hear whatever it was.

"Ask Jade if she'll help you download Skype onto your computer." He got up and retrieved the small pad of paper on top of the dresser. Scribbling something down, he tore the sheet off and returned to sit beside me on the couch. "This is my Skype name. Send me a contact request, and we can do a video chat. It's not the same as seeing each other in person, but it will have to do until I can figure something else out."

Taking the paper, I folded it and put it in the pocket of my jeans.

A knock on the door drew our attention. He stood and went to open the door for Cal and Jade. Our time together was over.

Chapter 19

Stephan
Saying good-bye to Brianna was almost as difficult as it had been the first time. The only thing that made it easier was the knowledge that our separation had an expiration date. I wouldn't be going four months without holding her in my arms again. That wasn't happening. If I had my way about it, I wouldn't be going a week without having some sort of physical contact with her. In order for that to occur, though, I would have to get creative.

When Jade and Cal arrived to pick up Brianna promptly at noon, they handed me a small black bag that had been propped up outside the door. Inside was a change of clothes for me. It didn't take a huge leap to know Lily was behind this. Only she would be brave enough to go to my condo, traipse into my bedroom, and rifle through my things. Why she hadn't gone and bought something new, I had no idea. Under normal circumstances, I'd be livid, but her actions made getting out of the hotel without drawing attention to myself much easier. If I'd had to wear my tux, I would have stuck out like a sore thumb.

It nearly ripped a hole in my heart watching the pain in Brianna's eyes as she left with Cal and Jade. I knew she wanted to come home with me, and if it had been possible without putting a proverbial target on her back, nothing would have stopped me from doing just that.

The risk was still too high, however. Since the press conference two weeks ago, I'd had more than one reporter jump out at me from the most unlikely of places. Even walking a block to get coffee was an adventure. Brianna wasn't ready for that. I'm not sure she ever would be.

At least talking via Skype was now an option. With Agent Marco no longer watching my every move, contact with Brianna was possible. We'd have to be careful, but at this point, I was willing to risk it. I needed her, and she needed me. Going back to the way we were wasn't an option.

After changing my clothes, I headed downstairs to the hotel lobby and out front to where the valets were located. Handing the young man my ticket from the night before, I waited while he jogged off to retrieve my car. It was raining, which somehow felt appropriate.

The valet appeared with my car, and I slid behind the wheel. Traffic was minimal downtown given it was a Sunday afternoon. I was also sure the weather had something to do with it. Fall was upon us, and with it came cooler temperatures that made you want to curl up in front of a warm fire, especially when you added in the rain. Like everyone else on a day like today, all I wanted to do was get home. It was already close to one, and I was sure Sarah was wondering where I was after ditching her last night.

As I pulled into the underground parking garage attached to my building, my cell phone vibrated in my pocket. I let it go to voice mail and waited until I'd put the car in park before checking to see who had called.

The number on the caller ID showed it was from Richard and Diane. I figured they were probably wondering about my disappearance last night as well. Diane was most likely worried something had happened with the case —for the last two weeks she'd been calling me almost daily to find out if I had any news. Checking the voice mail didn't give me any further idea as to what the call was about. It was Richard, and all he'd said was *"Call me when you get this."*

He didn't sound upset or agitated, so I hoped I was correct in that they were only checking up on me due to my unexpected departure from the gala. Figuring I might as well get it over with, I dialed their number and waited for someone to pick up.

"Stephan." There was a sound of relief in my aunt's voice. "I'm so glad you called us back so quickly. I hope everything's all right. You took off last night, and all Lily would tell us was that something came up and that you had to leave."

I smiled. Lily could have made a great politician with answers like that. "My apologies if I worried you, but Lily was right. Something came up that required my immediate attention."

"Nothing bad, I hope."

"No. Nothing bad." For some reason I couldn't wipe the smile off my face.

"I'm glad to hear that. With everything that's going on, I never know anymore."

There was a pause on the other end.

"Stephan, Richard would like to speak to you. I've got to get back to dinner anyway. Jimmy and Samantha are supposed to be here in about ten minutes." Diane hesitated. "You could still come if you'd like. There's plenty of food, you know."

"I appreciate that, Diane. Maybe next time."

She sighed. "Okay. Here's your uncle. Be safe."

Since Brianna's departure, I'd only been to Sunday dinner at Richard and Diane's once. I had to admit my uncle had been making a real effort lately. He was even somewhat sympathetic over my plight. I hated fighting with him, and I was glad that appeared to be behind us. Maybe we could begin working on rebuilding what we'd lost since Tami had driven a wedge between us with her lies. They were the only family I had left.

"Hello, Stephan. I trust everything is good with you or else your aunt wouldn't have given up the phone so easily."

"Nothing newsworthy." Although my relationship with Richard had improved over the last few months, I wasn't sure I was ready to bring up my renewed connection with Brianna yet.

"That's . . . good, I suppose."

I could hear the curiosity lurking behind his words, so I decided to get to the point. "I got your message. There was something you wanted to talk to me about?"

"Oh. Yes. I was wondering if you'd be home this afternoon. I wanted to stop by and speak with you about something."

"You can't discuss it now?"

There was a pause. "I'd rather do it in person. Will you be home?"

Now I was curious. "As far as I'm aware, I should be home. Do you have any idea what time?"

"I'll head over after dinner if that works for you."

I nodded even though he couldn't see me. "That's fine."

"Okay. I'll see you then."

The phone went silent as Richard disconnected the call from his end. Perplexed, I removed the cell from my ear and stared down at it. The last time he'd called me out of the blue needing to talk with me, we'd argued for two hours and didn't speak afterward for six months. What in the world did he want to talk to me about that was so urgent?

Figuring it was best to put it aside for now—after all, I'd find out what all the mystery was about in a couple of hours anyway—I grabbed my things and headed upstairs.

The downstairs of my home was empty when I entered. That wasn't unusual—Sarah spent most of her time in her room if I wasn't home. "Sarah?"

She bounded down the stairs toward me. I was still amazed she could do that with her growing belly. Sarah was in good shape, though. She'd worked out in my gym every day she'd been here. "Hey. You're home."

I smiled at her.

Her expression went from worry, to shock, and then a sly smile crossed her features. "I guess I don't have to ask what . . . or should I say *who* dragged you away from me last night."

"You don't?"

She laughed and rubbed her stomach lovingly. "Nope. You saw your lady love last night."

Although I hadn't planned to deny it, I wanted to know how she'd come to that conclusion. "Why do you think that exactly?"

Sarah ambled into the kitchen, shaking her head. "It's written all over your face." She glanced over her shoulder at me as she took a glass from one of the cabinets. "You're practically glowing. If I didn't know any better, I'd think you were the one that was pregnant."

She winked at me, and I laughed.

"See. That. If I'd said something like that yesterday, you would have rolled your eyes at me."

That only made me smile wider. Although I could feel the separation, seeing Brianna had given me hope. "Yes, I saw Brianna last night."

Sarah strolled into the living room with her water and folded herself onto the couch. "Well, at least I know you ditched me for a good reason." She patted the cushion beside her. "Come on. Spill. It's the least you owe me after abandoning me at *your* foundation's charity dinner."

Reluctantly, I set my things down outside my bedroom door and joined her on the couch. She was right about one thing—I did owe her an explanation. Sarah had been my date, and my dad would have ripped me a new one if he knew I'd ignored a woman like that, no matter what the reason. A gentleman never did that to a lady.

There was a light in Sarah's eyes I hadn't seen since she'd arrived. I wondered if there was a part of her that was living vicariously through my love life.

"So come on, did you go meet her somewhere?"

I shook my head. "Not exactly. She was upstairs in one of the hotel rooms."

"Oooh. So a late-night rendezvous, then. Romantic."

Again, I chuckled, and it felt good. "Something like that."

"And?"

"And what?"

She huffed. "That's all you're going to give me? That you met her in a hotel room? I mean you were there the *whole* night."

Instead of being angry, for some reason I was amused. It had to be the aftereffects of being with Brianna. "I'm not giving you the sordid details."

"Aha! So you admit there *were* sordid details." She moved both eyebrows up and down suggestively.

Shaking my head, I pushed myself up off the couch and stood. "I think that's enough information for you. I should check in with Lily and make sure something didn't come up last night that I need to address."

Sarah pouted as I walked away.

Leaning down to retrieve my things, I glanced back at her. "By the way, my uncle will be stopping by in an hour or two."

"Do you want me to leave?"

"That's not necessary. I just wanted to give you a heads-up."

"Okay. Thanks." She paused. "Oh, and Stephan?"

I waited.

She leaned forward, resting her chin on her forearms against the back of the couch. "I'm glad you got to spend some time with your girl."

My conversation with Lily mimicked the one with Sarah in a lot of ways. Lily, however, wanted to know more than just if Brianna and I had sex last night—not that I shared any more information with Lily on that front than I had with Sarah—but Lily also wanted to know how Brianna herself was doing. Their meeting had been brief, and other than seeing that she was physically fine, Lily hadn't gotten much more in the way of an update on Brianna's life. I shared with her what I knew, although it wasn't much. The little bit of talking Brianna and I had done last night had been on more personal subjects, not her life in general.

After I hung up with Lily, I made myself some lunch and joined Sarah in the living room. She was watching some old movie. It was black and white, and there was a lot of dancing. Not really my thing, but she seemed to be enjoying it. I'd observed over the past month that while Sarah was still very active, she wasn't as full of untamed energy as she used to be. Whether that was due to the baby or something that had happened over time, I didn't know.

Almost two hours on the dot since I'd spoken with my uncle, the security panel lit up, announcing we had a visitor. I stood and went to let Richard in.

"Stephan." He smiled, but it was tentative, which made me all the more curious as to the reason for his visit.

I stepped back and motioned for him to come inside. "Richard."

My uncle removed his overcoat and folded it neatly over his arm.

Across the room, Sarah switched off the television and stood. "Hello, Dr. Cooper."

"Hello, Sarah. It's nice to see you again."

"You, too." Sarah glanced over at me and then back to my uncle before picking up her water and the chips she'd been snacking on. "I'll head upstairs and give you two some privacy."

I waited to see if my uncle made any move to tell her that wasn't necessary, but he didn't. Whatever he had to say to me, he must have wanted to do so in private.

Once Sarah disappeared up the stairs, we made our way into the living room. He took a seat on the couch, and I lowered myself into my chair. I wouldn't ever be able to sit in my chair again and not think of Brianna. My arms always felt empty without her in them.

Not wanting to get too lost in my memories, I tried to focus on my uncle. He was looking out the large bank of windows at the Minneapolis skyline, appearing to be deep in thought. I considered asking him what he needed to talk to me about, but I decided to wait. He'd tell me whatever was on his mind eventually.

A heavy silence filled the air as time passed. Still he didn't speak. I noticed his jaw twitching and realized he was trying to find the right words to say whatever it was he'd come to say.

When he did finally speak, he didn't look at me. "Stephan, I need to ask you a question, and I know you will probably tell me to go to hell, but I need to know."

That wasn't exactly a promising opening.

He turned his head to look at me, his eyes guarded. "Is it yours?"

I was genuinely confused. "Is what mine?"

Richard's expression hardened, but I could tell he was trying to remain calm. "The baby."

"What are you—" My eyes widened as I realized what he was talking about.

He must have realized the moment I'd put the pieces together. "I've been a doctor for almost twenty years. Even with her efforts at concealment last night, it was impossible for me to miss. How far along is she—four, five months?"

"About four," I answered, still attempting to wrap my mind around what my uncle had just implied.

"What about Brianna? I thought you loved her. You loved her so much you immediately fell right back into your ex's arms and got her pregnant?"

There was no mistaking the disapproval in his voice, and I knew I needed to clear up his misconception immediately. "Sarah isn't carrying my baby."

"What?"

"It's not mine."

It was his turn to look confused. "Then why is she here—living with you?"

"Sarah is here to support me." I paused, not sure how much I wanted to share of Sarah's story. "And she needed some time away. I offered her a place to stay while she was here."

He didn't answer right away. "You have to know how this will look, don't you?"

"What are you talking about? She's a friend who needed a place to stay while she's in town. Nothing more."

Richard looked at me in disbelief. "Stephan, don't be so naïve. You have a young woman—one you used to date, no less—living with you, who happens to be pregnant with no other man on her arm but you. How exactly do you think that is going to look to the outside world?"

My gaze drifted to the stairs. "I hadn't really thought of it."

And I hadn't. Sarah had needed my help, so I offered it. She was a friend. Why wouldn't I provide what she needed when it was in my capacity to do so?

Richard was right, though. The outside world wouldn't see it that way. Even if they did, the local reporters wouldn't. They would see this as a scandal to sink their teeth into.

"Does Brianna know?"

My uncle's question brought my attention back to him. "No."

He shook his head. "How did your life get so complicated, Stephan?"

I laughed, but there was no humor in it. "I have no idea."

Richard leaned forward and clasped his hands over his knees. "What are you going to do?"

I sighed and mirrored his position. "I don't know that either."

To my surprise, Richard stood and picked up his coat. He strolled over to me and patted me on the shoulder. "You're a smart man. You'll figure it out."

Looking up, I met his gaze. "Thanks."

Richard walked over to the door, shrugging his coat over his shoulders. "Let your aunt and I know if you need anything. We'll help if we can."

I nodded, and then he was gone.

The severity of what he'd said weighed on me. I didn't want Sarah to leave, not when she didn't have anywhere else to go, but I wasn't sure her staying was a good idea anymore either. Richard was right. Sooner or later the press was going to catch wind of who Sarah was and that she was living with me. It was inevitable.

Still lost in my thoughts, I didn't hear Sarah come back downstairs until she was almost beside me. "He's right, you know."

I didn't bother to turn around to face her. "You heard?"

"I shouldn't have listened, I know, but I was curious."

"It's fine."

She lowered her voice to almost a whisper. "I'll go back to the hotel. I'm sure they'll have a room."

"No." I turned to face her. "You are not going back to that barely functioning hotel. Especially if it means you're going to be staying there for any length of time."

"I can't stay here, Stephan. You heard him." She shook her head. "I can't believe we were so stupid."

I stood and pulled her in for a hug. "We weren't stupid. We just didn't think."

She wrapped her arms around my waist, burying her face in my chest. "Same thing."

"I'll think of something."

"Stephan, you don't—"

I leaned back so I could look her in the eye. "I'll think of something."

Chapter 20

Brianna

"I don't like this." Cal stood in the doorway of my bedroom, his arms crossed, with a scowl on his face.

Jade snorted. "You don't have to like it." She was helping me set up Skype on my computer. I remember hearing about Skype in school, but I'd never had a reason to use it myself. Who would I have talked to?

"Maybe you should set her up on the main computer in the study. It has a bigger screen."

She stopped what she was doing momentarily and gave him an exasperated look. "Cal, when are you going to accept that Anna wants to have a relationship with Stephan Coleman? He's who she wants. Deal with it."

Turning her attention back to my laptop, she let him stew over her words.

"I just don't want him to hurt her. Why is it that I'm the only one who seems to be worried about that?"

"He won't hurt me."

Cal walked over and sat down on the edge of my bed. His movements were slow and steady so as not to frighten me. "I know you insist that's true, Anna, but what if you're wrong?"

"I'm not."

He sighed. "But what if you are? You've been hurt so much. I don't want to see you hurt anymore. I won't. I can't."

The last word barely made it out, and he sounded as if he were in pain. Jade noticed it, too—her fingers hovered over the keyboard as we both turned our attention to Cal.

Cautiously, I stretched my arm until I could touch the tips of his fingers with mine.

Cal slowly turned his palm over and squeezed my offered hand.

Jade moved my laptop to the side, and we both sat waiting for him to explain himself. "Don't look at me like that."

Jade scooted closer to him. "How else are we supposed to look at you?

There's obviously more going on here than just your dislike of Stephan. What is it? What aren't you telling us?"

Cal looked down and sighed before getting up and walking to the window. "It's nothing."

Jade and I looked at each other, neither of us believing his denial. She climbed off the bed and went to him.

He barely acknowledged her as she slipped beside him. It was slightly awkward watching them. I felt like a voyeur.

She laid her hand on his arm.

Cal didn't pull away from her . . . he didn't move at all.

"Talk to us."

He shrugged. "I just don't want him to hurt her. That's all."

Jade wasn't letting it go. "But why? Why are you so sure he's going to hurt her? He hasn't yet."

"I just know, okay?" His voice took on a hard edge.

I flinched.

Jade must have seen me out of the corner of her eye, because she glanced in my direction before turning her attention back to Cal. "No, it's not okay. This has gone on long enough. Give me one good reason why you think he's going to harm her."

"Because I've seen it before, all right?" He threw his hands up in the air, and instinctively, I pressed myself back against the headboard of my bed. "There. You happy now?"

I tried to take in one breath at a time. They were staring at each other. Cal's nostrils were flared with his agitation. If it were me standing there beside him, I would have been cowering at this point, not unlike I was now. Jade, however, stood her ground.

"No. I'm not *happy*. I need you to explain what you mean when you say you've seen this before. What, exactly, have you seen before?"

He didn't answer.

"Cal, honey, I need you to explain yourself. You're acting irrationally, and we need to understand why."

For the first time since he'd walked away, Cal looked over at me. His gaze met mine, and I realized he looked sad. "Our neighbor."

He paused, continuing to stare at me.

"We don't have a neighbor, Cal," Jade interjected when he failed to elaborate.

"Not here. When I lived with my dad." He hesitated. "We had a neighbor. She was really nice. She and her husband moved in next door when I was sixteen. Every afternoon when I came home from school, she'd have cookies for me, and I'd help her with things around the house. Mow her lawn and things like that, when her husband was away."

We waited.

"One night, I heard some noises coming from their house. I couldn't make out what it was, but it made me nervous for some reason. The next day, though, she was there to greet me with cookies just like before, so I let it go. A couple weeks later, I heard it again. This time, when she brought me cookies the next day, I saw her limping. When I asked her about it, she brushed it off and told me it was nothing I needed to worry about, just husband and wife stuff."

Cal sighed and ran a hand over his face. It was the first time he'd broken eye contact with me since he'd started talking. "It happened a few more times, so I asked my dad about it. He said she and her husband probably liked it rough and to mind my own business."

Jade stepped closer to him. "I'm assuming that wasn't what it was, right?"

"No. Yes." He sighed. "I don't know. One day I came home from school, and there was an ambulance there along with a police officer. I only got a glimpse of the neighbor who had been so kind to me, but what I did see left an impression I'll never forget." His gaze found mine again. "She had bruises down both sides of her arms—I don't know about her legs because she was wearing pants, but she was limping again, so I can only assume they were there, too. I heard the medic say something about rope burns." He paused again. "Back then, I didn't know what all that meant, but I know now. I won't let that happen to you, Anna."

I was speechless, and so was Jade.

When he realized that neither of us was going to say anything in response to his confession, Cal stormed out of the room, and a few seconds later, we heard the front door slam shut.

While he was gone, Jade finished setting up my Skype account, and I sent the contact request to Stephan. Jade explained I had to wait for him to accept it and then we'd be good to go.

She continued to reassure me that Cal would be fine, given time. We both picked at our food, intermittently glancing at the door until the dishes were washed, dried, and put away. When we finished, I went to my room and sat on my bed with my laptop open, hoping that Stephan would accept my request.

That was where I was when I heard Cal return. He didn't bother to come into the room to see me. Instead, I heard some murmuring and then the sound of their bedroom door closing.

I didn't know what to do. Should I stay and wait for him to come to me, or should I go to him? I felt responsible for the pain he was feeling. Memories were powerful things. I knew that better than anyone. It was my fault he had to relive what had happened.

A sound coming from my computer startled me. I almost threw it across the bed, away from me, before I realized what it was. The Skype icon at the bottom of the screen was lit up.

My stomach suddenly felt as if it had a hundred butterflies in it, all trying to get out at once. Shaking, I moved my curser over the box and clicked on it.

Are you there, sweetheart?
Excitement surged through me as I placed my hands over the keys.
Yes. I'm here.
☺ **Good. Are you alone?**
Yes.
I'm going to send you a request for a video chat. A box will pop up on your screen. Press the green button with the video camera, and then I'll be able to see you.
Okay.
I'd barely typed out the word before a black box with two green buttons and one red appeared on my screen. Following his instructions, I pressed the green button that looked like a video camera. Seconds later, Stephan's face appeared on my screen.

He smiled when he saw me. "Hello, Brianna."

"Hello, Sir." I smiled back at him. It was so good to see Stephan, even if it was only through a computer screen.

"Did you have any problems loading Skype onto your computer?"

I shook my head. "No. Jade set everything up for me. She said it was easy."

It felt somewhat strange talking to him like this. I was used to being able to touch him and feel his body pressed up against mine when we had our evening conversations. I missed sitting with him in his chair.

"What were you thinking about just now?"

I looked up again quickly. "I was thinking that talking to you over the computer like this . . . not being able to touch you . . . feels weird."

The corners of his mouth turned down a little. "I miss you being here with me, too. We'll see each other soon, though. I promise. Until then, this is the best alternative." He shifted, moving his laptop closer so that I could see more of his face. "Tell me about your day. What did you do after you left the hotel?"

"Not a lot. We came back here, and I read a little. Then Jade helped set up Skype for me."

"Did you eat?"

"Yes."

"Lunch *and* dinner?"

"Yes, Sir."

Stephan smiled, and I felt a little flutter in my stomach. "Good girl. I'm glad you're eating more."

"I'm trying . . ."

"Continue."

I looked down and tangled my fingers. "But sometimes it doesn't taste good."

"What do you mean it doesn't taste good? Is the food bad?"

Glancing back up at the computer screen, I took a moment to study

Stephan's face. I wanted to reach through the computer and feel him. "No. The food is fine." I wasn't sure how to explain. "Sometimes it tastes like dirt or paper or something."

He didn't respond immediately. "Last night you didn't appear to have issues with the food."

"The food last night tasted good."

Stephan's brow furrowed. "What about this afternoon?"

I lifted one shoulder before dropping it.

"Use your words, Brianna. I can't read your mind."

Feeling guilty, I looked down again.

"Eyes on me, Brianna."

Looking up again, I met his gaze. "The food tasted okay, but it wasn't the same. I wasn't really hungry, but I made myself eat something because I knew you'd be angry if I didn't."

"You're right, I would have been. You have to take care of yourself."

"I know. I'm trying for you, Sir."

His smiled lit up his eyes. "I know you are, sweetheart. Thank you."

I smiled back at him, again missing the feel of his arms wrapped around me.

"I know. I wish I was there to hold you right now, too," he whispered.

We sat for several minutes, neither of us saying anything. It might not be what I wanted, but having him there on the other end of the computer made me feel so much better. I'd hated not being able to talk to him these last four months. "Sir?"

"Yes?"

"Can I ask you something?"

"You can ask me anything, Brianna. You know that."

Pressing my lips together, I debated whether or not to say anything about what had happened with Cal today. I was confused, though, and Stephan could always help me make sense of things. "Cal was really upset today that I was going to talk to you over Skype. He'd been upset about the hotel, too, but Jade convinced him somehow." I paused. "I always knew Cal didn't like you, but today he said something, and Jade pressed him about it."

"What did he say?"

The sound of Stephan's voice soothed me, and I took a deep breath before continuing. "He kept saying that he was afraid you'd hurt me, and then he told us about a neighbor he had."

I shared the story Cal had told Jade and me, including the part where he'd come home one day to find the police and an ambulance at her house.

Stephan listened intently, not commenting until I was finished. "And Cal believes I would harm you like that?"

I nodded.

"What do you think?"

My eyes widened at his question. "You wouldn't hurt me. I know you wouldn't. And I told him that."

"You're right. I wouldn't. But knowing this does help me to understand why Ross had such a strong reaction to my being a Dominant. He equates BDSM with abuse."

"Yes."

Stephan leaned in closer to the computer, his eyes taking over most of the screen. "You did, too, once."

"It was all I knew."

There was a noise somewhere on his end. He looked up, over the screen, then back down at me once more. Leaning back, he sighed. "It's getting late. I should let you get some sleep. I want you to do something for me."

"Okay."

"I want you to think about us and our relationship. You know I want you in my life—that I want you to be my submissive. I want you to think about what that means, and I want you to write down any questions you have for me. We might as well use this time apart to our advantage. Otherwise it's just an irritation to us both."

"What kind of questions?"

"Anything you want to know. Think about what you know, what you've seen . . . even what Cal has said. Make a list if you'd like, and we can talk about it. I want you to think about what a relationship between the two of us would mean long-term. What it would mean to truly be my submissive. I know you can be what I want and what I need, but this is something you have to decide for yourself. Is this a lifestyle you want."

"But I'm not better yet. I'm working on it. Dr. Perkins says that it will take a while, but I'm trying. I want to be better for you."

I notice a small reaction in him when I mentioned Dr. Perkins. "Ah. Yes. Your therapist. You'll have to tell me about her next time." He paused. "For now, however, you need your sleep, and you have some thinking to do. I have a late meeting tomorrow that I can't get out of, so we won't be able to talk like we are tonight. Are you able to be online Tuesday night?"

"Yes, I think so."

"Good. I'll meet you on here Tuesday evening. Think about what I said, Brianna. I love you, and I want to share my life with you. That includes the kinky aspects as well."

"Okay."

Stephan smiled. "Good night, love."

"Good night."

Sherri Hayes

Chapter 21

Stephan

First thing I did on Monday morning was phone Oscar. I needed his help in procuring Sarah a place to live for as long as she remained in Minneapolis. The conversation with my uncle had opened my eyes to the fact that her living with me, especially now that her pregnancy was noticeable, wasn't in my best interest. I refused to let her go back to that hotel. It wasn't what you'd call sleazy, but it wasn't all that great either—especially long-term. Sarah still had no idea how long she was staying, so I wanted her to have a place where she'd be comfortable.

Oscar, who hadn't seen Sarah recently since she always retreated to her room when he stopped by, wholeheartedly agreed with Richard. My lawyer said he'd get back to me in a couple of days, so until then, Sarah and I had agreed it was best she and I not be seen entering and leaving my building together, although that usually wasn't a problem. She had her schedule, and I had mine. After our being seen together at the gala, however, I had a feeling it was only a matter of time before someone put two and two together.

Sitting down behind my desk, I swiveled my chair around so that I could look out the large bank of windows. I'd spoken to Brianna less than twenty-four hours ago, and already I wanted to log on to the computer or pick up the phone so that I could hear her voice. This separation was maddening. I wanted to know what she was doing, how she was feeling. I also needed to find the best way to tell her about Sarah before she found out in some other way.

I'd debated whether or not to bring it up last night, but given I had no idea how she'd react to finding out my ex was back in town, I thought it might be better to explain things to her in person. That was why, lying in bed last night, I'd begun brainstorming ways we could see each other. Going to a restaurant was out unless I rented the entire place for the evening. It was a possibility, but I wanted to explore other options. Dinner at a restaurant, no matter how private I tried to make it, would still mean other people would be around.

The telephone on my desk rang, forcing me to push my thoughts of Brianna to the back of my mind and focus on work. I needed to get through this day. My afternoon was booked with back-to-back meetings. After that, I had a business dinner scheduled with a couple who'd expressed interest in contributing significantly to The Coleman Foundation and our work with some of the local free clinics. As much as I'd rather spend my evening talking to Brianna, I couldn't neglect my job—especially now, when everyone's eyes were on me. I only wished things were different, and she could be there with me.

***

"It's nice to finally meet you in person, Mr. Coleman. My wife and I have heard good things about your foundation."

Caleb Haase smiled politely from across the table. He was older, probably in his early sixties, as was his wife. His crisp suit was a visible sign of wealth broadcast for all to see. I didn't tend to flaunt the fact that I had money most of the time. Yes, I dressed well, but while my suits were tailored to fit, they didn't cost as much as some cars.

"Thank you. We do try to help as many people as we can. Our teamwork with the local hospitals and clinics has been paramount to that effort."

The server, a man about my age, delivered our drinks and then discreetly left the table. The Haases had chosen the location for tonight's dinner. It was one of the most expensive restaurants in the Twin Cities. If the smallest crumb was dropped on the table, someone on the staff was there to sweep it up moments later. It was overly pretentious.

Vivian Haase took a sip of her fruity cocktail, her diamond jewelry reflecting off the light in the room and drawing attention from anyone who happened to be watching. "That's how we heard about you, you know. A doctor friend of ours works at one of the free clinics. When we mentioned wanting to help, he suggested we look into The Coleman Foundation. What we've learned so far has impressed us." She paused and pursed her lips. "I was happy to hear that rumor about you being involved in . . . shall we call them 'unsavory' activities . . . has been put to rest." She took another drink. "For the most part anyway. You'll always have the stray dog now and then trying to dig up a story just to cause trouble."

When the Haases had first requested we meet over dinner rather than at my office, I'd thought it was merely a personal preference. I was swiftly realizing this meeting wasn't really about The Coleman Foundation. Well, it was, but only indirectly. This was an interview of my character. If they found me suitable, they would donate to the foundation. If they didn't, they would take their money elsewhere.

It was a common game in these types of social circles, but one I tried to avoid whenever possible. I had to make a decision. Did I play their game and get the money for the foundation, or did I stand up and walk out with my pride. It was a difficult quandary.

"Yes, we thought maybe you'd be bringing your girlfriend tonight—the one you brought to the gala Saturday night. She's very pretty. Have you been seeing each other long?"

The ease with which Mrs. Haase was trying to weasel her way into my personal life astounded me. "She's just a friend from my college days." I quickly tried to redirect the subject. "Did you attend the gala, then?"

"Oh, heavens no. We would have been polite enough to introduce ourselves if we had. No. Caleb was catching up on his reading Sunday morning and saw your picture in the paper. I couldn't help but notice you and the young lady you were with."

I tried to school my features and not react to her news. Although I shouldn't have been surprised, finding out Sarah and I had been photographed together at the gala took me by surprise. We'd arrived before everyone else, and I hadn't noticed anyone snapping a picture beforehand. That meant someone inside the ballroom had taken the picture.

Luck was on my side, and the server appeared with our first course, meaning I could refrain from responding while he was there. I took the opportunity the lull in conversation provided to change the subject. "The last time we talked, you mentioned wanting to help specifically with the free clinic aspect of the foundation's work. Is that still the direction you're leaning?"

I said a silent thank you when Mr. Haase took the bait and began telling me about their doctor-friend's work and how it had it had inspired them. Thankfully we made it through the rest of dinner without delving back into my personal life.

It was well after ten before I made it back home. The lights were out, so I figured Sarah was already upstairs asleep. She'd been working at Daren's friend's office a lot recently. No doubt she would be up early to head there again.

The dinner had gone on longer than I'd anticipated. We had been served five courses over two and a half hours. By the time it was over, I could safely say the Haases were not my kind of people. I got the impression they gave of their money so they could brag about how generous they were to their friends. People like that irritated me, but I wasn't stupid enough to turn down their money, either. There were people out there—more every day it seemed—who couldn't afford basic healthcare, not to mention long-term care that was sometimes needed. Although it wasn't a part of my job I liked, I would smile and play nice with people like the Haases for the greater good.

After grabbing a drink of water, I ambled into my bedroom, undressed, and took a shower.

Showers were never the same without Brianna. Every time I stepped inside the marble enclosure, I was assaulted with memories of my time there with her. Closing my eyes, I could almost hear the sound of her breathing in my ear . . . her moans as I stroked and caressed her.

I leaned forward and rested my head against my forearms—the cool tile a stark contrast to the heated water spraying across my back. My body betrayed me as my cock stiffened at the thought of Brianna warm and wet beneath my hands, even as my chest clenched painfully with the knowledge that she wasn't here.

Breathing in a deep lungful of moist air, I pushed myself away from the wall and farther into the spray. She and I would get through this. We had to. Seeing her again had only confirmed what I'd already known. There was no way I could live without her being a part of my life.

The next day seemed to drag. Every time I looked at the clock, barely any time had passed. By five o'clock I was practically bouncing in my seat like an anxious toddler. It was shocking, the level of effect Brianna had over me, but I wouldn't change it for the world.

When I arrived home, Sarah was in the kitchen making something on the stove. She took one look at me and smiled a knowing smile. "I got home a little early today, so I made some soup. Nothing fancy, but I figured it was better than takeout."

I wasn't all that concerned with food, but I didn't want to be rude. "Smells good. Do you need any help?"

She shook her head. "Nah. I got this. I was just going to chop up the rest of the chicken and make us some sandwiches to go with it. Did you want one or two?"

"One's fine. Thank you." I wasn't even sure I could force one down my throat. It wasn't that Sarah was a horrible cook. She was decent—better than I remembered her being—but the last thing I wanted to do was eat. I knew I had to be patient, though. Brianna needed to eat dinner as well, so logging on to Skype early was only going to either pull her away from her meal or be a long, drawn-out frustration.

After changing into jeans and a long-sleeved shirt, I rejoined Sarah in the kitchen and helped her set the table. We worked silently for the most part— her smirks and barely stifled giggles providing the bulk of the communication.

Sarah was halfway through her dinner when she spoke. "Are you planning to talk to her tonight?"

"Yes."

She chuckled. "I figured. You have a nervous energy about you."

I nodded. It was true. There was no reason for me to deny it. Although Brianna said she wanted to be with me, we'd never discussed the nuts and bolts of her being my submissive before. In the past, things had just sort of evolved. I knew we could go back to that, but I wanted her to have some structure—know what to expect. She'd had too many unknowns in her life already. I didn't want our relationship to be one of them.

"I'm sure she's just as excited to talk to you. I mean, she did set up a secret meeting with you at the hotel, right? That has to mean something."

Suddenly having enough of my food, I pushed it slightly away from me and leaned back in my chair. Sarah was trying to help, but I didn't want to discuss my relationship with Brianna right now. "Oscar sent me an e-mail today. He has a realtor looking at properties around the city that can be leased on a month-by-month basis. According to the realtor, he should have some properties for you to look at by the weekend."

Sarah sighed and laid her spoon beside her bowl. "I don't understand why you are being so insistent about this, Stephan. I can just go back to the hotel."

"No. Sarah, you're five months' pregnant. You need somewhere you can live, relax . . . a place you can make feel like your home, even if it is temporary. A stark hotel room that has nothing more than a bed, dresser, television, and a bathroom isn't good enough."

She shook her head. "Still so overprotective. I'm not your sub anymore, remember?"

"No, but you *are* my friend. I'm not letting you live in some crappy hotel while you're here. If you can't stay here, then finding you an apartment is the least I can do."

Silence greeted my declaration. She stared at me, eyes narrowed, for several seconds. "Fine. If it makes you happy, then fine. But what if I decide to leave in a week or two? What then?"

"Then nothing. After that month's lease is up, it will be rented to someone else. Easy as that." I stood and took my dishes into the kitchen.

Sarah was still sitting there when I returned to the table. "You're determined to do this, aren't you?

"Yes. I am."

She shook her head and picked up her spoon again. "Go call your girl and leave me in peace."

Sarah winked, and I laughed.

"I can still spank you, you know," I said as I strolled toward my bedroom.

She chuckled. "That would be interesting with my belly now wouldn't it?"

I turned right outside my door and glanced down at her growing midsection. We were both smiling. "That it would."

When I logged on to Skype a few minutes later, I noticed Brianna was already online.

Good evening, sweetheart.

A minute later, a response came back.

Good evening, Sir.

Are you ready to talk?

Yes.

Needing to both see and hear her, I pressed the video call button and waited for her to answer. Only seconds passed before her beautiful face popped up on my screen.

I smiled. "Hello."

"Hi."

"How are you? Did you have a good day today?"

She nodded. "I spent most of the day reading . . . and working on my questions."

"That's good. I'm anxious to hear what you've come up with."

Brianna looked down, and I could see the uncertainty cross her features. This was so much harder when she wasn't in my arms, where I could feel every movement and response. "It was . . . hard. I don't know what to ask."

"What do you want to ask? There have to be things you've been wondering. Let's start there."

"Okay." She sighed and lowered her gaze again. "Will you beat me?"

I'd told her to ask anything, but I hadn't expected her to begin with such a loaded question. "Be more specific, Brianna."

She swallowed and looked back up at me. "Will you hit me?"

"I would never punch you, no, but I would like to spank you."

Her eyes went wide, and her voice lowered to almost a whisper. "Why would you want to spank me?"

"It's something I enjoy. I'd at least like to try it with you. We don't have to do that right away, but at some point I'd like to spank you and see what you think of it. Who knows, you may like it. Spankings, when done right, can be quite erotic."

I saw the doubt in her eyes, mixed with some fear.

"Brianna, have I ever forced you to do something you didn't want to do?"

"No."

"What about when I've punished you? Was it ever something so horrible or outrageous that you couldn't handle it?"

She shook her head. "No, Sir. Your punishments have always been fair."

I closed my eyes for a brief moment, reluctant to go where I knew I must. Meeting her gaze, I brought up the one subject I would have liked to avoid. "I'm not him, Brianna. I will never be him."

Her chest rose and fell rapidly, showing her distress.

"Stay with me, sweetheart. Look at me and stay here with me."

Brianna's gaze met mine, and I watched as her breathing slowly returned to normal.

"Good girl. Better?"

"Yes. Thank you."

The ache in my chest multiplied, and my next question came out much softer than I'd intended. "Do you think I would stop doing something if you hated it?"

"Yes."

"Good. Brianna, I want you to understand that what I want is a relationship with you. Yes, there are times when I will be in charge and I will expect you to do as I say, but you will always have your safewords, and I would never do anything to you that would break your trust in me."

"Okay."

"What else?"

She pressed her lips together, so I knew she was nervous about whatever it was she was going to ask. "What would you expect me to do? Would you . . . use me?"

I couldn't stop my smile. "I'd like to play with you, yes. I'd like to do all sorts of kinky things with you. I know when you say 'use' you are thinking all sorts of negative things—I can see it by the look on your face. It doesn't have to be. You enjoy it when I hold you down, when I have my way with you. I'm using you for my pleasure then, Brianna, and you find pleasure in it as well, don't you?"

Brianna nodded.

"As for what I'd expect you to do, I've been thinking about this, and I want to see how you feel first. In the past, I've kept my lifestyle confined to the weekends. I'm not sure that would work with us."

She scrunched up her nose, and I realized she didn't understand where I was going with this. I needed to be clearer.

"You know how you call me Sir all the time? You rarely call me Stephan. In fact, I do believe you've only called me by name once, and only at my insistence."

I smiled at her to let her know I wasn't upset about it.

"It doesn't feel . . . right."

I nodded. "I know. But this is what I mean. Typically, in a weekend-only arrangement, we would be a normal couple during the week. You'd call me by my given name just like everyone else does. Then on the weekend, during playtime, you'd call me Sir." I paused. "Or Master."

"You want me to call you by your name?" She looked nervous. More nervous than she had been when she asked if I would beat her.

"I may from time to time, yes, but that brings me to my point. You aren't comfortable with it. You like calling me Sir." I waited until I was sure she was looking at me. "And I like it, too. So I think a twenty-four-seven agreement would better suit us."

"What does that mean—twenty-four-seven?"

"It means that you would always act as my submissive. You would always defer to me, and ask my permission for certain things. It wouldn't be much different from now. Or should I say, it wouldn't be much different than when you were living with me. Is that what you want?"

"I think so."

This was so hard. I wanted to hold her. "But you're not sure?"

"It's just . . . what if I don't get better? What if I can't do the things you want to do?"

I saw exactly where her mind was drifting to. "Brianna, I explained about Logan and Lily. That won't happen again. Anything new we want to try, we will talk about it and then try it. Just us. No one else."

"Okay."

I waited. "Did you have any more questions for me?"

"No. It was really difficult to come up with questions. I don't know what to ask."

"That's all right. I'm sure you'll think of more as time goes by. But Brianna, I need to know if you want to move forward with this . . . with us. This doesn't have to be an all or nothing deal. We'll talk things through always, but I think you'd do well with some rules, and they would make me feel better as well."

"Okay." I wasn't surprised to see her relax her shoulders some at my suggestion. Brianna needed rules. She craved the safety and structure rules gave her.

"First, I want you to start keeping a journal again. I want you to write down what you did that day, how you felt, and any questions that come to your mind. And since we're apart for now, I want you to do your journaling in an e-mail to me. This way I know what's going through that mind of yours. Second, I want you to make sure you are eating three meals every day. Do you have any problem with those rules?"

"No, Sir."

"Good. 'Cause I have one more for now. I've gotten the impression that you've stopped cooking, is that correct?"

"Yes." She paused, and I waited. "Jade or Cal usually make something, or they order takeout."

I nodded. "Since it's Cal's home, you'll need to talk to him first, but I want you to start cooking again. I know how much you enjoy being in the kitchen, and I think it will help relax you. Tomorrow you will ask if it's okay for you to start cooking dinner on the nights you're home."

She swallowed but nodded in agreement.

Softening my tone, I reached out toward the screen. She was so close, yet so far away. "I love you, Brianna. We'll figure this out."

"I love you, too."

Glancing over at the clock, I frowned. It was later than I'd hoped. I wasn't ready to let her go just yet, though. "Tell me about this therapist of yours. I did some research on her. She seems . . . knowledgeable."

We spent the next twenty minutes talking about her visits to Dr. Perkins. I was still leery of Brianna seeing a psychiatrist, but I was attempting to hold my tongue. I didn't want Brianna to get hurt. She needed help and support, not judgment and ridicule.

So far, Brianna seemed to like Dr. Perkins well enough, although she admitted she was nervous about sharing our relationship. I understood her reluctance. Kink wasn't something all mental health professionals understood. There were those who were what they called "kink friendly," but in the grand scheme of things, they were few and far between. I only hoped this Dr. Perkins had an open mind. For now, I'd bide my time and wait. If she hurt Brianna, however, all bets were off.

Chapter 22

Brianna

The next morning I slowly crept out of my bedroom to join Cal and Jade for breakfast. It wasn't something I normally did, so they both were suspicious.

I didn't say anything until after I'd sat down with my bowl of cereal in front of me. "Cal?"

He paused with his spoon hovering in midair. "Yes, Anna?"

Swallowing, even though I had yet to take a bite of my breakfast, I looked down at my bowl as I spoke. "May I start cooking dinner?"

At first, he didn't say anything, and I began to get nervous.

"Now?"

The tone in his voice caused me to glance up at him. His brow was furrowed, and I could see that he was confused. "I'd like to start making dinner for us."

He still looked as if he didn't understand.

Luckily Jade interjected. "I think she means that she wants to be the one to cook dinner for us tonight."

I nodded, grateful that Jade had explained to him what I somehow couldn't.

"Oh." He resumed lifting his spoon to his mouth and then shrugged. "I guess you can."

Breathing a sigh of relief, I picked up my spoon and began eating. Throughout breakfast, I noticed that Jade kept glancing over at me, but she didn't say anything. I had a feeling she would after Cal left for work, though.

Sure enough, the moment Cal's vehicle disappeared from sight, Jade addressed me. "You didn't just mean tonight did you?"

I shook my head.

She pursed her lips and studied me. "Stephan wants you to start cooking again?"

"Yes." I paused, looking out the window. "He thinks it will relax me."

Jade hummed but didn't comment.

We sat there in silence for a long time watching a pair of birds on the lawn. Cal had installed a bird feeder, and with the cooling temperatures, the birds flocked to it. This was nice—sitting there watching—no pressure to be or do anything. The only thing that could have made it more perfect was if Stephan were with me.

Before I knew it, it was Friday and I was sitting in Dr. Perkins's office.

"How have you been this week, Anna?"

I smiled. "Good."

Dr. Perkins tilted her head to one side, and she lifted the right side of her mouth slightly. "I'm glad to hear you're in such good spirits. Anything you'd care to share?"

Stephan and I had talked for the last three nights, and we were going to talk tonight as well. Knowing I was going to hear from him tonight made my heart clench in my chest. He promised me that he was working on a way for us to see each other . . . a date. Thinking about it made me smile wider.

"This is a wonderful change for you, Anna. You're very pretty when you smile."

"Thank you." I'd talked to Stephan more about Dr. Perkins, and I knew he had mixed feelings about my seeing her. He didn't say much, but he held himself more erect whenever we talked about her, and his speech was very formal. He didn't seem to have a problem with Dr. Perkins specifically, so I imagined it was therapy itself. I hoped one day he'd share with me why he felt as he did.

"Do you want to talk about it? Or would you rather talk about something else today?"

Although I didn't know how she would react, I wanted to tell her. "I saw Stephan. And I've talked to him this week." My cheeks were starting to hurt with how much I was grinning.

"Ah. I see. And I'm gathering it went well."

I nodded enthusiastically.

"Where were you when you got to see him?"

Pressing my lips together, I debated whether or not to tell her.

"You look worried."

"I'm not sure if I should tell you or not."

Dr. Perkins leaned forward in her chair, setting her notepad to the side. "Anna, everything you tell me in here is between us. I'm here for you, to try and help you. It's become obvious in our short time together that this man is important to you—incredibly important if the change in your demeanor is any indication."

I thought about it for another minute. "Jade arranged for a room at the hotel."

She looked slightly taken aback but swiftly composed herself. "So he met you in a hotel room?"

"No. I was waiting in the room, and they brought him to me."

"I see. And did you stay in the room with him?"

I nodded.

"All night?"

"Yes."

She leaned back, reaching for her notepad, and scribbled something down before looking up at me again, her expression serious. "Do you have a sexual relationship with this man?"

It was my turn to look confused. Why would she want to know that?

Seeming to realize my reaction, she explained. "The reason I ask, Anna, is that given what you've been through, it's unusual that you'd be open to that type of a relationship. How long has it been since you were held against your will?"

I had to think about it, which surprised me. "A little over six months."

"And was this your first sexual encounter with Stephan?"

"No."

She didn't respond immediately, and I fidgeted. As her silence continued, I began to shake. What was she going to say?

I watched as several emotions crossed her face, before she seemed to settle on a frown. "Anna, I have to ask. Is he forcing you to have sex with him?"

My eyes went wide. "No! Stephan doesn't force me to do anything I don't want to do."

"So you wanted to have sex with him?"

With my hands clenched tightly together, I nodded. I wouldn't have a panic attack. I wouldn't.

A look of concern and sadness blanketed her features. "I'm going to be completely honest with you. I'm concerned. You went through something extremely traumatic, which you just told me ended only six months ago. It makes me wonder if this man, if he didn't force you, did he manipulate you in some way . . . convince you to sleep with him?"

"No." I was trying to be as firm as possible even if I was still shaking inside. Stephan didn't do anything wrong.

She sighed and held up both hands in surrender. "Okay. I believe you. I just don't want to see you get hurt, Anna. Because of what you've been through, you are in a very vulnerable state, and there are people out there who would take advantage."

"He isn't like that. Stephan helps me."

Dr. Perkins nodded, but I could tell she wasn't entirely convinced. "Maybe you could invite him to one of our sessions. He wouldn't have to stay the whole time, but if he's as important to you as you say, I'd like to meet him."

Instead of commenting, I just nodded. I didn't think Stephan would agree to come with me to see Dr. Perkins given how he felt about therapy, which was why when I told him about it that night, I was surprised to hear him say that he would go.

"You will?"

"Of course. She's clearly curious about me, and I'm certainly curious about her." He paused. "Do you not want me to go?"

"No. I do. I just didn't think you would." I glanced down at my lap before meeting his gaze again.

"I'm interested in anything that involves you, Brianna. Let me know when you need me to be there, and I'll arrange my schedule accordingly."

"Okay. Thank you."

He smiled through the computer screen. After talking to him nearly every day this week, I was finally getting used to communicating this way with him. It wasn't the same as face-to-face, but at least I was able to see him and hear his voice. Knowing he was there, that I could talk things over with him . . . I felt balanced.

"I have some good news."

The excitement in his face caused my heart rate to pick up.

"I've arranged for us to have the planetarium all to ourselves next Saturday night. Do you think Jade or Ross could drive you there?"

"I think so. I'll ask Jade in the morning." Thoughts of the last time I saw him flittered through my mind, and my body heated in response.

A knowing smile crossed Stephan's face. "Soon, Brianna. Soon."

We talked for another half hour, until he reluctantly said it was time for both of us to get to bed. I'd been e-mailing him my journal entries every night before I fell asleep, so once I disconnected from Skype, I pulled up my e-mail and began to type.

I know I usually start with the beginning of my day and work my way toward the end, but that's not what's on my mind right now. In eight days, I'll get to see Stephan again. I'm feeling a mixture of nervousness and excitement, but mostly excitement. Skype has been great, but it's not the same as being with him. I miss his touch, his smell . . . just everything.

The last time I was at a planetarium was for a school field trip. I don't remember much about it other than it was dark and the boy beside me wouldn't stop talking. The rest of it is kind of a blur. It was fourth grade.

My weekly appointment with Dr. Perkins was today. She noticed that I was unusually happy and wanted to know why. We talked a little about Stephan, and she wants to meet him. I was surprised when he agreed. Knowing they will meet makes me feel anxious. I like Dr. Perkins so far, but I love Stephan. What if something happens between them? I don't know what I would do. I want to get better for him, and Dr. Perkins is helping me do that, but if Stephan didn't want me to see her anymore, I don't think I could go against him. Maybe the two of them meeting isn't a good idea.

I paused musing over what I'd written. It was all true. Taking a deep breath, I continued.

Tonight I cooked chicken parmesan for everyone. Cal and Jade couldn't stop complimenting me, and I was so embarrassed. They both had second helpings, and Cal says he's going to need bigger clothes if I keep cooking. I don't think that's true, but I didn't say anything.

I skimmed over what I'd already written. Everything was there. The important stuff anyway.

As I read over it, though, something popped into my mind, so I quickly typed it into the e-mail.

Sir,

Should I still be calling you by name in my journal entries, or do you want me to address you as Sir? I know in the past you said it was okay, but I wanted to be sure.

Brianna

Before I could change my mind, I hit send. He would read over it in the morning as he'd done all week. Sometimes he'd bring up things I'd written the next time we talked, and sometimes he didn't. However, he always answered my questions whenever I had them. Even though I knew he wouldn't be angry—he encouraged it even—every time I asked a question, I felt as if I was holding my breath, waiting for the shoe to drop. I was learning that was because of what I went through. Because of Ian.

Shutting down my computer, I quickly went through my nightly routine and climbed into bed. When I woke up, there would only be seven more days to wait.

The next day, I waited for Cal to leave before approaching Jade. "Next Saturday . . ."

When I didn't continue, Jade stopped what she was doing. "Yes? What do you need?"

"Can you take me to the planetarium?"

She raised her eyebrows. "Um. Sure. Why do you want to go to the planetarium, though?"

"Stephan said he rented it out for the entire night."

Jade chuckled and went back to whatever it was she was working on. I assumed it was homework. "I see. So you aren't really going to be gazing at the stars."

Embarrassed, I ducked my head. I could feel my cheeks heating.

That only made her laugh harder. "It's okay, Anna. And yes, I can take you. Just find out what time he wants you to be there."

"Okay."

She refocused on her work, and I turned my attention to the television. I'd taken to watching some of the morning shows, but I didn't really have a favorite, so I ended up flipping through the channels a lot. Jade didn't seem to mind.

My hand stopped mid-flip as I saw Stephan's face pop up on the screen. The local talk show wasn't something I normally watched, as it focused more on celebrity gossip than anything else, but seeing Stephan I couldn't help but halt all movement . . . waiting to see what they said.

"Some of you may remember us talking about Mr. Coleman just a few weeks ago in relation to federal charges being brought against a well-known art dealer, Ian Pierce. Mr. Coleman has since been removed as a person of interest in that case, but now it seems he is drawing attention for other reasons. More personal reasons."

There was a new picture on the screen. This one was of Stephan and a woman. He was in his tux, and the woman was in a beautiful gown.

"It seems Mr. Coleman's recent legal troubles didn't slow down his personal life. Last Saturday night, Mr. Coleman was accompanied by a Miss Sarah Evans. Miss Evans and Mr. Coleman are rumored to have a history together, and sources say she's been spotted frequently coming and going from his home. We've also managed to learn that Miss Evans is expecting. Could Mr. Coleman soon be a daddy? Are there wedding bells in this couple's future?"

The television suddenly went dark. I had no idea if I'd turned it off or if Jade had. That didn't matter at the moment—nothing did.

My hold on the remote loosened, and it slipped from my fingers. Somewhere in my mind, I registered the sound of it hitting the floor.

I couldn't move.

Sarah Evans.

Was she his Sarah? The one from college? The one who'd been his submissive? Everything I couldn't be?

And they were going to have a baby?

Jade knelt before me, her hands cupping mine. "Anna? Can you hear my voice, Anna? Come on. Talk to me."

But I couldn't. I couldn't do anything. My mind and my body were completely numb.

Chapter 23

Stephan

The sound of my cell phone ringing roused me from sleep on Saturday morning. I'd been having a rather pleasant dream that involved me, Brianna, and the dining room table. Glancing over at the clock beside my bed, I noted it was only seven in the morning. Whatever this was, it had better be an emergency.

"Hello?" My voice was gruff from sleep, so I cleared my throat as I waited for whoever was on the other end to respond.

"Mr. Coleman, it's Michael James."

I sat up abruptly and tossed the sheets out of the way. For Michael to be calling me this early in the morning, he had to have found something about whoever had stolen the money.

"Sorry to bother you so early, but I know you wanted to be kept informed."

Getting out of bed, I strolled toward my bathroom with the phone pressed against my ear. "Don't worry about the time, Mr. James. What have you got?"

"As you know, I've had my computer guy digging through the files trying to locate the specific computer that was used for the transactions. He broke through late yesterday, and I spent the better part of the night going through all the surveillance video of the area that corresponded with those times."

He paused.

"Only two people were present in every instance."

"Who?"

"I think it's better if you see for yourself."

While I wasn't thrilled with this, I did understand. "I'll meet you in my office in an hour."

Sarah was already up when I walked out of my bedroom. She was sipping on a mug of coffee as usual. "Hey. You're up early."

"So are you."

"Yeah, but I have work to do." She looked me up and down, taking in my attire. "And from the looks of it, so do you."

I nodded. Although I wasn't in my usual suit and tie, I was more dressed up than usual for a typical Saturday.

Sarah was quiet as I made myself breakfast. She sat drinking her coffee and nibbling on a bagel.

I joined her at the table and offered her some of my food. She declined. "I'm going to look at a couple of those apartments this afternoon that your lawyer sent over."

"Hopefully one of them will work."

She sighed. "I still think this is ridiculous, Stephan."

Swallowing the last bite of my breakfast, I smiled. We'd had this conversation almost every day this week. My position wasn't going to change. "Call me when you find the one you want, and I'll have Oscar handle the paperwork."

Sarah glared at me as I took my dishes into the kitchen.

When I returned, she was still glaring. "You're impossible, you know that."

I laughed. "Why thank you."

Exasperated, she leaned back in her chair with her right hand casually resting on her belly.

"Call my cell if you need anything. I'll be at the office for a while, and then I should be home."

Sarah waved her hand in the air, effectively dismissing me. Her reaction made me smile wider.

The drive to the office was uneventful. It was another crisp fall day, and the traffic was minimal, which was good. It gave me time to think. If Michael had found something on the tapes, it would mean calling in the police. It would also mean that the media would catch wind of yet another scandal with my name attached to it. I knew, before we took any action, I would need to get Oscar involved. My lawyer had certainly been earning his retainer as of late. Every time I turned around, there was something else I needed his assistance with.

There were only a handful of cars in the parking garage when I arrived. Very few people at the foundation worked on the weekends, outside of security and technical support, and even those departments worked with a skeleton crew. Like my father, I believed employees should have family time. There would always be work to do and people to help, but we couldn't neglect our own lives in the process.

My CFO was already waiting for me when I stepped off the elevator. "Mr. Coleman."

"Good morning, Mr. James."

He motioned down the hall. "I set everything up in the conference room. I thought it would be easier to view the footage on the big screen than on a computer monitor."

Nodding, I followed him into the room we reserved for large group meetings.

We both took a seat, and he picked up the remote. "We narrowed down the times of three of the transactions—all of which were made first thing in the morning. Once I had the times, it was just a matter of going through the video."

Without commenting further, Michael hit play, and the screen came to life.

A picture of the fourth floor lobby appeared. The place was empty, much like it would be now if we ventured downstairs. The time-stamp on the video showed six forty-two in the morning.

Nothing happened for another few minutes, and then there was movement. Two employees stepped off the elevator. The first one I recognized right away as Megan, the fourth-floor receptionist. As usual, her top was way too tight, showcasing her breasts for all to see. Every time I had to go see Lily, Megan made a play for me. It hadn't mattered to her in the slightest that I'd showed no interest in return.

The woman with her looked familiar, yet I couldn't place her.

Michael must have realized my lack of recognition. "Greta Morris. She's one of Ms. Adams's assistants."

Once he said her name, I felt guilty for not immediately knowing who she was. Greta had worked for the foundation almost from the start. My mother had hired her personally. I should have remembered.

We watched for several more minutes as both ladies went to their desks and began working. Nothing noticeable happened until the next set of employees entered the room. At that point, Michael paused the video. "The transaction occurred between six forty nine and seven. Of that, we're certain. Given the sophistication of the IP scramble we encountered, I'm not willing to take anything for granted when it comes to locating the computer. This, however, doesn't lie. One of these two women is our thief."

The two of us spent the rest of the morning combing over the remaining security video. It was much the same as the first. Occasionally there would be one or two other employees present, but always Megan and Greta.

At noon, we took a break for lunch, and I put in a call to Oscar. He suggested pulling the phone records of both women. All the calls they made from the office phones were subject to monitoring and the property of the foundation, so legally we could listen to them without needing a warrant. Unfortunately, that meant neither Michael nor I would be going anywhere anytime soon.

By six o'clock, we were elbows deep in call records. We'd started with the ones immediately following the dates and times we knew the money had been stolen. Nothing.

Since both of us were determined to solve this mystery, we buckled down and kept searching. I sent a quick e-mail to both Brianna and Sarah to let them know I wouldn't be home this evening due to something at work. Not being able to talk to Brianna left an empty feeling in the pit of my stomach, but it couldn't be helped. We were so close, and yet we were missing an essential piece of the puzzle.

It was well after two in the morning before we had a breakthrough, and even when we heard it, we had to rewind it again to be sure.

"Did you get it?" You could tell the woman didn't want anyone around her to hear her conversation.

"Yep. I got it. You did good."

"Are you sure this is the best way?"

"How else were you going to get the money, Grams? This was the best way. They'll never miss it."

The woman sighed. *"I need to get back to work."*

"Don't worry about it, okay? I've got you covered."

The conversation ended, but I had to hear it a third time to be sure. Even then, it was hard to believe Greta Morris, who'd been working for my family for over fifteen years, had stolen from us. And from the sound of it, her grandson was the mysterious computer wizard who'd manipulated the IP signatures.

I rubbed the heels of my palms into my eyes. "I can't believe it was her."

"Don't feel bad. She wasn't on my radar either until I saw the video."

Michael fell back in his chair and closed his eyes, exhaustion taking over.

"When was the last time you slept?" I asked.

He open one eye and glanced over at me. "What time is it?"

"Almost three in the morning."

"Sunday?"

I frowned. "Yes."

"About forty-five hours."

Standing, I raised my arms over my head and stretched. "We both need a break."

"We have more recordings to go through. I'm fine."

"You're not fine. Besides, my eyes hurt, and I'm starting to see double. We both could use a break and a little rest."

"What about this?" Michael motioned to the files spread across the table.

"I have a key. The door will be locked."

Once in the privacy of my office, I collapsed on my couch. How Michael was still functioning on so little sleep, I had no idea. It hurt to keep my eyes open at this point.

Not bothering with anything more than kicking off my shoes, I settled into the couch and closed my eyes. Within seconds, I was asleep.

The first thing I noticed when I opened my eyes was the sun blazing through the large windows in my office. I'd been so tired, I hadn't thought of pulling the blinds. Glancing down at my watch, I realized it was just after nine—I'd slept about six hours. My back was slightly stiff from my choice of bed, but other than that, I felt rested. That was good since Michael and I had another long day planned.

After freshening up some in my bathroom, I ambled down the hall to the executive lounge where Michael had crashed. He was stretched out along the sofa at the back of the room, snoring. I decided to let him sleep for a while longer and went back to my office. There was a lot that needed to happen today.

The first thing I did was call Jamie and ask if she would pick up breakfast, along with an assortment of sandwiches, and bring them to the office as soon as possible. I could tell she was curious as to what was going on by her slight hesitation, but she didn't ask questions.

While I waited for her to arrive, I send out an e-mail to all the board members notifying them of an emergency meeting Monday at eight. I didn't want to sit on this. As much as I hated firing people, Greta had broken the law and my trust. I didn't have a choice—she had to be dealt with. I sent an additional e-mail to Lily asking that she stop by my office before the meeting. If Logan hadn't been home this weekend, I would have called her. He was scheduled to fly out of town again first thing Monday morning. I didn't want to interrupt their time—especially when there was nothing she would have been able to do at the moment.

My next order of business required a phone call to the head of our IT department. He'd been involved with Michael's investigation extensively already. Unfortunately, I was going to have to interrupt his weekend.

"Hello?"

"Good Morning, Erik. It's Stephan Coleman. My apologies for interrupting your Sunday."

There was a long pause on the other end of the line. "Is there something wrong with the servers?"

"No, but I'm afraid I'm going to need you to come into the office today. Mr. James and I are in need of your assistance."

Again, there was silence. I heard a door open and then close before Erik spoke again. "You found something?"

I decided to keep it simple. "Yes."

"Okay. I'll need about an hour. My wife is getting the girls ready to go to the park."

"I understand. Get here as soon as you can. And please pass along my apologies to your wife. If it could wait until Monday, I wouldn't pull you away from your family like this."

"No. I completely understand."

Hanging up the phone, I sighed. I was going to have to do something to make this up to Erik and his family. It was bad enough that I was having him come in on his day off, but to find out they'd had plans sent a wave of guilt through me. Family was important. Losing my parents had taught me that harsh lesson. It was also the reason why Richard's lack of faith in me hurt so much.

Pushing that to the back of my mind for the moment, I returned to my e-mail. The first thing I noticed as I began scanning was that there was no e-mail from Brianna last night with her journal entry. I frowned. Brianna was near perfect at following instructions. She never willfully disobeyed me. I immediately started wondering if something had happened. Had she been hurt? Was she not able to get to a phone or a computer?

Before I could second-guess myself, I fished my cell out of my pocket and dialed Ross's home number. It rang several times and then went to voice mail. I cursed and ended the call before leaving a message.

My next attempt was to Ross's cell. This time it sent me straight to voice mail. "Call me when you get this. I need to speak to Brianna, and no one is answering the home number."

I knew my message was rather direct given the fact that I wanted his assistance, but my level of anxiety was increasing. I needed to hear her voice . . . know that she was okay. Her not e-mailing me was secondary. I knew she had to have a good reason for not obeying my rule. Even if she didn't, I would deal with that *after* I knew she was safe.

Unable to sit still, I began pacing, which was how Jamie found me fifteen minutes later.

She knocked on my open door to announce her presence. "I have the food you asked for, Mr. Coleman. Shall I put it in the lounge or the conference room?"

Her arms were loaded down with bags, and I rushed across the room to help her. "We'll put them in the lounge." Jamie let me take the majority of the bags from her possession, and we made our way down the hall.

As we entered, Michael was sitting on the edge of the couch rubbing the sleep from his face.

"Good, you're awake. I asked my assistant to bring us some food."

Michael stood, still sluggish. I could only imagine how much his body was protesting. He had a good thirty years on me, and even after being awake for a good half hour, my back still didn't feel quite right.

Jamie stayed for another five minutes, making sure we had what we needed before taking her leave. Michael and I devoured almost half of what she'd brought. Neither of us had eaten anything since the dinner I'd ordered in last night around five, so we were both starving.

We were finishing our meal when Erik strolled into the room.

"I smelled food, so I thought I might find you here."

"If you're hungry, there are still plenty of sandwiches." I nodded to the brown paper bag sitting in the center of the round table.

"That's all right. We'd just finished eating right before you called."

Guilt started to raise its ugly head again.

Erik pulled out a chair, and sat down between us. "So you found some new information, I take it?"

"Better than that," Michael said, wiping his mouth with one of the napkins. "We've found our thief."

"Really? Who?"

"Greta Morris."

He scrunched up his nose at this new information. I could tell he was trying to place the name. Although the foundation wasn't exactly small, Erik came in contact with most people who worked in the building at one point in time or another. "Older lady who works for Lily Adams?"

Michael got up and went to refill his coffee. "That's her."

"Wow. Never in a million years would I have suspected her. She's so nice."

I could empathize with how Erik was feeling. It was the same way I felt when I heard her voice on the recording last night. To be honest, I was still trying to come to terms with it.

As Michael rejoined us at the table, I addressed Erik. "I need you to log in to her computer and copy all the data to a separate file. We'll have to turn all those records over to the authorities tomorrow."

"You're having her arrested?"

"I don't have a choice."

A short while later, Erik headed down to the fourth floor to begin working on Greta's computer. Michael and I went back to work in the conference room. The two of us still had months' worth of Greta's phone conversations to go through. We divided them up to make things go faster.

At nine, Michael and I called it a night, satisfied that we had everything we needed for tomorrow's board meeting. Erik finished with Greta's files about two hours earlier and had headed back home to his family. He'd be back bright and early tomorrow morning with the rest of us at the board meeting. Although he wasn't an executive or a member of the board, anytime we addressed something that involved technology, Erik was invited to sit in.

Driving home, it hadn't escaped my notice that Ross hadn't called me back. I didn't have an e-mail from Brianna either. The temptation to drive directly to Ross's house instead of my condo was tempting, and I argued with myself all the way home.

Sarah must have heard me come in because she came down the stairs moments later. "You look like something the cat dragged in."

Instead of addressing her comment, I asked the one question that had compelled me to drive home instead of directly to Ross's. "Any messages for me?"

She looked confused but shook her head. "No. Things have been pretty quiet around here."

I nodded.

"Don't you want to know how my apartment hunting went?"

Tossing my keys onto the table, I rubbed my hand along the back of my neck, and sighed. "Sure."

Sarah raised her arm, and I noticed a single key dangling from her fingertips. There was a huge smile on her face.

This news gave me a slight lift in spirits. "You found something."

"Yep. It's perfect and only five minutes away. So I can stop by and bug you whenever I want."

Shaking my head, I couldn't help but smile a little. "I'm happy for you."

For the first time since I arrived, Sarah seemed to take in my less than enthusiastic demeanor. "Everything all right? Did something happen with Brianna?"

"I don't know. I haven't heard from her since Friday."

"Do you think she's okay?"

"I don't know that either. I left a message for Ross earlier, but he's not returned my call." I paused. "Then again, Ross isn't my biggest fan. If I haven't heard anything after my board meeting tomorrow, I'll head over there."

It was her turn to frown. "Do you think that's wise?"

"I couldn't give a damn if it's wise or not. She was supposed to e-mail me last night, and it's not like her to disobey me. I intend to find out what's going on one way or another."

Chapter 24

Stephan

It was seven forty-five on Monday morning, and I stood staring outside my office window at the city. The beautiful day we had yesterday had been replaced by another day of rain and gloom. A few snow flurries had even pelted my windshield on my way to work. It was fitting given what was on the agenda today.

To add to my stress, Brianna had yet to contact me. I had no idea what was going on, but after today's board meeting, I was going to find out. With every passing hour, the sick feeling in my gut got worse. I had to see her soon or I was going to make myself physically ill with worry.

Just before eight, Lily knocked on my door. "Hey."

Her smile vanished as I turned around. I'm sure the solemn look on my face gave her some indication as to the seriousness of what was about to transpire.

"Close the door and take a seat."

She did as instructed.

I waited until she was settled in the chair before I began. "You're aware that we've been investigating the money that was taken, corresponding with your purchases for the fundraiser."

Lily nodded. "And signs point to someone in my department."

"That's correct." I paused. "We found evidence this weekend that we can't ignore, and Lily, it *is* someone in your department."

She sat up straight. "Who?"

"Greta Morris."

Her eyes went wide. "No. That's impossible. Greta is the sweetest woman in the world. She wouldn't do something like this."

"We have her on tape. A conversation with a person we assume is her grandson given that he called her Grams."

Lily's mouth fell open in disbelief.

"There's more. Erik found evidence of the corresponding transaction hidden in her computer. He hasn't found the others yet, but he's still searching." I stood and walked over to where Lily was sitting. Kneeling down, I placed a comforting hand on her knee. "Lily, I'm sorry. I don't like it either, but I know it has to be worse for you because you know her."

She looked at me, her eyes filled with moisture. "I just don't understand. There has to be an explanation. Someone used her computer without her knowledge. Something."

I shook my head. "We have her on video. She was at her own computer when the thefts occurred."

Closing her eyes, she took a deep breath. When she met my gaze again, I saw stubborn resolve shine through as she stiffened her posture. "That's what the board meeting is about this morning."

Nodding, I stood and resumed my place behind the desk.

"You're going to fire her?"

"That will be up to the board, but I'd say it's likely." I reached for my phone and pressed the call button for Jamie. "First things first, however."

Seconds later, Jamie opened my office door. "Yes, Mr. Coleman?"

"Jamie, could you please ask Greta Morris to join us in my office, as well as a member of Human Resources, as soon as possible."

Jamie swallowed before nodding her assent. "Yes, sir."

Once she'd left the room, Lily faced me, somewhat surprised. "You're going to give her the chance to explain?"

It was my turn to sigh. "She's worked for my family for over fifteen years, Lily. If for no other reason, I need to know why."

Twenty minutes later, I sat across from a bawling Greta Morris. When I'd confronted her with what we'd found, she hadn't tried to deny it. Instead, her shoulders had slumped, almost in relief, and she'd begun to cry.

Over and over again, she apologized for taking the money. There was one problem, though. The way Greta talked, she'd only taken money from the company once, to pay for her mother's medical bills. "I don't know what I was thinking, Mr. Coleman. I don't. I shouldn't have done it. I know I shouldn't have."

"Greta, how many times did you and your grandson pull money from the account?"

She looked up at me in shock. Her eyes were bloodshot from her tears. "You know about Frankie?"

"We have you both on tape. You called him from the phone at your desk. Those conversations are recorded."

With this new information, she started crying again.

I was getting irritated, although it wasn't entirely due to Greta and her situation. My anxiety was already piqued because of what was going on with Brianna, so I snapped. "Answer the question."

All three women in the room, Lily, Greta, and our HR manager, Tracy, jumped at my less than reserved outburst.

Taking a deep breath to try and calm myself down, I tried once more. "How many times, Greta?"

"Just once! Only once. I took what we needed. That's all. I swear."

Sighing, I leaned back in my chair to think. There had been five transactions, not one. If Greta hadn't made them, then that only left one person. "Greta, where did you get the idea to do this?"

She fidgeted, nervous. "My grandson."

"And where did he get the idea?"

Greta stopped moving, and her eyes grew round as saucers. "His girlfriend."

"And who is Frankie's girlfriend, Greta? Does she work here?"

"Yes. Megan Cartwright."

The rest of the morning was complete chaos. This new information changed things, and the board meeting turned into more of a meeting to bring everyone up to speed and decide what needed to happen next. Given Greta's remorse and her years with the company, I was willing to go easy on her, but only if she helped us go after Megan and her grandson. Megan wasn't a hard sell. Her grandson, however, who was looking to be the brains behind the operation, if not the mastermind, was a completely different story. I didn't want to see Greta spend time in prison if it could be helped.

The board was split down the middle. Half of them were so upset by her betrayal that they wanted to see her pay for her crimes, no matter that she was a minor player in the whole situation. The other half felt that, given her years of service and obvious manipulation by her grandson, she should be fired and allowed to go on with her life. Ultimately, the decision fell on my shoulders. With a fifty-fifty split, I had to make the final call.

"I need a few minutes." Without further comment, I stood and walked from the room.

Greta was being watched under guard in my office, so at the moment, that was off-limits. Turning on my heel, I headed toward the executive gym. Rarely anyone used the space besides me and Lily, but even if they did, everyone was sitting in the conference room awaiting my decision.

As soon as I was inside, I closed the door and locked it behind me. I needed to think, and I didn't want to be interrupted.

I wasn't in the right frame of mind for this, but it wasn't something that could be put off either. Megan was already being watched. She'd been pulled away from her desk to help one of the other assistants with some files. It was a task that could have waited, but we'd needed to get her away from her computer in case she got suspicious of what was happening and tried to delete any evidence. Plus, Erik needed time to make a mirror copy of her computer. We weren't taking any chances for evidence to disappear. Because of all that, I was on borrowed time. I had maybe an hour, max.

Pacing back and forth, my mind inevitably wandered to Brianna. What would she think of all this? Taking a seat on one of the padded benches, I closed my eyes and let myself imagine that I was sitting at home with Brianna in my arms. Almost instantaneously, I felt the tension begin to ebb from my body. What I wouldn't give to hold her at this moment.

Sighing, I opened my eyes and stared at myself in the long bank of mirrors. I understood those board members who felt betrayed, but I couldn't justify throwing the book at Greta given the circumstances. Especially since I, myself, had broken the law to do what I thought needed to be done as well, and I would never regret that choice. The Dom in me, however, felt there needed to be some price paid.

A half hour later, I strode back into the conference room. Everyone looked up at my arrival. Some of the board members were still sitting at the table, but many had gotten up and were scattered throughout the room. Everyone quickly resumed their seats once I'd retaken mine.

I met the gaze of each one of them before I spoke. "I've made my decision."

They all nodded, some of them looking more confident than others.

There was something I needed to know first, before I gave them my verdict. I directed my question to Doug, the head of the foundation's legal department. "What are the ramifications to the foundation if we press charges?"

"It's difficult to say since every case is different. I think we have a good chance at winning the case, but whenever the public is involved you never know what their reaction might be."

Michael interrupted Doug. "If I might interject—I've been doing this for a lot of years, and I've never seen a case like this end well for either side involved. Often, even though the organization itself may have done nothing wrong, the perception of irresponsibility lingers." He paused. "What I'm saying is that if we go public with this, press charges, there is always a possibility that the amount of donations the foundation receives each year would drop drastically. You may lose more than you would gain."

There were a few more comments made by various members of the board, but nothing that changed my initial feelings on the matter. In the end, I'd chosen to fire Greta, stripping her of her position. The foundation, however, wouldn't press charges against her if she agreed to work in the mailroom as a volunteer for a minimum of five hours per week until she'd paid back the money she owed us. The only other condition was that at no time was she to use a computer while she was doing volunteer work for us. If she did so, our agreement would be null and void, and we would pursue legal action against her.

As for Megan and Greta's grandson, Frankie, I was less concerned with their fate. They deserved whatever happened to them. A decision, however, did have to be made. I placed that task in the hands of Doug, Michael, and Lily. I felt Lily had a vested interest in whatever punishment the foundation chose to dole out. It had happened in her department, after all. The three were to meet, make a recommendation, and report back to the board on Friday.

When we brought Greta back into the conference room to let her know of our decision, she was more than grateful and readily agreed. She thanked me and the board profusely for not sending her to jail. There were a few on the board who didn't like my decision, and I saw some glares as they left the room. I wasn't all that concerned. They would get over it.

Megan would be pulled aside by HR and one of the firm's lawyers and be told she was being suspended on suspicion of theft. Since we weren't having her arrested—at least, not as long as she complied with whatever the board came up with as a suitable punishment for her crimes—she'd be on leave, without pay, until the final decision was made. For now, I wanted to see her relegated to the lowest job we could find for her and make her stay there for the foreseeable future. I wasn't sure that was the sane part of me talking, or if everything in my life was finally getting the best of me.

Erik mentioned he could place a type of tracker in Megan's computer that would show if anyone outside the company tried to access it and then track that person's movements. It would essentially give us full access to the hacker's computer. Right now, all we had on Greta's grandson, Frankie, was his single phone conversation with Greta and her confession. I wanted more. He and Megan were responsible for this, and I wanted everything I could get on both of them. It would give us leverage if they tried to weasel out of what they'd done and place the blame solely on Greta's shoulders.

One by one, everyone left the room, with the exception of my uncle. He lingered by the coffee until we were alone.

"Something on your mind, Uncle?"

He absentmindedly stirred his coffee, before throwing the little straw in the trash can. "I know you've been busy with this situation, so I was wondering if you'd read a newspaper lately or watched the news?"

I frowned. "No. Why?"

"Because you and Sarah are all over it."

"Me and Sarah? Why?"

"Because apparently you're expecting a baby together."

"What?"

"I told you this would happen, Stephan. The media loves to jump to conclusions, and they didn't have to leap very far for this one. Have you told Brianna, yet?"

At the mention of Brianna's name, my heart sank. "When did you hear about it? Where did you see it?"

Richard stood there with an exaggerated calm. "Last night on the news. I was at the hospital most of the weekend, though, and from the sound of the anchor's comments, this wasn't their first broadcast reporting it—they were giving an update, which included pictures of you and Sarah in college."

My heart started beating rapidly. "I have to go."

"Maybe you need to calm down first."

I ignored him, my only thought of Brianna. That had to be why she hadn't e-mailed, why she hadn't called. I had to get to her and explain.

Making a beeline for my office, I grabbed my keys, and then raced to the elevator.

Jamie yelled after me. "Sir?"

I stepped onto the elevator before I answered her. "I'm leaving for the day."

Her mouth opened to respond, but the elevator doors closed, cutting her off.

Sliding behind the wheel of my car, I started the engine, and then maneuvered out of the parking garage and out onto the street. It was then I noticed the extra news affiliates hanging around. Had there been that many this morning? I had no idea.

As I drove, it rapidly became clear that I had several of them following me. That wouldn't do. Even in my desperation to get to Brianna, I knew I couldn't lead them to her.

Making an unplanned right at the traffic light, I headed in the opposite direction of where I wanted to go. I dug my cell phone out of my pocket and hit Lily's number.

"Stephan? Where are you? Your uncle said you flew out of here as—"

"I'll explain later, I promise, but I need to borrow Logan's car."

"What? Why?"

"I'm being followed, and I need to lose them. That will never happen as long as I'm driving my car." She was silent on the other end of the line for too long. "Lily?"

"Um. Yeah. Sure. His keys are on the kitchen counter next to the toaster."

"Thanks."

Without waiting for her response, I hung up and sped toward Lily and Logan's apartment as quickly as Minneapolis traffic would allow. My only hope was that switching cars would throw the vultures following me off my trail.

Chapter 25

Brianna
"There's been no change?"

"No. None. We thought she'd come out of it by now. That's why we called you. We've never seen her like this."

A hand touched my forehead, and then two fingers pressed firmly against the side of my wrist. "She doesn't appear to be running any type of a fever, and her pulse is steady."

"Is there anything you can do for her?"

The voices moved farther away, although they were still close enough that I could hear them. "You could admit her to a psych ward for observation, but given her history, it may do more harm than good."

"I don't understand how this could happen. I thought she was getting better. She was acting better." That time I recognized the voice as Cal's. He sounded irritated . . . and worried.

"She *is* getting better, Mr. Ross, but Anna experienced trauma that left huge emotional scars. That isn't going to repair itself overnight."

They were all quiet for a long time, and then I heard what I thought to be Jade's voice. "So what do we do now?"

"Keep doing what you've been doing. Sit with her. Talk to her. Give her an anchor to reality. Anna has escaped inside herself because what happened . . . what she saw and heard . . . was too painful for her to deal with. This . . ." She paused. "This is how she's protecting herself. Unfortunately, there is no magic button that will bring her back. You're going to have to let her work it out on her own."

After that, the voices left the room, leaving me alone. There were no sounds other than a low hum that seemed to surround me. The sound only added to the feeling of emptiness, and eventually the black void pulled me into its embrace once again.

Raised voices tore at my subconscious, demanding I pay attention to them. I didn't want to. I wanted to go back to the void. There wasn't pain in the void.

The voices wouldn't go away, though. They kept getting louder. One voice in particular.

Cal's.

"You have a lot of nerve showing your face here."

I opened my eyes slowly, and the light that hit my eyes nearly blinded me.

Someone spoke, but I couldn't hear what they said. Their voice sounded muffled.

"You need to leave."

The muffled voice spoke again.

"Like hell you are. Leave now before I rearrange your face some more for you."

The muffled voice grew louder, and this time I was able to make out both the words—and the speaker. "I'm not leaving until I see Brianna."

Stephan.

My chest tightened painfully, and memories flooded my mind. Stephan was going to be a father. He was going to have a baby with his ex-girlfriend. No. If they were having a baby together then she wouldn't be his ex anymore, would she?

I heard more yelling but no words. Then there were sounds of things breaking.

Willing my legs to work, I stood up beside the bed. I felt weak, but I knew I had to do something. I couldn't stay in my room and hide no matter how much I wanted to. Stephan felt responsible for me. That had to be why he was here. He deserved to be happy, though, and Sarah could do that for him. She could do the things I couldn't. I had to set him free . . . let him know that he didn't need to care for me anymore.

When I shuffled into the living room, Stephan and Cal were both on the floor. Each looked as if they'd thrown a few punches. Stephan had a bloody lip, and Cal's nose was bleeding. Jade was towering over them, trying to break them apart, but she didn't look to be having much success.

"Stop," I squeaked.

They couldn't hear me over everything else that was going on.

I took a deep breath and tried again, this time putting all the energy I had left behind it. "Stop!"

Stephan halted his movements first, which caused him to double over from a swift punch Cal landed to Stephan's stomach.

I tried one more time. "Stop! Please, stop."

This time, Jade and Cal heard me. They froze.

Stephan used Cal's distraction to push him away. Cal grunted, but other than that, failed to react.

"Brianna." Stephan stood and took a step toward me.

I took a step backward.

My retreat didn't escape his notice, and he didn't continue to approach me. "I was worried when you didn't contact me. I tried to call you."

"Leave her alone, you bastard! She doesn't want to talk to you."

"Cal, honey, calm down. You're going to frighten Anna."

Cal's only concession to what Jade said was that when he spoke again, he was no longer yelling. "Haven't you hurt her enough? Leave."

Stephan didn't take his eyes off me when he answered Cal. "Not until I say what I've come to say."

Cal didn't like that answer. He took a step forward like he was going to attack Stephan again, but Jade blocked his path. "Let him talk, and then he can go."

"Why are you always on his side? You heard what he did. He doesn't deserve anything."

Jade sighed but stayed calm. "I'm not on his side. But the two of you fighting again isn't going to solve anything either. Let him say his piece, and then he will leave." She turned to address Stephan. "You will leave after you've said what you came to say, or I will help Cal throw you out. Understood?"

Stephan looked as if he were going to argue but gave Jade a single hard nod instead.

He looked me up and down, taking in my appearance. "Give us a minute."

"Not on your life." Cal's voice was hard once more.

Stephan sighed. "I'm guessing you heard the rumors going around about me and Sarah."

Cal snorted, but Stephan ignored him.

"Brianna, they're not true. Sarah *is* pregnant, yes, but it's not mine."

I didn't respond.

"Sarah came to visit because she needed some time away to think. She was pregnant when she arrived in Minneapolis."

He paused and took a tentative step toward me again. This time, I didn't move.

"I've never lied to you, Brianna, and I don't want you to think that I have. I had every intention of explaining Sarah to you, but I wanted to do it in person. I was going to tell you Saturday at the planetarium. We would have had time to talk, to be together . . . and I could have explained everything. I wasn't expecting the media to blow things out of proportion."

Moisture gathered in my eyes. I didn't know what to believe. They'd said the baby was his, but Stephan had never lied to me before. I wanted to believe him.

"Since I'm laying all my cards out on the table here, Sarah has been living in the upstairs bedroom at my condo since she arrived. This weekend she found a place of her own and is moving out as we speak."

She'd been living with him?

"Look at me, Brianna."

No matter how conflicted I was feeling, I couldn't deny him.

When my gaze met his, I could see the pain in them, and my heart broke a little more.

"I love you, Brianna, and I never meant to do anything that would make you question your trust in me."

"Okay, that's enough." Cal pushed forward, placing his hand on Stephan's chest.

Stephan wrapped his fingers around Cal's wrist. "I'm not finished."

"Yes, you are. You said what you came to say. Now you are going to leave."

When Stephan didn't move, Cal punctuated his words with a push. Stephan narrowed his eyes at Cal but took a step toward the door.

Cal positioned himself protectively between me and Stephan. Over the last few weeks, I wasn't as jumpy around Cal as I used to be, but it still made me nervous when he was like this.

Stephan opened the door and paused before stepping outside. He met my gaze again from across the room. No words were spoken, but what I saw spoke volumes. He was hurting. Every instinct inside me called out to comfort him, but before I could command my body to move, he was gone.

I listened to him start his car and then disappear down the driveway.

Closing my eyes, I collapsed onto the floor as the blackness took over again.

When I opened my eyes, I was back in my bed. I had no recollection of returning to my bedroom. The last thing I remembered was seeing Stephan walking out the door and my heart breaking in two all over again.

"Hey, you're awake." Jade sat in one of the kitchen chairs a couple of feet from the bed.

I met her gaze but didn't say anything.

"Are you hungry? I made some soup. It's not as good as what you can make, but Cal says it's edible."

I shook my head.

She sighed and reached out to touch the tips of my fingers where they were laying on the bed. "Anna, you haven't eaten anything in almost three days. You need to eat something."

"I'm not hungry." Even those three simple words took more effort than they should.

"Please eat something. For me?"

Reluctantly, I nodded. Jade had been so nice to me. I didn't know if my moving in with Cal would have worked if not for her. She'd allowed me to lean on her when I no longer had Stephan.

Stephan.

My eyes filled with tears again.

Two seconds later, Jade's arms were around me. "It will be okay. We'll figure it out. I promise."

She held me until I'd stopped crying. I felt dead inside except for the pain that seemed to be a permanent resident in my chest. It almost felt as if someone were sitting on top of me and wouldn't get up. Every time I breathed in, it wasn't enough to fill my lungs. It reminded me a little of my panic attacks, but this was different in that there wasn't a flashback or a *fear* of pain. This time there *was* pain.

Jade brought me in some soup and sat with me while I ate it. It didn't have much flavor. I didn't know if it was just me or if it was because Jade had made it. She wasn't very good with cooking, even with the few lessons I'd given her.

"You don't like it."

"It's fine," I said, sipping another spoonful into my mouth.

She didn't say any more until I'd finished the soup. Taking the bowl from me, she laid it on the nightstand beside the bed. "Cal wants to come in and see you, but I asked him to wait. Anna, do you remember what happened this afternoon?"

"Yes."

"So you remember Stephan coming to see you?"

"Yes. I remember."

Jade moved to sit on the bed beside me. "Did you want to talk about it?"

Did I?

"There's no pressure, but if you want to talk, I'll listen."

I thought about it for a few minutes. "Stephan has never lied to me before."

"Do you think he's lying now?"

"I don't know. The news . . ."

Jade shifted so that we were facing each other. "No one can tell you what to do, Anna. Well, Cal will probably try to tell you what to do."

She smiled, and I couldn't help the soft snort that escaped.

"My point is that you can't always believe what you hear on the news or read in the paper. Remember my friend I was telling you about? The one that was raped? The guy was a football player, and there were some people who thought she was lying. They spread rumors about her that weren't true, and some of those rumors were printed in the campus paper. I know it's not the same thing, but . . ." She sighed. "What does your heart tell you?"

"I don't know!" I cried.

She grabbed hold of my hands and held tight. "Yes you do. One way or another, you know."

Four days later, I sat across from Dr. Perkins in her office. It had been a long week. Stephan had come to see me again on Tuesday, but Jade had met him at the front door and told him that he needed to give me some space. I wanted to see him, but I didn't at the same time. He'd been my stability since he'd gotten me away from Ian. For the first time in months, I felt unsure of the one thing I'd always been certain of. Him.

I reached up and touched my collar. There were several times this week I'd almost taken it off. It didn't feel right for me to wear it anymore. Not when I was doubting . . . everything.

"You look like you have a lot on your mind today, Anna."

As if I'd been stung, I dropped my hand and wrapped my arms around my torso. I looked quickly around the room as if waiting for some unknown . . . something . . . to jump out at me.

I hadn't wanted to come today, but Jade and Cal had begged me to go. They thought it would help.

"This is a safe place. No one's going to hurt you here."

Meeting Dr. Perkins's gaze, I saw the same worry that had been on Cal's and Jade's faces since Monday. I didn't like making them worry about me, but I couldn't help it. My world no longer made sense to me. "You know what happened?"

"Your friends filled me in on some of it, but I'd like to hear it from you. If, that is, you'd like to share it with me."

Dropping my gaze to the floor, I raised my feet up onto the couch and rested my chin on my knees while hugging my legs. Every time I talked about it, I felt. I didn't want to feel.

When I didn't say anything after a while, Dr. Perkins leaned forward in her chair, and laid her pad of paper aside. "I know there has to be a lot going on inside your head right now, Anna, and I'd like to help you sort through it . . . make sense of it, if I can, but I'm going to need for you to talk to me."

Closing my eyes, I let the pain creep in. "I don't know if he's lying. I don't know."

The feeble dam that had been holding my emotions at bay broke wide open. My entire body shook violently with my sobs as I let the pain flow freely through me for the first time since I'd seen the pictures of Stephan and Sarah on television. The will to keep myself upright disappeared eventually, and I fell onto my side into a fetal position. It hurt so much, and this time no one could take it away.

For the next two weeks, the pattern continued to repeat itself off and on. Anytime someone would say something about Stephan, or anything that would remind me of him, I'd end up curled in a ball crying for what felt like hours until I no longer had the energy to cry anymore.

After that first Tuesday, Stephan didn't attempt to stop by Cal's house, but that didn't stop him from contacting me. He sent flowers every day after that first week, and when I logged on to my computer every day there was always an e-mail from him. I didn't read them, but knowing they were there was both a blessing and a curse. It didn't help me know what to do.

On Friday night, after yet another session with Dr. Perkins that was mostly made up of me breaking down in uncontrollable tears, I lay in my room staring at the ceiling. I needed someone to tell me what I should do.

Rolling over, my gaze fell on my laptop. I hadn't logged on to my e-mail today, but I knew that if I did, there would be another e-mail from Stephan. The pull to read them had become even stronger as the days passed. It was becoming difficult to resist.

Jade kept saying that eventually I'd figure it out . . . that I'd know what to do . . . what to believe. I wasn't sure she was right.

Reaching out, I ran my index finger over the edge of the computer as if it held the answer to my conundrum.

Before I could stop myself, I flipped open the screen and set the computer on my lap. As soon as it was booted up, it beeped, notifying me that I had new mail. Hesitating for only a fraction of a second, I clicked on the icon that would bring up my e-mail. There, staring back at me, were at least twenty messages from Stephan—at least one every day for over two weeks, and on some days there'd been two or three.

Pressing my lips together, I argued with myself. Should I read them or go on ignoring his attempts at communication?

As soon as the word *communication* popped into my head, I recalled how many times he'd gone on and on about how important communicating with him was. But he'd broken that rule, hadn't he?

Taking a deep breath, I closed my eyes and counted to ten. Before I opened them, my right index finger pressed down on the keyboard almost as if it were following its own command. When I looked at the screen again, there, in black and white, was Stephan's e-mail.

> Brianna,
> I have no idea if you're reading these e-mails I'm sending you or not, but I hope that you are.
> There is nothing that I can say or do to express to you how very sorry I am for not telling you about what was going on sooner. I wanted to explain the situation to you in person, not over some lifeless computer. I wanted to hold you so you'd have no doubt that what I was telling you was true.
> You must have questions, and I want to answer them for you. Please give me the chance. I love you, sweetheart, and I always will. Please, talk to me.
> Love,
> Stephan

I brushed the tears from my cheeks as I read his words. There was anguish in what he'd written, just as there'd been in his eyes the last time I saw him.

One by one, I read through the e-mails. Most of them were similar to the first one I'd read, only varying slightly and with increasing desperation. He was hurting, and no matter how confused I was or how much pain I was in, I couldn't deny his one request. Stephan saved me. Even if he had lied to me about Sarah and the baby, he'd still given me back my life when I'd thought all hope of anything past surviving had been taken from me. At the very least, I owed him this.

Setting my laptop to the side, I slipped out of bed and tiptoed out of my bedroom. The house was dark, and for the first time, I realized how late it was. I debated whether or not I should go back to my room or not, but tomorrow was Saturday, and Jade and Cal would most likely not have work or school. They'd been watching me like hawks lately.

As quietly as I could, I walked to the other side of the house where Cal and Jade's bedroom was located. Not giving myself the time to second-guess my decision, I knocked on the door.

Less than a minute later, Cal opened the door. His hair was standing on end, and he looked as if he'd just been woken from a bad dream. "Anna? What's wrong? Are you hurt?"

I shook my head.

He frowned. "What is it?"

Meeting his gaze, I took a deep breath to gather the courage I would need to make this request of him. "I need to talk to Stephan. Will you drive me?"

Chapter 26

Stephan

The sound of buzzing caused me to sit up in bed. Glancing over at the clock, I noted that it was three o'clock in the morning. Who in the world was ringing my doorbell at this hour?

Getting out of bed, I threw on a pair of jeans and headed for the door. Whoever it was, it had to be someone I knew or they would never have gotten past the front desk. At least, I hoped we never had another incident like what had happened with Brianna's father. Considering he was behind bars for the foreseeable future, I highly doubted it to be a likely scenario.

As I drew closer to the entrance, the security panel came into view. I almost tripped over my own feet when I saw Brianna standing there. Ross was beside her, but all I could focus on was her. I rushed the rest of the way to the door and flung it open. "Brianna?"

Ross scowled but said nothing.

Brianna looked nervous but determined. I had no idea what was going through her head. We hadn't spoken since I'd shown up at Ross's house almost three weeks ago.

"I read your e-mails."

At her confession, I breathed a sigh of relief. I'd not been sure that she would read them, but I'd hoped . . . prayed she would. "Would you like to come in?"

She nodded and stepped inside. Ross shadowed her.

I wasn't thrilled with his presence. The man had bloodied my lip the last time I saw him. I'd spent the rest of the evening icing the thing, and even then, it had been noticeable the next day. The newspaper had speculated it was a present from Sarah's father after the news had leaked that I'd knocked her up.

Leading them to the living room, I motioned for Brianna to sit down. Unfortunately, Ross sat down beside her. Sitting in my chair, I waited to see what she had to say.

Instead of addressing me, however, she turned to Ross. "Could you give us a minute?"

He looked at her as if she'd just asked him to jump off a cliff without a harness. "I'm not leaving you alone with him, Anna. No way."

"Please?"

Ross hesitated, and for a moment, I didn't think he was going to comply with her wishes. "Fine, but if he does anything, I'm going to rearrange his face again."

After giving me a hard stare—a warning—Ross stood and walked back out the front door. It didn't escape my attention that he'd made sure it remained unlocked when he stepped out into the hall. I could see him pacing on the security monitor.

I turned my attention away from Ross and back to Brianna. She looked too thin again, and I knew she'd not been eating properly. It hurt to know that this time I was the cause of her pain. "You said you read my e-mails?"

"Yes."

"And?"

"And I need you to explain it to me."

I took a deep breath. Okay. I could do that. "Let me start from the beginning, all right?"

She nodded and looked down.

"I need you to do something for me first, though?"

Brianna glanced back up to meet my gaze. "What?"

"I want you to promise that you'll look at me while I'm talking to you. I want you to be able to see that what I'm telling you is the truth. Will you do that?"

"Yes."

I smiled. It was weak, but I wanted her to know how happy I was that she was giving me this chance to explain.

"About two months after you left, Sarah contacted me. She'd heard about what was going on with Ian and your father and said she was coming to town." I leaned forward, desperate to touch Brianna but not sure if I should. "She arrived two days later, showing up at my office out of the blue."

No longer able to stand the distance between us, I stood and walked over to sit beside her on the couch. I kept my distance, not touching her, although it had to be among the toughest things I'd ever had to do in my life . . . right up there with letting her leave me in the first place.

Brianna held herself rigid, clenching her hands together. I didn't know if that was because she was afraid I'd touch her or to keep herself from reaching out to me. Maybe a little of both.

"That night she invited herself over for dinner. I know that might sound strange, but that's Sarah. She can be incredibly pushy at times." I paused. "She reminds me of Lily in that way. You never want to get in Lily's way when she's going after something she wants. She'll steamroll right over you."

"And Sarah wanted you." Brianna sounded resigned.

"No! Not at all." I reached out into the space between us. Reaching but not touching. "She wanted to know about you."

Brianna looked shocked. "Why?"

Again, I smiled. "Because she realized how important you are to me. I received a phone call from Oscar while she was in my office, and she could tell from my reaction how much I care about you. I've never loved anyone before you, Brianna. Sarah wanted to know everything she could about the woman who'd stolen my heart."

We both sat quietly for several minutes. I wanted to go slow this time. Before, I'd blurted out the vital information as swiftly as possible, not knowing at what point Ross would try and throw me out. This time it was different, and I was going to make sure Brianna knew everything.

"After dinner that night, Sarah told me she was pregnant. It's one of the reasons she came to visit me. Some things happened with her boyfriend, and she needed time to think. It was then I offered her a place to stay."

"Did you have sex with her?"

I couldn't believe she was asking me that, but I answered her anyway. "No. Sarah and I haven't been together in that way for years." I paused. "And just to be clear, I've not had sex with anyone but you since I met you, Brianna. No one but you."

"Really?"

I cocked my head to the side. "Yes. Why is that so unbelievable?"

She shrugged. "I don't know. I just thought that when I left . . ."

"No, Brianna. No."

Again, silence filled the room. I wished I could make her understand how ridiculous the notion was that I'd want to be with anyone but her, but I knew right now wasn't the time to try to convince her of that. This was my opportunity to set the record straight—maybe my only opportunity—and I had to clear the air once and for all.

"You know the locked room upstairs?"

"Yes."

"She stayed there while she was here."

"Not in my room?"

Again I resisted the urge to reach out to her. "No. That's *your* room, Brianna. Yours."

Brianna's gaze left mine and drifted over to the door that led to her room.

"Do you want to see it? It hasn't changed since you left."

She looked at me once more. I could see the conflict in her eyes, so I made the decision for her. Standing, I motioned toward her room and waited for her to rise.

It took her several moments before she got up from the couch and followed me into the room. I hadn't been in there myself for more than a week. Since she'd been gone, I'd rehired a maid to come in once a week and clean. This room had been off-limits to her. I hadn't wanted anyone to touch Brianna's things but me, so I cleaned the rooms myself when needed.

"It's the same," she whispered, her fingers grazing the edge of the bed.

I stood back and let her walk around the room. Every once in a while, she'd pick up something and then put it down before moving on to the next thing. She seemed to be in awe that everything was exactly as she'd left it, with the exception of the items I'd sent to her.

Once she'd made a complete pass around the room, she returned to stand several feet in front of me. I took a step forward, and when she didn't retreat, I took another one. "We weren't communicating when Sarah moved in, and when I saw you at the gala, all I could think about was how good it felt being with you again. If not for Lily, I wouldn't have even remembered that Sarah was my date, and that I'd left her downstairs. At the time, all I could think about was you."

Taking a chance, I tentatively extended my hand, hoping she'd take it.

She glanced down at my offering, and after a moment's hesitation, she linked her fingers with mine. Being able to touch her again was like a breath of fresh air.

We stood there holding hands for what felt like forever. I didn't want to break the connection, but eventually I knew I had to. There was more I had to say. "I want to be honest with you, Brianna. Telling you about Sarah's baby hadn't really crossed my mind until my uncle brought it up to me after the gala. It's Sarah's baby, not mine, so I didn't see the relevance. I realize now that was naïve of me, and I should have told you right away."

Pulling her a little closer, I waited until she looked up at me. "I meant what I told you at Ross's. I was planning to tell you when we met for our date at the planetarium. I was afraid if I told you over Skype, you would only hear that Sarah was living with me and expecting a baby . . . that you would panic and think I didn't want you anymore."

Reaching up with my other hand, I cupped her cheek. "I realize now that by not telling you right away, I ended up with exactly what I'd feared."

Brianna

I was trying very hard to stay focused, but it was difficult with Stephan's hand on my cheek. The only thing I wanted to do was close my eyes and melt into his embrace. It would be so easy to forget everything else and lose myself in him.

"Tell me what you're thinking, Brianna."

The heat of his hand was doing funny things—very pleasant funny things—to my insides. "I want to believe you."

He frowned. "You don't believe me?"

"I want to."

Stephan sighed and stepped away from me, leaving me cold and alone once again. I wrapped my arms around my waist in an attempt to warm myself.

The distance only increased, physically and emotionally, as he collapsed into the chair in the corner. I wanted to go to him, but I didn't know if I should. If anything, I was more confused than I'd been before. Everything in me wanted to believe him, but there was a little voice inside my head that sounded a lot like Cal telling me I shouldn't.

"Would you like to see the room Sarah stayed in? I haven't felt like doing much with it since she left."

Since I had no better suggestion, I nodded.

He got up, and I followed him out of the room. We passed through the living room, and I could see Cal on the screen Stephan had installed after I'd opened the door to John. He was sitting along the wall, tapping his fingers against his legs. He hadn't wanted to bring me tonight. If it were up to him, I would forget about Stephan and move on with my life. I wasn't sure I could do that, however. Stephan was too important.

We walked up the stairs and passed through Stephan's library before arriving at the room that before had always been locked. He opened the door and motioned for me to go inside.

The first thing I noticed was that the walls were a dark blue—darker than you'd normally find in a bedroom. There was also very little furniture in the room other than a bed, a single nightstand, and a dresser. Also, unlike the bedrooms downstairs, there was no carpet in this room. The floor was some sort of rubber, but a throw rug had been placed over a section of it to soften it. "This was her room?"

"Yes."

I stepped farther inside, not understanding. This didn't feel like a bedroom.

"You're probably wondering why I had the room locked before."

Glancing over my shoulder, I waited for him to go on.

"This used to be my playroom."

I sucked in a lungful of air.

"When you left, I didn't know if the police would want to search my condo or not, so I thought it best to remove anything that would make me look less than normal."

Although I'd suspected for a long time that was what had been in this room, hearing him confirm it sent my head spiraling. "Your playroom?"

He stepped closer to me, not stopping until he was standing only inches away. "I've never made it a secret what I am, Brianna. Nothing I can say will express to you how sorry I am for breaking my own rule and not telling you right away what was going on with Sarah. You should never have had to hear something like that on the news. It was my responsibility to tell you, and I failed. I can only hope that you can find it in your heart to forgive me."

I looked into his eyes. The pain was still there. Keeping my distance was hurting him. It was hurting me, too. I realized then it was fear that was holding me back. Fear that Cal might be right, that I might have been wrong in giving myself completely to Stephan. I didn't think I had been, though. He'd made a mistake, and now he was doing everything he could to make up for it.

Before I could rethink my actions, I launched myself into his arms. Stephan didn't hesitate. He wrapped his arms around me and buried his face in my hair.

"Oh, sweetheart, I've missed you. I was so scared you were never going to talk to me again."

With my head resting on his chest, I could hear his heart pounding against my ear. This, being in his arms, felt right. I didn't ever want to feel separated like that from him again. It was worse than when I'd left. Then, I'd known that there was a possibility for us even if it was in the future. This rift had been different. It was as if all the possibilities, all the future hopes and dreams I'd fantasized about, had disappeared and been replaced with utter desolation. I didn't like that abyss of nothingness. I wanted Stephan, and I'd take him even if he wasn't perfect.

Stephan leaned back, brushing the hair away from my face with his fingers. "May I kiss you?"

I nodded.

As soon as I'd given him the green light, Stephan bent his head and caressed my lips with his. It was featherlight . . . cautious.

"I love you," he murmured before pressing his mouth firmly against mine. Within seconds, the outside world ceased to exist. The only thing that mattered was this. Him.

My hands searched for purchase against the skin of his back. I wanted closer, to feel more. As if reading my thoughts, he ran his tongue along my bottom lip, requesting entrance. I opened my mouth, and his tongue slipped inside to begin its gentle exploration.

I wanted to keep kissing him forever, but before I knew it, he was ending it. His breathing was exaggerated, as was my own, as he rested his forehead against mine. "If we don't stop, I'm going to end up stripping you of your clothes and taking you on that bed there."

Right then, that sounded perfect. I'd missed him so much. All I wanted was to feel him over me again, his body pressing me possessively into the mattress.

He groaned. "That's not helping, Brianna. Ross is still downstairs. I'm surprised he hasn't come looking for you yet."

My enthusiasm faded. I'd forgotten about Cal. He wasn't going to like that Stephan and I had made up. "I should go talk to him."

Reluctantly, I stepped away from Stephan and headed toward the door.

"Wait."

I stopped and turned back around to face Stephan.

"Move back in with me."

"What?"

"Move back in with me. Here. You can stay in your old room if you want, just come back home. I've missed you like crazy, and this separation hasn't been good for either of us." He paused. "Even before my stupidity."

The offer was tempting. As great as Cal and Jade had been to me, Cal's house had never felt like home. My home was with Stephan. Even though my address had changed, that never had. "What about the reporters?"

"We'll figure it out."

Stephan took hold of my hands, stepping closer.

"You hardly ever go out alone anyway, and there is security here. You'd be safe." He placed my arms around his waist and held my face in his hands. "We'll figure it out. Together this time. Just say you'll come home."

I didn't want to say no, so I didn't. "Okay."

He smiled, his face alight with his obvious joy at my answer. "You'll move back in?"

I smiled back at him. "Yes."

Stephan placed a hard kiss on my mouth before grabbing my hand and heading downstairs. Now I just had to tell Cal and Jade. I wasn't all that worried about Jade, but Cal . . . that was an entirely different story. I just hoped that, in the end, he'd be happy for me.

Chapter 27

Brianna

"I think that's the last of it." Jade placed her hands on her hips. She hadn't said much when Cal and I returned to the house and I'd explained that I was moving back in with Stephan. Unlike Cal, who repeatedly gave his opinion on the matter. Stephan had wanted me to stay, but given how Cal was reacting, I'd thought it best to go and come back later with Jade. I didn't want them fighting again.

When she continued to stand there watching me, I started to think something was wrong. "What is it?"

For a long moment, she didn't say anything. "I'm just worried maybe this is happening too fast. Yesterday you weren't even speaking to him, and now here you are moving back in. Even Emma said she didn't think this was a great idea."

Emma, my lawyer, had stopped by Cal's while we were packing up my things. I'd been so focused on other stuff that I'd forgotten it was Saturday and that she'd be stopping by to check on me and give me an update as she usually did.

"I don't want to be away from him."

She nodded. "I know that. And I don't know what I'd do if our situations were reversed." Jade dropped her arms and came to stand in front of me. "Just promise me you'll stay in touch, okay?"

"I will."

Jade hugged me tight for a minute before stepping back. She looked over my shoulder into the main room. "Then again, I don't know if Cal would let you do anything else."

"He's really mad at me."

"No. He's not mad at you. He's furious with Stephan. In his mind, Stephan coerced you somehow into moving back in with him."

"But he didn't."

She brushed a loose piece of hair away from my face gently, meeting my gaze. "I'm not sure Cal's opinion on that will ever change. He views you as the little sister he never had. I don't know if you are aware of this or not, but there have been nights when he's woken up from nightmares yelling your name. When I asked him about it, he said it's always the same. You're in this dark place. He can see you, but for some reason he can never get to you." Jade sighed. "I think on some level he feels responsible for what happened to you. I know it's irrational, and I think he does, too, but you can't change how you feel."

I glanced out into the living room. Although I couldn't see Stephan from where I was standing, I could see Cal. He was glaring at something off to his left, and I knew that it had to be Stephan. "Should I talk to him about it?"

"Maybe. But not now. Even if you tried, I'm not sure he'd listen. He's so caught up in his own anger."

Nodding, I helped her put away the suitcases we'd used to bring everything over and then walked back out into the main room with her. I felt as if I needed to do something to mend this rift with Cal. He'd gone out of his way to help me over the last few months. I didn't want to leave him feeling as if I didn't appreciate it.

Crossing the room, I made my way over to Cal. As I neared, his expression softened, and I realized Jade was right. He wasn't mad at me. His anger was directed solely at Stephan.

Taking Jade's advice, I didn't try to reason with him. Instead, I circled my arms around his waist and squeezed. "Thank you."

Cal held his body rigid. I was beginning to think he wasn't going to react at all to my gesture, but then he relaxed his stance and rested his hands lightly on my back. He didn't reply, but it was enough for now. I didn't have many friends, and I didn't want to lose the ones I had.

Jade and Cal didn't stay long after that. I could tell Cal didn't want to leave, but Jade reminded him they'd both see me Friday afternoon to take me to my appointment with Dr. Perkins. Stephan and I hadn't discussed my continued visits with the psychiatrist. I knew he wasn't crazy about my going.

I stood watching the closed door after Cal and Jade left. They no longer appeared on the security monitor, so I was watching a screenshot of the empty hall.

Stephan came up behind me and wrapped his arms around my waist. I leaned back into him, enjoying the feeling of being in his embrace once again. Oh, how I'd missed that.

"Are you all right, sweetheart?"

"Yes."

"But?"

"I feel as if I did something wrong."

He stepped back some and turned me to face him. "Have you changed your mind about moving back in?"

I shook my head. That was the last thing I wanted him to think. "No. I want to be with you."

Stephan pulled me closer so that our chests were touching. He grazed his fingers against my cheek before tilting my chin up. "Then what is it?"

"I don't like to see Cal so upset."

"Is he ever not upset?" The right side of Stephan's mouth curled up slightly, so I knew he was trying to make a joke.

"Sometimes."

At my serious expression, Stephan sighed. "He doesn't like me, and I'm not sure he ever will. I think that's something we're both going to have to accept."

"I know."

He kissed the tip of my nose. "Maybe in time—when he sees you're happy—he'll learn to at least tolerate me."

I nodded but didn't say anything. Even though I wanted what Stephan suggested, I wasn't holding my breath. Cal was extremely stubborn, and given what he'd experienced with his neighbor, I wasn't sure he'd ever be able to accept my relationship with Stephan.

"Come on, let's get some lunch, and then I have to get some work done."

Frowning, I looked up at him. "You have to go into work today?"

Stephan placed a quick kiss on my lips before leading me into the kitchen. "I went in for a couple of hours after you left this morning. Unfortunately, there are some things going on right now that require my attention. Otherwise, I wouldn't have gone in at all and helped you move."

His news only made me feel worse.

"Hey," he said, placing the items he'd removed from the refrigerator on the counter. "Stop with the sulking. I chose to be here today when you returned with your things. That was my choice, not yours, so none of this feeling guilty. It was not your decision to make, Brianna."

I glanced down at the floor. "I could have waited."

He didn't like that response. "No. I want you here with me. I didn't want to wait, and I hope you didn't either."

Looking up, I could see he meant every word. "No. I didn't. I just don't want to be a burden. I've already—"

"Brianna, let's get one thing straight right now. You are not now, nor have you ever been a burden to me. Do you understand? Never."

"Even when I have my panic attacks and you have to change your plans because of me?"

He smiled and wrapped his arms around me, holding me against his chest. "Even then."

Stephan kissed the top of my head before letting go. "Come on. I'm getting hungry, and I want to spend some time with you tonight. Just the two of us. I've missed that."

I smiled up at him, happier than I'd been in a while. "Me, too."

Stephan

Sitting in front of my laptop going through e-mails was the last thing I wanted to be doing. Brianna was watching television in the living room, and I wanted to be right there with her. It took great effort on my part to keep my hands to myself while Ross and Jade were here. Of course, I could have thrown caution to the wind and given in to my impulses. Typically I would have done just that where Ross was concerned, but today was different. I could tell he was itching for an excuse to have another physical confrontation with me. Brianna didn't need to deal with that on top of everything else.

I'd told Michael, Lily, Doug, and Erik to keep me apprised of the situation with Greta, Megan, and Greta's grandson, Frankie. They'd divided the duties, trying to do a complete and thorough job by the time the board met again on Friday. Megan was suspended and told a decision regarding her fate, along with her boyfriend's, would be forthcoming and that if they cooperated, no charges would be filed. She seemed to be on board for the time being. Frankie was more reluctant, but it seemed Michael's initial meeting with him had changed his tune.

Movement drew my attention to Brianna. She walked toward me tentatively. "What do you need, sweetheart?"

She seemed hesitant. "I was just wondering if you wanted me to cook dinner?"

I glanced down at the clock. It was already four thirty. I was at least an hour away from being finished.

Pushing my chair away from the table, I stood, stretching. Dining room chairs weren't meant for long, drawn-out work sessions. I hadn't wanted to go upstairs and leave her down here alone, though. Not yet.

I reached for her, pulling her to me. "That would be wonderful."

Placing a soft kiss on her lips, I reluctantly went back to my makeshift desk. The sooner I got done, the sooner I could have her back in my arms.

Dinner was delicious. I'd missed Brianna's cooking, but more importantly, I'd missed eating supper with her. Her presence alone seemed to lessen the stress of dealing with what was going on at the foundation. I wasn't sure if she would ever completely understand the profound effect she had on me.

After helping her take the dishes into the kitchen and loading them into the dishwasher, I led her into the living room and over to my chair. I sat and pulled her down with me. She quickly snuggled close, getting into her favorite position. It was impossible to describe how good something as simple as having her sit with me in my chair again felt. There were no words that would do it justice.

I let us both enjoy the moment for a while before starting the conversation I knew we needed to have. "How are you feeling?"

She released a relaxed sigh as she wiggled closer, pressing her nose against my neck. "Good."

Pressing a kiss to her temple, I inhaled the coconut sent of her hair. It amazed me, all the simple things I'd missed. "Now that you're back home, there are some things we need to talk about."

"Okay." I was a little surprised by the lack of fear in her voice. She sounded utterly content.

There was so much I wanted to say—a lot that needed to be said. I decided to start with something simple. "Did you and Jade get everything situated in your room earlier?"

"Yes. She helped me put all the clothes away."

"Good." I ran my fingers through her hair gently. It was almost as if I had to remind myself that this was real, that she was home with me. "The room is yours, Brianna. You can do with it what you wish. If you want to paint it a different color, get new furniture, just let me know and we'll get it arranged how you want it. It's your space to do whatever you want with."

Brianna was playing with the buttons on my dress shirt and then suddenly stopped.

"What is it?"

"Does that mean I'm not going to be sleeping in your bed?"

I breathed a sigh of relief without even realizing how much the thought that she might not want to share my bed right away had plagued me. "That's up to you. If you'd rather sleep in your room for a while, I'd understand, but I want you with me, Brianna, and that includes having you in my bed."

She gripped my shirt briefly before going back to toying with my buttons. "I want to be with you, too."

Cupping her cheek, I guided her mouth to mine. Her lips were soft and pliant as I applied a gentle suction. I was torn between wanting to deepen the kiss and devour her and the need to make sure all was right between us before I took that next step.

Ending the kiss before things got too carried away, I tucked her head back into the crook of my neck. Brianna's enthusiasm when it came to our physical contact never helped quell my desire for her. "We need to talk about how we move forward in our relationship. Are you ready to do that?"

"Yes, Sir."

I inhaled a deep breath. It was the first time she'd called me Sir since our fallout. I couldn't believe how good it felt. "Do you remember the rules I gave you at Ross's?"

"Yes."

"What were they?"

"Eat three meals a day. Cook dinner every night. And e-mail you my journal before I go to bed."

"Good girl." I caressed her hair lovingly, letting her know I was pleased. "I want you to keep doing those things with one slight alteration. Since you're back home now, I've left a new journal in your nightstand for you to use. I still expect you to write in it every day, and I want you to present it to me every evening at dinner."

I felt her swallow hard. "Okay."

"Does that make you nervous?"

"A little."

"Why?"

She shifted against me and brought her hand up to graze the back of my neck, sending a shiver down my spine. "You'll be reading it in front of me."

I smiled. "Yes. And?"

"And what if I write something that makes you angry?"

"Then we deal with it as we always do." I made her look at me. "Brianna, there is nothing you could do that would make me stop loving you. Stop worrying about what my reaction might be. This journal is to help both of us. It will give me insight into your thoughts and feelings on what's going on in our lives and whatever we may do in our relationship. If something you write upsets me, we'll talk about it—simple as that."

Brianna glanced down. "I didn't like being . . ."

She sighed.

I waited.

"I didn't like not knowing if you'd lied to me or not. It hurt so much."

Tears welled in her eyes, and I took her face between my hands. With our noses touching, I met her gaze. "What happened was my fault, Brianna. Mine. You had every right to feel as you did. Although I'll do my best not to make the same mistake again, I can't promise that I'll never mess up."

"I know."

We stayed that way for a while, watching each other and taking in what we'd both almost lost. I would do my best to make sure that never happened again.

Brianna and I spent the rest of the evening sitting in my chair, talking, and touching. By the time we made it into my bedroom, I was about to explode. Guiding her into the bathroom, I turned on the shower and began removing her clothing. I watched her closely, looking for any signs that she wasn't ready—that this wasn't what she wanted—but there weren't any. Brianna appeared as ready as I was to reconnect in this most physical way.

My erection stood proud the moment I released it from the confines of my dress pants. I'd been hard for most of the evening but I'd been ignoring my needs so we could talk things out. We still had a long way to go. She'd forgiven me, but whether she admitted it or not, a level of trust had been broken. I had to rebuild that, and it would take time. After guiding her into the large marble stall we'd shared many times before, I reached for the shower gel and began to wash her.

Slowly, time began to melt away, and we were once more in a cocoon that sheltered us from the outside world. Nothing existed outside the marble walls surrounding us.

As I rubbed the soap onto her body, I relished every sigh . . . every moan. My cock ached painfully with the need to be inside her. Unfortunately, I'd not brought any condoms into the bathroom with us. It was tempting to throw caution to the wind and ignore rational thought, but I persevered. Somehow.

Normally I would have let her wash me, but I couldn't. I was afraid if she so much as touched me, I'd either explode on the spot or take her right then and there. To hell with precautions.

As it was, I rushed through drying both of us off and carried her into the bedroom. She lay spread out on the bed, her legs loosely parted. I climbed on top of her, wedging myself in between her thighs. I leaned over and reached into my drawer to retrieve a condom. Tomorrow I would have to talk to her about going back to see Richard for another blood test. It had been more than three months, and once the tests came back clean, I hoped I never had to wear anything that would separate us again.

Resting one elbow at the side of her head, I positioned myself at her entrance, rubbing up and down along her folds. She was wet, and heat radiated from her pussy. The whole evening had been foreplay, and we both seemed to not need any more stimulation.

I pressed forward with my hips, feeling her walls take hold of me, hot and pulsing. Rocking my hips, I slowly seated myself fully inside her. "I want you touching me tonight. Place your arms around my neck and hold on."

Obediently, Brianna wrapped her arms around my neck and held on as if her life depended on it. I began to move, pistoning in and out with ever-increasing speed. It didn't take long before I felt the first signs of my orgasm approaching. Lowering my head, I latched on with my mouth to the skin right above her collarbone while my right hand slipped between us to rub her clit. I listened as her breath hitched, and her pussy squeezed me tight almost causing me to lose control.

"Come." It was all I could manage to utter as I reached the point of no return.

I bit down at the force of my orgasm. Brianna screamed, and her back arched. Her pussy spasmed around me as she found her own release.

Coming down from my high, I looked beneath me at the woman I hoped to love for the rest of my life. She was flushed, and her eyes were barely open. There was a bite mark on her right shoulder. Her hair was disheveled from my hands, and it was matted around her temples from our exertion.

I'd never seen anything more beautiful.

Chapter 28

Brianna

As promised, Cal and Jade came to pick me up on Friday afternoon for my appointment with Dr. Perkins. Cal was quiet, pensive, but Jade was full of questions. She wanted to know how things were going and jokingly commented that Cal's house wasn't the same without me. I had little doubt that it was different without me there, but that was most likely a good thing. The two of them had to rearrange their lives to accommodate me and my issues. Now they could go back to the way things were before I'd changed everything.

The two of them waited in the lobby while I went in for my appointment. I sat down, clasping my hands together and resting them on my legs.

She always started with the same question. "How are you today?"

"Good."

Instead of asking her typical follow-up question—*did anything happen this week you'd like to talk about?*—she remained silent. Her expression held curiosity.

I started to get anxious. "Is something wrong?"

Her eyes widened at my question, and then she must have realized her reaction and reined herself in. "No. I mean, it's just that I've never heard you say that you were 'good' before. Usually when I ask you how you're doing, you say you're fine. Today, not only did you give a different answer, but you also appear more open than I've ever seen you. Your shoulders aren't slumped, and you don't have your arms wrapped protectively around yourself."

"Oh." I didn't really know what to make of her statement. It wasn't something I'd thought about.

"Something you want to share?"

I pressed my lips together, pondering how much I should tell her.

"Remember, Anna, anything you say in here stays between us unless you decide otherwise."

It probably didn't matter. She'd find out eventually anyway since I wasn't planning to ever leave Stephan again if I could help it. Neither one of us liked being apart. "I moved back in with Stephan."

If I thought she looked wide-eyed with curiosity before, then she looked downright flabbergasted with this new information. "You're no longer living with your friends who are waiting out in the lobby?"

"No."

"I see. And when did this happen."

"Saturday."

Dr. Perkins scribbled something down on her notepad. "So you've been living with Stephan for the last six days?"

"Yes."

She was quiet for a long minute. "Will you tell me about it?"

So for the next twenty minutes, I explained as best I could to her what had led up to my moving back home. Of course, she knew the first part. She'd visited me at Cal's, and I'd seen her three times since I'd watched the news broadcast.

"It sounds as if you talked things out. And I'm proud of you, Anna. You communicated your feelings well."

I tugged at the material of my jeans and noticed there were several loose threads. "It's easier with Stephan."

She cocked her head to the side. "How so?"

"I don't know. It just is. He . . . he listens to me."

"And you don't always feel others do?"

Shrugging, I glanced over at the door. "My mom did. But then when I moved in with John, he never had time."

"What about your friends now? Do they listen to you?"

"Sometimes."

Dr. Perkins leaned back in her chair. "How does that make you feel when they don't listen to you?"

"It depends."

"On?"

"On what it's about."

She nodded. "Can you give me an example of something recently?"

"Cal wasn't happy about me moving back in with Stephan. He was really angry about it, and he wouldn't listen when I told him that it was all a misunderstanding and that Stephan had apologized."

"And how did that make you feel—that he wouldn't listen to you?"

I thought about it for a minute. How did it make me feel? "Hurt, and a little angry."

She sat forward, clasping her hands in front of her. "That's understandable, Anna. You made a choice for yourself, and he didn't respect that choice."

"But why? I understand that he doesn't like Stephan, but why can't he accept that I want to be with him?"

Dr. Perkins smiled. "I think that's something you're going to have to ask him."

On the way home, I thought about what Dr. Perkins said. She was right. Only Cal could answer my question. But was I ready to know the answer?

"We're here." Cal sounded less than thrilled.

When I remained in the car, Jade poked her head back into the vehicle. "Everything okay, Anna?"

I was looking at Cal, debating whether or not to take Dr. Perkins's advice, but I nodded, answering Jade's question. When I still didn't move, Jade slid in beside me, reaching for my hand. I took it, needing the support for what I was about to do.

"Cal?" The words came out in a whisper, but when he turned, I knew he'd heard me.

"Yeah?"

"Why . . ." I swallowed nervously. What if asking only made things worse?

He furrowed his brow in confusion. "Why what?"

Closing my eyes, I forced the words from my throat before I could suppress them. "Why don't you respect me?"

"What?" His question echoed loudly in the small space of the car. "Anna, what are you talking about?"

I held Jade's hand in a death grip and opened my eyes. "Y-you don't like that I moved back in with Stephan. Y-you don't respect my choice."

He sighed. "Anna, it's not that simple."

"Why not?"

Cal let out a frustrated breath. "It just isn't."

Dr. Perkins said I should explain to him how what he was doing made me feel, so that was what I did. "It hurts to know that you don't accept my decision."

His expression turned angry, and I cringed back in my seat a little. "Did that shrink tell you to say that?"

"Cal!" Jade scolded.

"She's never said anything before, so that woman had to put the idea in her head."

Jade wrapped her arm around my shoulders. "You don't know that."

"What's going on here?" My head whipped around as I saw Stephan approach the car.

Not thinking twice, I opened the car door and ran into his arms.

He caught me, soothing me not only with his hands but with the steady rise and fall of his chest as he held me. "Are you all right, Brianna?"

I nodded.

Cal and Jade exited the car, and I could hear their footsteps as they approached.

"Why is Brianna shaking like a leaf?"

I didn't have to glance up to know that Stephan was looking directly at Cal.

"That's none of your business, Coleman."

"Brianna is my business, which means whatever is making her upset is my business as well."

"Oh, that's right. You're back in the role of protector. Everything you've done gets swept under the rug as you swoop in and save the day."

Stephan didn't respond right away. He tightened his hold on me. "This isn't the place to have this conversation. You can either accompany us upstairs or leave. It's your choice."

Without waiting for a response, Stephan turned us both toward the elevators.

Stephan

I was trying hard to control my temper. Brianna was trembling beside me as we rode the elevator with Cal and Jade. For a moment, I'd thought maybe they were going to leave, but Jade followed us into the elevator and Cal reluctantly did so as well. I had no idea what he'd said to make her so upset, but given how closely people were watching me lately, having an argument in a parking garage—even a private parking garage—wasn't a good idea.

As soon as we walked into the condo, I pulled Brianna off to the side. Holding her face between my hands, I searched her eyes. "What number, Brianna?"

"Four."

"Can you tell me what happened?"

Cal and Jade approached from my left, but I ignored them for the time being.

"It's my fault," Brianna whispered.

"I don't recall asking whose fault it was." I raised one eyebrow, letting her know that I was still waiting on an answer to my question.

Brianna glanced down, and I tightened my hold. She snapped her gaze back up to meet mine. "I asked Cal why he didn't respect my decision to move back in with you. He got upset, and I started to panic."

I glared at Cal. The man knew how Brianna reacted to aggression.

"Don't look at me like that, Coleman. It wasn't like I meant to yell at her. She completely blindsided me. How was I supposed to react?"

Gritting my teeth, I forced myself to speak in a calm, even tone. "Perhaps you should try listening to her."

He snorted. "You mean like you?"

I lowered my hands and wrapped my arms around Brianna's waist, positioning her in front of me. Her back was against my chest, so that we were both facing Cal and Jade. This discussion had been brewing for a long time. "I always make it a priority to listen to what Brianna has to say. She's very observant, and when she shares something, it's usually important to her. Having lived in the same house with her for four months, I'd think you'd have learned that."

That only made him angrier, but I didn't care. No one else appeared to be willing to tell him the truth. He needed to get his head out of his ass.

"You know nothing about me, Coleman."

"I know that you have a temper that you let get the best of you more than you should. You don't like me, and under normal circumstances that wouldn't bother me. However, given how much we both seem to care about Brianna, we are going to have to find some way to put those differences aside for her sake. I know you don't like the fact that I'm wealthy, and what happened with your neighbor has clearly defined how you view what I am."

His face turned red. "She told you about that?"

"Brianna doesn't keep secrets from me."

"Unlike you from her."

"I don't have to explain myself to you, Ross. Brianna has accepted my apology, and that's all that matters."

Ross clenched and released his fists several times. He didn't like my answer and was trying to rein in his temper. I was feeling just as frustrated as he was, but over the years I'd learned to control my anger—most of the time. If I was honest with myself, though, Ross pushed my buttons more than most.

"Ask him your question again, sweetheart."

Brianna continued to shake, but she did as I instructed. "W-why don't you respect my decision?"

I'd expected to see Ross's anger flare again, but instead he sighed. "It's not that I don't respect your decision, Anna. I just don't think it was really *your* decision."

She tensed in my arms. "I don't understand."

It was my turn to sigh. I rested my chin on her shoulder and whispered in her ear. "He thinks I talked you into it."

Ross snorted. "Manipulated her would be more like it."

Brianna stood up straight, and I didn't have to see her face to know she was getting angry. There weren't many things that would set her off, but attacking me was one of them. "He didn't. He asked me to move back in, and I said yes."

"Of course he did."

"You don't believe me." She sounded sad.

He was quick to try and correct her. "No. That's not what I meant. I believe that *you* believe that's what happened."

She tilted her head to the side. "That doesn't make any sense."

"Gah!" Ross pulled at his hair in frustration. "Anna, people like him . . ." Ross nodded in my direction. "They're experts at manipulation. They know how to get people to do what they want them to do and make it seem like it was their idea."

"He's not like that."

"How do you know, Anna?" Ross gestured to me with his right hand. "How do you even know what he told you about that woman is true? Have you talked to her? Has she confirmed his story? For all you know the baby really is his and he's just covering his tracks."

Brianna shook her head violently. "No. He wouldn't lie to me."

"But how do you *know* that?"

It was Brianna's turn to sound defeated. "I just do."

I hated seeing her like this. Kissing her cheek, I hugged her tighter. Sarah had been begging me to set up a meeting between her and Brianna, but the timing was never right.

No one spoke for several minutes. We seemed to have reached a stalemate.

As the silence continued, Ross seemed to lose his conviction. "I don't know what you want from me."

"Trust me," Brianna whispered.

I was so proud of her. She was speaking her mind even though I could feel doing so caused her heart to pound rapidly in her chest.

"I do trust you."

She shook her head. "You don't."

At this point, I was surprised he didn't stomp out. He did turn and walk away, but he only went as far as the couch. Ross sat down and held his head in his hands. I almost felt sorry for him.

Brianna twisted in my arms. She gazed up at me, her eyes pleading. "Should I go to him?"

I wanted to say no, but logic won, and I dropped my arms, releasing her. "Do what you need to do, Brianna. I'll wait here."

As I stood by and watched Brianna walk away from me to go comfort another man, I had to tamp down my jealousy. I knew she didn't feel that way about him, but it was instinctual, not logical.

"He really does care about her, you know."

I didn't take my eyes off Brianna when I responded to Jade's statement. "That's the only reason I allowed her to go with him in the first place. If I didn't think he cared, I wouldn't have let her leave."

"You know when you make statements like that it only solidifies Cal's position."

This time I did glance over at her briefly. "I will do whatever it takes to protect Brianna. I won't apologize for that."

We both watched as Ross and Brianna talked on the other side of the room. They kept their volume low, so other than a few words here and there, we couldn't hear what was being said.

I was attempting to read Brianna's lips when Jade broke through the silence with her next question—one I wasn't expecting. "How long have you been a Dom?"

"Almost six years."

"And this Sarah . . ."

"Sarah was my first submissive. We were together for almost a year and a half."

"Why did you break up?"

"She graduated and moved away."

"So you didn't want a long-distance relationship?"

Although I didn't mind explaining my relationship to Jade—I liked Jade —I wasn't willing to divert my attention from Brianna. Ross might mean well, but he had a tendency to do things that sent her into a panic. "Our relationship was never traditional, so it wasn't an issue."

Wanting to redirect the conversation away from my past relationship with Sarah, I decided to ask her a question. "Do you think Ross will ever be able to accept our relationship?"

She sighed. "I don't know. Maybe."

"She's right, you know. I would never hurt her. Not like he thinks I would."

"I sort of figured as much. The few times I've seen you with her, you've always been affectionate and loving . . . gentle even." She turned to face me, and I looked over to meet her gaze. "But just to be clear, if you ever do hurt her, I'll help Cal kick your ass."

Her ultra-serious expression caused me to chuckle. "I think you're safe there. If I ever hurt her, there would be a line of people waiting to do me serious harm. My friends Lily and Logan would be at the front of the line."

Ross asked Brianna a question I couldn't hear, and she nodded. The next thing I knew, they were hugging. Brianna smiled, and practically skipped back to my side.

"Feeling better?"

She nodded.

Ross joined our little group and, in another turn of events, held out his hand. I reached around Brianna and took his offering. "I'm still not sure about this whole relationship between you two, but as long as you don't prevent Anna from seeing us, I'll agree to keep my opinions to myself."

"Thank you."

We both dropped our arms, and I rested my hands on Brianna's shoulders.

"We should probably go." Ross focused on Brianna. "I have a meeting next week, but Jade will pick you up Wednesday and take you to your appointment."

"That won't be necessary. Brianna wants me to meet Dr. Perkins, and I'm taking Wednesday off."

Ross frowned but didn't argue. He looked pointedly at Brianna. "We'll call you."

Brianna nodded, and we saw them out. I doubted all was mended, but it was a start. As with any relationship, it needed to be built brick by brick. Like it or not, Ross and I were in each other's lives because of our love of Brianna. We were going to have to figure out how to function in each other's space without constantly trying to mark our territory. Brianna had made her choice. It was up to both of us to accept it.

Chapter 29

Stephan

Nearly two days had passed since Brianna's confrontation with Ross upon her return from her therapist. We'd had several conversations between that time—most of them revolving around my relationship with Sarah. No matter how many times I tried to reassure her that the feelings I had for Sarah couldn't compare to the ones I had for her, she still had doubts. I didn't think it was that she didn't believe me, but more that she didn't believe that much in herself. Either way it was disheartening.

After spending some time answering e-mails, I came downstairs to see how her preparations for dinner were coming, but I didn't see her anywhere. She was supposed to have gotten dinner started and then spent some time reading. The last thirty-six hours had been more stressful for her than what I would have liked, and I had a feeling dinner was going to be even more so for her.

"Brianna?"

She poked her head up over the counter.

I leaned to the side so that I could get a better look at her. She was kneeling on the floor. Her hair was pulled back, but I could see strands that were plastered against her face from sweat. This was not preparing dinner. Nor was it reading.

Taking a step closer, I zeroed in on a bucket and what looked like a scrub brush in her hand. I frowned. "Stop what you're doing and come over here."

She froze, and her gaze remained focused on the floor as she rushed over to where I was standing.

I stood with my arms crossed as she waited about a foot in front of me. Yesterday during one of our conversations, I'd suggested inviting Sarah over for dinner so that Brianna could meet her. Brianna had agreed but also asked if Lily could come, too. It was a simple request, and I was thrilled she'd spoken up. I'd called Logan right away and invited him and Lily to join us this evening.

What I hadn't expected was for Brianna to go into some sort of cleaning overdrive today. At first, I didn't think much of it. Brianna liked to clean— she'd done so almost every day when she'd lived with me before. I'd made some phone calls while she went around the house tidying up this morning. As far as I was concerned, aside from dinner, that was the end of it. Over lunch, I'd complimented her on the good job she'd done and commented that she could spend the rest of the afternoon taking it easy. Apparently Brianna had different ideas.

She stood before me with her hands behind her back and her head down, looking guilty.

"Look at me." I waited until she looked up, although she didn't lift her head. "What were you doing just now?"

"Um."

"Brianna." I knew perfectly well what she was doing, but I wanted her to tell me.

"Cleaning the floor, Sir."

If I wasn't so upset, I may have found her reaction to my displeasure slightly amusing. As it was, the fact that she knew what she was doing wouldn't make me happy only irritated me more. She'd been going nonstop for the last six hours. Sarah, Lily, and Logan were coming for dinner, not the queen of England. While I'd not made her afternoon activities a command, I'd thought I'd been clear that I didn't want her to spend it on more cleaning. "On your hands and knees?"

"I didn't want to miss anything," she whispered.

I didn't say anything for several seconds. She hunched her shoulders and lowered her gaze. "Go kneel on the floor by my chair, and stay there until I say otherwise."

She did as she was instructed.

Once she was kneeling beside my chair, I walked into the kitchen where Brianna had been cleaning. There was a scrub brush, a bucket full of soapy water, and a towel lying on the floor. I shook my head, dumped the water, and put everything away. She was overcompensating. I understood her anxiety, but I wasn't going to allow her to keep this up.

Confident things were back to normal in the kitchen, I strolled into the living room and took a seat in my chair. Motioning for Brianna to move closer, I guided her head onto my lap. Laying my hand on top of her head, I began stroking her hair. Little by little, I felt her relax.

Brianna was stressing herself out over this meeting. I wasn't exactly sure why. "Tell me why you were cleaning the floor."

She released a deep breath and snuggled deeper into my lap. "I wanted everything to be perfect."

I thought about that for a minute as I looked around. Everything was in its place. She'd vacuumed and dusted earlier today. I had to be missing something. "Why do you think everything needs to be perfect?"

"I don't know."

"Yes you do."

It took several minutes for her to answer. "She was your first. She took care of you. I wanted . . . I wanted her to see that I could take care of you, too."

Her confession caused me to pause, and when I stopped moving my hand through her hair, she tensed up. I resumed my motion. "Relax."

It took some time, but eventually she did relax.

I sat there and thought about what she'd said before responding. "Maybe I didn't explain this as well as I should have. My relationship with Sarah—if you want to call it that—wasn't anything like what we have. It can't even be compared. The only times she took care of me, as you put it, was on the weekends when we were in Dom and sub roles. Even then, it was relegated to what we'd agreed upon. She never went out of her way to do something special for me unless it was purely based on our friendship alone."

Lifting her head, I turned Brianna to face me. "There was no love. Sarah never took pleasure in serving me outside the bedroom."

"She didn't take care of you?" Brianna looked doubtful.

I rubbed my thumb along her cheek. "No. Not in the way you do."

Brianna was quiet as she processed this. I'd thought I'd made it clear to her after last night's talk that Sarah and I had only been friends with benefits. Granted, I'd focused more on generalities than details. I'd explained how we met, our friendship, and how we'd decided to start playing together. Sarah and I trusted and respected each other. That was all. There were no other feelings involved other than physical gratification.

"Talk to me."

"She let you do things to her that you can't do with me."

I cocked my head to the side, observing her expression, and something dawned on me. "Brianna, are you jealous?"

It took her a minute to answer, and when she did, she looked as if she were waiting for an anvil to drop. "Yes."

Sighing, I leaned down and guided her up into my arms. Once she was situated in my lap, I took hold of her face and brought it directly in front of mine so that our noses were touching. "You have nothing, and no one, to be jealous of, sweetheart. I love you. And I know you're worried about the sexual stuff, but you don't have to be. We'll figure it out along the way."

"But you could do that stuff with her. Maybe . . ." She pressed her lips tightly together, and I had a feeling I wasn't going to like the next words out of her mouth. "Maybe I could do the stuff you want."

The pulse in her neck raced under my fingers, and I could see the fear in her eyes even as she spoke the words.

"No."

Instead of calming her down, my response only made her heart rate speed up and her breathing become shallower. "No?"

"Take a deep breath, Brianna."

She closed her eyes for a moment and did as I said.

"Another one."

This time, she watched me as she inhaled a lungful of air and released it.

"Good girl. I want you to keep breathing slow and deep, understand?"

She nodded.

"Are you dissatisfied with our sex?"

Her eyes widened. "No!"

I smiled. "Good. Neither am I."

"But . . ."

"But?"

Brianna glanced down before meeting my gaze again. "But you want more."

"In time, yes. We can take it slow, though, and we'll talk about it ahead of time." I brushed the hair away from her face, and made sure she was looking at me before I said my next words. "I plan on having you in my life —and my bed—for a very long time, Brianna. There will be plenty of time for us to try new things together."

"You shouldn't have to wait for me."

"Shouldn't that be my decision?"

She went quiet. "What if I want to?"

Although I knew Brianna was nowhere near ready for any type of intense play, I decided to humor her. "Okay, what would you like to do?"

I saw the wheels turning in her head. She knew I'd want an answer after she'd laid down the proverbial gauntlet.

Suddenly her eyes lit up. "The rope."

"You want me to tie you up?" Although I was a bit skeptical, I would hear her out.

She nodded minutely. "You like that, don't you?"

"Sometimes I do, yes. And how would you like me to bind you?"

"However you want."

"Hmm." I needed to make a phone call.

Placing a hard kiss on Brianna's lips, I leaned back, separating us a little. "Do you have everything prepped for dinner?"

She nodded.

I'd told her to keep it simple, so she was making some sort of pasta dish with salad. The last thing I wanted on top of everything else was Brianna spending hours today in the kitchen. She needed to decompress, and reading always did that for her.

"Good. I want you to go to your room and take a nice long bath for the next hour. Take your book with you, and you can spend the time reading. After that, you may return to the kitchen. That should still give you plenty of time to finish before everyone arrives."

Brianna looked down, her guilty expression returning. "Yes, Sir."

I patted her leg, and we both stood. Bending down, I gave her a soft, lingering kiss, which she readily returned. I was tempted to change my plans and spend the next hour relaxing her in a very different way, but I held strong. Somehow.

Standing to my full height, I waited as Brianna left the room.

Once I could no longer see her, I headed upstairs to call Logan. Since I'd had all my BDSM items removed from my condo, I didn't have any of my Shibari books. If Brianna was really interested in giving rope-play a try, then I was going to do this with as much forethought as possible. I wasn't going to let her go into this blind. The last thing either of us needed was for her to have one of her panic attacks while she was bound.

I knew it might still happen, even with the preparation ahead of time, but I was hoping the extra effort would pay off. Maybe we would both be pleasantly surprised.

Brianna

As instructed, I spent an hour in the bathtub reading—or trying to read. I only made it through one chapter, and it wasn't a very long one. The book was interesting enough, but I couldn't focus on it. My entire body vibrated with anxiety over meeting Sarah—Stephan's ex-girlfriend.

I knew he said they were only friends, and aside from their sexual relationship in college, that was all they had ever been. What I couldn't understand was why? Stephan was wonderful. He was kind and loving, and he went out of his way to help others. Of course she would want to be with him. Wouldn't she?

When my hour was up, I bolted out of the bathtub. As quickly as I could, I dried off and put on clean clothes. Stephan had said not to dress up, and I didn't want to disappoint him again, so I selected a pair of jeans and a nice T-shirt.

Dressed, I made a beeline for the kitchen. Stephan was nowhere to be seen, so I assumed he was upstairs. Something major was going on at the foundation with some money that had been stolen. He'd explained a little of it to me, and it sounded like a huge mess. Since I'd been home, he'd spent more time on his laptop than I'd ever seen before. I understood, though. He was the boss, and he wanted to make sure everything was handled properly.

Most of the time he'd disappear for an hour or two upstairs after dinner, and while he was gone, he'd give me some sort of assignment in my journal. Sometimes it was easy, like writing about the one place in the world I most wanted to visit. Other times it would be things prompted by either my previous journal entries or our talks. Those were usually harder, like Friday night when I'd written about what happened with Cal that afternoon. He'd wanted me to think about what I might have done had Jade not been with me and if he'd not shown up when he did. I wasn't sure if I would have been brave enough to say anything if Jade hadn't been there.

As I started assembling dinner, I thought over my first week back with Stephan. Some things had changed, but most hadn't. We'd had sex every night so far, but it had been pretty tame. He was still in control of everything, but it was almost as if he were waiting for me to break at any moment. I missed the new things he used to do to me. Although my fear always reared its ugly head, I knew deep down Stephan wouldn't do anything to hurt me, and I wanted to do these things for him.

That was why I'd brought up the rope. I couldn't forget how his eyes lit up months ago when I'd mentioned it. He wanted to tie me up, and I had to admit that I was curious. Everything else was different with him, and I was hoping that would be, too.

At ten minutes to five, Stephan came down the stairs smiling. I turned my head to smile back at him before returning to my task. He walked over to where I was standing and wrapped his arms around my waist from behind, burying his face in my neck. "Something smells good."

"Thank you."

He hummed. "Anything you need me to do?"

I shook my head. For the last half hour, I'd been trying not to think about our dinner guests. Well, except for Lily. I was excited to see her. I'd talked to her once on the phone this week, but she was as busy as Stephan. I hadn't realized the theft had occurred in her department until she told me.

Stephan tightened his arms around me as his lips brushed from my shoulder up to my ear. "Are you still nervous?"

"Yes."

Suddenly he was moving and taking me with him.

We didn't go far, only a few feet. "Let's see what we can do about that, shall we? Do you have anything cooking that will burn in the next ten minutes?"

"No." My voice was shaky. I wasn't sure if it was more from nerves or excitement.

"Good. Place your hands on the counter in front of you and keep them there."

Leaning forward, I did what I was told.

Stephan still had his arms around my waist, but they didn't stay there for long. He trailed his hands up my torso until he was cupping my breasts. Then, before I knew what was happening, he pulled down both my shirt and the cups of my bra, exposing me. It wasn't cold inside the condo, but my nipples reacted as if I'd walked out naked into freezing temperatures. He took hold of my breasts and began massaging them roughly. I closed my eyes and moaned. I loved when he touched me like this.

"Do you like that?" His breath was warm against my ear, but it made me shiver.

"Yes."

Moments later, I sucked in a deep breath as his fingers moved forward to pinch and pull my nipples. "That's it. You like that, don't you? I bet you're wet for me, aren't you, Brianna?"

He pulled harder, and a surge of pleasure went to the spot between my legs.

"Hmm. Speechless, are you? I suppose I'll have to check for myself, then." Before my brain could register what he was doing, he removed his hands from my breasts and was lowering my jeans.

I opened my mouth, but words left my brain as he thrust two fingers inside me and began pumping vigorously.

The only sounds were my breathing and of his hand slapping against my very wet sex. I could feel my climax building, and I closed my eyes, trying to hold on. He'd not given me permission to come.

It wasn't long until I was teetering on the edge, and to make matters worse, he'd returned his left hand to my breasts. In an almost unbearable rhythm, he was alternating his attention between them—twisting and pulling my nipples. I bit down on the side of my cheek.

"Please."

"Please what, Brianna? Tell me what you want."

I gasped as his thumb grazed my clit. "Please. May I come, Sir?"

He licked up my neck as he continued his assault. "Not. Quite. Yet."

No? I was going to cry. I didn't know how much longer I could keep my orgasm at bay. Every muscle in my body was shaking . . . begging for release.

I felt him graze his teeth along my collarbone, and I almost lost it right then and there. "Don't you dare, Brianna. Not until I say."

Shaking my head, I tried to find something else to think about other than what he was doing to me. It was the only way.

Nothing worked, though. Everything that came to mind led straight back to Stephan and, consequently, what he was doing to me.

There was a noise in the distance, but I couldn't tell what it was. I was too lost in feeling.

Without warning, Stephan picked up the pace and pinched my clit at the same time he tugged hard on my nipple. "Come. Come now."

He didn't have to tell me twice. I came. Hard. My voice echoed throughout the condo.

When I could finally think clearly again, Stephan had one arm holding me up. His other hand was at his mouth as he sucked on his fingers. He had a huge grin on his face. "Feeling better?"

"What?" I had no idea what he was talking about.

He chuckled.

"I'll take that as a yes." He helped me rearrange my clothes. "Do you think you can stand on your own now?"

I nodded.

Stephan looked extremely amused for some reason.

He leaned in and kissed me, plunging his tongue deep inside my mouth. I could taste myself on him and realized the fingers he'd had in his mouth must have been the ones he'd had inside me. He'd been licking himself clean.

When he broke the kiss, that was when I heard it. The doorbell. My face flushed with heat as I realized that at least one of our guests had arrived.

Had they heard anything? Would they know?

As if he could read my mind, Stephan brought my forehead to rest against his. "I love you. Remember that."

Without uttering another word, he went to get the door.

Chapter 30

Stephan
I had to admit, part of my reasoning for bringing Brianna to orgasm
right as the doorbell rang announcing our guests was purely for my own
sadistic pleasure. There was an added benefit in that she'd been wound
tight with nerves over meeting Sarah, and I'd wanted to distract her.
Nothing did that faster than arousing her. It was also a direct reminder to
her that I was in control, and she needed to let go and allow me to guide her
through tonight.

Brianna was flustered and flushed. I couldn't help but chuckle to myself
as I opened the door. All three of our guests stared back at me—Logan with
a knowing smirk not unlike my own, and Lily and Sarah both with more
cautious expressions. My soundproofing may have muffled the noise, but
given the way Brianna had screamed, I doubted it had drowned out the
sound entirely. From the looks on their faces, I was right.

"You're right on time. Come on in."

As I took their coats and put them in the closet, I glanced over at Brianna.
She was busying herself with taking the food out of the oven. Not once had
she looked this way.

"Can I get everyone something to drink? We have iced tea, water, milk,
and lemonade."

After taking everyone's drink order, I strolled back into the kitchen. I
removed the items I needed from the refrigerator and set them on the
counter before pressing myself up against Brianna from behind. She stilled.
I knew she could feel my still semihard cock pressing against her ass.
"Later I will have you take care of this, but right now, I want you to
remember what just happened. I am in control. Stop worrying about the
unknown and enjoy the evening. Can you do that for me?"

"I will try, Sir."

I slid my hand suggestively over her abdomen. "You'll have to do better
than that, Brianna, or I'll have to take you into my bedroom and give you
another reminder."

She swallowed hard but didn't comment.

"How long until dinner's ready?"

"About five minutes." Her voice squeaked slightly, which only made me smile wider.

Kissing her shoulder, I stepped away before I forgot we had company and took her right then and there. "Let me know when it's done, and I'll help you bring it into the dining room."

Carrying the glasses into the living room where everyone was waiting, I left Brianna to finish. Logan grinned as I handed him a glass of iced tea. "Misjudge the time earlier?"

I smiled back at him. "Not at all."

He shook his head and took a drink.

When I gave Lily her water, she looked concerned. "Should I go say something? I don't want her to think we're avoiding her."

"I think that's a great idea. She's a little frazzled."

Lily stood and smacked my arm playfully. "No wonder. She's not used to the sadistic little games you Doms like to play."

Both Logan and I laughed, which caused Brianna to glance in our direction. She appeared to have calmed down some, but there was still too much tension in her shoulders for my liking. I'd give her some time, but if she was still tense by the end of dinner, I would be following through on my promise. Brianna needed to learn to let go. We were among friends tonight. Nothing was going to happen to her. There was no reason for her to be nervous.

I watched from my chair as Lily hugged Brianna and asked if she could help with anything. Once I was sure Brianna was relatively fine, I turned my attention back to Logan and Sarah.

"She's not thrilled about my being here, is she?"

I took a sip of my water and answered Sarah. "She's nervous, but Brianna is always anxious about meeting new people. It doesn't help that you and I have a history, though. Or that the two of us were recently splashed on the front page of the society section together."

Sarah frowned. "She sees me as a threat?"

"In a way."

"I don't want her to feel uncomfortable."

"Brianna will be fine. And besides, she wanted to meet you as well. End of discussion."

The frown didn't leave Sarah's face, but she didn't say anything more.

A few minutes later, Brianna tiptoed up beside me. "Dinner's ready."

I reached out to take her hand as I stood, pulling her against my side. "Brianna, this is Sarah Evans. Sarah, I'd like you to meet my girlfriend, Brianna Reeves."

Sarah offered her hand, and with only a slight hesitation, Brianna took it. "It's nice to finally meet you, Brianna. Stephan talks about you all the time."

Brianna looked up at me, seemingly shocked at this information.

I hugged her closer. "Don't look so surprised. Why wouldn't I tell my friends about the woman I love?"

Instead of answering my question, she looked down at the floor, her cheeks turning a beautiful shade of pink. "Dinner's ready."

"Thank you." I kissed the top of her head before releasing her and addressing Logan and Sarah—Lily had already made her way into the dining room. "If you want to take your seats at the table, we'll bring the food over."

Brianna walked back into the kitchen, and I followed her. We gathered the food and brought it to the dining room table. Pulling out Brianna's chair for her, I waited for her to sit. She did so but not before looking up at me, questioning. When we were out in public, I always held her chair for her, but this was the first time I'd done so at home.

Everyone piled food on their plates and began eating. I smiled when I heard the pleasantly surprised sounds coming from everyone. Brianna was a great cook, and I was blessed that she was all mine.

Logan was the first to speak up. "This is amazing, Brianna. You'll have to give me the recipe."

Everyone else hummed their agreement.

Brianna kept her gaze on her plate. "Thank you."

Her shy response was to be expected. I was happy she'd answered him at all.

Reaching over beneath the table, I squeezed her thigh. She looked up at me, unsure until she saw that I was smiling. Brianna smiled back and then went back to her food.

It seemed like it was up to me to get the conversation rolling. "How do you like your apartment, Sarah?"

She glanced over at Brianna before answering. I was hoping as the evening wore on everyone would stop being so on edge. "I love it. In a lot of ways it's like my apartment in St. Louis, only smaller."

Lily speared a piece of her chicken. "Any idea how long you're staying in Minneapolis?"

Brianna froze.

"Not really. I need to decide soon, though. I'm already six months along, and in another month or so I doubt I'm going to feel like traveling."

Lily shook her head. "No, you probably won't."

"Have you considered going back to California to have the baby? I'm sure your parents would love it." As I spoke, I kept Brianna in my peripheral vision. Even though she had her head down, I knew she was paying attention to every word.

"I don't know about that."

"What do you mean? Why wouldn't they be?" I knew I was being demanding, but Sarah's parents were wonderful people. They'd been devastated when Sarah and I broke up. I still kept in touch with them, even after all these years. There was nothing in my knowledge of them that would make me think they wouldn't be completely welcoming to Sarah.

Sarah squirmed in her seat. "Um. Well . . . I haven't exactly *told* them yet."

"Told them?" I paused, sure that I had to be misunderstanding. "You mean you haven't told them you're pregnant?"

She shook her head.

"Why not?"

"Look, can we not talk about this?"

"Not a chance. Why haven't you told your parents, Sarah? You just said yourself you're already six months along. Don't you think they should know?"

She threw down her napkin and stood. "Yes, they should, damn it, but I don't know how to tell them. Derrick was the first boyfriend since you that they liked. What am I supposed to tell them, huh? They're going to want to know where he is—why we aren't together anymore. Am I supposed to tell them he dumped me because I'm a sick freak who likes to be dominated in the bedroom? Huh?"

Before any of us could respond, Sarah bolted toward the door.

I pushed my chair back, ready to go after her, but Lily stopped me. "Let me go. You stay here with Brianna."

This was certainly not how I saw dinner going. Maybe I shouldn't have pushed it, but I couldn't believe Sarah hadn't told her parents. I understood everything she'd said and that it would be difficult, but I still knew her parents would stand by her no matter what. That was the kind of people they were.

Brianna reached out to take hold of my hand. "Are you okay?"

Logan excused himself and disappeared into the kitchen to refill his iced tea.

Smiling, I squeezed her hand and laced our fingers together. "I'm fine, sweetheart. You?"

"I'm okay."

"Good."

"Sir?"

At the look in her eyes, I wanted to pull her closer, but I didn't. "Yes?"

"Sarah's boyfriend left her because she's a submissive?"

I sighed. "Basically."

Moisture appeared in her eyes.

"What's wrong, sweetheart?"

"If he loved her, why wouldn't he love all of her?"

Leaning in, I rested my free hand against the side of her face. "I don't know. Sometimes it doesn't work that way. Sometimes you find out things about a person that you can't live with. I guess her being a submissive was one of those things for him."

A tear slid down her cheek. "That's not fair."

I wiped the moisture away with the pad of my thumb. "No, it's not, but remember that you didn't think you could be what I needed either. Maybe it was the same for him. We don't know what he was thinking."

Brianna

How could someone do that? I mean, if he really loved her, then how could he have left her because of how she liked to have sex? I didn't understand.

Stephan said it wasn't all that different than what I struggled with—not being enough for him—but I didn't see it as the same thing at all. My issues were because of my past. My doubts lingered only because of that. It wasn't the same.

Stephan tried to comfort me as best he could, but my heart was breaking for a woman who not an hour ago I was jealous of.

Logan rejoined us at the table, but I hardly noticed as the door opened and Sarah and Lily reentered the condo. Sarah looked as if she'd been crying.

They came back to the table and took their seats. I knew I had to say something. "Sarah?"

She looked in my direction.

"I'm sorry."

Sarah looked confused.

"Your boyfriend shouldn't have left you. He was wrong to do that."

"That's sweet of you." She smiled, but there was a sad quality to it. "I'll be okay. It's just an adjustment."

This time, Logan spoke up. "I'm with Brianna on this one. What he did was harsh. I get this lifestyle isn't for everyone, but leaving you high and dry after finding out you're pregnant? That's a special kind of low."

"He doesn't know."

Everyone at the table seemed startled by this news except Stephan. He must have already known.

Lily was the one to voice what was on all of our minds. "You haven't told him?"

Sarah shook her head. "No. He stormed out two weeks before I found out, and I couldn't bring myself to tell him. I was afraid he would think it was some kind of a ploy to get him back, but it's not . . . it wasn't. We were using protection. I'm not sure what happened." She took a deep breath. "It doesn't matter at this point. What's done is done. I can't change it."

"You should still tell him. I know I'd want to know if it were mine."

She gave Logan a hard stare. "Even if you thought the woman carrying your child was disgusting?"

He nodded. "Even then. He has a right to know."

Sarah sighed, deflated. "I know he does. And I'll tell him. Eventually. Not until after the baby is born, though. I don't think I could take another blowout with him while my hormones are such a mess."

Stephan squeezed my hand to get my attention. "Didn't you bake a cake earlier?"

I nodded. "Should I get it now?"

He smiled, and turned to address the rest of the table. "Excuse us."

Standing, Stephan helped me from my chair and led me into the kitchen. He removed the cake from the refrigerator and placed it gently on the counter before retrieving five plates from the cabinet. Following his prompt, I took the cake knife, along with five forks from the drawer. Before I could start cutting the cake, however, Stephan halted my movement. I met his gaze. "Are you all right?"

"Yes."

Smiling, he bent down to place a chaste kiss on my lips. "You are amazing, Brianna. I love you."

I smiled up at him. "I love you, too."

We worked together to cut and plate the cake and then to serve it. Everyone raved about it just as they had the baked pasta I'd made. It was embarrassing, but it made me feel good at the same time.

After dessert, Sarah politely thanked me for dinner and then said she needed to get back to her apartment before it got too late. It wasn't much after eight, but I think she was still feeling awkward about the earlier conversation. I understood why everyone felt she should tell the guy, but opening yourself up like that was scary. The only one I felt comfortable doing that with was Stephan, and that was because I trusted him completely. It didn't sound as if this guy had earned Sarah's trust.

"Thank you for allowing me to meet you, Brianna. You have a great man, and he loves you very much."

I shifted my weight, a little uncomfortable with her comment.

She smiled. "You're shy, too. I'm sure Stephan likes that as well. He was never big on my bratty nature."

Stephan wrapped his arm around my waist as he came up beside me. "No, I wasn't."

Sarah looked behind us to where Logan and Lily were sitting in the living room. "It was nice to see you both again as well. Hopefully we can all get together again before I leave."

A few minutes later, Sarah left, and Stephan and I joined Lily and Logan in the living room. I sat in Stephan's lap as I usually did, while they sat side by side on the couch. Logan had his arm around Lily's shoulders as she leaned into him. They looked like any other couple.

"Do they still have you traveling?"

Logan whispered something in Lily's ear before he responded to Stephan's question. "Unfortunately. The only upside is that I've been able to rearrange my schedule to where I'm home most weekends."

"I finally get to see him." Lily placed her left hand on his chest and rubbed suggestively along the buttons. I shuddered, remembering the last time I'd seen them together at their apartment.

"You okay?" Stephan's voice was soft in my ear.

"Yes."

He ran the back of his hand down the side of my face. "What is it?"

"I'm just . . . remembering. The last time."

Stephan paused for a long moment and then nodded. He tightened his hold on me and kissed my temple. "It's the four of us talking tonight, Brianna. Nothing else."

I nodded and cuddled closer to him.

We talked for another two hours . . . or they talked. I said a few things here and there, but most of their conversation was about work and the upcoming holidays. It was hard to believe Thanksgiving was just around the corner. I felt almost certain Stephan and I would be spending the day with his aunt and uncle. They were Stephan's family, so it only made sense.

At ten thirty, Logan and Lily said their good-byes. As they were leaving, I noticed Lily slipped Stephan what looked to be a book from her purse. He glanced down at it and smiled, thanking them. I'd hugged Lily good-bye before they walked to the door and went to clean up the kitchen. Being close to Logan still made me nervous, even though I didn't think he'd do anything.

Stephan closed the door. He lay whatever Lily had given him on the table where he kept his keys and walked over to where I was standing. Taking both my hands in his, he pulled me to him until my chest was touching his. "You did well tonight. I'm very proud of you."

I buried my face in his chest, inhaling his scent. "Thank you."

"Is everything off in the kitchen?"

"Yes. I already put everything away, too."

"Good girl." He kissed the top of my hair and guided one of my hands between us to the bulge in his pants. "I do believe I mentioned a slight problem I had earlier needing some attention."

I swallowed, excited. All thoughts of the book left my mind as I concentrated on the feel of him beneath my hand.

Without a word, Stephan removed my hand and started toward his bedroom. I followed, eager to find out what was going to happen.

He didn't stop until we reached the bathroom, where he immediately began removing our clothes. There was no finesse to it—as he removed an article of clothing, he tossed it haphazardly to the side.

When we were both naked, he led me into the large shower. He turned on the spray and proceeded to wash me as he normally would. There were no words, no conversation—only action. If it were anyone but Stephan, I would have been scared to death by his silence.

Finished, he handed me the body wash and the sponge . . . again with no instruction. I took it and went about my usual task of washing him. His penis stood fully erect the entire time, and it bobbed excitedly as I lowered myself to the floor to wash his legs and feet.

On my way back up, he placed a firm hand on my head. I looked up, thinking I must have done something wrong, but he shook his head. The heat in his eyes caused the muscles between my legs to clench.

With one hand he held the base of his penis, while with the other he placed pressure on the back of my head, telling me without words what he desired. I opened my mouth and took him between my lips. He groaned and applied more pressure.

This was the first time Stephan had allowed me to do this for him since I'd moved back in, and I didn't take the privilege lightly. I called upon all the skills I'd learned at the hands of those evil men to bring Stephan pleasure, sucking and licking his shaft.

Soon both his hands were tangled in my hair, and I knew he was close. His chest moved rapidly with each exaggerated breath, and he began pumping his hips in rhythm with my movements.

He twisted the strands of my hair in his fists and tugged. Pain shot down my skull, but all it did was add to my joy. Stephan was on the edge. He was experiencing amazing pleasure, and I was giving it to him.

"Swallow every last drop."

It was the only warning I received before he thrust deep into my mouth, his penis hitting the back of my throat. He tightened his hold on my hair even more as he reared back. His back arched, and I tasted his cum as it slid down my throat.

Following his instructions, I continued to lick and suck until he stilled.

He staggered back, slowly easing his hold on my hair.

I looked up, smiling. The pride I felt radiated off me.

Stephan smiled back down at me. He caressed my lower lip lovingly with his thumb, and I realized then that never in my life had I felt as happy as I did at that moment.

Chapter 31

Stephan
The alarm woke me way too early for my liking on Monday morning. The blowjob Brianna had given me the previous night sent me into some sort of a sleeping coma. I didn't think I moved once during the night.

While Brianna was making breakfast, I took the Shibari book Logan and Lily had brought last night up to the study and locked it in one of the drawers. I didn't want Brianna to find it before we'd had a chance to go through it together. Even though she'd expressed an interest in having me tie her up, I didn't know how she'd react to seeing the pictures displaying people in various states of bondage. From what she'd told me, Ian wasn't a fan of rope, but that didn't mean she'd never been bound. I knew for a fact that she'd been suspended with ropes while Daren caned her, and that had been a terrifying experience for her.

After a quiet breakfast, I kissed Brianna good-bye and drove to the office. Work was beginning to calm down. Erik was still combing through a few files, but for the most part everything surrounding the theft was wrapped up —including the three culprits. Greta, Megan, and Frankie had all been relegated to working off their transgressions and repaying every dime they stole. In the end, what Greta had stolen was a drop in the bucket to what her grandson and Megan had taken. Unfortunately, she'd most likely be working her portion off for much longer than they would since most of what they'd taken had been sitting in a bank account, unused. It was only a matter of having them close the account and give back the money.

Greta, however, had used hers to help pay her mother's doctor bills. I felt bad about that, so I'd been trying to find a way to help her. Unfortunately, I couldn't do it directly given the hows and whys. It wouldn't look right for me to bail her out after what she'd done, which was why I'd turned to my aunt. She had no direct connection to the foundation anymore since Richard held her spot on the board.

"So you believe her story, Stephan? The money was truly spent to pay her mom's bills?"

I nodded even though Diane couldn't see me as I leaned back in my office chair and looked out the bank of windows. "I do. Michael's looked into her bank accounts and the transactions she made right after the money was transferred. It's all accounted for."

"All right. Let me see what I can do. I'd like to meet this woman. Maybe you could arrange for her to come to the house for lunch after the holiday."

It wasn't as if I hadn't known Thanksgiving was fast approaching. I did. But with everything else that was going on, I'd intentionally pushed it to the back of my mind. Now it was only days away. "That shouldn't be a problem. At this point, I think Greta would agree to just about anything."

"Remorse will only work in her favor. I'll check my schedule and get back with you on what days will work for me. Now, speaking of Thanksgiving, what time should I expect you Thursday?"

"I need to speak to Brianna first, and then I'll let you know, okay?"

"Brianna? Are you two back together, then?" The excitement in her voice was unmistakable.

I chuckled. "Yes. She moved back in with me a little over a week ago."

My aunt squealed like a little girl on the other end of the phone, and I had to hold the receiver away from my ear.

"I take it you approve." I couldn't suppress my smile.

"Of course I approve. You have to bring her with you, Stephan. I won't take no for an answer."

"I'll talk to her about it tonight. I promise. Things have been a bit crazy lately with her moving back in and what's been going on at the foundation."

"Oh, I'm so happy for you. I'll get your room cleaned up for you, and the two of you can spend Thursday night here at the house. I need some extra time since I haven't seen the two of you in so long." She paused long enough to take a deep breath. It was as if I hadn't said a word. "I wonder if Brianna would want to go shopping with me on Friday. What do you think? Would it be too much for her?"

"Probably, but I'll leave that up to Brianna."

Diane seemed to deflate at the news. "I'm glad she's back in your life, Stephan. Even over the phone I can hear the difference."

The rest of the day dragged on as I met with several of the board members individually. Since everything had gone down with Greta, Megan, and Frankie, the majority of the board were taking more of an active interest in the foundation's inner workings. I could understand, but it only added to my list of things to do.

At five thirty, I pulled into the parking garage attached to my building. I'd called Brianna from the office letting her know I'd be a few minutes late. There were a couple of stops I needed to make before heading home. She, of course, was completely supportive and assured me dinner would keep.

When I walked through the door, Brianna ran over to me, throwing her arms around my neck. Feeding off her enthusiasm, I dropped my briefcase and picked her up, wrapping her legs around my waist before backing her up against the nearest wall. Holding her hips firmly against my growing erection, I kissed her hard.

Releasing her lips, I rested my forehead against hers as I used the leverage the wall provided and ran my right hand up the inside of her bare thigh. I loved it when she wore skirts.

As I neared her pussy, her arms tightened around my neck. "I missed you today."

Her whispered words only caused my need for her to grow. Who needed dinner anyway?

I made contact with her moist heat. She was already ready for me, and I'd been home less than five minutes.

"And what have you been thinking about today, Brianna?" As I asked the question, I slipped first one finger, then two inside her.

Her eyes rolled back in her head. "You."

"Hmm. What about me?"

"Last . . . last night."

She was killing me. "What about last night?"

Brianna gasped as I grazed her clit with my thumb and lowered my head to begin nibbling on the skin at the base of her neck.

"Tell me."

"When I was . . ." I could tell she was having difficulty concentrating. Whatever she'd been thinking about today, it hadn't been random thoughts. Brianna was very aroused. "When I was sucking you."

I hummed against her neck and then bit down.

Brianna squeaked, which only drove me to want more. I needed to be inside her.

She whined as I reluctantly pulled my fingers out of her pussy. I didn't want to, but I needed my hand. "Don't worry, sweetheart. I'm not nearly done with you yet."

Reaching into my back pocket, I pulled out my wallet. Finding the single condom I'd placed in there after our meeting at the hotel, where I'd been without, I plucked it out with two fingers before letting my wallet fall to the floor with a thud.

"Unfasten my pants, Brianna."

She scrambled to comply, seeming to be as desperate to feel me inside her as I was.

Once she had my zipper down, I adjusted my hold on her slightly so that my pants could be moved out of the way. She helped with that, too, which caused me to smile. "Eager, aren't you?"

"Yes, Sir. I missed you today."

I smiled before pulling her face toward me and giving her a passionate kiss. "So you said."

Not able to wait any longer, I tore the wrapper away from the condom and rolled it down my aching cock. Lining it up with her pussy, I pressed forward, feeling the heat of her surround me. Heaven.

I held her gaze as I dug my fingers into the flesh of her ass, thrusting into her in one swift movement.

Her mouth fell open, and I took the invitation to plunge my tongue inside. She moaned into my mouth as I continued to take what I wanted from her. There was nothing outside of her . . . us. Nothing that could compare to the feeling of my cock inside her as I marked her as mine over and over again.

I ground us together roughly as I felt my climax building. "Touch yourself. I want to feel you come around my cock."

When she didn't move immediately, I took her hand and placed it where I wanted it before picking up where I'd left off and pounding into her.

Little by little, she gained confidence in touching herself as the sensations began to take over. "That's it. Make yourself feel good."

The muscles of her pussy began contracting, almost begging me to come. I kissed her, pouring everything I had into it. I never wanted her to have any doubt how I felt about her—how much I wanted her.

Sucking her bottom lip into my mouth, I bit down, feeling the flesh of her lip give as I toyed with it.

Brianna was completely lost in sensation. Her eyes were glazed over, and her breathing was shallow and rapid. The walls of her pussy were gripping me with ever-increasing force, and I wasn't going to be able to hold on for much longer. "Let go, Brianna. Come for me."

I bit down again on her lip—harder this time—the salty taste of her blood hitting the tip of my tongue.

At the same time, Brianna's pussy clamped down on my cock, and she shuddered as she released a near silent scream.

Watching her was my undoing. My balls tightened, and a surge of energy shot up through my cock as I came. The only thing that could have made the experience any better was if I'd been able to feel her completely. It was a good thing she had an appointment to go get her blood work done on Wednesday, or I might have gone insane.

Brianna

I couldn't breathe.

Okay, I could, but it felt as if all the air had been knocked out of my chest when I climaxed. How did he do that? How did he make me feel as if I were floating and being knocked flat on my back at the same time? Sex before him had never felt good. Sex with him felt as if I were on a high I never wanted to come down from.

"Are you all right, sweetheart?"

"Uh-huh." I wasn't sure if I could form words at the moment.

This, of course, made him chuckle.

His thumb rubbed lightly against my lip, and I flinched. "I didn't mean to break the skin. I guess I got a little carried away."

I reached up, touching the spot. My lip was slightly swollen, but other than that, I couldn't feel anything different. When I removed my hand, though, there was a small drop of blood.

Stephan separated us and helped me to regain my footing. "Come on. It looks like we both need to clean up, and I'll get you some ice to put on your mouth."

As we ate dinner, Stephan continued to watch me closely. He looked worried.

"Did I do something wrong, Sir?"

He looked surprised. "No. Why would you think you did anything wrong?"

I shrugged, taking another bite of my food. "You seem worried about something. I thought maybe I'd done something that displeased you."

Reaching across the table, he took my hand in his. "No. You didn't do anything wrong. I'm wondering, however, if I did. I know I've bitten you before, but this is the first time I've broken the skin. How do you feel about that?"

"It hurts a little, but I'm okay."

He sighed. "I didn't ask if it hurt, Brianna. I want to know how you feel about my hurting you."

I stopped eating and looked at him. "You didn't hurt me."

"I injured you. I need to know how you feel about it."

What he was saying made no sense to me. Yes, he'd bitten me, but at the time it felt amazing. Even now it wasn't that bad. The worst was when he had cleaned it earlier. "You didn't mean to."

"That's irrelevant, Brianna. I *did* injure you. I drew blood."

I didn't know what he wanted me to say. This didn't even compare to what had been done to me, but the fact that he was worried about something so minor made me love him even more. "I love you."

Stephan looked taken aback for a moment. "I love you, too, but that doesn't have anything to do with what just happened. I got carried away. I shouldn't have—"

There was only one thing I could think to do to make him stop beating himself up over this. He hadn't done anything wrong.

Slipping out of my chair, I lowered myself to the floor until I was kneeling in front of him. I bowed my head and placed my hands behind my back, taking the position I'd held many times before I'd met him.

"Brianna, what are you doing?"

I remained silent.

"Answer me."

"I'm showing you, Sir, in the only way I know how. I'm yours and only yours. I trust you with all of myself—my heart, my body, and my soul. It was an accident. You didn't mean to cause me harm."

The minutes ticked by as I waited for his response.

No words were spoken as he placed his hand on top of my head. I could feel the heat seeping through my hair as a feeling of calm welled up inside.

Still, I waited. I would wait in this position all night if that was what he desired. I would do anything for him, and I needed him to understand that.

With his other hand, he reached behind me and took hold of my left wrist. I remained still, allowing him to manipulate me however he wanted. He placed my left hand over his beating heart. "Look at me, Brianna."

I raised my gaze slowly to meet his.

His eyes were intense, but unlike before, when he held me against the door, it wasn't passion I saw—it was determination. "I, too, am yours, Brianna Reeves. Yours and only yours. You own me completely, heart, body, and soul. And I promise you that I will do all that I can to be worthy of your gift to me, because it *is* a gift, and I will treasure it and you for as long as you will allow me."

Tears slid freely down my cheeks at his declaration. How did I get so lucky to have him find me, rescue me? He brought happiness back into my life and taught me that I could be loved . . . that I deserved it. There was nothing I could do to repay him for that, and my submission to him was such a small offering. That he saw it as more only increased my desire to serve him—to be the best submissive I could for him.

Time melted away as we sat there. It was as if we were trapped in a bubble and neither one of us wanted it to burst.

Of course, eventually it did. The phone rang, dragging us back to reality. He cupped my face and placed a reverent kiss on my lips, before going to answer the phone.

I waited.

"Hello?"

He paused.

"We were having dinner. No, I haven't talked to her about it yet. I will. Yes, I know. I'll call you tomorrow and let you know for sure. I love you, too."

I heard him hang up the phone and walk back to where I was kneeling on the floor.

Stephan helped me to stand. "That was my aunt. She asked me earlier today if we were going to their house for Thanksgiving. I told her I'd talk it over with you and get back to her, but apparently she's getting impatient."

I nodded. "I figured we'd be going to their house. It's what normal families do, isn't it?"

He smiled. "I'm not sure I'd call my family normal, but yes, it's what normal families do."

"Okay."

Stephan pulled me into his arms. "She's also requesting that we spend the night. It's sort of a tradition, but if you don't think you'll be comfortable, we can come back home. She'll have to adjust."

"She wants us to sleep there?"

"Yes." He tilted my chin so he could see my face. "How do you feel about that?"

"Would I be sleeping in the same bed as you?"

"Of course."

"Okay. As long as you're there with me, I know I'll be all right."

He placed a soft kiss to my forehead. "I'll let her know tomorrow. For now, we need to finish our dinners. Take a seat, and I'll pop them both in the microwave. I'm sure they're ice-cold by now."

At Stephan's encouragement, I retook my seat at the table and waited while he took our plates into the kitchen. This night hadn't turned out at all like I thought it would, and it wasn't over yet.

Chapter 32

Stephan

As I rejoined Brianna at the table with our reheated dinners, I tried to push what had happened out of my mind. She was correct. It was an accident. I hadn't meant to break the skin on her lip. I hadn't meant to lose control. Needing something to take my mind off it, I picked up Brianna's journal and started reading.

Going through her journal provided some great insights into the way she thought about things. Today she'd written about her meeting with Sarah the day before. She thought Sarah was beautiful, and she'd been intimidated at first. Brianna mused over Sarah's observation of my not caring for her bratty nature. In Brianna's mind, she couldn't understand why someone would intentionally try to get themselves into trouble. Brianna was such a good girl, so it didn't surprise me that she was having a difficult time wrapping her mind around Sarah's personality.

When I got down to the part where Brianna was talking about our time in the shower, I had to pause and adjust myself. She'd gone into detail as to how my cock felt in her mouth, the salty flavor of my cum, and how my pulling her hair added to her enjoyment. We'd had sex less than an hour ago against the door, and I was already contemplating taking her again.

I knew I needed to calm down, so I pushed her journal to the side for a few minutes and concentrated on my meal. There were things I wanted to do tonight that didn't involve sex—well not yet, anyway. I needed to focus and not allow myself to get carried away. Besides, Brianna's lip needed time to heal. I didn't think I could go very long without kissing her, but at least if I wasn't caught up in the heat of the moment, I could ease up on the amount of pressure I used.

Once I felt in control, I went back to reading. Luckily, after getting past her retelling of last night, she spoke of more mundane things, including a phone conversation with Ross. That was something that could cool my libido. From the sound of it, he was at least trying to uphold his end of the bargain by not harassing Brianna about moving back in with me.

Unfortunately, that was the only reprieve Brianna gave me, because after that she'd started reading her latest book, which apparently had some rather graphic sex scenes. It had gotten her all worked up and thinking about last night again, hence her jumping me as soon as I'd walked through the door.

I glanced over at her after I read the last words, which were *I can't wait until Stephan gets home. I need him.*

She met my gaze, and soon after, her pupils began to dilate. I knew they matched my own, which in no way helped my predicament. Brianna was able to do something to me that no other woman had ever been able to do— leave me in a near constant state of arousal. I always wanted her.

I took a deep breath and cleared my throat. "Are you finished?"

Brianna nodded.

Before my need overrode my common sense, I pushed my chair away from the table and stood. "Clean up, and I'll be back down in a few minutes."

Practically running up the stairs, I sought brief refuge in my study. I needed to get a hold of myself. There was no way I could have a conversation with Brianna about ropes and tying her up if I felt like this. Closing my eyes, I took several deep breaths.

My cell phone vibrating in my pocket caught my attention. I frowned when I saw the caller ID. Why was Agent Marco calling me and at this time of day?

By the time I hung up the phone, all thoughts of sex with Brianna had been sufficiently quelled. Ian Pierce. The man disgusted me. According to Agent Marco, Pierce wasn't taking the deal the feds were offering, even knowing Brianna had given the FBI her statement. It wasn't difficult to figure out the game he was playing. He didn't think Brianna would go through with it—testify against him. It would be a huge blow to the prosecution's case.

Gritting my teeth, I dug my fingers into the back of the leather chair. I tried to keep myself from dwelling on it since there was nothing we could do at the moment. Marco was still hopeful, but a trial date had been set for February fourth. I would have to inform Brianna of this new development.

Feeling, if not calmer, more in control of myself, at least, I unlocked the drawer where I'd put the book on Shibari. Brianna was nowhere near ready for most of the things in this book, but I was hoping we could work on changing her view of bondage in general. She liked it when I held her down. I also knew, although she said she wanted me to tie her up, the thought scared her. We were going to work on that.

Tucking the book under one arm, I made my way back downstairs. Brianna was still in the kitchen, loading the dishwasher. I smiled at her as I strolled across the room to retrieve my briefcase. It was still on the floor where I'd dropped it after she'd attacked me. I couldn't help but smile at that pleasant memory.

Picking up the briefcase, I carried it over to my chair and sat down.

Brianna would join me when she finished what she was doing. This was our routine—our ritual. It was something we both loved and needed.

Sure enough, roughly five minutes later, Brianna appeared beside my chair. I had my hands folded in my lap, so she hesitated. "May I sit on your lap, Sir?"

I opened my arms, and she smiled.

Once she was seated comfortably, I spent a few minutes holding her before I began our nightly conversation. "Ross sounds as if he's finally accepted your new living arrangements."

She nodded. "Yes, other than asking if I needed anything, he talked mostly about Thanksgiving. He's going home with Jade to meet her family. I think he's a little nervous."

"He's not met her family yet?"

Brianna shook her head.

"Haven't he and Jade been together for a while?"

"Almost two years. But her family lives in Georgia. He says they're ultraconservative, and they've been putting off the meeting because they don't know how her parents are going to react to the two of them together. Cal isn't very religious, and he and Jade are pretty much living together now."

"That would be tough." I almost felt sorry for Ross. Certainly for Jade. She would most likely take the brunt of it if things went badly.

Brianna continued to play with the buttons on my shirt. "What about you? How was your day?"

"Long, but things are slowing down some. Everyone's still on edge after what happened, which I can understand."

"I understand why the one lady stole the money—to help her mom—but the other two . . . I can't understand that."

"It was greed, pure and simple. The fact that they had the money stored in a bank account rather than using it to help with the medical bills Greta was stressing over proves that."

She shook her head, and her hair brushed against my neck, tickling me. I was still reeling from how good it felt to have her back. Every moment was precious.

Because of that, I dreaded the conversation we were about to have. "I received a call from Agent Marco while I was upstairs."

Brianna stilled. Her muscles tightened.

She pressed her nose against my collarbone. "I don't like him."

I chuckled. "Neither do I, love. Unfortunately, we have to deal with him whether we like it or not."

There was no reaction from Brianna.

Rubbing my hands up and down her arms in hopes that she would relax, I continued on. "He spoke to the prosecutor today. So far, Pierce isn't taking the deal they've offered him, and a trial date has been set for February."

Brianna gripped my shirt. Her hold was so tight that I thought she might rip it in two. "I'm going to have to testify."

I pulled her close against my chest, as close as I possibly could with the clothing between us and our current positions. "I'll do everything I possibly can to make sure that doesn't happen, Brianna. You've been hurt enough by that monster."

She didn't say anything right away. She would need time to process everything. This was huge. The fact that she hadn't gone straight into a panic attack was a remarkable accomplishment, and my pride in her swelled.

After several minutes, she brought her hand up to touch the side of my face. I looked down at her, and her eyes were full of worry.

I caressed her cheek, wanting to reassure her, but before I could speak, she did. "It will be okay."

Sucking in a deep breath, I let it out slowly before I responded to what she'd just said. *She* was worried about *me*. "Brianna, it's not me I'm worried about. It's you. I don't want you to have to go before a room full of strangers and relive what that man, and I use that term very loosely, did to you."

"But I deal with it every day."

I opened my mouth to protest.

"It's not the same thing, I know, but as long as you're there, as long as I can see you when I'm up on the stand . . . I think I can do it." She was quiet for a long time, but I could see she wasn't done. "He shouldn't get away with what he did."

Closing my eyes, I tucked her head up against my neck and rested my cheek against her hair. Whatever did I do to deserve her? "No, he shouldn't."

If I had my way, part of his punishment would involve spending several hours a day being tortured, beaten, and raped. He deserved to experience firsthand every injustice Brianna had. That was only fair. Unfortunately, the most I could hope for was that he was convicted and spent the rest of his life behind bars—his freedom taken from him permanently.

I hated that it was looking more and more as if she may have to testify. It only made me hate Ian Pierce more.

"Sir?"

"Yes, sweetheart?"

"Can we . . . can we talk about something else?"

I let out a breath I wasn't aware I'd been holding. "Sure. What would you like to talk about?"

She shrugged. "Is there something in your briefcase?"

Meeting her gaze, I raised one eyebrow in question.

"It's just that you brought it over and set it beside your chair tonight. You never do that."

Always so observant.

I smiled. "There is something in my briefcase, but we'll get to that a little later."

Shifting her in my arms slightly, I reached behind my back to retrieve the book I'd hidden. I held it out to her.

Brianna sat up and took the book from my hand. "What is it?"

Although *Shibari* was printed in large red letters across the top of the book, I wasn't sure Brianna knew what Shibari was. "It's a book about ropes . . . tying people up."

She looked up at me, wide-eyed. "Oh."

Brianna

He rubbed his thumb gently back and forth over the pulse in my neck. I knew my heart rate had picked up. I could feel it.

As I looked at the cover of the book, I began to wonder. "Is this the book Lily gave you last night?"

Stephan nodded. "Yes. I asked Logan if I could borrow it. All my books and toys are still in storage."

I thought about that for a minute. "Are you going to get them back?"

"My things? Yes. Hopefully I can arrange to have them returned soon since there's no longer a threat of my condo being searched. It doesn't have to be done immediately, though. They're safe where they are for now."

Nodding, I concentrated on the book I was holding. I didn't know what to say to that. Although I knew he had "toys"—I had to suppress a shudder—I wasn't sure I was ready to see them.

"They'll be locked away upstairs like they were before—at least until you're ready for us to explore some of them. I won't push you on it."

I also knew that while he wouldn't push me now, that didn't mean that would always be the case. Eventually I'd have to at least look at what he owned. It was part of him, and I had to accept that.

"May I open it?"

He knew I was once more talking about the book. "Go ahead."

The first couple of pages were what you'd expect in any book—a title page and a table of contents. Some of the chapter titles were interesting, though.

When I came to chapter one, I was surprised to find a picture of a naked girl kneeling. The only rope was the one she had draped across her lap. I guess I'd expected it to be . . . more.

I realized a few minutes later that "more" was only five pages away. The first chapter was all about safety, and the dos and don'ts of Shibari—Japanese rope bondage. Chapter two was where the actual bondage started.

At first, it was a lot to take in, and if not for the smiling women and even some men in the photographs, I would probably have reacted much differently. My pulse was still racing as I flipped through the book, but it wasn't as bad as I thought it would be. "Will you do this to me?"

"I'd like to do some of it, yes, but I'm not experienced enough to try the more intricate bindings." Stephan went back a dozen or so pages to a picture toward the beginning and pointed. "This is more along the lines of what I'd like to try with you after we get past some of your fears. Given your rather . . . enthusiastic response to breast play, I think you'd enjoy it."

The picture was of a woman with rope tied around her breasts. It wrapped around her back and also tied in the middle, separating each breast. "Is it painful?"

He shook his head. "No. Not if it's done right. What it does is restrict the blood flow just enough to heighten sensation."

"Okay."

Stephan turned me to face him. "Brianna, I would never do anything I didn't think you could handle. You said you were interested in rope—in having me tie you up. I thought this would give you an overview, an education of sorts. Most of what's in the book I would never attempt because I know I'm not that good. I'd be putting your safety at risk, and I won't do that. Understand?"

I nodded. "Yes, Sir."

"Good. Now for the second part of what I had planned for tonight."

He smiled, but there was something behind it that I'd never seen before.

Reaching down beside his chair, Stephan picked up his briefcase and laid it on my lap, directly on top of the book. Without comment, he opened the briefcase. Inside was a length of red rope. I swallowed, nervous.

Stephan removed the rope, and after closing the briefcase, set it back down beside the chair. "Here."

"Wh-what?"

"Take the rope. I want you to see what it feels like."

"Okay." My voice was weak, and my limbs were shaking, but I did what he asked. "It feels soft."

"It's cotton."

I didn't know what to do with it, so I held it loosely between my fingers until Stephan's hands covered my own. He took the section of rope from my left hand and ran it gently along my wrist. It felt strange, but not in a bad way.

He kept rubbing it back and forth until I relaxed against him. "Good girl. Now I want you to watch what I do, and if you start to get frightened, I want you to tell me."

Doing as he asked, I kept my gaze on his hands. His movements were almost hypnotic as he continued to brush the rope over my skin.

Slowly he began to unravel part of the rope and then fold it in two. Once he appeared satisfied with it, he resumed his ministrations.

With every stroke, I felt myself being lulled into a state where I almost felt as if I were floating. I closed my eyes without thinking.

The motion stopped. "Open your eyes, Brianna."

I snapped my eyes opened and immediately looked down at my wrist. What I saw shocked me. The rope was wound around my wrist and tied in a knot.

I flexed my fingers. It was tight but only to the point of pressure . . . not pain.

A rush of guilt for not obeying him bubbled up inside.

He kissed the bare skin between my neck and my shoulder. "It's all right. You got caught up in the moment more than I thought you would."

Although I nodded, I still felt a churning in my gut at not keeping my eyes open.

"Stop," he ordered.

I took a deep breath and tried to relax.

He tugged on the loose end, getting my attention. "This is what I want to do to start out. I will bind both of your wrists in this fashion and tie the other end of the rope to my bed." Stephan then took his fingers and placed them on the knot. "If something were ever to happen, you can pull here, and it will release the knot, setting you free. If both your hands are bound, it would take some concentration and effort on your part, but it's able to be done."

"I can untie myself?" This didn't make sense. I thought the point was for me *not* to be able to get loose.

"If necessary, yes. Brianna, whenever a Dominant binds someone, whether it be with rope or anything else, there should always be safety measures in place, whether that means the submissive's knowing how to untie a knot, or having a pair of scissors handy so they can cut themselves loose."

I still wasn't sure I understood, but I nodded.

Stephan finished removing the rope from around my wrist and handed it to me. "This is yours. When you're ready, bring it to me and I will use it on you. Until then, I want you to get comfortable with it. Just as with the dildo in my toy drawer, this is a tool, nothing more. It can be used to give pleasure, or it can be used for pain, depending on the intentions of the person using it."

The rope fell into my lap, and I stared—dozens of thoughts running through my mind at once.

His voice brought me back to the present. "Tomorrow, I want you to write about what we talked about tonight in your journal. I want to know how you felt having your wrist tied and what your fears are."

"Okay."

He kissed me and then patted my leg. "Let's get ready for bed. I've had a long day, and I have the distinct desire to ravish you."

Chapter 33

Stephan

I smiled as I woke up Wednesday morning. Brianna was lying beside me in my bed. She had her body contorted in what looked to me to be a rather uncomfortable position, but as she was still sleeping, I had to imagine it wasn't as awkward as it appeared. What had me amused, however, was that while she was facing away from me, her arm was stretched out behind her back, her hand inches from my morning erection.

Not wanting to frighten her, I gently tilted her head in my direction. "Time to wake up, my love."

She groaned, but gradually she opened her eyes. "Hi."

"Good morning. Did you have pleasant dreams?"

Brianna furrowed her brow in confusion. "I don't remember." She paused. "Did I do something I wasn't supposed to, Sir?"

Instead of answering her verbally, I took her hand where it still rested inches from my cock and placed it on top of my very prominent erection.

Her eyes grew wide. "Did I do that?"

I laughed. "No, but given your hand's very close proximity this morning, I'm wondering what thoughts were going through that head of yours while you were sleeping."

"I don't remember."

Unable to resist, I flexed my hips, pressing my cock into her hand. Instinctively, she wrapped her fingers around it, and I couldn't stifle my moan.

Covering her hand with one of my own, I guided her movements. I was hard as a rock, and the feel of her gripping me had my blood pumping through my veins in no time.

Flipping the sheet off her body, I wasted no time slipping my hand between her legs. She opened for me as I eased a single finger inside. Her body was always warm and inviting, and her pussy gripped my finger as I began to move it in and out.

I watched her closely as we both continued our movements. When I added a second finger, she began to flush as her body became increasingly excited by what I was doing to her.

As she kept up her efforts to milk my cock, I bent down to kiss her. She kissed me back, her breath hot against my face as she exhaled. My thumb played with her clit, causing her to take deeper breaths. With every inhale, her chest expanded, brushing against my chest. I could feel the hard peaks of her nipples getting more rigid as her climax edged closer.

I was getting close, and I wanted her right there with me. Releasing her lips, I lowered my head and latched on to one of her nipples. She tightened her hold on my cock, and I groaned, sucking harder on her supple flesh.

"Sir?" She was moving her hips in time with my hand, and I knew she was close.

Keeping her nipple between my teeth, I worried it as I answered her. "Yes?"

"May I . . . may I please . . ."

She gasped as I sucked her breast back into my mouth and at the same time began rubbing the spongy spot along the front wall of her pussy. Her muscles clamped down around my fingers as I continued to stroke.

Her voice rose in pitch. "Sir? Please, please, pleeeeasee."

I reached between us and clasped the wrist of the hand she was using to pump me and encouraged her to pick up the pace. Brianna wasn't going to last much longer, permission granted or not. I wasn't going to back off, though. Soon she was going to be teetering on the edge, which was exactly where I wanted her.

Brianna had her eyes closed, and her mouth hung open in a near constant, yet silent scream. Her breathing was fast and shallow, and her face was beet red.

She lifted her free hand from where it was holding the sheet in a death grip and threaded her fingers through my hair. I knew she was utterly lost in the moment when she pulled my hair harder than she ever had before. Surprisingly, that only added to what I was feeling, and I felt my orgasm approaching, fast and furious.

My climax hit me, and I released her nipple just long enough to give her the permission to come that she'd been begging for as I exploded into her hand and onto the sheets.

As my breathing started to return to normal, I realized she was shaking—and not in a good way. "Brianna, what's wrong?

She didn't answer.

Sitting up, I pulled her into my arms, and she began shaking her head. "Talk to me, sweetheart. Tell me what's wrong. Why are you shaking?"

"Off. I need it off."

"What—" It was then I noticed how she was holding her hand out away from her body. I picked it up, examining it . . . thinking that maybe, somehow she'd been hurt. It looked normal, albeit a little red from the friction of jacking me off.

When I heard a sob escape her throat, I held her closer and examined her hand again. The only thing I could see was that a good portion of her palm was covered in my cum. A little confused, I leaned over to grab a tissue from the nightstand and began wiping it off her hand.

Once all signs of it were gone, she began to calm down.

"It's okay. I've got you."

"I didn't . . ."

"You didn't what?"

"I couldn't . . ."

Holding her face firmly with my hands, I forced her to look at me. "Brianna, take a deep breath, and tell me what happened. I'm not upset, but I need to understand."

"They . . ." She closed her eyes and sucked in a lung full of air. "They used t-t-to on me. And I couldn't get it off. They wouldn't let me get it off."

Cocking my head to the side, I concentrated on both her words and her actions of the last several minutes. "The men used to spill their cum on you?"

She nodded.

"And feeling mine made you relive that?"

Again, she nodded, but this time she opened her eyes to look at me.

"Did you have another flashback?"

"Yes!" She flung herself into my arms, holding on to my neck so tight I had to loosen them slightly so that I could breathe. "They were standing over me. Taunting me. I felt . . . dirty."

"Shh. I've got you. Those men are far away, and they're never going to hurt you again, do you understand?"

She had her head buried deep in the curve of my shoulder, but I felt her nod.

I waited until she quieted again before moving us both toward one side of the bed. Once my feet were on the floor, I got a solid grip on her and stood with her in my arms. Brianna didn't seem to notice as she continued to cling to me.

We were both already naked, so I headed straight into the shower. I lowered her legs, guiding them to the floor so she could stand on her own. She still didn't release me. "I'm right here, Brianna. I'm not going anywhere."

She stayed with me step for step as I turned on the water and crossed the small space to retrieve the shampoo, conditioner, and body wash. She was shaken from her flashback, and it was going to take some time. All I could do at the moment was be there for her—to catch her if she fell. Brianna was strong, though. She'd get through this like she did everything else.

What threw me more than anything was that Brianna had jacked me off before—many times. It had always been in the shower, though, where the water had almost instantly washed all signs of my cum down the drain. It made me think that her reaction had more to do with the feel or texture as it began to cool on her skin than the actual act itself. There was no way I could know that for certain, however. Not yet, anyway.

Slowly, I washed first her and then myself. The good news was that she was still with me. Her eyes were focused for the most part, and if I asked her a question, she answered me. She hadn't gone into a full-blown panic attack, and for that, I was grateful. Every day she grew stronger, even if she didn't realize it.

After our shower, I dried us both off and took her into her bedroom to get dressed. Although she slept in my bed every night, her things remained in her room. I wanted her to have her space, somewhere that was hers and only hers.

As with the shower, she went along with whatever instructions I gave. It was robotic, however, and I didn't like it.

Showered and dressed, I led her by the hand out to the kitchen where I fixed us a simple breakfast of toast and some fruit Brianna had sliced up the day before. As I was assembling the food, I got an idea. After fixing only one plate with enough food for both of us, I guided her over to the dining room table. I took my seat, but instead of instructing her to take hers beside me, I ordered her to kneel.

Brianna complied almost instantly.

"Look at me."

She raised her head and met my gaze.

I picked up a piece of fruit and held it out to her between two fingers.

Brianna leaned forward, but I pulled it back out of her reach.

"Every time I present you with a bite of food, you are going to ask if you may have it. And when you finish eating it, you are to thank me. Understand?"

She nodded.

"Use your words, Brianna."

"Yes, Sir. I understand."

"Good." I held the food out to her once more.

"May I?"

"May you what? And look at me when you speak."

"May I have the piece of fruit, Sir?"

I smiled and pressed the strawberry against her lips. "Yes, you may."

As she chewed, I took a bite of watermelon.

She swallowed. "Thank you, Sir."

"Good girl. Now another," I said as I broke off a corner of toast and added some jelly on top.

"May I have some toast, Sir?"

This went on for the remainder of our meal, and by the end, Brianna was looking and acting more like her normal self.

Brianna

I was starting to feel more like myself. The numbness was fading with every piece of food Stephan fed me. I didn't completely understand it, but having to ask for every bite and then thank him for it centered me. Little by little, the memories faded into the background where they belonged.

He wiped his mouth with a napkin before handing one to me to do the same. I took it and quickly removed any remaining traces of my breakfast from my mouth.

"Feeling better?" Stephan smiled at me as I gave the napkin back to him.

"Yes." I paused. How he knew to get me out of my own head amazed and confused me, but either way, I was grateful. "Thank you, Sir."

Stephan extended a single finger and traced it along my collar. "It's my job to take care of you, Brianna. And now that I know your reaction, I'll make sure we avoid activities that would require you to have my semen on your body."

One more thing I wouldn't be able to give him.

"Hey. None of that. I'm not saying it will never happen again, not if it's something you want." He hesitated, and I began to worry. Stephan rarely hesitated. "Your blood test today—if it comes back clean, I was hoping that our joining would no longer require a condom. With your reaction today, I'm not sure that will be possible."

"You want to have sex with me without wearing a condom?" He'd never done that before, and outside of sex with Ian, I'd never been taken without the person wearing protection. It was one of Ian's rules. In my time with him, only one of Ian's friends had attempted to take me without one, and Ian had grabbed him by his ear and dragged him out of his house. The man was completely naked, but Ian hadn't cared. He hadn't returned the man's clothes either.

"What's that frown for?"

I refocused on Stephan. "Can we try?"

It was his turn to frown. "Can we try what?"

"Sex without a condom."

The creases in his face deepened. "Why?"

"I-I want to try, Sir. It's what you want, and I want to make you happy."

"This is not required for you to make me happy, Brianna. Just you being here with me does that."

"But it's what you want."

He kept frowning. I didn't want him to frown anymore.

Scooting closer, I wrapped my arms around his waist and laid my head in his lap. "Please, can we try, Sir? If I start to panic, we can stop, right?"

Stephan sighed and caressed my head. The tension left his body, and I couldn't help but smile.

"All right, we'll try. If it doesn't work . . ."

I hugged him tighter. "Thank you, Sir."

He laughed and tilted my chin so that he could look into my eyes. "You can be very stubborn when you want something. Once you get over more of your fears, things could get interesting."

Maybe if he weren't smiling, I would have taken what he said differently, but he didn't seem to be bothered by whatever might lie ahead for us, so I wasn't either. As long as the future included both of us together, I was okay with it.

"Come on. We need to get ready to go if we're going to get you to the lab for your blood work before your therapy session with Dr. Perkins."

Scrambling to my feet, I ran into my bathroom to finish getting ready. I was nervous about Stephan and Dr. Perkins meeting, but I was hopeful as well. Stephan helped me get better, and so did Dr. Perkins. As I stood in front of my bathroom mirror brushing my teeth, the doubts began to creep back in. What if they hated each other? What if she thought Stephan was manipulating me, like Cal did?

No. I couldn't think like that. I couldn't. It would be okay. It had to be.

Finishing up, I took one last look in the mirror, and I went to find Stephan.

He was waiting in the living room for me, dressed in clothes I normally only saw him in on the weekends. I smiled, and he smiled back. "Ready?"

"Yes."

The lab wasn't far from Stephan's house, but it took us fifteen minutes longer than it should have. When we pulled out of the parking garage, Stephan noticed a car following us. It took several turns through the business district to lose them. Only after he was sure that we were no longer being followed did he continue on to the lab. Although I'd heard about the reporters from Cal, this was my first personal experience, and I had to admit it was scary. I didn't understand why they couldn't leave us alone. Weren't there more important stories to cover?

We were in and out of the lab in less than ten minutes. I didn't know if that was because of Stephan, or because they weren't that busy. He left me to sit in a chair a few feet away, but in his direct line of sight, while he went up to talk to the woman behind the screen. Words were exchanged, but I couldn't hear what was said. When he came to sit beside me, he took my hand and smiled. About two minutes later, my name was called.

Because of the holiday, my Friday appointment with Dr. Perkins had been moved to Wednesday. The time had also been changed to eleven thirty in the morning rather than three in the afternoon when I usually saw her. I noticed right away that there seemed to be more people in the building. Was that because of the time or the day? Either way, I didn't like it, and I held tighter to Stephan's hand.

"I'm right here."

His warm breath tickled my ear as he whispered. It was the reassurance I needed, though.

Hand in hand, we walked down the hall until we reached the door to Dr. Perkins's office. Stephan opened the door, and we entered the small waiting area. I breathed a sigh of relief when I didn't see anyone else waiting.

The woman behind the desk greeted me with a smile. I'd learned her name was Monica. "Good morning, Ms. Reeves. Have a seat, and I'll let Candice know you're here."

It seemed to take forever, but I knew it was only a couple of minutes. Dr. Perkins never made me wait long. My nerves were getting the better of me.

When the door opened, I jumped, drawing the attention of Stephan, Dr. Perkins, and Monica.

Dr. Perkins walked toward us, more cautious than usual.

Stephan stood, and I followed.

He extended his hand to her, and she took it. "You must be Dr. Perkins. Brianna has told me a lot about you."

She looked curious. "And you are?"

"Stephan Coleman."

"Ah. The infamous Stephan. It's nice to finally meet you."

"Likewise."

I stood watching the exchange. It was polite, but I could tell they were sizing each other up. I wasn't sure if that was a good thing or not.

Dr. Perkins switched her gaze to me. "Anna, would you like Stephan to sit in on your session today, or would you rather it just be the two of us?"

"I'd like him to come in, too, if that's okay?"

She smiled, but it wasn't as relaxed as it normally was. "Of course, but I always like to see my patients alone for a few minutes to start." Her attention refocused briefly on Stephan. "If you'd wait out here for about five minutes, I'll let you know when we're ready for you."

Dr. Perkins motioned toward the door, indicating she wanted me to enter . . . without Stephan.

I looked up at him, questioning.

He leaned down and placed a chaste kiss on my lips. "It's all right. Go on. I'll wait here."

Taking a deep breath, I nodded and followed Dr. Perkins into her office.

Chapter 34

Brianna

I sat down on the couch in Dr. Perkins's office, but I kept glancing toward the closed door.

Dr. Perkins took her seat across from me. She smiled, and it was slightly more relaxed that it had been a few minutes before out in the waiting area. "I wanted us to have a few minutes alone, Anna. Before Stephan joins us, I wanted to see if there are any topics you don't wish to discuss while he's in the room with us. This is your session, so it's completely up to you. I don't want you to feel as if there is any pressure. If you're not comfortable with him being in here while we talk about something, then I will make him wait outside."

"You don't want him here?"

"That's not what I said. Besides, what I want isn't what's in question. It's what you want, Anna. Only you, not me, and not Stephan."

"I don't have any secrets from Stephan."

She relaxed her shoulders, and this time her smile seemed genuine. "Okay. I'll go get him."

It took longer than I expected for her to return with Stephan in tow. I smiled at him as he took a seat beside me on the couch and threaded his fingers with mine. What had taken so long, and why was Stephan holding himself so rigid? I was always nervous when I came to talk with Dr. Perkins, and I wondered if it was the same for him.

Dr. Perkins had never hurt me in any way, but I never knew what emotions I'd have to deal with while I was there. Today was different. Stephan was here with me. He'd take care of me no matter what happened like he always did. We'd be there for each other.

I snuggled closer to Stephan. He wasn't relaxing, though, which I didn't understand. Did something happen? Glancing between the two, I could feel the tension radiating off them both.

Deciding I didn't care if it was appropriate or not, I climbed onto Stephan's lap and held him. His arms circled around me, and I felt his chest rise and fall beneath me as he started to relax.

He kissed my forehead. "Thank you."

I nodded. "Is something wrong? Did something happen?"

Stephan glanced up at Dr. Perkins, and I noticed they exchanged a look before he refocused his gaze on me. "It seems your therapist was worried about our relationship." He caressed the side of my face lovingly. "She wanted to make sure I wasn't taking advantage of you."

"But you're not!" It was my turn to go rigid.

Dr. Perkins settled back into her chair and picked up her notepad. "I needed to make sure that you weren't being pressured in any way. This is meant to be a safe space, and you have choices here, Anna."

Stephan stiffened beside me, and my heart picked up its pace.

"Brianna always has choices, Doctor. I told you I make sure of that." He must have sensed my anxiety over the exchange and began rubbing his thumb back and forth along my index finger. It helped, but I remained fearful of what might have happened out in the lobby between the two. After another tense minute, he leaned over and whispered in my ear. "Take a deep breath and relax. Everything's fine."

I took a deep breath as he instructed, and it did make me feel better.

He squeezed my hand and smiled, letting me know he was pleased.

"You two seem to be very in tune with each other." She paused. "That can be a good thing, as long as one doesn't overwhelm the other."

I heard what she was saying, but I was paying attention to Stephan. He was still anxious, so I rested my head on his shoulder and began playing with the buttons on his shirt like I always did. Almost as if without thinking, he rested his head against mine as the rhythm of our breathing became in sync with the other's. This often happened when we were in his chair, and I loved it. It was almost as if his taking a breath prompted my own.

No one spoke for several minutes as all I could hear was the inhale and exhale of our breath and the beating of his heart. We both needed this moment.

This time when Dr. Perkins spoke, it was in a much softer tone, the same one she usually used with me. "How does it come into play when you deal with conflict?"

"What do you mean?" Stephan's defenses were up again, so I did my best to calm him.

"All relationships have conflict from time to time. From my observations, Anna is extremely nonaggressive. I'm wondering how that plays out during any disagreements the two of you have."

"Are you asking if I force her to do what I want and negate any feelings she would have on the matter?" He didn't raise his voice, but I could hear his anger boiling just beneath the surface.

"That's not what I said, nor is it what I meant. I'm merely asking how the two of you deal with things when you don't see eye to eye."

When Stephan didn't respond to her question, Dr. Perkins turned to me. "Maybe you'd like to answer, Anna. Would you like to share an instance when the two of you have encountered a conflict . . . had a fight as it were . . . and how you resolved it?"

"Um. I don't know."

Dr. Perkins wasn't satisfied with that answer. I should have known better. "What about when you thought Stephan lied to you? You obviously resolved it somehow?"

"We talked?" I wasn't sure what she wanted me to say.

"What did you talk about? Did he come to you, or did you go to him? Was there a compromise?"

I glanced over at Stephan. He looked relaxed enough with the exception of his mouth. It was too stern, so I knew he was wound tighter than he appeared. He didn't like therapists. I figured it had something to do with his parents' death given what little he'd told me and what I'd overheard. That was all I knew, though. "He came to see me, but I wouldn't talk to him. Then he sent me e-mails. I didn't read them right away, but when I did, I went to see him."

"And you talked?"

"Yes. He explained. And apologized."

"Ah. A man who knows when to say he's sorry." She gave Stephan a small smile.

Stephan tightened his hold on my hand. "A person who cannot apologize for their mistakes is a fool."

"Very wise observation." Dr. Perkins jotted something down. I was always curious what she was writing when she did that, but I never asked.

He snorted.

"Something the matter?" Dr. Perkins lifted one eyebrow in question.

Stephan sat up straighter in his seat. "I thought this was supposed to be about Brianna, not our relationship. You've not once asked her a question about her past, or how she's dealing with her flashbacks. When exactly will you be getting around to that?"

"Your relationship with Anna is just as important, if not more so, than what has happened to her in the past. She needs to be in a stable environment that supports her emotionally and is healthy. How the two of you deal with conflict is essential. Abuse survivors tend to shy away from conflict. They often don't stand up for themselves as they should and too often end up in another abusive situation."

Instead of answering her right away, Stephan took several keep breaths and began running his hand up and down my arm. I relaxed into him.

Stephan brushed the hair away from my face and placed a soft kiss on my temple. "You asked how we resolve conflict. This is how."

"By you holding her?"

"She calms me, and I do the same for her. Every night we sit in a chair in my living room, her on my lap, and we talk."

No words were spoken for several minutes. When the silence was eventually broken, though, it was by Dr. Perkins. She cleared her throat, and we both turned to look in her direction.

"The change in both of your body language . . . it's remarkable." Her eyes were wide and observant. A part of me wondered what exactly she was seeing besides me sitting on Stephan's lap. Her reaction made it seem as if there were more to it than that.

"When you're like this . . ." Dr. Perkins motioned toward us with her hand. "What do you talk about?"

"Everything. There are no secrets between us."

Dr. Perkins considered this for a moment. "You failed to tell her about the woman you had living with you."

"A mistake on my part. I'd wanted to tell her in person, and our face-to-face contact was limited at the time. That won't happen again."

"And how do you propose to accomplish that?"

"Simple. I won't allow it."

She pursed her lips. "That's a rather controlling attitude."

He shrugged.

I reached up to touch the side of his face. He met my gaze, and I saw the distance in his eyes melt away.

He kissed my forehead.

Dr. Perkins cleared her throat, and we both looked in her direction, the intimate moment gone. "Well. I don't know what to say."

"An apology would be good start." I had no idea what had happened between them out in the lobby, but I knew it had to be something big. Otherwise, why would Stephan ask her for an apology?

It was her turn to look uncomfortable. "My apologies. I feel rather protective of my patients, and I suppose I may have gotten a bit carried away. Your situation is unusual."

Stephan nodded. "Yes, it is, but it works for us."

The rest of my session was tense, but they didn't fight. At the end, Dr. Perkins walked us to the door. "It was nice to finally meet you, Stephan. You're not exactly as I expected you'd be."

He pulled me against his side and released a noise that sounded somewhere between a snort and a laugh. "I suppose I should take that as a compliment."

She smiled and then looked toward me. "I hope you have a nice Thanksgiving, Anna, and I'll see you next week at our normal time."

I nodded, and Stephan led me out into the hall.

Stephan

I was not overjoyed with Brianna's psychiatrist. Her questioning was beyond irritating, and uncalled for. Everyone questioned my relationship with Brianna, and I was sick of it. I loved her. I wanted to spend my life with her. End of story. We should not have to justify ourselves to anyone.

In my opinion, what had happened out in the lobby when she'd returned to bring me into Brianna's session crossed the line.

She approached me with her arms crossed as I stood upon her reentering the waiting area. That was never a good sign, no matter who it was. "Mr. Coleman, as much as the world may revolve around you outside these walls, here it most certainly does not. I couldn't care less who you are or how much money you have in your bank account."

"What are you talking about?"

"Anna is vulnerable right now, and I want to make sure you aren't abusing the situation."

"You think I'm abusing her?" I couldn't believe the gall of this lady. Who did she think she was?

"I don't know. Are you?"

"No." I spit out the word through gritted teeth.

"Anna told me that the two of you have a sexual relationship. Considering what she's been through and the short time that has passed, I question your motives. And your intentions."

"Why is it that everyone finds it so hard to believe that I love her? Is it that you all find it difficult to love her? Because I find it's the opposite. Brianna is very easy to love. She is selfless and caring. Strong. Resilient. And determined. Even with all she's been through, she has a heart of gold. Again, I ask you, why is how I feel about her so unfathomable?"

I tried to shake off the memory, but after that experience, I needed some time to decompress. There was no better way of doing that than to spend time with Brianna. Not quite ready to head home, I drove out of the city, until I reached the park I'd taken her to months ago. The leaves were no longer green—in fact, most of them had fallen off their branches leaving the limbs bare, but the ones that hung on were an array of oranges, yellows, and browns. It looked like a completely different place.

Looking around, I made sure we were alone before opening the car door and stepping out onto the asphalt of the parking lot. There was a brisk wind, and I pulled up the collar on my coat to shield my neck from the cold. I walked around to Brianna and opened her door, helping her out. Once we were both as buttoned up as possible given our clothing, I took her hand and headed toward the trail we'd walked down the last time.

She was quiet beside me as we strolled down the path that was littered with leaves. It was peaceful and calm—exactly what we both needed.

Instead of turning off as we had last time to go to the clearing, we continued on down the path until we came to a creek that ran along the back edge of the park. It wasn't as wide as the one behind my aunt and uncle's house, but I hadn't forgotten when Brianna told me about sneaking off at her father's house to spend time by the water. It was soothing for both of us, which was perfect given the last two hours.

I found a boulder about half my height along the side of the bank and guided her over to it. Leaning against it, I turned her so that her back rested up against my chest and circled my arms around her waist. "Are you ready for Thanksgiving tomorrow at my aunt and uncle's house?"

She snuggled closer to me. Whether it was for warmth or because of the topic of discussion, I didn't know. "Will Jimmy and Samantha be there?"

"I doubt it. Jimmy is a first year resident. They usually stick the first years with the shifts no one else wants, and most people will want to spend Thanksgiving Day with their families."

Brianna nodded. "Good."

Although I would have like to see her face, I didn't want to relinquish my hold on her yet. "Do you not like Jimmy and Samantha?"

"Jimmy is okay, but sometimes he makes me nervous when he moves too fast or he's too loud." She paused, and I could only imagine the expression on her face. "I don't like Samantha."

I hummed. "She's not my favorite person either."

"Samantha doesn't like you."

Giving her a gentle squeeze, I rested my chin on her shoulder. "We've never gotten along. Most of that's my fault. Samantha always wanted to go into psychology, so she was always trying to psychoanalyze everyone around her. We butted heads. Even back in high school. Time hasn't changed that."

"So it's not because of me?"

I shook my head. "No. Not really. Samantha just likes to put her nose in other people's business, and I refuse to let her have any say in my life. She doesn't like that."

We stood for several minutes listening to the water as it trickled over a grouping of rocks nearby.

"May I ask you something?"

"Brianna, you can ask me anything you want. You know that."

"I know. But it's . . . it's about your parents."

Kissing the side of her neck, I buried my chilled nose in her hair, inhaling her scent and absorbing her warmth. "What do you want to know about them?"

"Not about them really, I guess. More, it's because of what happened to them that you don't like therapists, right?"

I tightened my hold on her involuntarily. "Yes."

My hands rested lightly on her abdomen, and she reached down to lace our fingers together. "Will you tell me why?"

Sighing, I closed my eyes before reopening them and beginning my story. "I've told you that right after my parents died I retreated into myself for months."

She nodded.

"My uncle insisted I needed therapy—someone to talk to, to share my feelings with." I paused, half lost in my memories. "The first woman he sent me to . . . well, it was a waste of time. It was right after, and I wasn't saying anything to anyone. She suggested they give it a little time and maybe try again in a few months. There was no sense in paying her to sit there for an hour each week while I said nothing. She was right. I wasn't going to talk until I was ready."

I squeezed her fingers before I continued. "When I did finally start talking, Richard was adamant that I go back into therapy. He was worried I would start to internalize again if I didn't get it out. The problem was the lady I'd seen originally didn't have any openings, and Richard wasn't willing to wait until that happened, so he found someone else. Looking back, it would probably have been better if I'd gone back to see that first person."

"Did they hurt you?" The concern in her voice made my heart melt.

"Not physically, no. The man Richard found was supposed to be one of the best in the area at dealing with grief. At first, it wasn't horrible, although I didn't much care for the guy. He was arrogant, and most of the time he didn't seem to like my answers to his questions. After a couple of months, though, things began to change. According to him, my feelings of guilt were no longer valid. I was being a spoiled, overprivileged brat, and I needed to get over myself."

Every muscle in Brianna's body tightened. "He said that to you?"

"Yes. And unfortunately, the teenager in me took that as permission to rebel. It was shortly after that when I started sneaking out. I guess you could say I began acting like the spoiled brat he accused me of being."

What felt like moisture hit the back of my hand. I looked up toward the sky, but I saw no sign of rain or snow.

Feeling another drop, I lifted my hand and turned Brianna's face toward mine. She was crying. "Shh, love. It was a long time ago."

"He was a bad man."

I smiled and kissed each of her wet cheeks. "Yes, he was. What he did nearly caused me to destroy my life. If not for my aunt, I wouldn't have graduated high school or gone on to college. I would have proved him right."

Suddenly she turned and wound her arms around my neck, hugging me. I held on tight. "I love you."

"I love you, too, Brianna. Always."

Chapter 35

Stephan
We were running late.

It was partially my fault. Okay, completely my fault considering I could have told her to stop, but that was the last thing I'd wanted. We'd slept in since we were up late the night before watching a movie together . . . well, that and fooling around. I had an extremely difficult time keeping my hands to myself.

This morning had been a rare occasion when Brianna woke up before I did, and when I had finally opened my eyes, she asked if she could service me. Brianna had a smile on her face, and I had no doubts that it was something she desired.

As I drove us out of the city toward Diane and Richard's, I grew hard again remembering. What Brianna could do with her mouth was amazing. Sarah enjoyed giving blowjobs, but she had rarely taken me all the way in —her gag reflex was too strong. She'd tried to overcome it but hadn't been completely successful while we were together. Brianna, however, had no issues whatsoever in swallowing every last inch of me. The feeling of being completely consumed by her was something I couldn't describe. It was exhilarating yet humbling. I felt powerful but honored at the same time.

"Everything all right, Sir?"

I glanced over to see the concerned look on Brianna's face before returning my attention to the road. Reaching for her hand, I placed it in my lap close to my erection. "Just remembering this morning."

"Oh."

I couldn't miss her smile, and it caused me to chuckle. With every day that passed, Brianna became more confident in her sexuality. It was hard for her to believe how much she affected me sometimes, but she was slowly learning. This morning was a perfect example of that.

"Did you want me to help you with it?"

It was impossible to suppress my groan. Yes, I would love to feel her lips wrapped around my cock again, but we were already running late, and I wasn't crazy enough to get a blowjob while driving. I wasn't a teenager anymore.

Squeezing her hand, I threaded our fingers together. "Later. As it is, we'll barely make it on time. Diane won't be happy if we're more than a few minutes late. She goes all out for the holidays."

Brianna scooted closer to me, wrapping her arm around mine, and laying her head on my shoulder. I kissed the top of her head, and relaxed back into the drive. There hadn't been any paparazzi outside my building today, and I was grateful. Maybe they decided spending time with their families was more important than trying to catch me doing something noteworthy. Or maybe they'd found someone more interesting to harass. I could only hope.

We pulled up to the front of my aunt and uncle's house with a minute to spare. How I'd managed even that was a miracle in and of itself. They lived nearly an hour from my condo, and we'd left fifty minutes ago.

As I exited my car, my cell phone beeped, letting me know I had a message. I quickly dug my phone out of my pocket, perplexed by who it might be. It was from Sarah.

Going home. Thank you for everything.

Smiling, I slipped the phone back into my pocket. Sarah and I had talked earlier in the week about her going home for the holidays. It looked as if she'd made her decision.

I helped Brianna out of the car and retrieved our bags from the trunk. We were going to give spending the night a chance, but I'd promised Brianna that if at any time she wanted to go back home to let me know. I wanted this to be a positive experience for her. She'd come out of her shell so much in the last seven months since I'd known her. It was almost hard to believe she was the same woman who'd sat in my living room that first full day in pain because she refused to go to the bathroom without permission—the same woman who had cowered in fear when I touched her.

With our bags over my right shoulder, I reached out with my left hand for Brianna's and headed for the front door.

As usual, the door opened before we were able to reach it. This time, however, it was my aunt who greeted us. "Get in here. I was starting to get worried."

I gave Diane a kiss on the cheek. "My apologies. We were running a bit late today."

She smiled knowingly. "I bet you were."

Brianna leaned into me, hiding her face in my shoulder. The girl who'd once been a sex slave now blushed at being called out on our implied sexual activities.

I chuckled. "Dinner ready?"

"Not yet. Why don't you and Brianna take your things upstairs, and then you can join Richard in the den while I finish things up? Maybe you can get him out of his medical journals."

Diane strolled back toward the kitchen, and I guided Brianna up the stairs toward my old room. I quickly deposited our bags down on the bed and pulled Brianna into my arms. Even though I couldn't take things too far, I still needed to taste her before we went down to dinner. Since she'd been back, my craving of her had only increased.

Her lips were soft beneath mine as I sucked them into my mouth one at a time. She held on to my shoulders, and a low hum reverberated from my chest.

Dipping my tongue inside her mouth, I languidly explored, taking my time . . . savoring.

A throat clearing pulled us apart.

I looked up to find Richard hovering right outside the door. "Your aunt wanted me to let you know she's putting dinner on the table."

He looked embarrassed at catching us kissing.

Smiling, I glanced down at Brianna. She was slightly flushed from our mini make-out session, but otherwise she was fine. I took hold of her hand, and we all headed downstairs to see what kind of spread Diane had put together this year.

When we ambled into the formal dining room, even I was somewhat stunned. Diane had outdone herself this year. The table was decorated with all manner of miniature pumpkins, squash, and colored leaves. There were only four place settings, confirming Jimmy and Samantha wouldn't be joining us today, but barring that, one would think Diane was hosting a high-society dinner party.

"It looks lovely, my dear." Richard kissed Diane's cheek before taking his seat at the head of the table.

"Thank you."

I pulled out Brianna's chair and then took my own beside her.

Dinner was fairly uneventful. Richard was on his best behavior. Not once did he try to question my relationship with Brianna. It was progress.

Afterward, we all retired downstairs to Richard and Diane's theater room. Neither were huge football fans, but Thanksgiving was the one day they both made an exception. I settled into one of the plush recliners and pulled Brianna down into my lap as Richard turned on all the equipment. A few minutes later, the big screen along the front wall came to life.

As we continued to watch the game, I started paying more attention to Brianna's reactions. Diane, Richard, and I would occasionally react or make a comment when one of the teams scored or if there was a big play—something we understood—but Brianna was reacting to more than that. She would tense up or shift her weight after plays that meant absolutely nothing to me.

When a commercial came on toward the beginning of the second game, I tilted her head so that she was looking at me. "You like football?"

She nodded. "John liked football. It was the only time he'd talk to me."

I brushed her hair back from her face and gave her a soft kiss on the lips. "Something I didn't know about you."

The game came back on, and I turned her back around so we could watch the game together. I had to admit it was a more enjoyable experience than it had ever been in the past. There was no doubt in my mind that was because of Brianna. She made everything better, and I derived pleasure from watching her become caught up in what was happening on the screen.

Once the second game was over, we all went back upstairs for some pie. Again, Diane had outdone herself. There was pumpkin, apple, cherry, and pecan. Brianna and I took a seat at the kitchen island as Richard and Diane brought the pies over.

My aunt loved to cook, and she was good at it. Not as good as Brianna, but good enough that my mouth was watering as I scooped up a mouthful of apple pie and ice cream.

It had been several hours since dinner, which was the only reason any of us had room for dessert. Brianna sat next to me with a piece of the pumpkin pie. She was eating and smiling. It was nice to see.

Diane and Richard sat across from us whittling away at their pieces of pie as well. We chatted about Christmas and New Year's—they'd been invited to a party by one of Richard's doctor friends on New Year's Eve. This was the first time in a while that we felt like a family. Richard and I weren't fighting—he appeared to have finally accepted my relationship with Brianna—and Samantha wasn't here to add unneeded, and unwanted, tension to the situation. It was pretty close to perfect.

"Brianna? I was wondering if you'd like to go shopping with me tomorrow."

Shocked, Brianna looked at my aunt before turning to look at me. "Um. I don't know."

I laced my fingers with hers and brought her hand to rest in my lap. "It's completely up to you, Brianna. Do you want to go?"

She looked torn. "Will there be a lot of people?"

"Probably. Although that will depend greatly on where you and Diane go."

Uncertainty took over Brianna's features.

Diane stood and began clearing the plates. "I'm not a big fan of crowds myself, so I tend to avoid them whenever possible. I would, however, like to hit a few of the specialty shops. You never know what they're going to have on sale the day after Thanksgiving."

It was evident by the emotions flittering across Brianna's face that there was a war of indecision waging inside her. I stood, and encouraged Brianna to follow, as I addressed Diane. "What time were you planning to leave tomorrow?"

"Nine, maybe. I haven't decided yet."

I nodded. "I think Brianna needs some time to think about it. She'll let you know in the morning."

Diane looked somewhat concerned. "All right." It was then she noticed that we'd both gotten up from our seats. "Are you heading upstairs, then?"

After giving Brianna's hand a quick squeeze, I released her and walked over to give my aunt a kiss on the cheek. "Thank you for dinner. It was delicious."

She smiled and patted my cheek. "You're always welcome, Stephan."

With a single nod to Richard, I rejoined Brianna. "We'll see you in the morning. Good night."

"Good night."

Brianna

Stephan didn't say anything as we trudged up the stairs to his bedroom, but I didn't mind. It had been a good day. Even Richard was nice to Stephan. He was smiling and seemed happy.

Diane's asking me to go with her tomorrow caught me off guard. Stephan had said I could go if I wanted to, but what if there were a lot of people and I panicked? Logic told me I would be safe with Diane, but there was always that little voice in my head that told me danger was right around the corner.

When we reached Stephan's bedroom, he shut and locked the door behind us. I wondered if that was to keep anyone from waking us up in the morning, or if he had plans for us tonight that he didn't want interrupted. Maybe both. I could only hope.

The first thing Stephan did was turn up the thermostat. It was a little cool in the room, although not what I would consider cold. Then again, the temperature was supposed to drop tonight. I could already see what looked like snow falling outside the window.

Once that was done, he took me by the hand and led me over to the padded window seat. He sat down and then guided me to sit between his legs. I leaned back against him and soaked up his warmth as he held me.

"I know you'd like to go with my aunt tomorrow. Tell me what your fears are?" His hot breath caressed my ear as he spoke.

"People. What if someone touches me and I freak out?"

I felt Stephan nod behind me. "That's a very real fear, and I don't see it going away any time soon. But the only way you're going to get over your fear is to slowly push through it."

"So you think I should go?"

"I think you need to look inside yourself and weigh the pros and cons of going. If the press were not watching my moves so closely lately, I would go with you. As it is, I think if you do decide to go, you'd be better off without me there. There is always a chance someone would recognize me, which is the last thing you need when out among strangers."

We sat there looking out at the snow fall for a long time. He hadn't turned on the light when we entered the room, so the only illumination was from the moon. The longer I sat there staring out at the night, the more confused I became.

He started to massage my shoulders. It wasn't until then that I realized how stiff I'd become. "Talk to me, sweetheart."

"Tell me what to do."

"I won't do that. This is something you have to decide for yourself."

"But I don't know."

"What does your gut tell you? Which is stronger—your fear or your desire to go?"

I thought about that for a minute. It was a tough call. One minute, my fear was the more prevalent emotion. The next, my desire to spend time with Diane, to get to know the woman who meant so much to the man I loved, was pushing to the surface.

Stephan slid his hand along the inside of my thigh, startling me. "Shh. Relax. Lean back against me and stop thinking for a little while. I've got you."

Nodding, I did as he asked and leaned back against his chest. He shifted slightly and positioned my head so that it was resting on his shoulder.

Without words, he unbuttoned the sweater I was wearing over my dress. He signaled for me to lift up slightly, and then he slowly pushed the garment off my shoulders and down my arms.

After dropping my sweater on the floor nearby, I lowered my head back to his shoulder, and he reached between us. Without preamble, he unzipped my dress. He slid the straps down my arms and kept going until the dress was pooled around my waist.

Brushing my hair out of the way, he began peppering kisses along my neck. I tilted my head to the side to give him better access. His lips sent shots of electricity through my body every time they connected with my skin, which was often.

I was so distracted by his mouth that I barely noticed when he unclasped my bra and discarded it until the cool air of the room hit my nipples. Almost immediately, though, he reached up and began playing with them. He massaged my breasts and pulled on my nipples, all the while continuing to kiss my neck. The area between my legs was tingling, and I lifted my hips, silently begging for more.

"Greedy tonight, are we?"

"Yes, Sir."

Stephan smiled against my neck, and he gave my nipples an extra hard pinch. I squeaked. "Shh. You have to be a good girl tonight and be very quiet. We wouldn't want to be overheard by Richard and Diane, would we?"

I shook my head. That was the last thing I wanted. Richard was nice to Stephan today. I didn't want to ruin that. "I'll be good."

"Mmm. I know you will, my pet."

Before I knew what was happening, Stephan stood, taking me with him.

Without saying anything, he divested me of the rest of my clothes and removed all but his boxers. "Lean over and put your hands on the cushion."

I complied, feeling the uncertainty bubbling to the surface. Was he going to take me from behind tonight? He'd only done that once before. Would he do it again? Here? Now?

"Spread your legs," he ordered from much farther away than he'd been moments before.

I spread my legs.

"Wider."

Following his instruction, I opened wider, feeling extremely exposed.

He knelt down behind me and ran his fingers up the inside of my thigh. I shivered.

His hand remained where it was, but then I felt pressure against my entrance. "Relax. It's just my other hand, Brianna. You're fine."

I took a deep breath and willed myself to relax. This was Stephan. He'd take care of me. I was okay. I'd be okay.

"Good girl."

Mere seconds after the compliment left his mouth, two of his fingers pushed inside me. He'd had his fingers inside me many times before, but for some reason this felt different. Maybe it was because of my position, and his. My legs were spread, and my behind was thrust high into the air.

Stephan removed his hand on my thigh. "Look outside, Brianna. Watch the snow falling and remember to keep quiet. I'd use a gag on you, but you're not ready, so I'll have to trust that you'll be able to control yourself. Can you do that, pet?"

All the time he spoke, he continued to thrust his fingers. It was becoming hard to concentrate. "Yes, Sir."

He reached up to caress one of my breasts until my nipple was hard and aching. Soon I wasn't thinking about what position I was in or where we were. All I could concentrate on were his hands and what they were doing to my body.

He removed his fingers from inside me. I felt empty but not for long. Seconds later, his penis was filling the space his fingers had been. As he pressed forward, I felt stretched . . . full . . . as I always did when he took me. It was even more so in this position.

When he was all the way inside, he used his now free hand and wrapped it around my hair. Although the position made me nervous given this was only our second time, knowing what was coming sent a surge of heat where we were joined.

"Brace yourself, Brianna. This is going to be hard, and fast. Are you ready?"

I braced my hands against the cushion as best I could. "Yes."

Stephan did not exaggerate when he said he was going to take me hard and fast. He used both my breast and hair as leverage as he both slammed into me with his hips and brought me back to meet each and every one of his thrusts at the same time. I opened my mouth in what was, thankfully, a silent scream. My entire body was screaming. I could feel him from the top of my head to the tips of my toes.

It was . . .

It was . . .

His hand left my breast and flattened against my clit. His motions were erratic, but it didn't matter. I was on the edge, ready to fall off.

He pulled back hard on my hair, causing my neck to arch. "Come."

The word was whispered, but it was what my body had been waiting for, and my world exploded.

Chapter 36

Brianna

Light was coming through the window the next time I opened my eyes. Stephan was lying beside me in the bed, his arm wrapped possessively across my stomach. The last thing I remembered about last night was how my orgasm had hit me like a freight train. I didn't understand how or why my body responded like it did to him, but I loved it. That it made him happy, too, was a huge bonus.

"You're awake?"

I glanced up to see Stephan smiling down at me. "Good morning."

He brushed his fingers down the side of my face. "How are you feeling?"

"Good. Rested."

That seemed to amuse him. "That's good. You were out of it after your orgasm last night. I had to carry you to bed." He leaned down and softly kissed my lips. "Sometimes your reactions amaze me."

Stephan didn't allow me to respond to his observations. He deepened our kiss and wrapped me further into his embrace, tangling our legs together.

When we broke apart, he took my face between his hands and gave me one last hard kiss. "Have you decided whether or not you want to go shopping with Diane?"

I hadn't. I hadn't thought of much of anything after he began touching me last night. "No."

"No you don't want to go, or no you haven't thought any more about it?"

"I hadn't thought any more about it." I paused, knowing he was going to want an answer one way or another. He said it was my decision, so I knew I had to decide. To my surprise, the thought of going shopping with Diane this morning didn't produce the fear it had last night. I wasn't sure if that was because it wasn't there, or if I was just so relaxed from what Stephan had done to me that I couldn't be frightened. Had that been his plan?

"If you're going, then we'll need to get up soon so that you have enough time to get ready and eat something. If not, then I'm sure I can think of other ways to occupy our day." The smile on his face was wicked, but I wasn't scared.

"I think . . ." I hesitated. "I think I want to go."

The next hour was spent getting ready and eating breakfast. Diane was thrilled when I told her I'd be going with her. She promised she wouldn't leave my side for a moment.

When Diane trotted off to the bathroom, leaving Stephan and I alone for a few minutes in the entryway, he pulled me into his arms. "You have your phone?"

"Yes, Sir."

"Your credit card?"

"Yes."

Kissing my lips, he reached into his back pocket and handed me several bills. "Put this in your pocket, not in your purse, and only use it in case of an emergency."

I took the money from him and did as he'd said, putting the money in the pocket of my jeans rather than the purse I was carrying.

Diane rejoined us in the entryway. "Ready?"

"Yes." My voice was shaking, but it was the best I could do given the circumstances. As the time grew closer for us to leave, my nerves had made a reappearance. Stephan said that was only natural and assured me that he was only a phone call away.

"Try to relax and have fun, all right, sweetheart?"

"I will."

Diane was quiet as she drove. Due to the snow the night before, the roads were slick in spots. I was glad she was concentrating on driving and didn't require me to keep up any sort of conversation, because I was trying to talk myself down from a ledge. Had I made the right choice in agreeing to go? Should I have stayed with Stephan? What if something happened? What if I freaked out and caused a scene? What if—

"Everything okay?"

I jumped but then forced myself to breathe. We hadn't even gotten near people yet. "Yes. I'm just . . . nervous."

"About the crowds?"

"Yes."

"That's understandable, which is why we're only going to make two stops today. One is to an art gallery, so there shouldn't be too many people hanging about. They have a fairly exclusive clientele, and most of them buy via a buyer, the Internet, or at events the curator hosts. I, however, prefer the one-on-one approach."

"Okay."

"Our second stop is a boutique. They carry woman's clothing that I absolutely adore. We may encounter more people there, but I think most after-Thanksgiving shoppers will be heading to the mall or the larger retailers. Personally I don't much care for them, but to each their own, right?"

I'd never heard Diane talk so much before, but I appreciated her breaking things down for me. It helped. "Thank you."

"Brianna, if you don't mind me asking, is there something you need me to do if you do freak out as you fear you might?"

That was easy to answer. "Call Stephan. He can calm me down better than anyone."

She smiled. "I'm glad he has you, Brianna. For the longest time he was so closed off. Even when he smiled, it never reached his eyes—not since his parents died anyway. The way I see him look at you . . . it warms my heart."

It was my turn to smile. I loved knowing that I made Stephan happy. With everything he helped me deal with, sometimes it was hard to see what he got out of it, but there was obviously something I gave him that no one else had before.

"You love him."

There was no reason to deny it. "Yes."

"And he loves you."

I felt my cheeks warm. "He does."

Diane didn't say anything more after that, but she didn't stop smiling.

The art gallery was just as she said it would be. There were hundreds of paintings and photographs hanging on the walls or in glass cases scattered around the room. We were the only people in the gallery besides the older lady who helped Diane find what she needed. She was looking for a picture to go on the wall in Richard's office. She wanted it to be special since that was his space and he spent a lot of time there going over patient files and other paperwork.

Once we were finished at the gallery, she drove another few blocks before stopping in front of a small clothing store. At least it looked small from the outside, minuscule even, but once we got inside, I saw that the outside was deceiving. The building was longer than it was wide, and it had an upstairs. There were clothes everywhere.

We worked our way through several racks, and Diane selected a few pieces she liked, draping them over her arm and then moving on to see whatever else she could find. I walked behind her, looking at some of the clothes but paying more attention to the other people in the store than anything else.

"Have you thought about Christmas? Did you want to get Stephan something? I know I said we were only going to two stores, but if there is somewhere you want to go, I'd be more than happy to take you."

I hated to admit the thought hadn't even crossed my mind. Christmas was just over a month away. "I don't know what to get him."

She sighed. "You and me both. That man is notoriously hard to shop for. Of course, most men are."

"What do you normally get him for Christmas?"

"Hmm. Let's see. Last year I got him a watch and some gift certificates for books and movies. He loves both, although he has so many already I have no idea how he keeps track of what he has and doesn't have." She waved her hand in the air dismissively. "But those are my go-to items—books and movies. I always try to find him something else, though, that he's not expecting."

Stephan did like books and movies. Most of the time we spent together that didn't involve talking or sex included reading or watching one of the movies Stephan had in his collection. I'd asked him once why he had so many movies that most people would consider chick flicks since before me he'd never lived with a woman. He'd said that Sarah had commented once when they were together that he never had any movies she wanted to watch, so he'd gone out and bought a handful of movies the store clerk had assured him his girlfriend would love. Sarah had appreciated the gesture, and since then he'd made it a point to keep his collection diverse.

We moved upstairs, and I noticed they had lingerie. Stephan had never expressed a desire for me to wear lingerie, but I also knew he enjoyed seeing me in the bra and panty sets Lily had picked out. As I continued to look, a couple of items caught my eye, but I pushed the thought aside. I had no idea what Stephan liked, and if I wore anything, it would be for his pleasure, not mine.

Diane finished her shopping, and we headed back toward her house. Overall, it had been a good day. I didn't buy anything, but I didn't have one of my panic attacks either.

I was on such an emotional high that I ran out of the car as soon as Diane parked it in the garage and rushed into the house to find Stephan. He was in the hall talking to Richard. I made a beeline straight for him.

He scooped me up in his arms and laughed.

"I missed you."

"I missed you, too. Did you have a good time?"

"Yes."

"Did you buy anything?"

I hesitated. "No."

Stephan looked at me, curious. I knew there would be questions coming, but I was glad he didn't ask me in front of his uncle.

Richard cleared his throat, and again I was embarrassed. "If you'll excuse me, I'm going to go see if my wife needs help carrying things in."

Stephan

I'd been glued to my cell phone since she'd been gone. Richard shook his head a few times but otherwise didn't comment. Given her smile when she got back, it seemed she had a good time.

Richard helped Diane carry in the few bags she had, and then we all gathered in the kitchen for leftovers. We made a dent in what Diane had made but not a big one. I already knew Brianna and I would be taking home leftovers. She wouldn't need to cook for a few days, at least.

After lunch, I disappeared upstairs for a few minutes to grab our bags. As I was turning to leave, I noticed Richard lingering in the hallway again. "Hey."

"Stephan."

When he didn't say more, a knot began to form in the pit of my stomach. He'd been pleasant during our visit thus far. I was hoping that wasn't going to suddenly change. "Something wrong?"

He shook his head. "No. I just . . . I wanted to say that maybe I was wrong. Before."

I raised my eyebrow in question.

"You aren't going to make this easy, are you?" He sighed. "I realize that I jumped to conclusions all those months ago when Tami came to see me. When she showed me pictures of her bruises and said you'd caused them, I immediately went into doctor mode. Over the years, I've seen too many cases of domestic violence, and the thought that you might be one of those abusers turned my blood cold. I was angry, and I admit I didn't listen to you as I should have. I'm sorry."

To say I was shocked was an understatement. Never had I thought I'd get an apology from Richard—not about that anyway. "Thank you."

"Don't get me wrong. I still don't completely understand your need to . . . to . . ."

"Be a Dom?"

He released an exaggerated breath. "Yes. I suppose that would be the easiest way to put it. I don't get it, and I don't think I ever will, but even I have to admit Brianna seems happy. She doesn't appear to be afraid of you in any way. In the end, I'm a scientist, and I have to take the evidence for what it is."

"Thanks. I think."

Richard chuckled. "I'm not doing this very well, am I?"

I smiled, letting him off the hook. "I think you did all right. Richard, if you have questions about my lifestyle, I will be more than happy to answer them for you, but only if you go into it with an open mind. If all you want to do is condemn, then I think it's better we just agree to disagree on the subject."

He nodded but didn't say any more.

The drive home took longer than usual. It seemed as if everyone was out and driving the exact same way we were—into the city. I would have thought people would be heading home at this point in the day but apparently not. Of course, it didn't help that we hit every traffic light—that, in and of itself, added another fifteen minutes to our drive.

Back in the condo, we unpacked and Brianna put away the food. Although the time at Richard and Diane's had been relaxing, there was something about being home.

I walked up behind Brianna as she unloaded the dishwasher. She melted back into me, and my arms wrapped around her waist. "What were you thinking about earlier?"

There was no need to specify when. Brianna knew what I was talking about. "Diane and I went to a clothing store today. They had lingerie there, and I wondered if that was something you liked?"

Burying my face in her neck, I chuckled. "Brianna, I don't think there are too many guys out there who don't like to see their women in lingerie."

"Okay."

"Of course, I like you naked as well. I'm not picky." To drive home my point, I reached up and found her cloth-covered nipple and gave it a quick pinch.

She let out a squeak.

I smiled and took a step back. "I'll be upstairs for a while. Once you're finished, you can read or watch television. I'll be down once I'm finished sorting through e-mails."

After giving her a quick kiss, I disappeared upstairs.

The next few weeks were relatively uneventful, with the exception of our meetings with Oscar and Emma. They were both concerned. Ian Pierce was holding firm, and it was looking more and more every day like we were going to have to go to trial. To make matters worse, Emma delivered another blow that afternoon. John was requesting to see Brianna.

I was angry Emma even brought it up, but she stood her ground and insisted that, as Brianna's lawyer, she wouldn't be doing her job if she kept something like that from her client. Oscar agreed, which didn't improve my mood.

"You don't have to decide right away, Anna." Even Emma's tone was grating on my nerves, although I had no idea why. She wasn't talking any differently than she normally did. "Think about it and let me know."

"Are we done?"

Oscar, Emma, and Brianna all abruptly turned their attention to me. I could feel the disapproval radiating from my lawyer. Whether he liked my attitude or not was irrelevant, as was Brianna going to see her father, in my opinion. Hadn't the man done enough damage? Now he was skirting the system, enlisting the help of one of his friends in law enforcement, to make contact with Brianna he wasn't supposed to have.

"Yes, I think we're finished. For now."

I didn't wait for Oscar, or Emma, to add anything more before standing and ushering Brianna toward the door.

"Anna?"

Brianna looked over her shoulder at Emma while I tried to calm myself down. Why was it that I was the only one who appeared concerned with *protecting* Brianna . . . shielding her from more hurt. Everyone else seemed content to throw her to the wolves and hope she made it out relatively unscathed.

Once Emma reminded Brianna that she'd be stopping by our condo next Saturday to go over some things with her, we left. All I wanted to do was get home, sit in my chair, and hold Brianna. With every day that passed, I hated Ian Pierce more and more. As for John . . . I wanted to see him rot in a jail cell for the rest of his life. I pictured something cold and dark and devoid of normal human interaction.

"You're angry."

"Yes."

"Did I do something?"

I sighed and tried to calm myself. "No. It's not you."

"You don't want me to see John."

I wasn't going to lie to her. "No, I don't."

"Why?"

Glancing over at her, I shook my head. "Because I don't see the point. We don't even know *why* he wants to see you." I paused. "Do *you* want to see him?"

She shrugged. "Not really. I guess I'm curious. He kept asking to see me after he was arrested, but then he stopped. Now he wants to see me again. Why?"

I guess I could see her point. He was, after all, the only living family she had left. I gripped the steering wheel hard, my knuckles turning white. "As much as I hate to admit it, Emma is right. It's your decision. I won't stop you if you want to talk to him but, Brianna, I want you to think about this long and hard. John hurt you. A lot. He's the one ultimately responsible for you ending up in Ian's clutches for ten months. You don't owe him anything. If you want to go see him, fine. I won't stop you. But don't do this for him. He doesn't deserve it."

Brianna nodded and reached for my hand. I took it, and after placing a soft kiss on her fingers, placed our joined hands in my lap. Starting the vehicle, I maneuvered out into traffic. We drove home in silence, both of us with a lot to think about.

Chapter 37

Stephan

As promised, Emma stopped by the following Saturday. It was less than two weeks before Christmas, and it was anything but the joyous time I'd hoped it would be for Brianna. Because of that, I hovered like a mother hen over their meeting. Emma gave me the evil eye a few times, but I pretended not to notice. There was no way I was leaving Brianna to deal with whatever Emma needed to go over with her alone.

It turned out to be copies of Brianna's statement. There were a few items the prosecution wanted clarified since it was looking like we'd be going to trial come February. I could tell Emma was attempting to make the ordeal as easy as possible, but reliving any part of that nightmare was difficult for Brianna.

When I heard her voice become monotone, I intervened.

I knelt down beside her chair. "Look at me, Brianna."

Emma startled a little at my brisk tone, but I dismissed her reaction and focused on Brianna. She slowly turned to meet my gaze, but her eyes were unfocused. I knew she wasn't truly with me in that moment.

Reaching out, I took hold of both her hands and brought them to the side of my face. I wanted her to be able to feel me here with her. "Take a deep breath."

She did.

"Another."

Her chest rose and then fell as she sucked in the calming breath.

"Good girl. What number?" I knew it was probably high, even though by all outward appearances she wasn't having a panic attack. This was how Brianna had coped, and it was something I feared she might always fall back to.

"Six."

I nodded and glanced over to Emma. "She needs a break. We'll be back shortly."

Helping Brianna to stand, I picked her up and carried her into her bedroom. I would have taken her over to my chair in the living room, but I wanted her away from Emma for a time so that she could decompress. The next best option was the chair in her room.

Getting us both comfortable, I let her cling to me for a few minutes. It was what she needed, and I gradually felt her heart rate slow to a normal pace.

I kissed her forehead and ran my hands through her hair. As much as I hated what Emma was doing, I knew it was a necessary evil. There was a good chance that in less than two months Brianna would have to go before a jury and testify—telling the world what Ian had done to her. She was going to be forced to come face-to-face not only with her abuser but to recount the details of her captivity. I wasn't going to be able to help her, no matter how much I wanted to. She would have to sit up on that stand alone and hurting. The thought of it ate at me.

I'd asked Oscar if there was anything we could do to prevent what appeared to be inevitable. Unfortunately, the law stated that Ian Pierce had the right to a fair trial. Unless he changed his mind and took the deal between now and February, all of our hands were tied.

"Thank you," she whispered.

"No need to thank me, love. I'm always here for you. I only wish I could do something to make this easier."

She snuggled closer. "You do. Knowing that you're here—that you love me no matter what—that helps me."

"I wish I could do more—make it all go away for you."

"You do."

I looked at her skeptically.

Brianna took on a rather serious expression as she sat up to face me. It was a complete one-eighty from the frightened woman I'd brought into the bedroom a few minutes before. "You do. There are times when I don't think about what Ian did to me. At first, no matter what was happening, I'd always relate it back to the bad stuff. That doesn't always happen anymore. There are times when I don't remember, and it's only what's happening in the moment."

Unable to resist, I kissed her. She met my lips enthusiastically, and it ended up getting more out of control than I'd intended. When I finally pulled us apart, we were both panting. "Emma is still in the other room."

She looked deflated. "I know."

I laughed and gave her another kiss that told her how much I wished we were the only two in the condo.

Brianna straddled me, and I could feel her heat through her jeans. I dug my fingers into her thighs, pressing her down against my growing erection. This was quickly getting out of control, and I knew I needed to stop, but she felt too good.

"Everything all—"

We broke apart and turned toward the door. Emma was standing there red-faced, with her mouth hanging wide open.

"Um. Perhaps I should come back later." Before I could speak, Emma turned on her heel and left the room.

Sighing, I helped Brianna stand and walked with her back out into the main room. As much as I wished all the things Emma had to go over with Brianna didn't have to be done, I knew better, and waiting wasn't going to make it any easier.

It took a little convincing, but Emma stayed and finished going over everything she needed to with Brianna. One of the points the prosecutor wanted clarified was where the abuse had taken place in the house. Ian's property was still closed off. Given how big the house and surrounding property was—and that the entire scope of it held potential evidence— they'd been combing through it room by room, acre by acre. I had no idea where Alex was staying if this was still the case. I knew Agent Marco had talked to her, but my understanding was that she was denying anything out of the ordinary had happened to her while living with Ian.

This time around, I sat beside Brianna, holding her hand. It made a world of difference. She didn't go into her robotic mode again and was able to answer Emma's questions.

As Emma was leaving, she took hold of Brianna's hand and held it. "You're seeing a psychiatrist, aren't you, Anna?"

Brianna nodded. "Yes. Dr. Perkins."

Emma smiled. "You might want to talk to her about this. The upcoming trial, I mean. She might be able to give you some techniques to help you through your testimony. Having Stephan sitting with you, holding your hand, seemed to help, but you won't have that in court."

"Okay."

I pulled Brianna into my arms as Emma walked out the door. We stood there watching the monitor as the elevator doors opened and then closed behind her. This was going to be a very long seven weeks, and I began to think of ways I could distract Brianna. The last thing she needed was to spend that time fretting over what was to come. It wasn't as if either one of us could change it.

As we sat in my chair later that night, I brought up something that had been lingering on my mind since the conversation we had with Richard and Diane on Thanksgiving. "Did you and your mother have any Christmas traditions?"

She furrowed her brow, seeming to be deep in thought. "We used to bake cookies. Is that what you mean?"

I smiled and cuddled closer to her. This day had been rough on both of us. "Yes. That's exactly what I mean. What kind of cookies would you and your mom make?"

"All different kinds. Gingerbread. Chocolate chip. Sugar cookies. And these ones Mom called monster cookies with M&M's in them." Although she had her head resting on my shoulder, I could hear the smile in her voice.

The topic had successfully distracted her, so I kept going. "Did you make them on Christmas Day or before?"

"The weekend before. Mom and I would go to the grocery store and buy all the supplies early Saturday morning, and then we'd spend the rest of the weekend baking."

Brianna's voice drifted off. "Your mom would be very proud of you, you know."

"Why do you say that?" She sounded far away.

I sat her up, so that I could see her face. She looked sad. "Because from what you've told me, she sounds like a great mom. She loved you, and she'd want to see you happy. You're taking back control of your life, Brianna. Control that was taken from you without your consent. How could she not be proud of the strong daughter she raised?"

A single tear slid down her cheek. "I don't feel strong."

"But you are. You are the strongest woman I've ever known. Every time you've come up against a wall, you fight and you push through it. It may take time, but you do it. You don't give up. That's strength. Anyone can appear to be strong if that strength has never been tested. Yours has been tested, and then some, and you survived, Brianna. You survived. That, my love, is true strength."

Tears were flowing freely down her face. I attempted to wipe them from her cheeks, but as soon as I brushed one away, another was there to take its place. "It's you. You help me. You're the strong one."

I shook my head and brushed my lips against hers. "No, that's all you. *You*, Brianna. If you didn't have that strength inside you, what I did to help wouldn't matter."

Leaning my forehead against hers, I met her tear-filled gaze, trying to will her to understand how I felt. "I know your mom would be proud of you, because I'm proud of you. There is no way the woman you've told me about wouldn't feel the same way."

Brianna wrapped her arms around my neck and buried her head against my shoulder. "I couldn't do it without you."

"Yes, you could, but I'm very glad you've chosen not to."

I waited for her to calm down some, rubbing her back, trying to provide what comfort I could. "Would you like to tell me some more about how you used to celebrate Christmas with your mom? Surely you had other traditions. Like . . . when did you open presents? Christmas morning, or did you open them early on Christmas Eve?"

She giggled, and I was hoping that was a sign the worst of it was over. "Christmas Eve. Mom said once I knew Santa wasn't real, there was no point in waiting."

"Ah. Smart woman."

Brianna

It was the Friday before Christmas, and I still hadn't figured out what to get Stephan. I'd asked Lily, but she wasn't able to help me much. Stephan didn't really need anything. I'd been thinking about it nonstop for days, but I had yet to settle on something I thought wouldn't just take up space or was something generic. He always took care of me, and I wanted his Christmas present to be special.

Jade arrived to take me to see Dr. Perkins. It was my last meeting for two weeks since she was taking next week off. She said I could always call her service in case of an emergency, and they could track her down.

"How have you been this week, Anna?"

It was the same question Dr. Perkins asked me every week. Usually I responded by telling her I was fine, but today I decided that I wanted her help. That was what she was for, right? "Frustrated."

She scribbled something down on her notepad. "What has you frustrated?"

"Christmas. I don't know what to get Stephan."

"Ah, yes. Sometimes finding gifts for those in our lives can be hard. I find that men especially can be difficult to buy for."

"That's what everyone keeps telling me, but it doesn't help me figure out what to get him. It has to be special."

Dr. Perkins set her pen and paper down and leaned forward resting her elbows on her knees. "Does he have any hobbies? Something he likes to do in his free time?"

"Yes, but he has lots of books and movies."

"Okay. Well, is there anything else he likes besides books and movies?"

It took me a minute, but suddenly a lightbulb went off in my head. Although it wasn't really a gift exactly, I knew it was something he wanted, and he'd been putting off doing it because he was unsure of my reaction. I'd need some help, though, to pull it off.

"You're smiling. You must have thought of something."

"I did."

Dr. Perkins sat back in her chair. "It's good to see you happy, Anna."

"Stephan makes me happy."

"I can see that."

We'd talked about Stephan a lot since he came with me the day before Thanksgiving. Dr. Perkins hadn't pressed the issue about my sexual relationship with Stephan, but I knew she was still worried. I'd become good at reading people during my time with Ian, and I knew she was holding her opinion on the subject back. Every time we talked about my relationship with Stephan in any depth, she would bite the inside of her cheek. It was barely noticeable, but after a few times, I'd picked up on the subtle reaction.

She picked her pad of paper back up. "So now that we've solved that little dilemma, what else has been going on in your life this week?"

I glanced down and started to pick at my jeans before I told myself to stop it. Stephan had noticed some loose threads in my jeans and asked me about it. When I'd told him, he'd given me that look that said he wasn't happy. I had to at least try not to ruin any more of my clothes due to my fidgeting.

Pressing my palms flat against my legs, I took a deep breath to steady myself. "Emma—my lawyer—she came by to see me Saturday."

"And what did she have to say?"

"They . . . Agent Marco and the prosecutor . . . wanted more details on some things I said in my statement."

"I imagine that was stressful for you."

I nodded. "I don't think I could have gotten through it if Stephan wasn't there." Pausing, I took another deep breath. "Emma thought so, too. She said I should talk to you . . . see if you could help me prepare for the trial."

Dr. Perkins didn't answer me right away, and when she did, her voice had taken on a sympathetic tone. "Anna, I wish there was something I could say or do that would make this easier for you, but I don't think there is. We've talked some already about breathing techniques and having something you can touch to ground you to reality so that you can pull yourself back from a flashback. Those are all things you can use, but in the end there's no way to know how you're going to react until you're up on the stand."

"I know. I don't know what Emma was hoping you could do. You can't even help me decide what to do about John—"

"Wait. John? Your father?"

I nodded.

"Anna, what's going on with your father? Did something happen you didn't tell me?"

Shrugging, I squirmed in my seat. It felt as if I were being scolded. I'd meant to bring it up last week, but we'd started talking about other things, and there was no time. "He wants to see me."

"I see. And do you want to see him?"

I brought my knees up to my chest and hugged them. "I don't know. I mean, why does he want to see me? Why now?"

"I don't have the answer to that, Anna. No one does but him."

"I know."

Dr. Perkins was quiet for several minutes. "What's the best memory you have from when you were living with your father?"

That was easy. "Watching football. Especially if his team was winning. He was always in a good mood then."

She nodded and asked me to go into specifics, which I did. Not every moment at John's house was horrible, but most of it was. The bad had easily outweighed the good.

Before I knew it, Dr. Perkins glanced over at the clock. "Anna, I want you to do something for me before the next time we meet. I want you to write down a list of pros and cons of going to see your father. Make sure not to leave anything out. It needs to be a comprehensive list. You don't have to show it to anyone—not even to me. This is for you, so you can say anything you want on it. Including calling him nasty names if you want to."

She winked at me, and I laughed.

"Can you do that for me?"

"Yes."

"Good." She smiled. "Our time is up today, and remember, I won't see you again until after the New Year. Try not to let all this dampen your holiday. You're strong, and you'll get through this."

I held her gaze. "That's what Stephan says."

Jade was waiting for me when I walked out of Dr. Perkins's office. I waved good-bye to Monica as Jade and I left.

It was snowing when we walked outside, so by the time we reached Jade's car, we were both damp and cold. She started the car and then grabbed a blanket out of the backseat that she used to cover us both. "Just until the car heats up. It's freezing out there. That wind rips right through you."

I huddled under the blanket but didn't comment.

"How was therapy?"

"Okay."

"Just okay?"

I nodded.

"Is that your way of telling me you don't want to talk about it?"

"I'm just anxious. I need to get home and make some phone calls."

That got her attention. "Phone calls?"

"I finally figured out what I'm getting Stephan for Christmas, but I need some help."

"Anything I can do?"

I thought about that for a minute. "Can you take me to a store?"

She froze. "You want me to take you to a store?"

"Yes."

"With people?"

I nodded.

"Um. Okay. What store did you want to go to?"

I sagged in my seat, feeling the weight of what I wanted to do. How was I going to pull all this off? Christmas was only four days away. "Somewhere that sells fountains. The ones people put on their desks or in their offices."

As understanding hit, Jade got a huge smile on her face. She gathered the blanket that was covering us and threw it into the backseat. "I know the perfect place."

An hour later, I entered the condo and rushed straight into my bedroom to hide Stephan's gift. It had taken only five minutes for me to find the fountain I wanted to get. It was fairly simple, but it was exactly what I'd wanted. It had three levels. The one at the top was the smallest, with each consecutive level a little wider than the one above it. The rock the fountain was made of reminded me of Stephan's rock behind his aunt and uncle's house. It was almost perfect, but I wanted one other thing to go with it.

Stephan was due home in less than twenty minutes, so I knew I had to hurry. Using my cell phone, I dialed Diane's number. She'd given it to me when we'd gone shopping in case for some reason we'd gotten separated.

She answered on the third ring. "Hello?"

"Diane? It's Brianna."

"Brianna? Is everything all right?"

I felt bad for frightening her. "Yes. Everything's good. I was wondering if you could help me with something."

"Of course. What did you need?"

I explained to her what I was looking for and why. She squealed with excitement. "Oh, that's perfect! He's going to love it."

"Do you think so?"

"I know so. You put a lot of thought into this, and Stephan is the type of man that will appreciate it."

"I hope so."

Diane made a dismissive sound. "Now, do you want me to bring it over to you sometime before Christmas, or do you want to wait and add it when you get here?"

"Can I give the fountain to you to keep until Christmas? I'm afraid he'll see it ahead of time. Plus, I have no way to wrap it up for him."

"Of course. I'll stop by Monday and pick it up. No worries."

"Thank you."

After saying good-bye to Diane, telling her I needed to go start dinner, I quickly made my final phone call. When he picked up, I swallowed, nervous. My hands were sweating, but I knew I had to do this. For Stephan.

"Hello? Logan? It's . . . it's Brianna. I need your help with something."

Chapter 38

Brianna

On Monday morning I was a bundle of nerves. Even though I knew Stephan couldn't be here with me, I wanted him nonetheless. He could calm me like no one else. As it was, I was standing in the kitchen pulling apart the remains of a bagel while waiting for Lily and Logan to arrive. Diane had already come and gone first thing. I was glad to get that marked off my to-do list at least.

The whole weekend was stressful, and Stephan noticed how on edge I was. He thought it was because of the upcoming trial and John. I was anxious about that, yes, but that wasn't what had me on pins and needles.

Stephan tried to distract me with everything from putting up a small Christmas tree that he dug out of the back of his closet to baking dozens of cookies. I had no idea what we would do with the cookies. There were way too many of them to eat all on our own. Mom and I used to deliver them to the neighbors, but I couldn't see Stephan going to the other floors and presenting them to the residents. We barely saw anyone else who lived in the building, let alone knew who they were.

I glanced over at the stacked containers full of cookies sitting on the counter, and before I could stop myself, I reached over and grabbed one. Removing the lid, the smell of sugary goodness floated up to my nostrils. I reached in and took a cookie, stuffing it into my mouth unceremoniously.

It would figure that right as my mouth was full of cookie the security panel would come to life, letting me know Lily and Logan had arrived. I could see them walking briskly toward the door, and there was no way I was going to be able to finish chewing and swallowing before they rang the doorbell. Running over to the trash, I promptly spit out the cookie, rinsed my mouth out with a drink of water, and rushed to answer the door.

Flinging the door open, I faced Lily and Logan. After a second, their relaxed expressions turned into ones of concern. "Are you all right, Brianna?"

I nodded but didn't move. The initial rush of answering the door slowly faded, and I felt unease take its place. Logan wasn't acting aggressively at the moment, but it didn't matter. He was a male, and an alpha male at that. The whole reason why I'd asked if Lily could come, too, was that I didn't think I could handle being alone with Logan—even if he was Stephan's best friend.

"Can we come in?"

At Lily's question, I jarred myself into action. "Yes."

As soon as they were inside and the door was shut behind them, Logan took charge, and I felt myself shrink a little. "He's gone?"

"Yes."

Logan must have realized how his tone had been perceived, and he softened it. "Are you sure you want to do this, Brianna? It's going to mean having a handful of strange men going in and out of the condo for most of the day."

I wrapped my arms around my waist as if that, somehow, would protect me. "I'm sure. I want to do this for Stephan."

He nodded. "All right. I'm going to go finalize things with Tom at the front desk so he knows what's going on. Why don't you and Lily get what you need and take off for your appointment. Lily can call me when you're on your way back, and I'll make sure the guys stay out of sight until you're back in the condo. I'll handle things here—that way you don't have to be involved or around people you don't know." Without waiting for me to respond, he walked toward the door.

"Logan?"

"Yes?" He stopped and looked back over his shoulder.

"Thank you."

He smiled. "No thanks needed. I'll be back in about a half hour."

Lily took hold of my hand and marched me to my room. Without a word, she packed a small bag for me and hoisted it over her shoulder. "Your appointment with Julie is in twenty minutes."

For the next hour and a half, Lily sat beside me as Julie waxed all the unwanted hair from my body. I knew how much Stephan liked it when I was bare. He hadn't said anything since I'd moved back in with him, but I knew it was something he desired. It was something I could give him.

Before we left the spa parking lot, Lily called Logan to let him know we were on our way. When we arrived back at the condo, there was no sign of Logan or any of the men.

Lily took my hand and led me into the kitchen. "Come on. We're going to need supplies if we're going to be cooped up in your room most of the day."

"Thank you for staying with me, Lily. And for this morning."

She glared at me for a second before she began digging through the cabinets and drawers. "You can stop thanking us, you know. We want to help. Simple as that."

We gathered an armful of snacks and drinks before heading to my bedroom. I didn't argue with her, but it wasn't simple. Not at all. Not only would it take up Logan and Lily's entire day, but it also required Logan to get other people to help him with only two days' notice. It was also Christmas Eve.

Lily and I crawled onto my bed along with my laptop and settled in to watch a movie.

About twenty minutes in, Logan knocked on the door, causing us both to look up from the computer. "I wanted to let you know that the guys and I are back. We're going to be in and out for about the next hour, so if you hear a lot of commotion, it's only us."

We both nodded.

"Did you need anything before we get started?"

Lily answered. "Nope. I think we're good."

He smiled. "I'll let you get back to your movie, then." Logan shut the door behind him, and we returned to watching our movie.

It was only a few minutes later that we started hearing voices. Lots of voices. Male voices.

As if sensing my discomfort, Lily placed her arm around my shoulder and pulled me against her side. It wasn't the same as Stephan, but it helped.

The noises in the main room ebbed and flowed for the next two hours. I heard several different voices, but I couldn't tell how many of them there were. How many guys had Logan brought with him to help?

At lunchtime, Logan knocked on my bedroom door again before strolling inside with two plastic bags. "I brought you ladies some food."

Lily scrambled off the bed and took the bags from Logan so that he didn't have to come too close. They both knew he still made me nervous.

She looked in the bag and got a big smile on her face. "Italian?"

He shrugged. "I figured if you were going to be shut up in this room, you deserved substantial sustenance."

Lily stretched up on her tiptoes and gave Logan a kiss. It started out as a chaste peck, but then she kissed him again, and he wrapped his arms around her, pulling her closer.

I looked away.

Once Lily returned to the bed and started pulling out the food, I gathered my courage and met Logan's gaze. "How are things going?"

My voice sounded weak, and I knew it.

"It's going well so far. I'd say we've got another hour or so tops. Most of the holdup is remembering where he had everything. I helped him dismantle it, but before that, I'd only been in there a handful of times—and it had been a while."

I looked down. "I've never been in there."

"At all?" Lily sounded shocked.

"No."

"Then why . . ."

Glancing over at her, I could see her confusion. I guess it made sense.

"Because I know he misses not having his things here."

Logan took a step closer, drawing my attention back to him. "Brianna, if you're not ready, then don't push it. Stephan will understand."

I shook my head. "I'm not. I just want him to have his stuff back, so that when I am ready . . ."

Lily placed her hand over mine in a comforting gesture. "So that when you're ready, it will be there."

I nodded.

She smiled. "Makes sense."

Lily and I spent the next hour eating the food Logan had brought for us. She told me about their plans for Christmas. Tonight they were going to a party—a BDSM party. Tomorrow they were starting the day with brunch at her parents' house and then going over to his brother's. Lily told me that Logan's parents had moved to Florida two years ago, so as a family they did a sort of Christmas in July thing. Logan and his brother and sister still tried to get together on Christmas Day, though. I got the feeling that Logan's parents were a little self-involved. Then again, I didn't know them.

"Logan still makes you nervous."

It wasn't a question, and I didn't deny it. "Yes. A little."

"Can you tell me why?" She paused. "Other than the fact that he's a man."

I shrugged. "That's part of it, but it's also because he's . . . he's . . ."

"A Dom?"

"Yes. No. Not exactly."

"What then?"

We were so involved in our conversation that before we knew it, Logan was knocking on the door again. "We're all done."

"Okay."

"I'm guessing you don't want to see it?"

"Um . . ."

"It's all right. There's no pressure, Brianna." He paused. "Did you want me to leave it unlocked or lock it like Stephan had it before?"

That was a good question. I didn't know, but I figured when in doubt, locking it was probably better. "Can you lock it, please?"

He smiled. "Of course."

When Logan left the room, Lily turned to face me on the bed. She didn't say anything, only stared. I realized she was waiting for me to answer the question she'd asked before Logan had interrupted. "Logan is . . . confident? I'm not sure if that's the right word, but that, added to the fact he's a man, makes me unsure of him."

Lily reached out and took hold of both my hands. "Logan would never hurt you, Brianna. Ever. First of all, I'd go postal on his ass, and that's not even factoring in what Stephan would do to him. Plus, Logan isn't like that. Do you think he and Stephan would be best friends if he were?"

"I guess not."

She smiled and gave me a hug.

Logan and Lily didn't stay long after that. They had to get ready for the party that night. Plus, Stephan would be home soon. He was getting off early since it was Christmas Eve. According to him, there had to be some perks to being the boss. He hadn't wanted to go in at all, but he had a conference call he couldn't miss or something. To be honest, I'd missed most of his explanation because I'd been so distracted. I hadn't considered that he'd not be going to work, even if it was Christmas Eve.

After saying good-bye to Lily and Logan, I went back into my bedroom and dug out the rope Stephan had given me from the drawer where I kept it. Over the last few days, I'd picked it up whenever I could, attempting to get used to it. I'd even wrapped it around my wrist, trying to remember how it felt. When he used it on me, I didn't want to panic—that was my biggest fear.

At a quarter after three, I laid the rope down neatly on the end of my bed and strolled out into the living room to wait for Stephan. I only hoped this night went as planned and that he liked his gifts.

Stephan

I was so glad this day was over. Half the employees had taken the day off since it was Christmas Eve. If I'd had my way, I would have done the same. Jamie had asked for the day off to spend with her family, and I'd granted her request. I didn't feel it was right to make her be here when all I wanted was to be at home with Brianna myself. If not for the conference call I'd had to take with a hospital executive in New York, I would have been.

Traffic was sparse driving through downtown. Most people were already home with their loved ones, which was exactly where I was headed. Brianna had been distracted all weekend—I knew everything was getting to her. I'd tried my best to keep her busy. The best part of the weekend, in my opinion, had been making cookies. Of course, I had some fun with her toward the end, and I'd ended up taking her—both of us covered in flour—on the kitchen floor.

I chuckled, remembering. We'd had to take a shower afterward, even before we could clean up the mess, because flour was in places it shouldn't be.

After parking the car in my spot, I grabbed my briefcase and walked toward the elevator. It opened fairly quickly, and I stepped inside.

On the ride up, I reevaluated my plan for tonight. Three weeks ago, we'd gotten a letter in the mail with Brianna's lab results. Everything came back negative. She was clean.

Since then, she'd asked twice if we could try to have sex without a condom. We'd talked about it, and I'd had her jack me off with her hand in the shower several times in the last two weeks to gauge her reaction.

The first time, I'd observed her actions and reaction after. It was subtle—so subtle, I hadn't picked up on it before—but seconds after she released her hold on me, she'd twist ever so slightly into the spray and wash the evidence down the drain. It was done in such a way that I wasn't sure she was aware she was doing it.

When I had her do it the second time, I latched on to her wrist immediately after and held it in place, preventing her from washing my cum off her hand. I watched her closely and counted the seconds. As I reached fifty-two in my head, her agitation started to increase. I made her focus on me and try to breathe through it, but when her chest continued to rise and fall rapidly, I directed her hand under the spray and removed the remnants of my climax.

Over the course of two weeks, we'd worked on extending the time. She'd gotten up to five minutes two nights ago, which gave me hope. Five minutes was enough time for us to separate comfortably and for her to make it to the bathroom to clean herself.

I walked confidently into the condo and glanced around, searching her out while I removed my coat. She peeked up over the back of the couch when she heard me enter. The smile on her face showcased how happy she was to see me.

Brianna jumped up and tossed what I assumed was the book she was reading down on the couch before running across the room to greet me.

I planted a firm kiss on her lips and hugged her. "Hi, sweetheart."

"Hello, Sir."

Since I was home earlier than normal, I decided to spend some quality time with my girl before we thought about dinner. I removed my suit jacket, and placed it, along with my briefcase, on the table beside my keys. Grabbing hold of Brianna's hand, I led her over to my chair while loosening my tie. We sat down, and Brianna positioned herself in my lap. She immediately began playing with my buttons.

"How was your day?"

She hesitated for a moment. It was almost nonexistent, but I'd caught it. "Good. I'm glad you're home."

I kissed the top of her head and started running my fingers through her hair. "Did something happen today that you need to tell me about?"

Brianna nodded. "Can I wait to tell you until after dinner?"

Her response surprised me. Why did she want to wait? I knew I could press the issue, but if she wanted to wait until after we ate, I would give her that—as long as she *did* tell me. "All right."

"Thank you." She pressed her lips against my neck, giving me a gentle kiss. It was sweet and loving and perfectly Brianna. "How was your day?"

"Boring. Over half the staff had the day off, so it was pretty much a ghost town. I put on some Christmas music, and—other than answering some e-mails and that conference call I told you about—I spent most of my day reorganizing my desk. It's shocking how things accumulate."

"I can clean it for you if you want."

I smiled at her suggestion. "That's okay. We have a couple that comes in to clean the building once a week. They make sure everything is dusted and the floors are swept."

She nodded.

We talked a little more about my day before going into the kitchen to start dinner. I'd told her this morning not to worry about it until I got home since I knew I would be leaving the office early. While cooking wasn't my favorite pastime, it was always fun helping her. It was the only time she told me what to do, not that she was really telling me. It was more giving me direction. I was typically put in charge of making a salad or chopping up vegetables.

The best part, however, was finding opportunities to touch her. I'd wait until Brianna was completely focused on whatever she was doing and then reach over to touch her arm or wrist. Other times, I'd step up behind her and nuzzle her neck while she was mixing something together.

I remember the first time we worked in the kitchen together. She held herself stiff as a board, afraid of doing something wrong. How time had changed things. As we worked together side by side, we talked and laughed. It was relaxing and exactly what we both needed.

After we ate, I helped her clean things up and then went to change into something more comfortable. I was used to wearing suits, so they didn't bother me, but there was something to be said about jeans and a soft cotton T-shirt.

When I reentered the main room, I found Brianna kneeling with her arms behind her back. Straightening my shoulders, I strolled over to her with measured steps. A few feet away, I stopped and waited to see what she would do.

Several minutes passed, and I saw her swallow multiple times. It was clear she was nervous about something. Still, I waited.

She took a deep breath but kept her gaze on the floor in front of her. "May I give you your Christmas present now, Sir?"

Ah. So that was what this was about. "You may."

Brianna looked up, meeting my gaze. There was a note of uncertainty in her eyes, which made me wonder what, exactly, her present was.

Bringing her arms around from behind her, I watched as she gripped the red rope I'd given her in both hands and held it out to me.

I glanced at it and then back to her. "This is my Christmas present? You want me to tie you up?"

Her pulse pounded in her neck. "Yes. Part of it."

"Part of it?"

She nodded.

"What is the other part?"

Nothing.

"Brianna."

She lowered her gaze back to the floor. "It's upstairs. I-I-in Sarah's room."

It was probably good that she wasn't looking at me at that precise moment, because I was utterly confused. What in the world would she have gotten me that she'd need to hide upstairs in a room we didn't use?

I figured it was time to find out. She'd brought it up for a reason, so there was no point in delaying. It was meant to be my Christmas present after all.

Extending my arm, I took the rope from her with one hand and offered her my other to take. "Come on. Let's go see this present, and then we'll see about putting this rope to good use."

Brianna hesitated for a second longer than normal before placing her hand in mine. That was unusual. It made me even more curious as to this mystery present. Was she worried I wouldn't like it?

Slowly, we made our way hand in hand up the staircase, and through the library. When we reached the door to the room Sarah had used while staying with me, I realized that it was once again locked. I looked down at her, perplexed. "The door's locked."

She nodded. "Logan locked it."

"Logan?"

"Yes. He . . . he helped me with your present."

"I see."

Releasing her hand, I left her standing there while I went to get the key out of my desk. When I came back, I noticed Brianna had wrapped her arms around her waist and she was shaking. "Hey. What's wrong?"

"Can I . . . can I wait out here while you go inside?"

I had no idea what was going on, but given Brianna's reaction, I agreed. Turning my attention back to the door, I slipped the key in and turned the knob. I took one step inside the room and stopped. All my stuff was there. Everything—my toys, my spanking bench. Everything. Exactly the way I'd had it before.

Chapter 39

Stephan

I no longer wondered what Logan had to do with her Christmas gift to me. Brianna didn't even want to enter the room. She must have asked Logan to set my playroom up for her, but why? Only Brianna had the answer to that question, so without more than a cursory look over everything, I turned on my heel and went back out into the hall.

Brianna was exactly how and where I'd left her. She was still holding herself, as if somehow by doing that she would be able to keep her nerves under control. Seeing how she was visibly trembling, I didn't think it was working.

"Come here." I pulled her into my arms. "Deep breaths. I've got you."

Her chest rose and fell as she inhaled and exhaled. She held tight to my shirt, twisting it in her hands so tightly I was afraid it might rip.

"D-do-do you like it?"

"Tell me why." My playroom obviously still upset her, so why have Logan assemble it?

"I couldn't find anything to get you. Something you wanted. But I knew you wanted your things back. Your . . . toys." She was struggling to get her words out—her voice was shaking.

I sighed. "Thank you. But you didn't have to do this if it was going to make you so uncomfortable. I would have survived without them for a while."

"I know, but I wanted to. I wanted to do this for you."

Sometimes I truly wondered if I'd ever understand what went through her head. "It scares you."

"Yes."

"Why? What about it frightens you so much?"

Brianna gripped my shirt tighter, if that were possible, and I thought I felt some of the fabric near my lower back give. "Can we go back downstairs now?"

"Not until you answer my question."

A shudder rippled through her frame.

"There are things in there that could hurt me." Her words were muffled as she held her mouth against my chest.

I rubbed my hands up and down over her back to help comfort and calm her. It appeared to be helping, if only a little. I was sure that being just a few feet away from the room she was so fearful of wasn't making things easier, but I wasn't quite ready to take her away yet. "What have I told you about *things* hurting you?"

"Tha-that it's the person using them, not the things themselves."

"That's right. And the only two people in this condo are you and me. Are you afraid I'll use them to hurt you?"

"No!" It was the first clear response I'd gotten out of her since we came upstairs.

"Do you plan on using them to hurt yourself?" I knew she didn't, but I wanted her to acknowledge it.

"No."

Tipping her chin up, I made her look at me. I softened my voice to let her know I wasn't upset with her in any way. "Then why are you afraid? If you know I won't hurt you and you aren't going to hurt yourself, then they are just things—inanimate objects."

"What if . . . what if I remember? What if I have a flashback? If I start to . . ." She closed her eyes as if fighting off said memories.

I felt her panic rising, and I took her face in between both of my hands. "Open your eyes. Look at me."

Brianna opened her eyes, and they were full of fear and panic.

"Good girl. Focus on my eyes. It's just you and me. Stephan and Brianna. No one else. Breathe."

Gradually her breathing slowed. The panic faded from her face, but the fear was still there. I wanted to take the fear from her, too, like I wanted to take every other negative thing in her life, but as with so much of it lately, I couldn't. This was something she was going to have to face and push through on her own.

We stood there for a long while, staring at each other. The pulse in her neck beat rhythmically against my pinky. It was strange how something so simple made me feel even more connected to her than I already did.

Her pulse started to pick up its pace again. I was about to inquire as to what was wrong, when she answered my question for me. "I . . . I want to see."

I tried to school my reaction, but she'd caught me completely off guard. "What do you want to see?"

"Your pl-play . . . room."

"Sweetheart, you're shaking again. Brianna, are you sure?"

She nodded. "Will you . . . will you help me?"

I brought our foreheads together, never losing eye contact with her. "Of course I will, love. I'll be right there with you every step of the way.

Whatever you need."

Pressing her lips together, she closed her eyes briefly before meeting my gaze once more.

Without another word, I stepped back, putting a little space between us. I saw her fear skyrocket almost instantly, so I quickly repositioned myself in front of her and linked our fingers together. Standing still for a moment, I let her get her bearings. "Breathe with me. I'm right here. It's just the two of us. When you're ready, walk forward."

Nothing happened for a long time. We stood there together, holding hands, her eyes focused only on me.

Then she took a step. It was small—so small that I didn't have to move.

It was another forty seconds before she took the second step. This time, I moved with her.

Every step she took was measured, cautious, but I understood. I'd be with her all night taking baby steps if that was what she needed.

It didn't take all night for us to reach the doorway to my newly reassembled playroom. When we made it to the entryway, though, she stopped cold.

I waited to see what she'd do.

She looked over my shoulder into the room. "It looks smaller."

"That's because there is a lot in here. Before, there was just a bed and a dresser. The equipment takes up more space." I squeezed her hands, wishing I could hold her, but she needed me in front of her where she could see me and I could help to keep her in the here and now.

I knew when her gaze fell on my Saint Andrew's cross. She swallowed hard and took a small step back.

"Remember, it's only a thing. It can't hurt you."

She was quiet for almost five minutes. "You use . . . it?"

"I have, yes. I've used everything in this room at one point in time or another."

A shiver ran through her.

"Do you want to get a closer look?"

Brianna shook her head.

"Okay. We'll stay right here, then."

For the next fifteen minutes, we stood in the doorway to the playroom. Every now and then, she'd ask me about an item, but for the most part, she just took everything in. I wanted so badly to know what she was thinking, but I wanted to give her time to process everything. This was a huge step for her.

When she was ready, we walked back out into the hall. I closed the door, but this time I didn't lock it. "If you ever want to go inside and look at anything, Brianna, you may. I don't want you to be afraid of anything in that room."

I returned the key to my desk, and we went back downstairs. Although she'd given me the rope earlier, I had no idea if she was up for playing after the emotional roller coaster she'd been through. We both needed some downtime.

With that in mind, I had her wait for me on the couch while I made us some hot chocolate, lit up the little Christmas tree, and turned down the lights. I placed the mugs on the coffee table before sitting down beside her and lifting her on my lap. Once we were both comfortable, I reached for both our mugs and handed her one.

Brianna snuggled up to me. We sat drinking our hot chocolate and looking at the tree. It was all very peaceful and exactly what we'd both needed. I couldn't think of a better way to spend Christmas Eve.

Brianna
As I began to wake up, memories of last night seeped into my consciousness. We stayed cuddled on the couch together until well after midnight. Neither one of us had wanted to move, but eventually Stephan had said we needed to go to bed or we'd both fall asleep. I had been perfectly okay with falling asleep on the couch, but he hadn't thought it would be all that comfortable.

What he hadn't said, but what I knew from experience, was that Stephan preferred to fall asleep next to me without any clothes between us. I couldn't disagree with his desire, though, since I loved that part of going to sleep, too. There was something about feeling his warm skin against mine. If someone would have told me a year ago that I'd enjoy sleeping naked next to a man, I would have sworn they were lying.

Before I could roll over, he tightened his arm around me and pressed his lips against the back of my neck. "Merry Christmas, sweetheart."

I smiled. "Merry Christmas, Sir."

He slid his hand up my front until he was cupping my breast. "Are you ready for today?"

We were going over to Richard and Diane's for a late breakfast and then opening presents. I had no idea how long we'd be staying, but Stephan said we wouldn't be spending the night this time. "Yes."

"Good." He paused, and I felt him turn his head, then he went back to kissing my neck. "We have to get going soon, but I can't let you out of this bed without giving you something to get your day started off right, now can I?"

Not giving me a chance to answer him, he picked up my leg with his other hand and placed it on top of his thigh, spreading my legs wide open.

Stephan used his fingers to spread the moisture between my folds and up to my clit. Every pass he made teased me more, until I began moving my hips in an attempt to gain friction.

It didn't take him long to have me forgetting all about anything but what his hands were doing. My limbs were shaking as he worked his magic with his fingers inside me and on my breasts. Stephan was relentless with his mouth as well. He had every inch of my body tingling and hovering on the peak of pleasure before he finally gave me permission to come.

As I floated back down to reality, he continued to caress me. My bones felt like jelly, yet his hands were stirring that familiar tingle all over again. I could also feel his erection pressing into my backside, and I wondered if he was going to take me.

"Hmm. I'd love to spend the entire day in bed with you, Brianna, but I promised Diane we'd be at her house no later than ten. We'll have to finish this later."

He pulled away from me, leaving me feeling chilled as the cooler air hit my damp skin. I watched from the bed as he stood and stretched beside the bed. The muscles in his back flexed, as did those in his backside and legs. The sight was making me feel warm again.

Stephan looked over his shoulder and caught me ogling him. He smirked at me and then reached for my hand. I took it and flung the covers off me.

Once I was standing beside him, he pulled me flush against his naked body. I tilted my head up so I could look into his eyes. "I promise that we will have plenty of time later, love."

With that, he leaned down and captured my mouth with his own. I could feel his hard penis pressing against my stomach, and I moaned as I held on to his arms.

Unfortunately, the kiss ended too soon. "You make it way too easy to forget that we have plans today that involve clothes and other people."

I giggled, pleased that I could make him feel that way.

He laughed and shook his head. "Let's go, pet, before I get us both into trouble with my aunt."

Nearly two hours later, we arrived at Dr. Cooper and Diane's house. As we walked up to the door, it had a large wreath covering almost half of it. Even though it was much bigger, it reminded me of the one my mom used to hang on our door at Christmas time. I wondered what had happened to it. Not only the wreath, but to all her things.

No one greeted us at the door this time. Instead, Stephan opened it and ushered me into the kitchen where both Diane and Dr. Cooper were dressed in matching aprons. I'd seen Dr. Cooper in the kitchen before, but the apron made him look corny.

"Ah. There you are. We were beginning to think you weren't coming." Dr. Cooper handed each of us a basket. "Take those to the table, will you? Everything should be ready in a few minutes."

Diane smiled at me. "Merry Christmas."

I smiled back shyly. "Merry Christmas."

Stephan laid his hand lightly against the small of my back and guided me into the dining room. He took my basket from me and laid it on the table next to his before helping me into my chair. Once we were both seated, he laced our fingers together and brought the back of my hand up to his lips. He didn't speak, but everything he needed to say was right there in his eyes. Stephan loved me, and he was glad I was here with him. I was glad, too.

Christmas wouldn't have been the same this year without him.

Breakfast was casual, even though we were eating in the formal dining room. Everything that had been prepared could be eaten with your hands, like biscuits, fruit, and even little quiches. There was no real order to things as everyone dug in and nibbled as the conversation flowed. I was starting to relax more and more around Diane—and even Dr. Cooper, now that he wasn't always giving Stephan the evil eye. It was nice.

After breakfast, we all moved into the family room where the large Christmas tree was decorated. Beneath it were several presents, and it hit me that I hadn't gotten Diane or Dr. Cooper anything. I'd been so focused on Stephan that it hadn't even crossed my mind.

Stephan must have noticed what I was looking at because he hugged me from behind, and whispered in my ear. "If you're wondering about gifts, don't be."

"But I didn't—"

He turned me around and placed a brief kiss to my lips. "Don't worry. What I got them is more than enough for both of us."

I tried to do what he said as we sat down on the couch together. Diane and Dr. Cooper sat together on the loveseat. It was cozy, which wasn't what I expected. We sat there for almost an hour as everyone talked about the weather and reminisced about Christmases past. Stephan even talked a little about his mom and dad, which was nice. I mostly remained quiet and listened while I snuggled into Stephan's side.

Eventually Diane stood and announced that it was time for presents. She ambled over to the tree and began passing out gifts. I was surprised when she handed me two.

Stephan didn't seem surprised, and he kissed my temple before accepting the gifts Diane handed him. I knew right away which one of them was from me. It was bigger than the other two. When he took it from her and felt the weight, I could see the wheels turning in his head as he tried to figure out what it was. I turned my head away to hide my smile, giddy that I'd been able to pull off all my surprises without him finding out ahead of time.

Diane and Dr. Cooper opened their gifts first. Stephan—we—got Dr. Cooper a very nice set of hand-turned pens for work. They were made out of some sort of exotic wood and were very pretty. Each one was engraved with his initials.

Diane's gift was a vase that was painted with blue and yellow flowers. It was beautiful. "Thank you both. I love it. I know just the place for it."

Next I was informed it was my turn. I picked up the first package and read the card. It was from Diane and Dr. Cooper. The box contained an envelope, and there was a gift card inside to the boutique Diane and I had gone to the day after Thanksgiving, along with a note.

> I may be Stephan's aunt, but I'm not a prude. I saw you
> looking at the lingerie, and I know you were too shy to buy it

that day for yourself. As tempted as I was to go ahead and buy you something, I didn't want to embarrass you, so I figured this was the next best option. If you want me to go with you to pick something out, I'd be more than happy to, but I know this—every woman deserves to dress and feel beautiful for her man.

My cheeks heated as I read the note. Stephan leaned over and read it, too, when he noticed my reaction. He chuckled and kissed my cheek. "Looks like we need to go shopping."

I looked up at him, my eyes wide.

That only made him smile more.

"You have another gift to open." He tilted his head to indicate the remaining present still in my lap.

Picking it up, I eyed it warily before opening it. I didn't bother looking at the tag, although in hindsight, I probably should have. This present wasn't from Diane and Dr. Cooper. Inside the box was a beautiful set of earrings. They were silver with blue jewels.

"They're sapphires. To match your eyes."

I met his gaze with tears in my eyes. The earrings were beautiful . . . and perfect.

He laid his palm flat against my cheek and brushed his lips against mine. "I love you, sweetheart. Merry Christmas."

When I finally had myself under control again, I looked over to find both Diane and Dr. Cooper smiling at us. I smiled back but looked down, feeling overwhelmed and embarrassed by our display.

"Your turn, Stephan," Dr. Cooper announced.

The first two gifts he opened were from Dr. Cooper and Diane. Both held envelopes similar to mine, and his also held gift cards—one for a local bookstore and another for a store that was known for their vast movie selection. He saved my present for last.

Stephan picked up the weighted box and set it firmly on his lap before he examined the card. When he saw my name, he looked over at me, surprised. "This is from you?"

I nodded.

He smiled, wrapped his hand around the back of my neck, and brought our lips together. "Thank you."

"You don't know what it is yet."

"Doesn't matter. It's from you, so I know I'll love it."

I didn't understand his reasoning, but he was happy, so I was happy.

Stephan turned back to the package and began removing the decorative paper. Diane had put it in an unmarked box, so until he opened the cardboard, he had no idea what was inside. He lifted the miniature fountain out of the box and set it on his lap. "I got it for your office. It reminded me of—"

"My rock." He finished my sentence for me, and I was thrilled he saw the resemblance like I did.

I pointed to the new addition to the fountain that hadn't been there when I'd bought it. "This rock didn't come with the fountain. It's from down by the creek. I wanted you to have a piece of your special place with you at work."

Before I knew what was happening, Stephan had lifted the fountain off his lap, placed it on the floor, and had me pinned to the couch with both his body and his mouth. I kissed him back with equal fervor, completely forgetting we weren't alone until I heard coughing.

Even then, Stephan didn't stop kissing me right away.

"Um. Stephan? I think your aunt and I are going to go refill our coffee in the kitchen and give you two a moment."

Stephan pulled back enough to separate our lips but nothing else. His body remained plastered against mine, holding me firmly to the couch. I couldn't move if I'd wanted to. He was breathing hard, and so was I. "How did I ever get so lucky to find you, Brianna?"

"You like your present?"

"It's perfect. And once we get home, I plan on showing you just how much I love it."

Chapter 40

Brianna

We didn't stay long after Stephan opened his present from me. Diane asked us to stay for a late lunch, but Stephan insisted he wanted to get home before it started getting dark. I didn't mind the cold so much during the winter. It was the daylight—or lack thereof. By the time we left his aunt and uncle's house, it was close to two o'clock. During the summer months we would have had plenty of daylight left. In December, it meant we had two and a half hours. Maybe. It was only an hour drive, but if we'd stayed for lunch, it would have been cutting it close.

Thirty minutes into our drive home, Stephan reached over and tapped two fingers along my inner thigh. "Spread your legs."

I'd worn a nice dress for our visit, so when I spread my legs, the only thing between me and his hand was the thin pair of silk panties I wore. Even though he had the heater on in the car, the air that rushed up under my dress was cooler than I'd anticipated.

Stephan kept his eyes on the road, but the hand he had on my thigh edged upward, pushing my dress up until it was around my waist. My entire lower half was exposed. Maybe some part of me should have been afraid someone might look inside the car and see me, but for some reason I wasn't. The only thing going through my mind was *what is he going to do next?*

He didn't leave me waiting for long. "Give me your hand."

I complied.

Wrapping his long fingers around my wrist, he lifted my hand up to his lips and put two of my fingers into his mouth. He began sucking and running his tongue in between and around them. For some reason, it reminded me of having his penis in my mouth, sucking and licking. Between the memory and the sensation, I felt heat and moisture rush between my now parted legs.

A few minutes later, he pulled my fingers out of his mouth and guided them back toward my lap. He didn't release them, however. Instead, he nudged my panties aside, exposing me even more to the cooler air. Placing my now damp fingers directly over my sex, he began rubbing in a circular motion, making me feel even hotter there than I had before.

Without warning, he stopped the circular movements and positioned my two fingers directly outside my entrance. He released his hold on my wrist and brought his hand to rest back on the steering wheel. "Push your fingers inside, Brianna."

What? I wasn't sure I understood him.

"Put your fingers inside yourself, Brianna. Now. I want you to finger yourself for the rest of the drive home. You aren't to make yourself come, do you understand?"

"Yes. I-I think so."

He glanced over at me and smiled. It was that wicked smile of his, and for some reason, it made the space between my legs feel even hotter. I didn't understand it at all.

Stephan had turned his attention back to the road, but he seemed to know I hadn't moved. "I'm waiting, Brianna."

Taking a deep breath, I pressed the two fingers he'd sucked into my moist heat. I hadn't touched myself like this since that night we'd had sex for the first time. It felt strange, just as it had that night, but I did what he said and started moving my fingers in and out. I'd seen girls do this before to themselves, and of course, I'd had it done to me, but doing it to myself was different.

At first, it felt strange, but then it began to change. The spongy texture was no longer my main focus. I was too caught up in how good it felt.

We stopped at a traffic light, and Stephan reached over, placing his hand over mine. He slipped one finger down into my opening in sync with my two fingers. After a few times, he removed it and brought it up to my mouth. "Open."

I was too far gone at that point and did what I was told. He inserted his finger between my lips and coated my tongue with the wetness he'd picked up between my legs. Tasting myself was always weirdly mesmerizing. There was no other flavor I could compare it to, yet something about having it on my tongue and knowing where it had come from made my arousal increase.

His finger slipped out of my mouth and down my chin before disappearing altogether. I looked over at Stephan. He was concentrating on the road. We were moving again. I hadn't even noticed.

Every now and then, he'd glance over, making sure I was still following his instructions. He'd smirk and then turn back to the road. By the time he pulled into the parking garage, there was a wet spot on my panties, and most of my hand was soaked. I'd been fingering myself for almost a half hour.

Once he'd parked the car, he removed his seat belt and then leaned over the center console—using one hand to position my head the way he wanted it—and kissed me, thrusting his tongue deep into my mouth. "Do you have any idea how hot it was watching you, Brianna?"

He didn't give me time to answer. Instead he took hold of my wrist and removed my fingers from where they'd still been moving inside me. He brought my hand up to where our mouths hovered a breath away from each other and started devouring my fingers.

The sight . . . the feel . . . neither was helping relieve the ache between my legs.

Stephan kissed me again, this time bringing my hand with him. It was almost like having a third participant as he mingled my fingers in with our tongues.

When he finally pulled back, we were both panting. It was as if I couldn't get enough air in my lungs, but in a good way. I wanted him to take me. I didn't care where we were.

He smiled, seeming to be able to read my mind. "Oh no, Brianna. I'm not going to make it that easy, pet. You'll get your reward, but only after we've had some fun first. Remove your panties and hand them to me."

It took a moment for his request to work through the fog in my brain. I reached down with both hands and, after lifting my hips a little, slid the pink panties down my legs and handed them to him.

Stephan pressed them to his nose and took a deep breath. He smiled that wicked smile again and then stuffed my panties into his pants pocket.

After helping me lower my dress so that my now naked bottom half wasn't showing, he stepped out of the car and strolled to the passenger side. As he opened my door, a rush of cold air made its way into the vehicle. It floated up under my dress and brushed over my now bare skin.

Instinctively, I reached down with my free hand to make sure my dress didn't fly up. Stephan chuckled and leaned in to whisper in my ear. "Don't worry, Brianna. No one can see anything. No one knows you don't have any panties on underneath your dress but you and me."

Before he stepped away, he brushed his lips against my neck, sending a tingle of electricity down my spine and right between my legs. I didn't know if I was going to be able to walk let alone make it all the way to the condo. He might have to carry me.

Stephan

I was having way too much fun. Brianna was having a good day—we both were.

Last night hadn't gone as planned after she showed me her "present." I was still attempting to wrap my mind around her reasons why. Brianna couldn't even step fully into the room. Why did having my playroom set up in the condo matter if we weren't going to be able to use it? I had to admit, though, that having my playroom and all my toys at my disposal would be useful . . . even if we didn't actually set foot inside the room itself.

Once we were back inside our condo, I instructed her to go into my bedroom, remove all her clothes, and wait for me on the bed. I'd left the rope I'd given Brianna upstairs, plus I wanted to get some other items as well.

It took me roughly fifteen minutes to get what I needed out of the playroom. Logan did a good job putting it all back together. Only a few things were out of place, but not by much. He had a good memory.

Once I had everything I needed, I paused only long enough to grab Brianna's other Christmas present from where I'd stashed it before heading back downstairs. Brianna was waiting for me, and I couldn't wait to get started. I was hoping this would be a fun and memorable evening for both of us.

When I walked into my bedroom, Brianna was sitting naked on the edge of my bed as I'd asked. She looked up upon my entrance and smiled. Her arousal from earlier had diminished, but that was all right. It was early, and I planned to take my time with her.

I deposited everything I'd brought with me from upstairs onto the dresser right inside the door, with the exception of her remaining Christmas present. Walking over to stand directly in front of her, I concealed the item in my fist as much as possible and held it close to my side. "Are you ready for the rest of what I have planned for tonight?"

"Yes, Sir."

I smiled and helped her up.

"Close your eyes, Brianna." I didn't want her to see what I had in my hand until I was ready.

"I want to give you your second Christmas present."

Her nose scrunched up a little. I wasn't sure if it was in concentration or confusion. "Okay."

I took the pink dildo I'd gotten her and pressed it up against her hand. "Take it."

She wrapped her hand around the object and looked down.

It was easy to tell the moment she realized what she was seeing because her eyes opened wide, her hand fell open, and she dropped the dildo on the floor.

I chuckled and bent down to retrieve it. "It won't bite, you know."

"I didn't mean . . . I mean, I wasn't expecting . . ." She lowered her gaze to the floor.

I retrieved the dildo and placed it back in her hand. She didn't drop it this time. "Does it still frighten you?"

"A little."

"Tell me why?"

"I remember how they felt. How much they hurt sometimes. I know it's not the same, but . . ."

I reached out and cupped her cheek, lifting her head so I could see her face. "But the memory remains, right?"

"Yes."

She looked sad, and I didn't want that. "I want to help you to make happy memories, Brianna—together."

Brianna nodded. "I want that, too."

Smiling, I placed a reverent kiss on her lips before taking the dildo from her and putting it on the nightstand. Leaving her to stand by the bed for a few moments, I walked back to the dresser and retrieved the rope.

When I returned to stand in front of her, I held the rope in both my hands and waited to see what she'd do.

It didn't take long. She glanced up at me, meeting my gaze, and then held out her wrists. There was uncertainty in her eyes, but I also saw determination. I lifted both of her wrists to my mouth and placed a soft kiss to the underside of each one. "You have your numbers, Brianna. Use them. For tonight, if you reach a six, I want you to say yellow, and we will slow things down, understand?"

"Yes, Sir."

"Good girl."

Like I had the other night, I started by rubbing the rope gently along her wrist, letting her get familiar with the feel of it, letting it caress her skin. Slowly her eyes began to flutter shut, and I knew she was ready for the next step.

Careful to keep part of the rope touching her at all times, I folded the rope in half and wound it around both her wrists in the same way I had the other night. Once I had everything secure, I told her to open her eyes. "How does it feel? Is the rope too tight?"

"No, Sir. It's not too tight."

"Good. Do you remember how to untie yourself if you need to?"

"Yes."

Testing how she would react to being bound, I used the rope to pull her against me. I wasn't all that rough about it, but there was still a tone of possession in the action.

A shudder ripped through her body, but I didn't get any indication that it was from fear.

I pressed my cheek against hers and spoke directly in her ear. "Are you ready to continue?"

"Yes."

Giving the rope some slack, I guided her closer to the bed. "Climb on and lie down with your head on the pillows."

She moved into position much quicker than I thought she'd be able to. It made me wonder how many times she'd had to be mobile while restrained in some fashion in her past. I rapidly pushed the thought aside. If this had any hope of working, I had to pay attention. Tonight we were going into uncharted territory, and I needed to be alert and attentive to Brianna's needs. She trusted me to take care of her.

I leaned over her and tied the loose ends of the rope to the bed. She looked up at me, watching. Normally I'd blindfold a submissive for this type of sensation play, but given Brianna's history, I didn't think that was a good idea. We were pushing enough boundaries tonight as it was.

Leaving her lying there for a minute, I went back to the dresser and picked up the rest of what I'd brought down with me. Bringing them over to the bed, I showed them to Brianna one at a time. The first was a fur glove. She wrinkled her brow, but other than that, she had no reaction. "Has anyone ever used one of these on you?"

She shook her head. "I don't think so."

Without putting it on, I placed it close to her hand where she could touch it and feel how soft it was. "It's made out of rabbit fur."

"It's soft."

I smiled. "Yes."

The second, however, got a bigger reaction. I'd grabbed a pair of tweezer clamps I wanted to try on her tonight. Brianna loved having her nipples pinched and pulled. I had no doubt she'd like clamps. It was only a matter of getting her past her fear. "Do you know what these are?"

"Yes."

"We're going to try them tonight, and see what you think of them. If you don't like them, we can always remove them, all right?"

"Okay." There was no conviction behind her voice, but she trusted me, and I wouldn't let her down.

Again, I brought the clamps up near her hands. This time, however, I placed one of the clamps on her index finger. She looked up, watching my movement. "This part here allows me to tighten and loosen the clamp—like this."

I slowly pushed the clasp up the tweezers to tighten the hold. She furrowed her brow in concentration.

"It should feel like it does when I pinch your nipples, but it will be more of a constant pressure."

She swallowed. "Okay."

I knew they were going to be a mental challenge for her because they did cause some level of pain, but I was glad she was willing to try them, at least.

Setting the clamps down beside the bed, I reached for the last item I wanted to use tonight—her new dildo.

Brianna's eyes opened wide, and her chest moved up and down more rapidly. "We're going to try to have a little fun with this tonight, too. Do you think you're ready for that?"

"I . . . I don't know."

I bent down and kissed her lips with soft pressure. "Thank you for being honest. We'll go slowly. I promise."

She swallowed and nodded, closing her eyes as if she were bracing herself.

Straightening, I removed my shoes, socks, and belt and tossed them on the back of the chair. By the time I turned back around, Brianna was looking at me again.

I smiled at her, brushing the back of my fingers along the side of her cheek. "I love you. Remember that. This isn't about pain. This is about pleasure."

"I trust you."

Taking a step back, I picked up the glove, the clamps, and the dildo and climbed on the bed with Brianna.

Chapter 41

Brianna

I laid there with my arms secured over my head to the bed as Stephan positioned himself between my legs. Being naked in front of him didn't bother me anymore. He'd seen and touched all of me many times. The ropes didn't bother me either, which surprised me a little. No, it was the items he held in his hands that had my heart thundering in my chest.

"How are you doing, Brianna? What number?"

Taking a deep breath, I met his gaze. "Three."

He nodded and set the glove, the clamps, and the dildo down on the bed next to my hip. The dildo rolled a few inches into the dip my body made in the mattress until it came to rest against my side. I sucked in a breath and began chanting Stephan's name in my head. If I remembered it was him, I'd be okay. He wouldn't hurt me. I knew he wouldn't.

In a smooth motion, Stephan pulled his shirt over his head, leaving the top half of his body naked. He still had on the khakis he'd worn to Diane and Dr. Cooper's. They were thicker than his usual dress pants, but they did nothing to hide the bulge of his erection. Whatever Stephan had planned for tonight, he was excited about it. I only hoped I liked it, too. I wanted to like it for him.

Stephan ran his hands up my legs and then back down until he came to my knees. Lifting slightly, he encouraged me to bend them, which only opened me more to him. He placed his hands on the inside of my thighs, holding me in position. "Beautiful."

I watched as he looked over every inch of me. Last night, when he saw I'd waxed for him, he'd gotten a look in his eyes, and he'd kissed me long and deep to the point where my head was spinning. There was almost that same something in his gaze as he stared down at me now that made me want to squirm. It sent the butterflies in my stomach fluttering like mad. What was he going to do?

A minute later, I got my answer. He reached over and picked up the fur glove, sliding it over his left hand. Out of all the items he wanted to use on me tonight, the glove was the only one that didn't make me anxious. The fur was soft. I knew it wouldn't cause me pain.

The first place he touched with the glove was my stomach. He rubbed the fur in all different directions, gradually branching out to my legs, my breasts, my neck, and even my arms. It was relaxing, and I felt my eyelids drifting closed.

"What number, Brianna?" His voice was soft, almost mimicking the feel of the fur.

I sighed. "One."

As the glove continued to move over my skin, his other hand began touching me as well. He would run the glove over a part of my body, and then his uncovered hand would brush lightly over the same area. The contrast caused me to shiver at times. It felt amazing, and all my nerve endings were on alert waiting to see where he'd go next.

Just when I thought it couldn't get any better, Stephan changed things up and added his mouth to the sweet torture. Sometimes he'd kiss a spot on my body. Other times, he'd lick or use his teeth. I nearly jumped off the bed when he ran the fur glove down my side and followed it up by licking the same area with his tongue and then blowing along the wet trail he'd left. It tickled, and made me twist and pull against the ropes. Stephan smiled in response and then grazed his teeth along the same path, sending a much different sensation coursing through my body.

I had no idea how long he spent touching and kissing me like this, but I knew I'd never felt anything like it. A part of me wanted to touch him like he was me, but there was another part that was enjoying the rope that was wrapped around my wrists. It reminded me of Stephan holding me down—securing me—making me feel safe. I stopped thinking and allowed myself to just feel.

Closing my eyes, I reveled in the sensation of Stephan's mouth as he sucked one of my breasts between his lips. Everything felt . . . more intense as he used his tongue to toy with my nipple. I heard someone moan, but I couldn't tell if it had come from me or him. What he was doing felt so good that I didn't care.

He released most of my breast, with the exception of the tip of my nipple. Rolling it around between his lips, he tugged slightly, making it harder, then released it completely and blew on it.

"Open your eyes, Brianna."

I did.

"Good girl. Now keep them open. I want you to stay with me. Do you understand?"

"Yes, Sir."

I saw movement out of the corner of my eye, but I didn't remove my gaze from him. He looked down and took the breast he'd been playing with moments before into his left hand. The glove was no longer covering it.

When he pinched my nipple, I knew what was coming and tensed up, waiting for the pain. "Relax, sweetheart. It won't be any different than when I pinch your nipple, I promise."

Instinctively, I closed my eyes.

"Brianna." His firm voice made me snap my eyes open and look at him. He was frowning.

It took me a minute to realize I'd disobeyed him. I immediately felt guilty. "I'm sorry, Sir."

He brought his fingers up to caress my face. "You're forgiven, but I need your eyes on me. I need to see how you're reacting. All right?"

I nodded. "Yes, Sir."

"Good."

Without any further delay, Stephan removed his hand from my face and brought it back down to my breast. He took my nipple between two of his fingers and twisted before pulling up, almost as if he were trying to lift me off the bed by my nipple alone.

Pain zinged through my breast straight to the spot between my legs. It made no sense, but I loved when he did that.

Before the feeling between my legs subsided, I felt something replacing his fingers. It wasn't warm like his hands. It was cold, like metal.

The metal constricted around my nipple, holding it. At first, I barely felt it apart from the cool texture. Then Stephan began to tighten it. I sucked in a lungful of air when I felt the start of the pain I'd been waiting for . . . and dreading.

Only the horrible pain didn't come. It hurt, yes, but not like I remembered. This was a dull pain. Stephan was right—it felt similar to when he pinched my nipples, except there was no let up. It was constant.

"Is that too much, Brianna?"

I shook my head. "No, Sir. It hurts, but . . ."

"But you like it."

He was right. I did like it. But why? I didn't like pain. Why did I like this?

"Shh. I know what you're thinking, love, and it's different. A little pain can heighten the senses. There's nothing wrong with liking it."

"But why do I like it now and not then?"

Stephan leaned forward. Hovering over me, he pressed our foreheads together, looking me directly in the eye. "Because I'm not trying to cause you harm. I'm attempting to increase the endorphins your body naturally creates to make things more pleasurable for you—for both of us."

As he spoke, he reached down and began tweaking my other nipple. I moaned.

"That's it. Keep your eyes on me and stay with me in the moment. Let yourself feel . . . experience."

I looked into his eyes and gradually felt a calm come over me. It was mixed with the butterflies and the pulsing between my legs, but it was still there. This was Stephan, and I trusted him to take care of me.

He must have sensed the shift in me, because he pushed himself back up between my legs and continued working on my other breast. When the nipple was hard like he wanted it, he placed a clamp over it, too, and began tightening it. This one pinched like the other one, but I was expecting it, so it wasn't as shocking.

After taking in every inch of me again, he placed a soft kiss to the top of one of my nipples—the first one he'd clamped. When his lips touched, a spark of electricity shot through it, and I felt moisture rush to my sex. How was this possible? He did the same thing to the other one. My breathing was becoming more labored, and I saw that wicked smirk return.

Stephan reached over and put the fur glove on his left hand again and resumed running it over my body, including my now very sensitive nipples. I couldn't believe how much the sensations changed. I felt as if I were on fire. Not just my nipples but everywhere. I had to concentrate to keep my eyes open because all I wanted to do was close them—and feel.

Stephan

Brianna was doing well. She'd had a moment, but with a little work, she'd made it through. My pride in her was almost more than I could contain.

Being able to touch her like this, play with her even in the simplest of ways, was exciting on many levels. Every step she took forward gave me confidence that one day she could, and would, move past what had been done to her. I was under no illusions that it wouldn't take time—a lot of time—but it was possible. Brianna fought for what she wanted. That inner strength would see her through no matter what life threw at her. I was just happy she was allowing me to be part of it.

Brianna gasped as I rubbed the fur glove back and forth over her nipples. She was reacting as I'd hoped to the clamps. Seeing her laid out before me like this, with her hands tied above her head and the silver clamps on her nipples, had my cock straining against the confines of my pants. I knew better than to get completely undressed yet, though. If I did, this would end much sooner than I wanted it to.

Sliding the glove off my hand, I tossed it to the side and bent down to press my lips to the tips of her breasts. She was watching me with hooded eyes. "Number?"

She released a ragged breath. "Two."

I smiled and pushed myself up her body a little farther until my face was level with hers. My chest grazed her sensitive nipples, and I enjoyed the way her eyes rolled back in her head slightly.

Using her distraction to my advantage, I took possession of her mouth with mine, slipping my tongue between her parted lips. Tasting her did nothing to calm my arousal, but I attempted to ignore it and focus on my mission. Keeping myself propped up with my left arm, I reached between us with my right and found the slick moisture waiting for me between her legs. She was so wet, I knew that she was almost ready for the dildo.

I took my time, however, and kissed her slowly while I rubbed my fingers up and down the folds of her pussy. Every now and then, I'd venture upward and circle her clit, but for the most part, I kept my attention lower. This wasn't about her coming . . . yet. I wanted her so worked up—so on edge—that she wouldn't think twice about the dildo I was going to insert inside her. She was almost there, but not quite.

After another pass with my fingers around the outside, I pushed two fingers inside her pussy. Her muscles contracted around the intrusion almost immediately, and I deepened the kiss. Brianna was so far gone at the moment, I wasn't sure she knew the specifics of what was happening. She was with me, though—here and now. That was what mattered.

When her hips began to buck against my hand, searching for friction, I knew it was time. A whine escaped her throat when I removed my fingers. I raised my head to look down at her.

She opened her eyes to look up at me. Her pupils were fully dilated and glazed over. I brushed some of the hair out of her face with my left hand, keeping her focus on me, while I retrieved the pink dildo I'd bought her.

I shifted slightly, which caused her to suck another strangled breath as her nipples absorbed the added stimulation. Using the distraction, I kept my gaze on her face as I pushed the dildo the first few inches into her pussy.

The moment what I was doing registered, Brianna's eyes opened wider and lost some of that glazed look. "It's okay. I promise it won't hurt. Relax."

I readjusted my hand, freeing my thumb to brush light circles around her clit. It took her a couple of minutes, but she nodded and took a deep breath.

Removing my thumb from her clit, I slowly began moving the dildo inside her until she gradually accepted it all. Little by little, the tension in her body left, and she let the feelings take over again. It was a sight to see, watching her reactions as I thrust the dildo in and out of her.

When I knew Brianna was getting close, I repositioned myself between her legs. Keeping the dildo moving with my right hand, I used the thumb of my left hand to tease her clit again.

The reaction I got was nothing short of thrilling. She began raising her hips up off the bed in time to meet the thrusts of the dildo. Her gaze never left mine, but it was so glazed over I wasn't sure if she was actually seeing me or not.

She gasped for air, her limbs shaking. I moved my hands so that the thumb on my right was able to graze her clit with every inward push of the dildo, freeing my left hand. Using my now free hand, I brought it up to her right nipple. She'd had the clamps on for long enough. They needed to be removed, and what better way to do that than as I gave her permission to come.

I grabbed the clamp between my fingers and lowered my mouth to her nipple. "Come."

At the same time, I loosened the clamp, allowing the blood flow to return to her nipple, and began licking the extremely sensitive area.

Brianna screamed. It was different from her usual screams of passion but similar at the same time. She pulled at the ropes holding her to the bed and bucked against me. Her orgasm lasted much longer than normal, which put a huge smile on my face.

When she calmed down, I checked in with her. "Are you all right?"

"Yes." I could tell she was still trying to catch her breath.

"Good. I need to take the other nipple clamp off. It will hurt a little, but I'll try to make it as painless as possible."

She nodded, and pressed her lips together in concentration.

Repeating what I did with the other side, I bent over her breast, and as soon as the clamp released her nipple, I sucked it into my mouth. Brianna let out a squeak of pain and then a sigh as my tongue eased the hurt.

Once I was sure she was okay, I placed all the toys back on the nightstand and stood over her. "How are your arms feeling?"

"Fine."

"No tingling? Numbness?"

"No, Sir."

Just to be sure, I ran my index finger around the edges of the knot to make certain it wasn't pulling after her thrashing about. It wasn't.

Satisfied that there were no circulation issues, I walked the short distance into the bathroom and got her some water. We'd get some food shortly, but I didn't want her to dehydrate in the meantime.

Brianna drank the water with my help. She was starting to come down from her high, which meant it was time to get back to work. I placed the now empty glass on the nightstand and stripped out of the rest of my clothes.

Rejoining her on the bed, I laid beside her this time, instead of on top of her. The ropes were loose enough that I could roll her over to face me. I wrapped my arm around her, drawing her close, and kissed her. This wasn't a soft kiss. It was one that reminded her who she belonged to, and I felt her body's response almost immediately.

Grasping her leg, I brought it up to rest on my hip, opening her to me. I grabbed her ass and pulled her closer, letting her feel how much I wanted her. She pulled at the ropes, and I knew she wanted to touch me. This only made me more excited.

I slid my fingers lower until I reached her pussy. This time, I didn't dance around the issue. Instead, I thrust two fingers inside her without preamble.

Brianna accepted everything I gave her, and by the time I removed my fingers and pushed my cock inside her, she was dripping wet and moaning with every thrust of my hips.

It took Brianna a moment to realize what was happening, because she'd been so caught up in the moment. I knew exactly when she did, because her eyes popped open. "Sir?"

"This is what you wanted?" I punctuated each word with a thrust of my hips. "You wanted to feel me inside you without a condom. Wanted me to come inside you. Didn't you, Brianna?"

"Y-yes, Sir."

Her nipples were still very sensitive, and our position meant that with every movement, my chest brushed against hers. It didn't take either of us long to reach the point of no return.

"Come for me, pet," I whispered against her lips.

This time she wasn't as vocal, but I felt every spasm of her orgasm around my naked cock as she milked me. The feeling was too much, and I couldn't hold back any longer. With another hard thrust, I emptied myself into her for the first time.

Sherri Hayes

Chapter 42

Stephan

As my breathing returned to normal, I reached up and released the ropes binding Brianna's wrists. Her arms fell to either side of her head as if weighted down. She appeared to be utterly relaxed, and so far she'd not shown any signs of discomfort or agitation from my cum. I hoped that continued to hold true, but I wasn't going to push it. This had been a positive experience for her so far—our first real time playing together with toys and bondage—and I wanted to keep it that way.

I separated us enough so that I could lift her into my arms. Once I was sure I had a solid hold on her, I swung my legs off the bed and stood.

Brianna's only response was to turn her head into my chest and hum. Her arms hung limp, with one dangling down toward the ground. I wasn't even sure she was conscious of anything besides me. The only reason I knew she was aware of my presence was by the way she leaned into me and smiled. Placing a soft kiss on her temple, I carried her into the bathroom.

Although it took some maneuvering, I kept her on my lap as I leaned over and turned on the water for the tub. Brianna needed some aftercare, and she needed to get cleaned up. This would kill two birds with one stone.

Once the water was ready, I sat her down in the tub. Again, it took some effort on my part. Brianna wasn't difficult for me to carry if I were walking from one room to the next, but sitting her down in a bathtub was a little more challenging, especially without much assistance from her.

Somehow I managed and then stepped in behind her. I eased myself down until my back was against the hard edge of the tub. Pulling Brianna back against my chest, I wrapped my arms around her and began massaging her wrist with my fingers.

She tilted her head back and slowly opened her eyes.

I smiled and brushed my mouth against hers. "How do you feel?"

Brianna blinked several times as if the sound of my voice was bringing her out of the fog she was in. "I feel . . . rubbery."

I chuckled. "Rubbery?"

She nodded and sighed as she leaned her head back against me. "Like my bones are made of rubber."

"Ah." I rested my cheek against her head as I continued to work my way up her arm.

When I reached her elbow, I lowered her arm back into the water and started working on the other one. Aftercare was extremely important, especially if a submissive went into subspace, which I was fairly certain had happened to Brianna. I wanted to make sure she came down slowly and that she felt loved and taken care of. This was an important part of play, and one I'd always enjoyed to a certain extent. I had to admit, though, it was different with Brianna, as so many other things were. With Sarah and Tami it had felt more like part of my job—my responsibility as a Dom. Working out any knots or tension in Brianna's arms and shoulders was an extension of my showing her how I felt about her.

Positive I'd taken care of any stiffness she might have after being tied to the bed, I took my time washing her. Brianna sighed as I ran the loofah over her body. She even moaned a few times as I brushed it over her nipples. They remained extremely sensitive and probably would for the rest of the day. I was looking forward to that.

Eventually the water started to turn cold, and we had to get out. Once we were both dried off, I wrapped her in a robe and threw on a pair of boxers before leading her into the kitchen. It was almost four, and neither one of us had eaten anything since breakfast.

Brianna and I spent the next hour curled up in the living room eating leftovers. The last thing I'd wanted to do was waste time cooking.

I broke off a piece of cookie and fed it to her. "Brianna, we need to talk about this afternoon. Are you up for that?"

She swallowed and nodded.

"What did you think of being tied up?"

Brianna rested her head on my shoulder. "It wasn't what I expected. I thought . . . I thought I'd feel trapped."

"But you didn't?"

"No." She shook her head. "I felt . . . safe. Like I do when you hold my wrists down."

I brushed my lips against her forehead. "I'm glad you felt safe. I always want you to feel safe with me, Brianna."

She ran her nose up the side of my neck, and a shiver ran down my spine. Brianna had no idea the power she held over me sexually. When she figured it out, I would be in trouble.

Taking a deep breath, I continued. "What about the fur glove?"

I felt her lips curve up into a smile. "I liked the glove."

"How about the nipple clamps?"

Brianna didn't answer me right away, but I waited, giving her time to gather her thoughts. "They hurt, but . . . but they felt good, too?"

It wasn't all that surprising that she was confused. Given her view of pain, it was going to take a while for her to reconcile the difference between good pain and bad pain in her mind. "Do you remember how we talked about how you like it when I pull your hair?"

She nodded.

"It's the same thing, sweetheart, and it's okay that you enjoy it. What we do together is completely different than what was done to you before."

Brianna placed her hand over my heart and then lowered it to begin rubbing her fingers over my nipple. I closed my eyes and took a deep breath. We needed to get through this conversation, but if she kept that up, I'd be cutting it short.

Reaching for her hand, I lifted it to my lips and kissed the inside of her palm before placing it safely back in her lap. "Do you see the difference, Brianna?"

"I don't know."

"What's confusing you?"

She began to raise her hand again, but this time I caught it and laced our fingers together. "You had me tied up. I couldn't . . . I couldn't stop you."

"Yes, you could have. You could have said your safeword, and I would have stopped. You know that, or else you would have panicked."

"I know it's different, but I don't understand. I don't." I felt the moisture against my shoulder before I heard the first sob leave her throat. Brianna had come so far, but she was still struggling. I knew she would for a while.

Setting the rest of our food down on the coffee table, I reached for a throw blanket and wrapped it around the two of us. Holding her close, I let her get it out of her system. I suspected some of her emotional state was an aftereffect of subspace, but I knew that was only part of it.

The sun had long set before I took her back into the bedroom. Brianna had stopped crying, but she refused to let me go very far. We took turns in the bathroom, but I saw her struggle with whether or not to allow me to leave her sight. She still had reactions to hearing me urinate even after all this time, so she ended up sitting on the edge of my bed waiting for me. I could see the relief in her eyes when I reemerged and joined her. I took her by the hand, and led her over to the side of the bed. It was early, but I could think of no better way to spend the rest of our evening together. I gathered her into my arms, and she curled up against my chest.

"I don't like being scared," she whispered.

I rubbed a hand up and down her arm and rested my chin against the top of her head. "I know you don't."

She was quiet for a long time. "I hate him."

My heart skipped a beat. "Who do you hate?"

"Ian." Her voice as she said his name was soft, yet hard. I heard both her fear and her resolve.

What could I say to that? I hated the man, too. Him and every other man who'd hurt her—used her. If I had my way, I'd castrate every last one of them.

"My mom said I shouldn't hate anyone, but I hate him."

I ran my fingers through her hair, hoping to relax the tension I felt building in her body. "I think in this instance, it's perfectly okay for you to hate him. I think your mom would understand."

Brianna slid her hand up my chest until it was around my neck. She buried her head in the hollow above my shoulder, and I felt her shudder.

She cried for over an hour before falling into a fitful sleep. It hadn't been the Christmas evening I'd pictured, but it was what she needed. The trial was less than two months away. She was going to have to stand up and testify against the man who had done things to her no human being should ever be subjected to. Brianna had every right to hate Ian Pierce. I was sure there was a very special place for men like him in hell.

Brianna

Stephan surprised me the next morning by announcing he wouldn't be working for the rest of the week. The foundation closed between Christmas and New Year's, and the conference call on Christmas Eve was the last obligation he had until after the New Year. I was beyond excited.

We ended up spending most of the week at a cabin about three hours outside the city. Stephan said he wanted to get away from everything for a while, that we needed the alone time. I completely agreed with him. It seemed as if so many things were bombarding us lately, between his work, the reporters who always tried to follow his car, to the upcoming trial . . . even my therapy with Dr. Perkins. All of it cut into our time together. It was nice to leave it all behind—even if it was only for a week.

On New Year's Eve, Stephan turned on the small television in the cabin, and we curled up on the couch to watch the ball drop in New York City. It was the start of a new year. For many, it marked a new chapter in their lives. My new chapter, however, had begun eight months before, when I'd been summoned to Ian's study.

I was in my room, or what passed as my room, when Alex came to get me. The sound of the lock turning made my blood run cold. "Master wants to see you, slave."

Alex released the cuff from around my ankle, led me down the long hallway, and we descended the single flight of stairs. When we reached the main floor, I heard voices coming from Ian's study. I braced myself. I knew what was coming next. Ian had a friend over. The only reason he would be calling for me would be to service his friend. He didn't share Alex often. Alex was his. I was his, too, but only in that I belonged to him . . . that I was his property. Alex was shown affection. I was not.

Knowing from experience that it was best to comply with whatever was about to happen, I obediently entered the room with my head down. I listened to the men talk, and then the stranger took hold of my chin and brought my head up. Averting my eyes, I made sure not to look directly at him. I'd made that mistake before.

The man's hands were hard and commanding. I held my breath waiting to see what he would do to me next.

Who would have known that less than an hour later, my life would change forever.

"Are you all right, sweetheart?"

I twisted my head so I could see him. Smiling, I ran my hand over the side of his face. *All mine.* "Happy New Year."

He smiled and kissed me. "Happy New Year."

Stephan kissed me again, and it wasn't long after that our clothes were discarded and flung into a pile on the floor. The television played on in the background, but we didn't pay much attention to it. All thought of anything happening outside our tiny space ceased to exist. The only thing that mattered was him pressing me down into the couch as he took me. This was how sex was supposed to be.

Sadly, we had to drive back into the city on New Year's Day. Stephan had to return to work the next day. Life outside the two of us went on, and we couldn't hide from it any longer.

As things returned to normal in our schedules, I began thinking more about John. I hadn't forgotten my father's request. Questions as to why continued to plague me—so much so that I decided to bring it up in my next session with Dr. Perkins. "I think I might want to go see John."

"Your father?"

"Yes."

Dr. Perkins nodded and wrote something down on her pad. "Why do you 'think' you 'might' want to go see him?"

"He wants to see me." I paused. "And I'm curious."

"Completely understandable. He's your only living relative, isn't he?"

"Yes."

"Only you know what's best for you. Don't feel like you have any obligation to him or anyone else. You said you 'might' want to go see him. What's stopping you?"

"Stephan doesn't want me to. And I don't know if I should. The last time I saw him, he tried to kidnap me."

"Is Stephan preventing you from going?"

I looked up at her, confused. "No. He told me he didn't want me to go, but that if I did, I should go because I wanted to, not because it was something John wanted."

"And do you want to?"

"I don't know what he wants from me."

Dr. Perkins sat forward. "That doesn't answer my question, Anna. What do *you* want? Only you can answer that. Seeing him might give you some closure, though."

"I don't understand."

She cocked her head to the side. "What don't you understand?"

"Why? Why did he do it? Why didn't he look for me? How could he just leave me there?"

Tears fell freely down my cheeks. Dr. Perkins handed me a tissue and waited until I was no longer sobbing. "I can't answer that for you, Anna. I'm sorry. And if you decide to meet with him, you need to accept the possibility that he might not be able to either."

I nodded and glanced down at the damp tissue I held between my fingers. There was only one person who might be able to answer my questions. I knew that. Even then, the thought of seeing my father again filled me with dread and panic. Still, I knew what I had to do.

When Cal pulled into one of the guest spots in the parking garage at Stephan's building, he turned off the car and started to get out until he realized I hadn't moved.

"Is something wrong, Anna?" Cal's voice startled me, and I turned to look at him.

"No." I paused and looked down at my hands. "I . . . I wanted to ask you for a favor."

"Anything. You know that."

I bit the inside of my cheek, trying to find the words to ask him what I needed.

"Anna?" Apparently I'd been quiet for too long. Jade looked worried, too.

"Will you . . ." I took a deep breath, closed my eyes, and spat it out. "John wants to see me. Will you take me to see him?"

Silence met my request, and I opened my eyes to find both Cal and Jade staring back at me. Cal had a blank look on his face. "You want me to . . . to take you to the prison to see your dad?"

I nodded.

"Why?"

"He's asked to see me, and . . ." It was difficult to put into words all the whys. "I want to hear what he has to say. I want to know why he did it. How he could."

Cal sighed and ran a frustrated hand through his hair. "Wouldn't you rather have Coleman take you?"

I shook my head. "He doesn't want me to go."

He snorted. "I can't say I'm thrilled with the idea myself."

"So you won't take me?"

"I didn't say that." Cal let his head fall back against the headrest and gave me a sideways glance. "When did you want to go?"

Suddenly I felt nauseous. This was really going to happen. "I have to call Emma. She . . . she has to arrange it."

He nodded. "Just let me know when. I'll rearrange my schedule to take you."

I think I nodded, but I wasn't sure. My nerves were getting the better of me.

Cal must have realized I wasn't completely myself. He and Jade rode up with me in the elevator as they always did, but they didn't leave right away.

I took the opportunity to call Emma. It was something to do. Also, I was afraid that if I waited, I would chicken out.

Emma promised to look into it, but she also reminded me that I still had a restraining order against my father. She doubted the prison would allow a meeting because of that, and if they did, it would take probably take months at best to make it happen.

I told her I understood, and she agreed to call me back as soon as possible. That turned out to be fifteen minutes later. The meeting was set up for next Wednesday at two in the afternoon. It wasn't going to be at the prison, though—Emma had been right about the restraining order and their not allowing me to visit because of it. Instead, Emma had contacted Agent Marco, and the meeting was going to occur in his office. John would be brought to Agent Marco and custody transferred to him temporarily.

Emma confirmed that John would be restrained, and she, Agent Marco, and anyone else I wanted would be present. She didn't want me to be alone with John. No one did. I thanked her and hung up the phone before relaying the information to Cal and Jade.

Jade walked over and hugged me. "It will be okay. I can come, too, if you want."

"You have class."

"I can skip it."

It wasn't that I didn't want her there, but I needed to do this on my own. Cal would be there with me, yes, but while he would protect me if need be, I wouldn't lean on him like I would Jade. That was the same reason I hadn't asked Stephan to take me.

Stephan. I'd have to tell him, and I knew he wouldn't be happy about it. He didn't want me to go, but I had to. For some reason . . . I had to.

Chapter 43

Brianna

As expected, Stephan wasn't happy that I'd decided to go see John. We were sitting in his chair on Friday night when I told him. He got really quiet for a long time before murmuring a barely audible "okay."

It wasn't until the next day that he asked me when I would be going. He was going to make arrangements to take the day off so he could take me, but I explained that Cal had agreed to do it. Stephan didn't like that either. "I would rather take you myself, Brianna."

"Cal will keep me safe."

He twisted his mouth in distaste. "I'm sure he will, but that's not the point. Keeping you safe is my responsibility."

We were lying in bed, enjoying a relaxing Saturday morning. His arm was around me, holding me securely to his side. I tucked my head into his neck and tried to explain. "I'm afraid . . ."

Stephan looked down at me, lifting my chin and making me meet his gaze. "What are you afraid of?"

"I'm afraid if you go with me that . . . that I'll lean on you too much. That I won't go through with it."

He frowned. "You don't *have* to go through with it. He deserves nothing from you."

"I know."

Sighing, he cradled my head back against his chest. "I want you to call me as soon as you leave Agent Marco's office, and you are to come straight home once you're finished."

"Okay."

"And you are to do exactly what Agent Marco and Emma instruct you to do."

I nodded. "I will. I promise."

Stephan combed his fingers through my hair. "I don't want you touching him, Brianna. Not for any reason. I don't trust him."

A shiver ran through me. "I won't, Sir."

He took a deep breath and hugged me tight before kissing the top of my head. "I'm going to worry every minute you're there."

That was the last thing I wanted. I kissed his chest. His neck. Anywhere I could reach. "Tell me not to go, Sir, and I won't."

Before I knew what was happening, I was lying flat on my back with him poised over me. He looked down at me with a level of intensity in his eyes that had nothing to do with sexual desire even though I could feel his growing erection straining against my thigh. With one hand along the side of my head, gripping possessively, he brought our foreheads together. "As much as I want to do just that, I won't. I won't take that decision from you, Brianna. I won't be like him."

"You're not." Stephan was nothing like John or Ian. He always put me first. Always.

He skimmed his hand down my face to my neck until he reached my collar. A deep rumble erupted from his chest, and his mouth descended. He pressed his lips almost brutally against mine. I'd been kissed like this before, but not by Stephan. Memories began floating in my head, and I had to force my eyes open. Even then, the panic seemed to be rising faster than I could quell it.

Stephan must have sense my unease, because he pulled away, breathing hard. "I didn't mean to do that. I'm sorry. It's just . . ."

He shook his head and rolled over on to his back, taking me with him. I took deep breaths, trying to calm my racing heart.

"I scared you."

I shook my head.

"I shouldn't have kissed you like that. I let my emotions get the best of me."

We spent the rest of the day lounging around the condo holding each other and talking about everything except John and my upcoming trip to see him. That night we had sex, but it was a complete departure from the aggressive kiss that morning. He kissed every inch of my skin before entering me, chanting over and over again that he loved me.

Wednesday arrived before either of us was ready for it. When Stephan left for work that morning, he hugged me longer than usual. I could tell he didn't want to leave me, but eventually he did. My heart ached, and I wanted to ask him to stay with me. It was weak, but I needed him.

I spent the morning cleaning everything I could find to wash, dust, or vacuum. Usually cleaning helped to relax me, but it didn't this time. As the day wore on, and the time for Cal to pick me up got closer and closer, I began to feel sick to my stomach.

My phone rang, and I rushed to dig it out of my pocket. It was Stephan. "Hi."

"How are you doing?"

I wouldn't lie to him. "I'm nervous. Scared."

"Have you changed your mind?"

"No." There was no conviction behind my voice, but it was the best I could do.

Stephan sighed, and I knew if he were here, I'd see the same frustration that had been on his face for the last four days. "What time is Ross coming to pick you up?"

I checked the clock. It was almost noon. "He said he'd be here about one thirty."

"Have you eaten anything since I left this morning?"

"No." I could feel his disappointment over the phone.

"Go make yourself a sandwich. I know you're nervous, but you need to at least try to eat something."

"Okay. I'll try."

"Once you've eaten, go take a shower, and try to relax a little. I want you to wear your favorite jeans, and the dark green sweater I bought you. No other jewelry besides your collar. Understand?"

"Yes, Sir."

"You'll do fine, Brianna. You're strong—stronger than he is. Stronger than he will ever be."

I sat back on the stool I'd been leaning on and let the tears fall. "Thank you, Sir."

"Now, go eat. I'm only a phone call away if you need me."

We said our good-byes, and I placed the phone back in my pocket before going into the kitchen and doing as I was told. I still wasn't hungry, but I did feel a little better. Hearing his voice always had a calming effect on me.

Stephan took the decisions out of my hands by telling me exactly what to do and what to wear. If he hadn't, I would have stressed myself out even more trying to decide what was best to wear given the circumstances and where I was going.

As it was, I came out of my bedroom right as the phone rang. It was Tom, letting me know Cal was here. I told Tom it was okay to let Cal come up and went to grab my purse and keys. Since I'd moved back in, Stephan had eased up on his insistence that I not be alone with Cal. He still didn't like it, but he'd lifted the restriction. Stephan hadn't, however, added Cal's name to the list of approved guests—Cal still had to go to the front desk first and have them call up to the condo.

When I opened the door, Cal stood, his frame taking up most of the doorway, looking ready for battle. "Stephan isn't here."

He blinked. "I know. I talked to him about ten minutes ago."

"You talked to Stephan?"

Cal chuckled. "Yes. I talked to Coleman." He looked down at the purse in my hands. "Are you ready to go?"

A few minutes later, we were on our way to the FBI office. It was only about fifteen minutes from Stephan's condo, but Cal wanted to make sure we had plenty of time in case we ran into any traffic. It was a good thing, too, because for some reason there seemed to be more cars downtown than usual, and we arrived at Agent Marco's office with only five minutes to spare.

Cal parked the car in the parking garage directly across from the building. He stayed close to me as we exited the garage and crossed the street to the front of the FBI building. The sky was overcast, and it looked like it was going to start snowing again at any moment. I pulled the lapels of my coat closer together, although I wasn't sure if that was more to keep out the cold or just to have something to do. My insides were churning.

He paused before we entered the building, and I glanced up to look at him, wondering if something was wrong. "Are you ready for this?"

I opened my mouth to speak, but nothing came out, so I nodded.

He extended his hand, offering it to me. I looked down at it, unmoving.

Cal, completely out of character, stood motionless as I contemplated if I wanted to take his offered hand or not.

Hesitantly, I reached out and slid my hand into his.

Emma was waiting for us when we entered. "You made it."

"Sorry. We ran into some traffic."

She nodded. "Are you ready, Anna?"

"I don't . . . I don't know." It felt as if there were something lodged in my throat all of a sudden. "Is he here?"

"Yes. They brought him in a few minutes ago."

Whatever was lodged in my throat seemed to grow. "Okay. I'm . . . I'm ready."

Emma turned and led us down the hall to a set of elevators. When the doors opened, we all got in, and Emma pushed the button for the fourth floor.

No one said a word on the ride up, which was probably best.

When we arrived on the fourth floor, Emma led us down another long hallway before stopping abruptly and knocking on a closed door.

"Enter." I recognized Agent Marco's voice.

Emma opened the door, and we stepped into the room.

"Ms. Reeves." Agent Marco nodded a somewhat gruff greeting. "Mr. Ross."

Agent Marco extended his hand, and Cal took it. I kept my one hand clasped to Cal's and the other balled into a fist at my side.

Emma, Cal, and Agent Marco conversed for a minute or two before he addressed me. "I have your father in a holding cell. If you're ready, I thought we could use one of the interrogation rooms across the hall."

I nodded, pressing my lips together. It was the best I could do at the moment.

"All righty, then." Agent Marco rounded his desk and led us two doors down and across the hall to another room. It held a table and three chairs— two on one side, one on the other. "Wait here."

Agent Marco left the room, and Cal guided me over to the two chairs on one side of the table, positioning himself so that he was closest to the door.

Emma took up a position in the far corner.

"Not too late to back out."

I didn't look at Cal. My eyes were focused on the door to my right, on the other side of Cal. The one we'd just come through, the one John was going to walk through in a matter of minutes. "I-I-I have to do this."

Five minutes passed before the knob began to turn. The door opened, and John shuffled in. He had cuffs around both his wrists and ankles. Both were linked with a chain. It prevented him from walking normally. Seeing it instantly brought me back to Ian's dungeon. I knew how it felt to have cuffs around your wrists and ankles, holding you in place. The cold metal binding you . . . preventing you from escaping . . .

"Anna? Anna?"

I blinked several times and stared up at Cal's worried face.

"Anna." Cal breathed a sigh of relief.

"I'm . . . I'm okay."

The sound of a chair scraping against the floor caused me to turn my head. There, across from me, sat my father. He looked . . . different . . . yet the same. There was more gray in his hair than I remembered, and he had wrinkles around his eyes that were new.

Agent Marco held on to John's upper arm until he was firmly in his chair, and then he walked over to stand by the door.

John shifted in his seat, and the chains binding him rattled. "I didn't know if you'd come."

This was going to be harder than I thought. "Why?" I swallowed. "Why did you want to see me?"

"They want me to testify next month at Pierce's trial. I didn't know if they'd told you or not. They want me to testify to the timeline or some such lawyer nonsense. I didn't want you to be surprised when I showed up. I know I'm not one of your favorite people right now."

I didn't know what to say to that, so I remained silent.

"For what it's worth, Anna, I'm sorry. I didn't plan for this to happen. I didn't mean for it to get so out of control. It just . . . did."

Neither of us spoke for several minutes, and I knew this was my opportunity to ask him what I needed to. "Why did you borrow money from that man?"

"Dumas?"

I nodded.

He sighed. "It's complicated."

Cal spoke up. "Why don't you try to explain it?"

John glanced briefly over at Cal before returning his gaze to me. "When I found out your mom was sick . . . that she was going to die . . . I don't know. I lost it, I guess. Chad, one of my deputies, took me gambling to try and get my mind off things, and it worked. It worked too well. Before I knew it, I was spending every waking minute I wasn't on duty at the casino. When I ran out of money, I borrowed against the house."

He shifted in his seat, and the chains clanged against each other again. A shiver ran down my spine. *It's not real. It's not real.*

"They were going to take the house, until someone gave me the name of a guy that might be able to help me. Dumas gave me a loan. I was able to pay off the casino and keep the house. I thought I'd be able to pay him back, but then your mom died and everything changed. You came to live with me, and my world was turned upside down. There were cuts that had to be made in the department, and instead of having the money to pay Dumas back, I barely had enough to make ends meet."

John looked me directly in the eye. "I thought I had more time. I thought . . . I didn't think he'd take you as collateral. I didn't know . . ."

Cal tightened his hold on my hand as I spoke.

"You didn't look for me."

"I did, baby girl. I promise you, I did."

Moisture pricked at my eyes. "Why didn't you look harder? Why didn't you . . ." I was sobbing uncontrollably.

Emma handed Cal a box of tissues. "Thanks."

Once I'd calmed down some, John continued. "I should have tried harder. At first, I thought he was just hiding you away somewhere until I came up with the cash. It wasn't until I approached him a month later with the money, after selling the house and nearly everything I owned, that I realized he no longer had you. After that, I widened my search, but I couldn't find even a trace. A few neighbors saw you get into a vehicle, but other than a general description, I didn't have anything else to go on."

Anger welled up inside me. "You should have tried harder! Do you know what happened to me? Do you know what he did?"

John visibly swallowed and had the decency to look somewhat ashamed. "No. All I've been told was that he held you captive for ten months."

For some reason, I wanted to show him rather than tell him. I wanted him to see what Ian had done to me.

Standing, I turned around. "Cal, can you help me pull up the back of my sweater?"

Cal looked up at me in question, but he stood and did as I asked, being careful to go slow and not touch me any more than he had to.

I heard two gasps as my shirt was lifted, revealing the scars on my back from the whip Ian and his friend had used on me.

Without being told, Cal lowered my shirt a few seconds later and helped me back into my chair.

When I looked up, both John and Agent Marco had paled. "How? What . . . what did that to you?"

"Ian whipped me for not remembering the proper kneeling position." I paused. "I was a slow learner."

His eyes looked as if they might bulge out of his head.

"If you'd looked for me harder, maybe . . . maybe I wouldn't have these."

"I'm so sorry. I had no idea. I—"

"You left me there."

"No. No I didn't. I looked for you. I did."

"You didn't file a missing person's report."

John sat back, deflated. "No. I didn't. After what happened, I was ashamed. If I'd known, though . . ."

I closed my eyes and asked the question I most wanted to know. "You put yourself before me. You thought of your well-being before mine. Why do you think you deserve a chance to be in my life again?"

"I'm your father. I love you."

I shook my head. "No. You don't do that to someone you love. You don't put your needs ahead of theirs."

"I don't know what you want me to say, Anna. I didn't mean for any of this to happen. None of it."

I stood abruptly, needing to get out of there.

"Where are you going? Our time isn't up yet. Please, don't go."

Cal walked me to the door, but I stopped before opening it. I didn't look back but spoke loud enough that he could hear me. "Ian beat me. He tortured and raped me and allowed his friends to do the same. I have someone now who loves me, who would do anything for me. He would move heaven and earth to keep me safe . . . to protect me." I paused and glanced over my shoulder to meet my father's gaze. "Good-bye, John."

Cal opened the door, and I walked out into the hall. I was able to keep myself together until I heard the door close behind me. Then I collapsed onto the floor and began sobbing uncontrollably.

Chapter 44

Stephan

As soon as I received the phone call from Brianna saying she and Cal were leaving Agent Marco's office, I grabbed my things and told Jamie I was leaving. I'd already cleared my schedule for the next day. It was hard to tell what state Brianna would be in after her visit, and I wanted to be prepared. It wasn't as if I'd been all that productive anyway for the past six hours. I was too worried about Brianna's meeting with her father.

Traffic was unusually heavy for the time of day, but I managed to get home before she did. I wasn't sure if that was a good thing or not, since I spent the agonizing minutes pacing the floor and glancing at my watch.

When the security monitor lit up, giving me my first glimpse of her, I knew straight away it was going to be a long night. Her shoulders were slumped, and she was looking down. Cal, walking beside her, didn't look much better, although his stance was more protective than weary.

I opened the door for them, not waiting for Brianna to fish out her key. The minute she saw me, she rushed into my arms and pressed her body as close to me as she possibly could. It felt good to have her close, to know she was safe with me. Taking a deep breath, I inhaled the scent of her hair . . . her skin . . . letting it wash the tension away.

Cal entered, and I stepped back, keeping an arm securely around Brianna. He looked at her and then up at me. No words were spoken between us, but I saw volumes in his eyes. Something happened, and it wasn't good.

"I'll call you tomorrow, Anna. If you need anything before then, you have my number. And Jade's."

When he hesitated, I knew he must be reluctant to leave. "Thank you for going with her."

He nodded and turned toward the door.

"Cal?" Brianna's voice was muffled with her cheek pressed against my shirt.

Looking back at us, Cal met Brianna's gaze.

"I'm sorry you had to see that."

He blanched, but at the same time, I saw him harden his features. "You don't ever need to apologize for anything that monster did to you, Anna. Ever."

She nodded slightly and averted her gaze.

Cal sighed, and his gaze lowered to her back. It took me a moment to understand the significance, but when I saw a shiver rock his body, I knew Cal must have seen her scars.

With one more glance at Brianna, Cal strolled out the door, closing it behind him and leaving Brianna and I alone.

I kissed the top of Brianna's head and gave her a gentle squeeze. "Come on. Let's get you out of these clothes and into a nice, relaxing bath."

Brianna walked, plastered to my side, into my bathroom. As the tub filled with water, I began undressing her. She stood still as a statue as I removed her sweater and jeans. It wasn't until I reached behind her to unclasp her bra that she spoke. Unfortunately, it was in that robotic tone she used when she was distancing herself emotionally. "I showed John my back. Cal saw, too. And Emma. And Agent Marco."

Tilting her chin up, I brushed my lips lightly against hers. "What did John say when he saw them?"

"He asked what they were from." Her voice sounded dead.

"Did you tell him?" I kept my voice soft and low. She was here with me but not completely.

"Yes." She paused and looked up at me. "But I don't know if he believed me."

With every new thing I learned of Jonathan Reeves, I liked the man less and less. I seriously wondered if he had one fatherly bone in his body. How could anyone see scars like Brianna's and not immediately want to rip off the head of the bastard who did it? Or at the very least show some compassion for what she'd obviously been through.

Wrapping one hand around the back of her head, I pulled her against my chest, giving her what comfort I could. I hated feeling so helpless, especially when it came to Brianna. "Let's get you in the bath. You can lie here and relax while I order us some dinner."

She glanced up at me, and I saw moisture in her eyes. "You're not getting in with me?"

My heart broke seeing her like this. "Let me call for the food, and then I'll be in, all right?"

Brianna lowered her gaze. "Okay."

I helped her into the tub and quickly went to order the food. It didn't take me long, and I was back in the bathroom in less than ten minutes, stripping off my clothes and climbing in behind her. She let her head fall back against my shoulder, and I held her close.

After a long silence, Brianna spoke. "He doesn't love me."

Although I happened to agree with her, I was curious as to how she'd arrived at that conclusion. Before when she'd brought it up, it had been phrased more as a question. This had a finality to it. "What makes you say that?"

"He cared more about himself than he did me." She paused. "He still does. When I asked him why he didn't look for me harder, he made excuses."

I placed a kiss on her bare shoulder. There was nothing I could say to make it better, because what she was saying was true. He was selfish. The world revolved around him, not his daughter, even after he'd confirmed she'd been sold to pay off his debts.

We lay there until the phone rang, letting me know the food had arrived. I helped Brianna out of the water and quickly dried us both off. "Go get in my bed. Don't bother getting dressed. I'll be in with the food in a few minutes."

By the time I slipped on a pair of sleep pants and reached the front door, the deliveryman was already there waiting. I paid him and went into the kitchen to grab a tray. Once the food was unpacked and loaded onto the serving tray, I carried it into the bedroom where Brianna was waiting. She was lying down, under the covers, facing the bathroom. When I ambled into the room, she shifted to look at me.

I set the tray on the nightstand beside the bed, stripped out of the pants I'd thrown on to answer the door, and climbed in beside her. She immediately crawled to my side, and I held her for a few minutes, basking in her closeness. "I know you probably aren't hungry, but I want you to try to eat something."

She didn't respond.

I leaned over and brought the tray to rest on my lap. Stabbing a piece of chicken with my fork, I lifted it to her lips. Brianna took the offering and chewed slowly. I speared another bite and popped it into my mouth.

It was slowgoing, but she swallowed down eleven bites before she glanced up at me and said she didn't think she could eat any more. I gave her a soft kiss and tucked her back into my side while I finished eating. She'd eaten more than I'd thought she would.

We spent the rest of the evening cuddled up in my bed watching movies. Every now and then, we'd talk, but we avoided anything that would lead back to John. She and I would discuss that more later, but she'd had her heart crushed by her visit—I knew she'd had high hopes that had been dashed.

At two in the morning, Brianna awoke from a nightmare. It was the first one she'd had since moving back in, and I had no doubts as to the cause. John was very lucky he wasn't within arm's reach at that moment.

She awoke twice more after that. It was a long night.

The next morning, I let her sleep in while I got something to eat and checked my e-mail. When she finally opened her eyes, I was sitting several feet away in a chair with my laptop. It reminded me again of some of her first nights with me, except this time, she was in my bed and not her own.

"Hi." She brushed her hair away from her face and sat up with her back against the headboard.

"Good morning. How are you feeling?"

"Tired."

"Considering how many times your sleep was disrupted last night, that's not surprising." I paused and closed my laptop. "Are you hungry?"

"A little."

I stood, set my computer down on the chair, and went to get her robe. Slipping the silk up over her shoulders, I made sure it was securely wrapped around her before placing a sound kiss on her lips. "Let's go get you something to eat, and then we'll talk."

Breakfast was a quiet affair—even more so than usual. I allowed her to mull over her thoughts while she ate and was happy when she finished all of the eggs and fruit I'd placed in front of her.

When she was finished, I led her over to my chair, and she curled up in my lap, gravitating to her favorite position. "We need to talk about your visit with your father."

"I know."

"How did it feel seeing him again?"

Brianna ran her hand absentmindedly over my chest. Normally she'd be playing with the buttons on my shirt, but I wasn't wearing one. "Nervous. Scared. Even though I knew he couldn't hurt me with Cal there, all I could think about was the last time I saw him—when he sent me the flowers and tried to take me away."

"I'd say that's a pretty natural reaction."

"I just thought it would be different. That he'd be different somehow."

"In what way?"

"I guess . . . I guess I wanted him to apologize for what he did. I was hoping he'd be sorry."

I kissed her temple, wishing I could give her what she'd wanted.

"I told him what Ian . . . what he did to me."

"Did he say anything to that?"

She shook her head. "I didn't give him a chance. I told him, and then . . . then I left."

All I could do was hold her and let her grieve. In a way, she'd lost her second parent. That was never easy no matter how it happened.

I didn't end up going in to work at all that day. Brianna needed me too much, and to be honest, I needed her. Her visit with her father had been trying for us both.

Over the next few weeks, Brianna and I rehashed her visit with her father several more times. Her nightmares continued, but none were as severe as those she'd had that first night. I wasn't completely sure they were entirely because she'd seen John again. The trial was inching closer, and soon she would come face-to-face with her torturer once more.

I had her journal about it multiple times as she worked through her feelings. While the visit hadn't been what she was expecting—hoping—it had provided a few more insights into John's thinking. He'd still been in love with her mother. It was obvious to me as soon as Brianna shared that aspect of the conversation. It took her a little longer to wrap her head around it. She'd always believed their divorce had been a mutual decision —that they'd fallen out of love with one another. Brianna wasn't sure how she felt about the new information.

Toward the end of January, contemplation of John's motivations were put on the back burner as preparation for the trial ramped up. We both took several trips to the prosecutor's office to prep. It was tedious and highly emotional. It also didn't help with Brianna's nightmares.

Two days before the trial, I decided it was time to present Brianna with the charm I'd bought for her. She'd surprised me in many ways over the last several weeks. After talking to John, she'd seemed to gain more resolve to see this thing through to the end. She wanted Ian punished for what he'd done, not only to her but to at least two other young women.

Brianna was in the kitchen cleaning up after lunch when I came up behind her and kissed her shoulder. "Hi."

She giggled. "Hi."

Brianna was truly amazing. She was so beautiful and all mine. I took the cloth out of her hand and threw it in the sink. Leading her into the main room, I instructed her to kneel. I could tell she was confused by the look on her face, but she did as I instructed.

With my empty hand, I lifted her chin, holding it in a position where she was forced to look up at me. "Brianna we've talked a lot about your being my submissive. You wear my collar, but when I gave it to you, it was meant to give you a feeling of security . . . safety. Although I hope you still feel safety and security wearing my collar, I'm also hoping you want it to mean more, as I do."

Releasing her chin, I opened my hand.

Brianna stared at the ornate charm I held in my palm. A small sigh left her lips as she opened her mouth and released a breath.

I'd had the charm custom made for her after she'd returned home. It was a solid platinum heart with an eternity symbol carved in the center. I'd planned to hold on to it for a while—until she was ready—but things felt different between us. Brianna wasn't the scared little girl anymore who didn't know what she wanted. She'd made her choice to be with me—as my submissive. I wanted to acknowledge her choice—and mine.

"Will you give every part of yourself to me, trusting me to make sure your needs are met? Protecting you? Cherishing you? Loving you?" I paused and knelt down in front of her. "Will you accept this heart—this symbol—and wear it to show the world that you are mine?"

Brianna nodded, and I saw her start to tear up.

Cupping the back of her head, I brought our mouths together. I put everything I was feeling into the kiss, trying to show her how happy she'd made me with one simple nod of her head.

"I love you," I whispered, breaking the kiss and resting my forehead against hers.

Brianna reached up and ran her index finger gently along the seam of my lips. She watched her finger moved back and forth several times and then smiled up at me with an almost mischievous look in her eye.

I laughed. She really was going to be a handful once she got over her fears. Brianna might not have realized it, but I had a feeling she had a playful side in there. I didn't think she would ever be like Sarah or Lily, but I could see her being playful once in a while, and that was okay. We'd figure it out, just like everything else.

Standing, I helped her turn a little so I could add the charm onto her collar. I was careful not to remove the collar from her neck, only unclasping it enough to slip the heart onto the circular ring.

She placed her hand over the heart and smiled up at me. "Thank you, Sir."

I took her face between both my hands and kissed her gently . . . reverently. "No. Thank you, Brianna. I am truly honored."

Brianna leaned into my hands, and I moved to sit on the couch. Lifting her onto my lap, I proceeded to kiss her. It was rather innocent at first— well, as innocent as our kisses ever were. That was until she squirmed just right, and my cock decided it had been ignored long enough and wanted in on the action.

Brianna

Stephan leaned me back on the couch, pressing me down into the cushions. The heart he added to my collar felt heavy as it lay against my collarbone. I was his now, really and truly his. There were no more questions as to whether or not I could be his submissive. The occasional doubt surfaced in my mind every now and then, but Stephan always said we'd figure it out as we went, and we always did. He never made me feel that my fears were stupid. Instead, he acknowledged them and set out to find a way to dispel them.

He kissed me while his hands explored. It was cold today, so I'd worn a sweater, but that didn't seem to deter him. Stephan slid his hand up underneath my shirt and palmed my breast, kneading and squeezing.

It didn't take long before he was working the sweater over my head and throwing it over his shoulder. I had no idea where it landed, but I didn't have much time to care as he pushed the cups of my bra down and went to work on my nipples.

All too soon, I was writhing beneath him. He was sucking on one of my nipples while pinching and pulling on the other. Shots of electricity pulsed from my breasts directly between my legs.

I let out a low whine when he stopped what he was doing to my breasts and reached down between us to unfasten my jeans. He chuckled.

"Patience, Brianna."

Without waiting for a response from me, he removed my shoes and shimmied my jeans down my legs, leaving me only in my panties and my bra—although the bra wasn't covering much. I thought he would finish removing the rest of my clothes, but he didn't. Not right away, anyway. Instead, he removed all of his own clothing, including his boxers, and stood near my head.

He cupped the back of my neck with his right hand and drew my mouth toward his erection. There was no need for instruction. I knew what he wanted, and I gladly provided it.

The salty taste of his penis as it hit my tongue only made me want more. I loved the taste, the feel of him in my mouth. He groaned and tightened his hold on my head as I sucked harder.

I ran my tongue along the head and thrilled when he jerked his hips, causing him to go deeper into my mouth. Soon he started to move his hips in shallow strokes as I continued to lick and suck as if there were no better taste in the world.

He was close. I could feel it in the way his body moved, in the rhythm of this breathing. Stephan surprised me, though, by pulling out of my mouth. He looked down at me and smiled, running his thumb along my bottom lip. "Not yet, my pet. As much as I love coming inside your pretty mouth, I will be inside you when I come this time. You are mine."

Stephan ran his index finger along my collar and palmed the heart he'd recently added. He looked up, meeting my gaze. "Mine."

Releasing the heart, he lowered his hand to first my left breast and then my right, cupping each one, weighing it in his palm, before pinching the nipple. He held my gaze. "Mine."

Ever so slowly, he trailed his hand down over my stomach, rubbing my skin lovingly, before continuing downward. He cupped his hand over my sex and pressed firmly. Heat and moisture pulsated under his fingers. "Mine."

I swallowed and nodded. Yes, I was his. Completely and totally his.

He didn't lower his gaze as he removed my panties and slipped two fingers inside me. With his free hand, he started playing with my nipples again. It didn't take long until I was moaning and arching my back. How he could do this to me, I had no idea, but I loved it.

Kneeling between my legs, he removed his fingers. Seconds later, I felt the head of his penis slide inside.

Stephan rocked his hips back and forth, entering me inch by inch. The slow progress was driving me crazy. I wanted to feel him. All of him. I wanted that completely full feeling I only got when he was seated inside me to the hilt.

Once every inch of him was inside me, he wasted no time pulling almost completely back out and thrusting in again. This time, however, there was no slow. The inward thrust of his hips was hard and fast, and my muscles surrounding his erection reacted to the pleasant intrusion.

He kept up a steady pace as I climbed higher and higher toward the peak. It felt so good. With every thrust of his hips, the heart charm bounced against my neck, almost as a reminder of his possession. I felt my climax building, edging closer, and Stephan leaned down to whisper in my ear. "Come for me, my pet. Let me see that beautiful face of yours as you climax around me."

His words had the desired effect. I grabbed hold of his upper arms, arched my back, and moaned through my orgasm.

Stephan kept moving his hips, not letting up for a moment. About a minute passed . . . or I thought it was about a minute . . . I really didn't know. My mind was fuzzy. All I could do was feel as my body continued to tremble from my release. I felt something brush against my hip and then press against my clit. It wasn't until he began moving it in a circular motion that I realized it was his thumb. "That's it. One more time for me. Let go and feel."

I couldn't believe it, but the heat began to build again, just as strong as before. Stephan started pistoning faster and moved his thumb in time with each of his inward thrusts. He kissed the pulse point in my neck and then latched on to it, sucking hard. It was all I needed to send me into another mind-blowing climax.

Chapter 45

Brianna

I was shaking as I got dressed the morning the trial was scheduled to start. Although I wouldn't be testifying that day—wouldn't even be going to the courthouse—I was nervous. I couldn't explain it exactly, but I was. Knowing that the next several weeks would decide Ian's fate was nerve-racking. What if the jury didn't believe me? What if I got up there in front of all those people and froze, unable to speak?

Stephan told me not to worry too much. He'd be right there, and Dr. Perkins was working with me on what to do if I started to feel that my anxiety was getting the better of me. She also told me that if I couldn't look at Ian while I was up on the stand, that was okay.

Even if I didn't look at him directly while I testified, I would know he was there, watching me. I would be coming face-to-face with Ian for the first time since Stephan had taken me away, and I had mixed feelings about seeing him. On one hand, I was scared to death—hence the shaking. On the other, I wanted him to see that he hadn't broken me—that I had survived despite everything he'd done to me.

Slipping my shirt over my head, I caught sight in the mirror of the heart Stephan had given me two nights ago. It was beautiful. The heart was solid, with the exception of the infinity sign that had been carved into it.

Placing my hand over the heart, I took a deep breath and looked at myself once more in the mirror. I remembered standing months ago in my bathroom, questioning who and what I was once Stephan had informed me I was no longer a slave. That girl had been lost. She'd had no direction. Fear of the unknown had been almost worse than knowing she was nothing more than someone else's property.

I was no longer that girl.

"Everything all right in here, sweetheart?" Stephan strolled into my bedroom in jeans and a long-sleeved shirt, looking extremely casual for a Monday morning. He'd made arrangements to work from home until the trial ended. His uncle and the senior vice president were stepping in to cover the meetings and conference calls Stephan wouldn't be able to attend. I was grateful and was once again reminded of how lucky I was that he'd rescued me. Unlike my father, Stephan knew I needed him.

"I think so." My voice trembled with my anxiety.

He opened his arms, and I went immediately into them, surrounding myself with the solace he was offering. Stephan brushed his lips lightly against my forehead. "Are you sure you want to watch the news coverage?"

We'd discussed it last night, and he'd agreed to let me watch the morning news so I could hear what was going on. Emma had explained the first day would consist of opening statements by both the prosecution and defense. No one would testify today, but it would set the tone for what was to come.

I wasn't allowed to be in the courtroom yet. Neither was Stephan. Those testifying couldn't be present until after they took the stand so that their testimony couldn't be influenced. In a way, I was glad. It meant I didn't have to be in the same room with Ian yet.

"Yes. I want to hear what they have to say." I paused.

"And?"

"And . . . I don't know how I'm going to react when I see him again. In person, I mean. I want to . . . I want to try and prepare myself."

He sighed and hugged me closer. "All right. Let's get us both some breakfast, and then we can turn on the TV for a while." Stephan tipped my chin up so that I was looking at him. "If you start getting agitated, I'm turning it off. Understand?"

I nodded. "Yes, Sir."

Twenty minutes later, we sat down in front of the television, me on Stephan's lap. The weatherman was talking about a large snow storm that was going to be coming through in the next few days. A minute later, the camera switched to a woman behind the anchor desk.

"And now we go live to Marcy who is standing outside the courthouse. Marcy?"

A female reporter came on the screen. She was bundled up in a heavy coat and a stylish hat to try and ward off the cold, but the wind seemed to be getting the better of her as her hair blew into her face over and over again even as she tried to move it out of the way. Behind her, I could see people. Lots of people. Some were going inside the courthouse. Many others, were standing outside, braving the cold. It wasn't every day that a local man went on trial for human trafficking.

"Good morning. I'm standing outside the courthouse where we are awaiting the arrival of the accused, Ian Pierce. Pierce is well known in the art community, and he has a reputation for dealing in rare and expensive artifacts. And although some of those priceless pieces have put him in the spotlight before, the attention he's getting now is of a different sort. This business mogul is accused of several counts of abduction, rape, human trafficking, murder, as well as money laundering and receiving stolen goods."

There was a long list of charges against Ian. Agent Marco had read them off to me, but I'd lost track given the enormity. They were expecting the trial to last for at least six weeks. I wasn't looking forward to it. I didn't want to see Ian any more than I had to.

The prosecution felt my testimony would be the most damaging, so I was going to take the stand last. They also warned me Ian's attorney would try his best to discredit me or catch me in a lie. Emma told me to be completely honest and not to hold back on my descriptions unless I didn't think I could keep myself together. Even then, she told me to ask for a break if I felt I needed one. I was dreading it.

I tried to pay attention to what the reporter was saying, but I was distracted by the people behind her. All too soon, it would be my turn to go to the courthouse. I'd have to face not only Ian, but all of those people.

Stephan nuzzled my ear, and I turned to look at him. "Is what she's saying upsetting you?"

"No. I . . . I wasn't really paying attention to what she was saying."

He raised one eyebrow.

"I was looking at all the people. There are so many."

"There are. This is a big case, and it's drawn a lot of attention."

Before I could respond, I heard the reporter say Ian's name, and I redirected my attention toward the screen. There he was. He was in a van, but he was looking out the window, so I could see his face clearly as the cameraman zoomed in to get a better picture. A shiver ran down my spine, and I felt cold.

Stephan saw him, too, and he hugged me tighter. His arms felt like a cage around my body, shielding me . . . protecting me.

The camera followed the van as it made its way around the side of the building. Moments before it disappeared out of sight, Ian turned toward the camera, and I saw the look on his face. It was smug, yet slightly irritated. I'd seen that look from him many times, and it had never boded well for me.

The screen went blank.

Whipping my head around, I looked at Stephan. There was an angry crease in his brow, and he held his lips in a hard line. I could see the pulse pounding in his neck and felt his fingers flexing against my leg.

"Sir?"

Stephan blinked and frowned. Closing his eyes, he took a deep breath before relaxing his fingers and cradling my head against his shoulder.

His breath blew gently through my hair, and he shuddered. "Are you all right?"

I nodded.

Stephan released a sigh and leaned back to look at me once more. He held my face between his hands. After a few minutes of silence, he pulled me against his chest again and started petting my hair. It was as if he couldn't decide whether or not to hold me close or have me in a position where he could look directly into my eyes. "I want to tell you something, but I'm afraid it will scare you."

"You promised no more secrets."

"This isn't a secret exactly."

I could feel the tension in his body, and I tried my best to soothe him as he attempted to do the same for me. This was love, I realized. Being there for the other person when they needed you. Being there for each other. "Please, tell me?"

He ran his lips along my forehead before tilting his head back to look up at the ceiling. "I want to kill him. There have been many times when I've wanted to hurt him for what he did to you, but just now? Seeing him riding in that van all smug and looking as if this is nothing more than an annoyance to him? I can honestly say that I wanted him to die."

I didn't respond. There was no need. Maybe Stephan's declaration should have scared me, but it didn't. I knew him, and he wasn't a violent man. As much as he wanted to see Ian dead, he would never go that far. Stephan didn't have it in him. It was against his nature. He wasn't that type of man.

Stephan

It took me a while to calm down after seeing Ian Pierce's face on the news. The first time I met him, he'd given me the creeps. Then, I had no idea as to the damage he'd done to the woman who'd now become the most important person in my life. Now, I knew that he'd almost destroyed this beautiful woman—nearly reduced her to a mindless zombie.

I held Brianna, drawing on the peace only she could bring me. It worked, and I caressed her hair, enjoying the feel of it between my fingers. She was here, and she was mine. That was what mattered.

We sat there until I glanced up at the clock and realized over an hour had gone by. I needed to check my e-mail and call Jamie. Although I'd made arrangements not to go in to the office while the trial was taking place, there was no way I could walk away completely for a month or more.

Cupping the side of her face, I lowered my mouth to hers and slipped my tongue inside her parted lips. There was still a hint of the orange juice she'd had this morning mixed with her own distinct taste as I slowly explored her mouth.

When Brianna ran her hand down the front of my chest, I knew I needed to stop. While I was always up for sex with her, there were things I needed to get done today. Giving in this early in the day would make it too tempting to blow everything off and go back to bed.

Moving my lips from her mouth to the side of her neck, I continued to place soft kisses along her skin. "I need to get some work done."

"Mmm. Okay."

I chuckled as her hand on my chest continued to descend. Wrapping my fingers around her wrist, I stopped her progress. "That's not helping."

She giggled, and it vibrated her entire body, which didn't help the state of my cock either.

Sighing, I leaned back, separating us a little. She was still on my lap, but at least I couldn't feel her breasts brushing against my chest as she moved. I needed a distraction—for both of us. And I needed to get to work. "Why don't you go get one of your books and read for a bit while I work? It shouldn't take me too long, and then we can do something together."

Brianna looked slightly disappointed, but she nodded and stood. These next few weeks were going to be interesting if they all began like this one.

Over the next two weeks, I tried for normalcy as much as possible. We worked out in the gym upstairs, read together, watched movies, and I helped her in the kitchen whenever I didn't receive a call from work that needed my attention. Richard had rearranged his patients so that he was able to spend three days a week at The Coleman Foundation. I hadn't asked. He'd offered. It was completely unexpected. The downside, however, was that Richard no longer had a hand in the day-to-day operations of the foundation. He was doing the best he could, but there were some decisions he wasn't comfortable making without my input.

It was the day before Brianna and I had to go to the courthouse for the first time. The prosecutor had called earlier in the day to say there was a good possibility I would be testifying. There was also a chance they'd be ready for Brianna, as well, so he wanted both of us there just in case. I'd already called Logan and Lily, along with Cal and Jade, to let them know. Logan was currently out of town, but I had a feeling he'd be there regardless. I knew the other three would as well.

I'd gone into my bedroom to take a call from my uncle and Jamie. They were having difficulty finding a report I'd been working on. As it turned out, I had a copy of it on my laptop and was easily able to e-mail it over to them. Unfortunately, that discovery had taken longer than I'd expected. Confident Jamie and Richard had the document they needed and could handle things from there, I said good-bye and strolled out into the living room to find Brianna.

She wasn't there.

She wasn't in the kitchen either.

"Brianna?"

No response.

Peeking my head into her room, I saw no sign of her. That only left upstairs.

Trudging up the stairs, I'd fully expected to find her in the study going through the bookshelves. When given time to read, Brianna could easily get through a book in a single day. Lily had brought other another large bag full of books last week, and Brianna had already made a sizable dent in them.

Brianna wasn't in the study.

My anxiety was building. Where was she?

Walking up the additional three stairs that took me up to both the gym and the playroom, my heart rate went into overdrive as I saw the door to the playroom standing open.

I stood out in the hall, almost afraid to go inside in case I would startle her. It was the first time since Christmas that she'd come near the playroom. I'd been inside a handful of times to retrieve and replace various items, but for the most part, the room had sat undisturbed.

Brianna stood roughly halfway inside the room, and she looked as if she were ready to bolt at any given moment. Instead of confronting her, I decided to stand back and watch. I wanted to see what she'd do on her own.

Nothing much happened over the next ten minutes. She barely moved, with the exception of a few nods of her head. I figured out that she was talking to herself. I couldn't hear what she was saying, but I had to wonder if she was giving herself a pep talk given the nodding.

Just when I thought all she was going to do was stand there in the center of the room, Brianna took a step forward. Then another. And another.

I held my breath as she stopped in front of the rack that held my floggers and crops.

Brianna reached out her right hand and hesitated, dropping her arm back down to her side and turning away quickly. When she turned around, however, her gaze fell on me standing in the doorway. She gasped and looked around, frantic. I wasn't sure if her reaction was because she thought she was in trouble, or because my presence made her feel trapped. I was hoping it was the former.

"May I join you?"

She wrapped her arms around her waist protectively and looked down.

I strolled into the room, taking my time, hoping not to spook her further. She never glanced up.

I stopped directly in front of her and waited.

"I'm sorry, Sir. I didn't mean . . ." Brianna still didn't change her stance.

Gently taking hold of first one hand and then the other, I brought her palms up to rest on my chest. "Look at me."

Tentatively, she looked up—first through her lashes and then by raising her head.

"Good girl." Leaving her hands where they were, I reached up and caressed her face with the back of my right hand. "I didn't expect to find you in here."

She started to lower her eyes.

"No. You are not to look down. I want to see your eyes."

Brianna snapped her gaze back to meet mine.

I had no idea what she was doing in here, but I had a feeling it was significant. "I don't care that you're in here, Brianna. I told you before that you could enter whenever you wanted."

"I wanted . . . I wanted to see if I could do it."

We were going to the courthouse tomorrow, and it was possible that she would see Ian again for the first time since that night in his study. I knew she was terrified about it, and I wondered if stepping inside this room—

something that also scared her—was her way of coping. "You wanted to see if you could face your fear?"

She nodded. "Yes."

Smiling, I brushed my thumb over her bottom lip. "Do you want to stay or leave? It's up to you."

Brianna swallowed. "What . . . what happens if we stay?"

I shrugged, wanting to reassure her that there was no pressure. "I thought maybe we could look around some more. Maybe you'd want to touch some things. Ask questions."

She pressed her lips together in a tight line, and I knew she was thinking about what I'd said. "We won't . . . play?"

"No. And you don't have to touch anything you don't want to."

There was a long stretch of silence, and then she nodded. "Okay. I'd like to stay."

I bent to give her a brief kiss before straightening and grabbing hold of her hands again. "How about we start over there?" I motioned toward the row of floggers and crops behind her that she'd been examining.

As patiently as possible, I waited for her to make the first move. I'd be lying if I said I wasn't anxious. This was what I'd been waiting for. It was the first step in getting Brianna over her fear of this room. I wasn't going to kid myself, though. We still had a very long way to go. Her being able to walk into the room on her own wasn't the same as her being comfortable enough to allow me to use any of my equipment with her.

Brianna turned back around, and I stepped to the side so that I wasn't directly behind her. I wasn't sure how she'd react to that should she begin to panic. She mimicked the position she'd been in earlier. "Remember, they're just things."

She took a deep breath and released it before cautiously grazing the tips of her fingers over one of the floggers. The one she'd directed her attention to was one of my heavier ones. "Does it hurt?"

I stood at her side, holding her left hand in mine while she continued to touch the flogger with her right. "It can. It can also be used to tickle and tease."

"Tickle?" She scrunched up her nose.

"Yes, tickle. If I hold the flogger in both my hands and just run the tips of it along your back, it would create a tickling sensation."

Brianna didn't respond to that and after a few minutes moved on to one with much narrower falls. "What about this one?"

"This one can be used to tease and tickle as well, but when it's thrown, it has more of a sting. Think of someone snapping a rubber band against your wrist."

She cringed a little.

"Remember what I told you before. Pain is relative."

"So you think I might like it." There was a remoteness to her voice that I didn't like.

"Maybe. Maybe not. It's difficult to tell what you'll like a few years from now."

Brianna looked up at me, eyes wide. "Years?"

I cocked my head to the side. "Months, years, decades. This goes at your pace, Brianna. Just like with the rope, we aren't going to try something if you're not ready. Plus, unlike the rope, these things have sounds that come along with using them, and we both saw how hearing Lily being spanked affected you. You're not ready for that kind of sound stimulation yet."

Swallowing, she took another brief glance at the floggers and then turned toward my spanking bench. "May I touch it?"

"Of course. You can touch anything you want to in this room."

Bravely, she walked forward. I stayed behind her and off to the side, letting her go at her own pace.

Like with the floggers, she reached out a hand and softly caressed the leather. She looked back at me. "It's padded."

"Yes."

"Ian's . . ." She swallowed. "Ian's wasn't padded."

"Ian was out to cause pain. That's not my primary objective. I've always wanted my submissives to enjoy themselves."

Brianna thought about that for a minute. "You . . . played . . . with Tami in here?"

"Yes. And the one time I played with Lily was in here as well." I wasn't going to keep secrets from her ever again, and especially not about this.

She nodded and to my surprise, she strolled over to my Saint Andrew's cross. "What is it?"

"It's called a Saint Andrew's cross. The shape allows a person to be tied spread-eagle to it for teasing, flogging, whipping . . . whatever the Dominant has in mind."

There was a long pause as Brianna considered my explanation. "His was different."

"Different how?"

"It was wood, like this, but it wasn't shaped like an X."

Brianna was talking, and that was good. It meant she was here with me and not lost in her thoughts.

She continued. "It was tall. Straight. But it had two metal rods sticking out of the top."

I thought about what she was describing, and a whipping post came to mind. It made sense. Ian was about force, and pain. Although it wasn't impossible to get someone attached to a Saint Andrew's cross without their cooperation, it was more challenging. With a whipping post, all that was needed was to have the intended's hands bound together. After that, their wrists could be attached to the top of the pole. It stretched them out, making for an easy target. "A whipping post."

"Yes." Brianna closed her eyes for a moment and then turned to face me. "I'm ready to leave now."

Nodding, I extended my arm, and she gave me her hand. She'd made another huge leap today. Tomorrow, she'd take another. It was one step at a time, and I was okay with that.

Chapter 46

Brianna
I pumped my arms harder, faster, trying to get away. There were trees everywhere, leaves and branches brushing and scraping against my legs as I ran. Where was I? I couldn't see anything but trees, trees, and more trees.

Something snapped in the distance, and I knew he was closing in. I had to run faster.

My heart pounded in my chest as I moved through the vegetation, searching for something . . . anything that would allow me to escape. I had to find a way out. I had to get away. I had to—

A hand clamped down on my shoulder, and I screamed.

"Brianna? Brianna, sweetheart, wake up."

I opened my eyes and saw Stephan hovering over me. His brow was creased with worry.

"That's it. It was just a dream. You're safe."

Flinging myself into his arms, I clung to him as I tried to calm down. A dream. It was only a dream.

As my breathing returned to normal, I felt sticky and in desperate need of a shower. I didn't want to let go of Stephan yet, though. Not yet.

"Shh. I've got you." He brushed my sweat drenched hair away from my face, my neck as he caressed me. Every touch eased the fear that had been racing through my veins.

"Someone was chasing me. I couldn't . . . I couldn't get away." I wrapped my arms tighter around Stephan's waist.

"Do you know who it was?"

I shook my head. "No. I couldn't see him. I just knew I had to get away."

The panic started to grip me again, and Stephan readjusted us so that he was leaning back against the headboard. He brought me with him, positioning me so that I was lying almost entirely on top of him. "I'm right here. No one is going to hurt you, love. No one."

Stephan continued to console me, his hands never stopping their ministrations, and eventually I closed my eyes and fell back to sleep. The only reason I knew that was because when I opened my eyes again, there was sunlight streaming in through his bedroom window. Before, it had been dark.

I blinked several times before tilting my head back to look up at Stephan. His eyes were open, and he was watching me. "Thank you."

He smiled and leaned down to brush his lips lovingly against mine. "It's getting late. We need to get showered and dressed soon, or we're not going to make it on time."

My heart sank in my chest as I recalled what today was. We had to go to the courthouse.

"Hey. It will be okay. And when it comes time for you to testify, I'll be right there. You can look at me the whole time if you want." He rubbed his thumb against my cheek. "You can do this, Brianna. I know you can."

"But what if I can't?"

Stephan smiled, but his face looked more sad than happy. "Do you want to testify?"

"Yes."

"Then you will. Somehow you'll find a way. You are the strongest person I've ever had the privilege of knowing, Brianna. If anyone can do it, you can."

I hiccupped and began to cry. Stephan held me, letting me get it out of my system.

All too soon, it was time to get ready. We showered together, dressed, and Stephan insisted I eat some toast. My stomach was churning, and I felt as if I were going to throw up.

Emma had arranged for us go to through a side entrance, so we were able to avoid most of the reporters. Since there were a few hanging out inside the courthouse, we couldn't sidestep them entirely. As soon as they saw us, they descended.

Stephan held me tight to his side as Emma guided us down the hallway. Before too long, Agent Marco, along with a security guard, appeared and ushered us into a room, out of the reporters' reach. Agent Marco firmly closed the door in one reporter's face. "Sorry about that. They're vultures."

Neither Stephan nor I responded to Agent Marco. I was trembling again. How was I going to do this?

"You can both stay in here until they're ready for you. Did you want anything? Water? Coffee?"

"Water. Thank you."

Agent Marco nodded at Stephan and glanced down at me. I saw a flicker of sympathy behind his eyes before he left to go get the water. The first few times I'd met Agent Marco, I hadn't liked him. He still wasn't my favorite person, but I had to admit that since I'd agreed to testify, he hadn't been such a hard nose. At least to me he hadn't.

Several minutes later, Oscar entered the room bringing the bottles of water Agent Marco had gone to fetch. He was followed closely behind by

Lily, Jade, Cal, and Logan. The room wasn't huge, and with all the additional people it felt even smaller.

Stephan guided me to a chair and then pulled another one up beside it and sat down. Emma took one of the water bottles and handed it to Stephan. He unscrewed the bottle before handing it to me. "Take small sips. I don't want you getting dehydrated today."

I did as instructed. They were all watching me.

Emma was the one to speak first. "The prosecutor has been laying out the case against Mr. Pierce. So far he's concentrated mostly on the financials, although the last two days included testimony from the family and friends of the other two missing girls."

Glancing up at all of them, I saw the looks on their faces. It wasn't encouraging. "Was it bad?"

This time it was Oscar who answered. "We're not allowed to give you specifics, but the defense did a good job of tearing holes in most of what was said." He paused. "I think you need to be prepared. Both of you. They are going to come after you with everything they've got."

As if sensing my unease, Stephan pulled me to him, cradling me against his side. "You'll come get me when they're ready for me?"

Emma nodded, and both she and Oscar left.

Our friends paired off in opposite corners of the room, almost as if they were standing watch. Occasionally someone would comment or ask a question, but for the most part, everyone appeared to be lost in their own thoughts. I wanted this to be over, behind me, so Stephan and I could get on with our lives.

Right before the clock struck noon, Oscar popped his head into the room and asked what we'd all like for lunch. When he returned with our sandwiches, he informed Stephan that he would be up soon. I nearly lost the two bites of my meal I was able to choke down, and it was only Stephan helping me breathe through the panic and nausea that helped keep the food down.

Less than an hour later, there was a knock on the door before Emma, Agent Marco, and a guard walked in. Oscar wasn't with them, so I assumed he was already in the courtroom waiting.

"They're ready for you, Mr. Coleman."

Stephan nodded and turned to face me. He held my face between both of his hands and rested his forehead against mine. "I'll be right back."

I nodded.

He faced Lily, and there was some sort of unspoken communication between them. She nodded and stepped forward.

Reluctantly, Stephan stood and trudged toward the door where Agent Marco and the guard were waiting. Lily quickly filled the seat he'd vacated moments before. Stephan paused at the door, looking back over his shoulder. His gaze met mine. There was an almost scary quality to his eyes, and I knew right then and there that he wasn't scared of facing all those people and telling them what he'd done to save me. He was going to put his entire reputation on the line by admitting he'd broken the law—that he'd bought another human being.

"Stephan?"

He froze. "Yes, Brianna?"

"I love you."

Stephan's eyes hardened, and he marched back across the room to where I sat. Lifting me out of my chair by my arms, he planted a hard kiss on my lips and then circled his arms around me, hugging me to his chest.

Before he released me, he palmed the heart that hung from my collar and looked into my eyes with an intensity that made my heart hammer in my chest for reasons that had nothing to do with fear or panic. He didn't speak, but I heard what he was saying loud and clear. I was his. He was mine. Whatever happened, nothing would change that.

Stephan

I didn't make it more than three steps outside the room we'd been holed up in before the questions began flying from reporters.

"Why are you here, Mr. Coleman?"

"Are you testifying?"

Questions began mixing with other questions until I was no longer able to distinguish one from another. They all wanted to know the same thing, though. Since Agent Marco had publicly announced that I was no longer a person of interest in the case, one by one the media had begun going elsewhere for their stories. Whether I liked it or not, that was once again going to change.

Keeping my chin up, my shoulders back, and my eyes forward, I followed Agent Marco to the courtroom. He peeked inside before opening the door. I watched him nod to someone inside the room, and then he stepped inside, motioning for me to follow.

As I slipped inside the large courtroom, away from the flashing cameras, the first thing I noticed wasn't all the people in the seats or even Ian Pierce himself. It was Brianna's father. He was being led past Ian and out a side door. What struck me most wasn't that he was there—I knew he had been scheduled to testify—it was the look in his eyes as he stared at Ian. I'd never seen that look from Jonathan Reeves. If looks could kill, Ian Pierce would be a dead man. Maybe, just maybe, Jonathan Reeves was beginning to grasp the horror his daughter had lived through.

"Who is the prosecution's next witness?" The judge's voice drew my gaze away from Reeves and back to the front of the room.

"The prosecution calls Stephan Coleman to the stand, Your Honor."

Standing up a little straighter, I walked confidently to the front of the room. The bailiff met me once I passed by the tables where the lawyers and Ian were set up, and escorted me to the witness chair. "Please raise your right hand."

I followed his instruction and lifted my right hand so that it was level with my shoulder.

"You do swear that the evidence you shall give relative to the cause now under consideration shall be the whole truth, and nothing but the truth. So help you God."

"I do."

"You may sit."

Lowering my arm, I sat down. It wasn't the most comfortable chair, but at least it had some padding to speak of. Thoughts of padding brought back the comment Brianna had made regarding Ian's spanking bench. I directed my gaze to the man in question and hardened my stare. He smirked back at me. Unless he knew something I didn't, he was being overly confident given the circumstances.

"Can you state your name for the record?"

Reluctantly, I turned my attention back to the prosecutor. "Stephan Coleman."

"And Mr. Coleman, do you know the defendant?"

"Yes. I do."

"How do you know Mr. Pierce?"

"I met him last May at his home. We'd conversed over the phone on two separate occasions prior to the meeting to set it up."

"And what was the meeting about, Mr. Coleman?"

When meeting with Agent Marco and the prosecutor to prepare for trial, they'd instructed me to look directly at the jury when I delivered this next piece of information. Every last one of them was staring right at me, waiting for my answer. "I met with Mr. Pierce to inquire about purchasing one of his slaves."

Several gasps were heard throughout the courtroom, including a few from those among the jury. It was followed by a flurry of commotion, and the judge banged his gavel several times to restore order. "Silence."

Once things quieted down, the prosecutor continued. "So you met with Mr. Pierce at his home to discuss buying one of his slaves?"

"Yes."

"And how did it come to your attention that Mr. Pierce had a slave to sell?"

"A friend of mine ran into Mr. Pierce and his two slaves at a party, and the subject came up that Mr. Pierce may be willing to part with his newest slave for the right price."

"And your friend brought this to your attention?"

"Yes, he did."

The prosecutor let my confirmation linger for several moments. "So your friend told you about Mr. Pierce and his slave—the one he may be interested in selling for the right price—and you went to meet Mr. Pierce at his home."

"Correct."

"Could you tell us about your meeting with Mr. Pierce?"

I nodded. "When I arrived, a young woman, who I later learned to be Alex, invited me into the house and took me to a room where Mr. Pierce was waiting. After greeting me, he dismissed Alex, leaving us alone in the room. I introduced myself, and we briefly discussed my reasons for coming. He followed that up by asking if I would like to see the merchandise."

The prosecutor cleared his throat. "To clarify, the merchandise being discussed is a person? A young woman?"

"Yes."

He nodded. "Continue. What happened next?"

"Mr. Pierce called Alex back and instructed her to go get Brianna and bring her to him. It wasn't long before Alex returned with another young woman. The woman, Brianna, was instructed to stand in the middle of the room while I inspected her."

"Inspected her, Mr. Coleman?"

"That's right." I wasn't going into detail. The experience itself had been humiliating enough for both me and Brianna. I couldn't see how knowing every move I'd made would be beneficial to the jury.

"What happened after you 'inspected' her?"

Again, I looked at the jury. "He asked if I liked what I saw and offered to let me try out her oral skills if I wanted."

There was a collective gasp, and the judge was once more banging with his gavel. "Now that's enough. One more outburst and I will begin removing people from the courtroom. Is that understood?"

He leveled a stern gaze over the expanse of the room before looking over at me and nodding. "You may go on, Mr. Coleman."

"Thank you." Turning back to face the prosecutor, I went on with my story. "I declined his offer and asked how much he wanted for her."

"Did you buy the young woman from Mr. Pierce?"

"Yes. I did."

"And what was this woman's name, Mr. Coleman?"

"Her name was Brianna Reeves."

The prosecutor nodded. "One more question, Mr. Coleman. Why did you buy this young woman from Mr. Pierce?"

"My friend, the one who saw her at the party, got the impression she wasn't there of her own free will. After seeing her myself, I agreed with his assessment. I couldn't, in good conscience, leave her there."

"Why not call the police?"

"And tell them what? I had no evidence, just my gut telling me something wasn't right. I had to do something, and I did."

The prosecutor had me confirm that I had been granted immunity for my participation in a crime in exchange for my cooperation. Some of the jurors looked disgusted. Others had a mix of interest and confusion on their faces. Human trafficking cases in the US weren't an everyday occurrence. I'm sure a few of them were at least trying to decide whether or not to believe my story. They were trying to figure out if the man on the other side of the table was capable of selling another human being. I knew for a fact he was. He was capable of that and a lot more.

Ian's attorney kept it brief. He had me state my name, my profession, and to reiterate how I'd met Ian. I thought he was going to return to his seat after that, but he stopped and pivoted on his heel, facing me once more. "How old are you, Mr. Coleman?"

I was confused, but I answered him. "I'm twenty-five."

"And as a twenty-five-year-old man, you have certain . . . needs, shall we say?"

Although I had a feeling I knew what he was trying to get at, I wasn't going to make this easy for him. He was trying to defend the enemy, after all. "If we're being literal, we all have needs. You're going to have to be more specific."

Instead of answering my question, he asked me another. "This woman you supposedly bought from Mr. Pierce, do you currently have a relationship with her?"

Ah. I knew where he was going. "Yes. I do."

"And would you classify that relationship as being an intimate one?"

I took a deep breath and answered, attempting to keep my frustration out of my tone. The prosecutor warned us this was a possibility. The defense was going to be grasping at straws. "Yes. Brianna and I developed a relationship . . . an intimate relationship. She's my girlfriend."

"And she lives with you, does she not?"

"Yes."

"I see. So you're here testifying against a man who you claim held your girlfriend against her will. A man who you say then sold you the woman you are, by your own admission, currently living with."

Gritting my teeth, I spat out my answer. "Yes." I was beginning to understand what Oscar was talking about. With a few simple questions, Ian's attorney had planted the seed of doubt as to my motives.

"Thank you. That will be all for now." He returned to his seat and ended by asking the judge for permission to call me to testify again at a later time.

As I stepped down off the stand, irritated and in desperate need to hold Brianna in my arms again, the judge announced a fifteen-minute recess. I supposed he wanted to give everyone, including the media that was sitting inside the courtroom, the opportunity to vocalize their shock over what they'd heard since he'd put a stop to it earlier.

The only thing I could concentrate on was getting back to Brianna. That was easier said than done, though, when I was waylaid from leaving the courtroom by the prosecutor. "You did well, all things considered."

"Thank you, but I'm not so sure about that."

He shrugged. "We knew the defense bringing up your relationship with Ms. Reeves was likely. How's she holding up?"

I glanced over my shoulder to where Ian was being taken out of the courtroom through the side door Reeves had disappeared through earlier. "As well as can be expected. She's nervous, and rightly so."

"I'll do my best to protect her, but they are going to go on the attack. I'm surprised your cross-examination wasn't worse than it was."

"He wants to call me back up on the stand later."

"Yes. That's not unusual. And he will probably do the same with Ms. Reeves as well. It will give him time to dig up dirt . . . try to catch you in a lie or find something to tarnish your reputation in some way." He paused. "Any skeletons in your closet I need to know about?"

I met the prosecutor's inquisitive gaze. Before I could respond, however, there was a commotion toward the back of the courtroom. I glanced back to see Logan poking his head through the door. He saw me and motioned for me to come.

Excusing myself from the prosecutor and his questions, I strolled down the aisle to meet Logan. He nodded out into the hall, and I followed him. I saw Brianna searching through the throng of people. When her gaze landed on me, I saw some of the panic ebb from her eyes.

Reaching out for her, not caring who was around us, I pulled her into my arms. A large puff of air left her lungs blowing hot against my neck.

I stood there holding her for as long as I could, but all too soon, everyone began reentering the courtroom, including the judge.

Brianna stood a few feet outside the door, flanked by our friends. Jade and Lily were directly by Brianna's side. They'd each been holding one of her hands when I'd walked through the door. Logan and Cal stood guard next to them. It was a rather impressive sight. I noticed Emma hovering directly behind Brianna. The five had her surrounded on three sides.

Through the closed door, I could hear the judge bang his gavel, bringing the court back to order. "Who is the prosecution's next witness?"

The prosecutor's voice sounded bold and confident. "The prosecution calls Ms. Brianna Reeves."

Ready or not, it was time.

Chapter 47

Brianna

The judge's voice echoed through the closed doors. If it was that loud standing out in the hall, I could only imagine how loud it would be inside the courtroom.

Stephan held tight to my hand as we waited. I could hear movement and some murmuring on the other side of the doors but nothing specific. There were too many things going on in the hallway where we were waiting. Heels clicked on the tile floor, and a there were a couple of men talking quietly along the wall.

No one bothered us as we waited. I wasn't sure if that was because they were too wrapped up in their own comings and goings, or if it had to do with the overwhelming presence of my bodyguards. And that was what they were—bodyguards. When Stephan had left to testify, Emma stayed in the room with me, along with Cal, Jade, Lily, and Logan. While Lily and Jade had stayed by me, holding my hand and trying to distract me as best they could, Logan and Cal had taken up positions about halfway between the door and where Lily, Jade, and I sat at the back of the room. They'd stood with their arms folded over their chests, almost daring anyone to attempt entrance.

A minute or so went by before I heard the prosecutor announce my name. The door opened, and Agent Marco motioned for me to enter. My limbs, however, wouldn't move.

"It's your turn, sweetheart," Stephan's voice whispered softly in my ear.

I felt Ian's stare on me from across the room and instantly wanted to crawl into Stephan's lap and bury my face against his shoulder. I knew that wasn't an option, though, given where we were, so I held his hand in a death grip instead.

All eyes were on me, and I felt the panic begin to swell. I closed my eyes, blocking out everything, but it was too much. I couldn't do this. I couldn't
—

A hand cupped the side of my face—a familiar hand. One that was soft yet firm. It turned my face to the side, and when I opened my eyes, Stephan was there, inches away from me. "Take a deep breath."

I did.

"Again."

The second breath came a little easier as I continued to focus solely on him.

"That's it. You can do this. Just keep breathing and look at me."

"Okay."

I have no idea how long we stood there, but no one around us moved or said anything. The weight of their stares pressed on me, but I stayed focused on Stephan. He never took his eyes off me. "Are you ready?"

"I think so."

He smiled and dropped his hands from my face. I took two steps forward before I realized Stephan hadn't moved.

When I looked back over my shoulder, Stephan reached out his hand, squeezing my fingers. "I have to stay out here. I'm not allowed to come in with you."

"Why?" I felt my throat constricting.

"The defense has asked permission to recall me to testify. Because of that, I can't be in the courtroom." He walked the two steps it took to reach me, and a guard took a step forward, silently telling him that he couldn't proceed any farther. "You'll be fine. I'll be right here. And you won't be alone."

Stephan nodded toward Logan, Lily, Cal, and Jade.

As if they'd both been prompted by some silent signal, Lily and Jade stepped up on either side of me and offered me their hands. Reluctantly, I turned away from Stephan and took the offering.

They walked beside me until we reached the last row of seats right behind the lawyers. "We'll be right here," Lily said as she and Jade each released my hand and slid into the empty seats.

I felt as if I were about to lose it, but I nodded. They sat down, and Lily motioned that I should continue to go on without them. I didn't want to. I wanted Stephan there with me. It would be so much easier if he was.

He couldn't, though. I knew that. Even if he'd been able to be inside the courtroom, I had to do this on my own. Taking a deep breath, I walked forward.

It was a long way to the witness stand. At least, it felt that way. The bailiff approached me halfway there, and I flinched. I had to force myself not to run in the opposite direction.

After the bailiff swore me in and I was seated behind the wooden partition, I felt a little better. The closest person to me was the judge, and although he was imposing sitting above me, I was fairly confident he wouldn't harm me. I wasn't sure why I felt that way, but considering how I was shaking inside due to all the other people in the room, including Ian, I was going to take it.

"Hello, Ms. Reeves."

"H-Hi."

The judge's voice startled me, causing me to jump. "You're going to have to speak a little louder so we can hear you."

My heart thudded in my chest, feeling as if it would burst through at any minute. I found Lily in the crowd, and she lifted her hand to her neck, dragging her fingers lightly along her collar. It took me a moment to realize what she was doing, but then I got it. Closing my eyes, I let myself feel the weight of my collar hanging around my neck. Stephan's collar.

"Ms. Reeves?"

I opened my eyes, and this time looked at the prosecutor.

"Can you state your name for the court, please?"

"Brianna. Brianna Reeves."

"Thank you." He smiled, and I knew he was trying to put me at ease. "Could you tell the court how you know the defendant?"

The prosecutor motioned toward Ian, and without thinking, I followed his movement. My gaze landed on Ian, and I nearly lost it. I closed my eyes against the memories that flooded through my head. Tears rolled down my cheeks, and I couldn't stop them.

"Ms. Reeves?"

I pinched my eyes closed, trying to block everything out. *Go away. Please, go away!*

A loud bang sounded, and my eyes flew open looking for the danger, ready to bolt.

For some reason, my gaze once again fell on Ian. He was laughing . . . amused.

He thought he was going to win.

"He was my Master." My voice rang out loud and clear through the courtroom, even though my insides felt as if they were vibrating out of control. "I was his property. He owned me."

The courtroom fell silent.

I knew I had to get it out now, or I never would. My hands were trembling, and I pressed them flat against my legs trying to keep them still. "The first time I met him, he had two men hold me down while he . . . while he beat me." I took a deep breath. "And then he placed a leather collar around my neck. He said . . . he told me I was his now and that I would do as he said or face the consequences."

"How long were you held against your will by Mr. Pierce?"

"Objection."

The judge's angry voice ripped through the courtroom in response to the defense's outburst. "Overruled." He paused. "Continue, please, Ms. Reeves."

My insides felt as if they were going to burst and I would lose the little bit of lunch I'd eaten. "Ten months."

"And that was when Mr. Coleman purchased you from Mr. Pierce, correct?"

"Yes. Stephan saved me. If he hadn't . . ." The tears started flowing again. I couldn't stop them. "If he hadn't, I would probably be dead by now."

"Objection. Speculation, Your Honor."

The judge turned his attention to me. "Please stick to the facts, Ms. Reeves."

I wrapped my arms around myself protectively and nodded.

There was a long pause while the prosecutor waited for me to collect myself. I was trying not to fall apart—really, I was. "Could you explain to the court what your life was like with Mr. Pierce?"

"I-I-I don't know if I can."

"Try? Please?"

Someone handed me a tissue. I didn't know who. "The first night I was there . . ." The words got caught in my throat. "I was . . . I was locked in the basement. It was cold. And dark. I remember . . . I remember being so scared. I didn't understand what was happening or why. What had I done to deserve this?" The last part came out on a strangled cry. I'd asked myself that question time and time again. Not only that night, but many nights after that.

"I thought . . . I thought it couldn't get any worse, but . . ."

"But it did get worse, didn't it, Brianna?"

I closed my eyes and nodded as more tears fell. "Yes."

"Take your time, but can you tell us what happened?"

"The next morning . . ." I had to clear my throat. "He . . . he came downstairs to get me. I tried to . . . I tried to fight him off . . . I tried! But I was too weak from the beating the day before. He attached a leash to the collar he'd put around my neck." I reached up, cupping my neck. The cool metal of Stephan's collar pressed into the palm of my hand, and I took another deep breath trying to calm myself, to get through this. I was wearing Stephan's collar now, not Ian's. Stephan's. And it was by my choice. No one could take that away from me. Not even Ian.

"I was taken . . . to another room on the main floor." I swallowed. "Later I learned he called it his—his playroom. He . . . he . . ." I shook my head begging the memories to go away. I didn't want to remember.

"He placed thick cuffs . . . around my wrists." It was almost as if I could feel the metal bands digging into my wrists. I glanced down through my tear-filled eyes just to make sure they weren't there. "And with the help of the same . . . the same two men from . . . from the day before . . . they placed my wrists high at the top of a wooden pole."

Just as Dr. Perkins had taught me, I sought out something that could ground me to the here and now. Sights. Sounds. Textures. "I couldn't move." My voice came out in not much more than a whisper. "My feet could barely touch the floor."

"What happened then?" The prosecutor's voice was equally as quiet.

"He . . . he whipped me."

I stopped, trying to breathe through the panic that threatened. "I don't know . . . I don't know with what. I couldn't see. But by the end, I was covered in blood."

"And then?"

"They took me down." I closed my eyes, remembering as if it were yesterday. Every part of my body hurt from my hands, all the way down to my feet. "They placed me face down on a bench." I paused and found Cal's gaze. He was staring back at me with wide eyes. I'd never gone into detail with him about what had happened. Now he knew. "One by one . . ." I swallowed, feeling bile rise in my throat. "They raped me."

I fell apart then, hunching over in my chair and sobbing.

Instead of asking me another question, the prosecutor addressed the judge. "Your Honor, I would request a recess so that the witness can compose herself after such emotional testimony."

There was a short pause. At least, it felt short. "Given it's almost four o'clock, we'll adjourn for the day and resume testimony tomorrow morning at nine. Court dismissed. Bailiff?"

Everyone stood except me. I felt as if a weight was pressing me down into my chair. I did it. It wasn't over yet, but I'd gotten through the first day. Ian didn't win. I didn't let him.

Arms wrapped around my waist, lifting me from the chair. I sighed. Stephan. I held on tight, never wanting to let go.

"You did great, sweetheart. I'm so proud of you."

I cried. I couldn't help it.

"Come on. Let's get you home, and then we can curl up in my chair. How does that sound?"

I smiled against his neck. My nausea was slowly receding. "Like heaven."

Stephan kissed the side of my face and smiled. "I couldn't agree more. Let's find our way out of here."

Stephan

If I'd thought Brianna's nightmares during the last month had been bad, they had nothing on what occurred the night after she testified. Every time her breathing evened out and I thought she'd finally fallen asleep, she would crinkle her nose and ball her hands up into fists. Less than five minutes after that, the thrashing and screaming began. The cycle repeated itself over and over again. It was a very long night.

At four, I gave up on either one of us getting any sleep and dragged Brianna into the bathroom with me for what I hoped would be a relaxing bath. I massaged her shoulders and back, keeping everything as innocent as possible. That was until she looked up at me and begged me to take her. I was unsure at first, but then she explained that she needed me to reassure her nothing that happened yesterday had made a difference. That she was still mine. That I still wanted her.

Her words tore at the very fiber of my being. Gripping the back of her neck, I brought her lips to mine. I took my time, touching and tasting her . . . slowly making love to her with my hands and mouth before positioning her over my cock and entering the warm depths of her pussy as the water moved around us.

We'd made love before, even though Brianna never referred to it as such. She always called it *sex* no matter if it was rough, or if it was sweet and gentle. I knew that had to do with her past. But even if she couldn't consciously acknowledge the difference, I knew subconsciously she did in the way her body reacted. Her pussy pulsed around me as I rocked her hips against me, grinding her clit against my pelvic bone.

Our lovemaking wasn't hurried. And when we both finally reached our climaxes, it was with our mouths hovering over the other's, and our gazes locked on one another's. It was a truly spiritual experience—and exactly what we'd both needed.

All too soon, it was time to get ready to go back to the courthouse. I wasn't looking forward to another day spent in the hallway waiting while Brianna gave her testimony. Although I knew a lot of what she'd gone through, there were details she and I hadn't talked about. Details she'd felt the need to share with me last night. I'd known she was beaten, collared, and then thrown in a dungeon. I'd also known that the next day Ian had raped her. Finding out she'd been beaten further and then gang raped by Ian and his friends was new information. It was difficult to sit and listen to, especially knowing that she'd had to sit up in front of a roomful of strangers—and Ian himself—and pour her heart out. He really was a bastard.

The drive to the courthouse seemed to take no time at all, and before I knew it, I was looking for a place to park.

Seconds after I turned off the engine, there was a loud bang, followed by several other similar sounds—four in total. I had no idea where the sounds had come from, but instinctively, I grabbed Brianna and ducked.

Several minutes passed, and eventually there was screaming and people running in every direction. People were panicked. I lifted my head up, taking in the scene. Something had happened, and it didn't look good. When we'd arrived, there had been only a handful of uniformed police scattered throughout the area. Looking now, I counted at least twenty.

I was weighing my options—stay in the car and wait to see what happened, or get out of the car with Brianna and try to get some answers—when my cell phone rang. It was Logan.

"Where are you?"

"We're still in the car, on the north side of the courthouse. What's going on?"

"I don't know exactly. From the looks of it, though, at least one person has been shot. Stay where you are, if you can. The police are locking down everything. No one who could have seen or heard anything is going anywhere anytime soon."

I nodded, even though he couldn't see me. "Call me when you have more information."

Slipping the phone back into my jacket pocket, I reached for Brianna and hugged her against my chest.

"What's going on?"

"Someone's been shot."

She looked up. "Who?"

I shook my head and began threading my fingers through her hair. Whatever was going on, I had a feeling we were going to be here a while. The police didn't take public shootings lightly. "Logan didn't know. He's going to call us once he finds out more."

Five minutes later, Ross called. He and Jade had arrived a minute or so before and were also stuck in their vehicles. When they'd tried to exit, they'd been order by an officer to stay put. No one seemed to have any answers at that point.

All that changed when my phone rang again. Almost twenty minutes had passed since we'd heard the first bang.

I checked the caller ID before I answered. It was Agent Marco.

His voice was clipped. "Where are you?"

"In my car, on the north side of the courthouse."

"Is Ms. Reeves with you?"

"Yes."

"Stay where you are. I'm on my way to you."

He didn't give me time to respond before disconnecting, and that sinking feeling in the pit of my stomach increased. What had happened?

Before I knew it, Agent Marco came trotting toward our car. He looked over his shoulder and then motioned for us to get out of the vehicle. I got out first and then went to help Brianna. Her fingers dug into my arm even through the fabric of my thick coat.

"Follow me."

I kept Brianna close as we followed Agent Marco across the snow-covered lawn and up the steps of the courthouse. He had to flash his badge more than once before we finally entered the building. Once inside, he took us upstairs into a room very similar to the one we'd waited in the day before.

"You might want to have a seat."

"That's okay. We'll stand." I'd had enough of all the cloak and dagger. "Are you going to tell us what's going on?"

He glanced down at Brianna, but she wasn't looking at him. "Roughly twenty-five minutes ago, Ian Pierce was shot."

Brianna tensed.

"How?"

"We don't know much yet."

I was getting frustrated, and Brianna was clinging to me as if I were going to disappear at any moment. "What *do* you know?"

"Pierce was on his way into the courthouse when a man shouted his name and fired. The guards returned fire on the shooter, and he was hit. So was Pierce. Both men have been taken to the hospital."

Wrapping my other arm around Brianna, I kissed the top of her head. "Did either of them survive?"

"I don't have that information. Not yet."

As much as I didn't like not knowing, yelling at Agent Marco for not being able to tell us more wasn't going to help matters. "Will you let us know when you hear something?"

"Of course." He paused. "Will you two be all right in here for a while?"

I nodded. "We'll be fine."

He opened the door and stepped back out into the hallway, leaving Brianna and I alone in the room. I guided us over to the corner and removed both our coats since I had no idea how long we'd be waiting. It took some effort on my part since neither of us wanted to release our hold on the other.

Once we were both free of our coats, I dug out my cell and called Logan. "Hello?"

"It's me. We found out what's going on."

"What? I asked one of the cops, but no one will tell me anything."

Pulling over a chair, I sat down, positioning Brianna on my lap. Her head gravitated to my shoulder, and I traced patterns lovingly down her arm with the tips of my fingers while I spoke. "Someone shot Ian. He and the shooter have both been taken to hospital."

"How—"

"Agent Marco found us. We're in a room on the second floor of the courthouse, waiting."

"What do you need us to do?"

"Nothing at the moment. Right now we're just waiting."

Logan let out a frustrated breath. I knew exactly how he felt. "Call us if you need something. We'll stay here for as long as they'll let us."

"Thanks."

My next call was to Ross. The conversation was almost identical to the one I'd had with Logan. It was amazing, the fierce protectiveness Brianna brought out in those around her.

"I hope he's dead." Brianna's voice was muffled since she had her face pressed up against my neck. I could feel every breath she took, and I could feel her heart beating against my chest.

Resting my head on top of hers, I closed my eyes and took a deep breath. I couldn't help but agree with her. "So do I, sweetheart. So do I."

Chapter 48

Stephan

We were all walking around on eggshells for the next three days. The shooter turned out to be the father of the first young woman Ian had taken nearly five years ago. There was no note, no explanation as to why he'd suddenly snapped. He'd been shot three times in the chest and was pronounced dead when he arrived at the hospital.

Ian didn't make it so easy. The bullet hit him in the chest and pierced the bottom of his lung before getting lodged in between two of his vertebrae. He was on life support in critical condition, and we were all holding our breath to see whether or not he got better or worse.

The media was camped outside the front of my building again. It was worse than before, if that was possible. Security had already removed two guys who'd thought they could sneak inside the building through the parking garage.

Ross, Jade, and Lily were near-constant visitors in our home. They all helped keep Brianna busy and not thinking about Ian and whether or not he was going to survive. Brianna had been shy at first with them, unsure how they were going to treat her now that they knew more details about her captivity. Jade and Lily had quickly put her mind at ease, though, by hugging her and dragging her in front of the television to watch a chick flick. The three of them sat huddled together eating junk food for hours.

Brianna's nightmares persisted. The only thing I found helped was when she lay with her head directly over my heart. Hearing my heartbeat steadily in her ear was the one thing that lulled her to sleep. The problem was that when I drifted off to sleep myself, one of us inevitably moved. Her nightmare would return and so would the screaming. Needless to say, neither of us got much sleep.

The two of us were lying on the bed watching a movie Saturday afternoon, Brianna's head resting on my chest, when the main phone rang. I kissed her forehead and jumped up to answer it. "Hello?"

It was the front desk. "Mr. Coleman, there's an Agent Marco here to see you. Should I send him up?"

I glanced back in the direction of my bedroom where Brianna was waiting. "Yes. That will be fine, but give us ten minutes, please."

"Will do, Mr. Coleman."

"Thanks." Hanging up the phone, I ambled back into my bedroom. Neither one of us had bothered getting dressed yet. "We need to put some clothes on. Agent Marco is on his way up."

"Ian?" She fisted the blanket in her hands, and I could see the pulse pounding in her neck.

I strolled over to stand in front of her, and one by one, I pried her fingers from the blanket. "I don't know yet. All I know is he's here to see us, all right? Let's get some clothes on and find out what he wants."

"Okay."

Bending down, I brushed my lips lightly over hers. "Good girl."

I threw on some clothes, leaving my feet bare, and then went with Brianna to her room so she could do the same. She was already on edge, and knowing Agent Marco was on his way up to deliver some type of news wasn't helping with her anxiety level. Twice she dropped the bra she was attempting to put on, because she was shaking so badly. I ended up having to help her with it, or else she wouldn't have finished in time. As it was, the doorbell rang right as we were walking out of her room.

Brianna stood close to my side as I opened to door to Agent Marco. "Come in."

"Thank you."

He stepped inside, and I closed the door behind him. "Can we get you anything to drink?"

"No. Thank you. This shouldn't take long."

I nodded and motioned for him to have a seat on the couch.

With a grace that contradicted his size, he lowered himself down on the couch, resting his elbows on his knees and clasping his hands together. I guided Brianna over to my chair and situated her on my lap, readying myself for whatever news he came to deliver.

Luckily he didn't make us wait. "I received a call from the hospital about an hour ago. Pierce developed a blot clot, and had an aneurism early this morning in his brain. They rushed him to surgery, but they were unable to stop the bleeding in time. He was pronounced dead at just after eight this morning."

Brianna sucked in a lungful of air and fisted my shirt in her hands. "He's . . . he's dead?"

Agent Marco nodded. "Yes."

"What happens now?" I had to know, and so did Brianna.

"For you? Not much. There's some paperwork that has to be done on our end, but we can't very well try a case when the defendant is no longer living." Then to my surprise, Agent Marco directed his attention to Brianna. "You did good the other day, by the way. My one piece of advice? Don't let that bastard win. Get your life back any way you can. Live and grow and be strong. Don't let him keep you a victim. Be a survivor."

I smiled and kissed Brianna's temple. "We're working on it."

He smacked his hands down on his knees and stood. "Good. Now, I need to go prepare for a press conference." Halfway to the door, he stopped and pivoted back in our direction. "I might suggest you hold a press conference of your own, Mr. Coleman. After your testimony, people are going to have questions."

Without giving me time to respond, he headed back toward the door, and within seconds he was gone. I remained where I was, cradling Brianna in my arms.

"People are going to hold it against you that you helped me, aren't they?"

I answered her honestly. "I don't know. Maybe."

"Will you hold a press conference?"

"I need to talk to Oscar first, and the board, but it probably wouldn't be a bad idea. The foundation relies on donations, and what's happened could put a bad taste in the mouths of some of our donors."

"I'm sorry."

"Don't be sorry. I'm not."

We sat there comforting each other until our stomachs began demanding we feed them. I knew there would be fallout, had expected it. The potential cost was worth it in my opinion. Agent Marco was right, however, a press conference might help with damage control.

After we ate lunch, I called Oscar and told him about Agent Marco's suggestion. He agreed it was a good idea, so I called a board meeting for Monday morning, and Oscar was going to arrange for a press conference immediately following. This meant that I would have to leave Brianna, which neither she nor I was thrilled with.

"Can I come with you?"

"You want to come with me to a board meeting?"

She looked down at her shoes. "But it's about me."

I walked over and tilted her chin up. "No. It's about me. About what I did."

"To help me. To save me."

Curling my fingers at the base of her neck, I hugged her to my chest. "You need to stop feeling guilty about this. It was my choice, and I don't regret it for one moment."

She circled her arms around my waist and sighed. "I want to help you. Please, let me help you?"

Sighing, I leaned back and looked into her eyes. I knew what she was asking. Brianna would defend me against anyone, including the throng of people outside that scared her to death.

Closing my eyes, I rested my forehead against hers. When I opened my lids again, meeting her gaze, hers eyes were almost pleading, and I realized that on some level she needed to do this. Not only for me, but also for herself. "All right."

Brianna breathed out a sigh of what felt a lot like relief. Did she really think I would say no after she pleaded with me like that?

"There are conditions, though." I gave her a stern look.

"Okay."

"You are to stay by my side at all times holding my hand. If things begin to get too much for you—if you reach a seven or higher—you are to squeeze my hand twice, like this." I reached for her hand and demonstrated. "The minute we go outside, people are going to start shouting questions at us. At you. You are to ignore them. At least until we get to the press conference."

She nodded.

Sighing, I pulled her back against my chest. I was not looking forward to Monday.

Brianna

The strange thing was, Monday morning felt more normal than the previous three weeks had. Neither of us slept much on Sunday night. But then again, neither of us had gotten a good night's sleep all week—all because of my nightmares.

Stephan tried to help. He'd sacrificed a lot of his own sleep so that I could rest. I don't know what it was about hearing his heartbeat that chased the nightmares away, but it was the only thing that worked. He would lie there reading a book or watching television while I drifted off to sleep, fighting off his own need for slumber so that I could get some of my own.

There were bags under his eyes as he got dressed in his usual suit and tie on Monday morning. I made us both breakfast, and we sat at the kitchen table eating. Normal. The only difference was that this morning, I was going to the office with him. He'd picked out one of the dresses I'd worn to have dinner with his family once. The press conference was going to be in the lobby of the foundation, so we didn't have to worry about the weather. That was good, because according to the news, we were supposed to get three or four inches of snow before nightfall.

He worked beside me to clean up after breakfast and then helped me into my coat. "Are you sure about this? You can still stay home."

"I'm sure. I want to do this for you. For us."

Stephan smiled, but his eyes were full of worry. "Okay. Let's get this over with."

We walked hand in hand out the door to the elevator. The moment we stepped off, into the parking garage, a camera flashed. Another reporter had breached security.

Just as that thought occurred to me, Stephan turned to shield me from the cameraman as much as possible, and two burly men—security—came rushing through a side door and practically tackled the trespasser. He kicked and screamed. Not about them attacking him, but because once they had him on the ground, one of the guards took his camera.

Stephan didn't wait around to see what happened next. He ushered me into his car, and we wound our way out of the parking garage.

As soon as we pulled out onto the street, I realized I'd underestimated the amount of media attention today's press conference was going to receive. When I'd moved back in with Stephan, there'd been roughly ten reporters hanging around his condo building. Today, there were at least fifty. I saw logos for every news outlet in the Twin Cities, plus all the national ones. My stomach began to do flip-flops, and not in the good way it did when Stephan walked into a room.

I reached for Stephan's hand, needing reassurance, and he laced our fingers together, squeezing. "We'll be home by lunch."

"Promise?"

He smiled and kissed the back of my hand. "Promise. And when we get home, we can cuddle up in bed and stay there for the rest of the day."

I couldn't help but smile at that. Spending the rest of the day in bed with Stephan sounded perfect to me, and I knew from experience it wouldn't only involve watching movies. There would be sex as well. Stephan didn't like for me to wear clothes in his bed, so he rarely did either. The two of us naked together in his bed was pretty much a guaranteed avenue to sex.

Rounding the corner, Stephan drove into the parking garage for The Coleman Foundation. I hadn't gotten a good look at the front of the building, but I had to imagine the scene was probably similar to the one outside his condo. We were the big news of the moment.

Stephan parked the car in his spot, which was thankfully not far from the elevators, and helped me out. We held hands as we rode up to the top floor that housed his office and the boardroom.

The elevator doors opened, and I saw Jamie. She looked up and smiled. "Good morning, Mr. Coleman."

"Good morning, Jamie. Is everything set for the meeting this morning?"

"Yes, sir. Everything's in the conference room."

"Wonderful. I'll be in my office. Once everyone's here, come get me."

Stephan steered me into his office and shut the door. Before I knew what was happening, he had my back pressed up against the door, and his mouth was covering mine. It was totally unexpected, but I responded eagerly. A kiss from Stephan was always welcome.

He plunged his tongue into my mouth and lapped possessively against my tongue, my teeth, and the inside of my cheek. I dug my fingers into his arms and held on.

When he pulled back, he was panting, and so was I. "I'd say I'm sorry, but I'm not. I needed that."

I smiled, happy I could give him what he needed, even if it was only a kiss.

"Come. I want to hold you for a while before we have to go face the sharks." I had no idea if he was talking about the board or the press conference to follow.

We were only able to spend about ten minutes cuddling on the couch before there was a knock on the door. Jamie stuck her head in. "Everyone's waiting in the conference room, Mr. Coleman."

"Thank you, Jamie."

The board meeting went about as well as could be expected. Some of the members wanted Stephan to step down, resign. Others, while not approving of his actions, felt that asking him to walk away from the foundation, which was essentially his family's charity, was a bit harsh. All of them, however, were afraid of the media backlash.

By the end of the meeting, it was decided that Stephan would take a leave of absence. I could tell this decision wasn't what he really wanted, but everyone felt it was best for the foundation if he took a backseat for a while —at least until the media frenzy died down.

Stephan and I made our way downstairs to the press conference. The moment the elevator doors opened to the lobby, there were shouts of both our names and questions.

"How did it feel to buy another human being, Mr. Coleman?"

"Brianna, is Stephan forcing you to be his girlfriend?"

I stiffened and edged closer to Stephan's side. He squeezed my hand and walked forward. Thankfully there had been a barrier set up with a stand and microphone for the press conference. Stephan stepped up in front of the microphone, and as if by magic, the room grew quiet. The only exception was the sound of cameras flashing. There were no shouts of questions, though. Everyone was waiting to hear what Stephan had to say.

"Thank you all for coming. I know there has been a lot of speculation lately regarding my activities in relation to the charges and trial of Ian Pierce. Earlier this week, I took the stand at Mr. Pierce's trial for the prosecution. Much of what I said on the stand has already been publicized, so I won't reiterate it here today."

There were a few groans that sounded from the crowd.

Stephan glanced down at me briefly, before readdressing the reporters. "We found out Saturday morning that Ian Pierce did not survive his injuries. I'll be honest in saying I have mixed feelings about this, and so does Brianna. He did horrible things, and he deserved to be punished for them. Death almost seems too easy."

A shout sounded from the back of the room. "What about what you did, Mr. Coleman?"

At first, I thought Stephan was going to ignore it, but he surprised me by answering the woman. "What about what I did? I saw a young woman who needed my help, and I acted on it."

"But you admitted on the stand that she's now your girlfriend."

"Yes, she is."

Stephan looked down at me, his eyes softening. I smiled up at him, trying to ignore the mass of people.

"Brianna? Did Mr. Coleman force you to be his girlfriend?"

I swallowed.

"You don't have to answer them if you don't want to." He said this loud enough for the reporters to hear.

Even though he said I didn't have to answer, I knew that I did. If I remained silent, then everyone would believe he had forced me, and that wouldn't be good for him.

Taking a deep breath, I held Stephan's hand in a death grip and faced the reporters. "No. He didn't force me."

More questions were shouted, including a few about our sexual relationship. I didn't like those, and neither did Stephan. He held up his hand to silence the crowd. "Brianna and I will not be answering any specifics regarding our relationship other than to say that yes, we are in a relationship and that we're happy. This has, however, been a very trying and difficult time for us emotionally with the trial and the media attention. Because of that, I will be taking a leave of absence from The Coleman Foundation. I need to focus on what's most important in my life right now."

He paused and took a long, lingering look over the crowd.

"Thank you all again for coming."

Before they could get over the shock of his announcement, Stephan stepped away from the podium, pulling me with him. A man I didn't know held the elevator door open for us, and we disappeared inside, leaving the reporters shouting questions behind us.

Epilogue

April 11th

Five years ago today, my life changed forever. It was the day I first saw the man I now call my husband.

So much changed for both of us that day. My life certainly changed, but so did his.

I wasn't what he was expecting. I know that now. We've talked about it many times since he bought me five years ago. He thought he'd pay Ian, give me some money, maybe set me up in an apartment, and have me go on with my life. It didn't quite work that way.

As it turned out, I'm glad it didn't. The life I have now is much better than I could have ever hoped it would be. That doesn't mean that we haven't had our share of bumps in the road, though, because we have. A lot of them.

After Ian's death, and Stephan's press conference, he spent the next week transferring everything to the senior vice president of the foundation. Glenn, who I've gotten to know well over the last four years, is a very nice man, and he's done a great job with The Coleman Foundation.

Stephan planned to step away for six months—a leave of absence—to let things die down and to give the two of us some time together. Six months turned into a year, and then two. Eventually Stephan decided it was best to make it official, and he stepped down as president of The Coleman Foundation. He was still on the board and took an active role in what was going on, but it was all behind the scenes. Glenn was now the face of the organization.

Another thing that changed was that Stephan and I no longer live in Minneapolis. Once Stephan realized that he would no longer be head of the foundation—that he didn't need to stay in the city—we talked about it and decided it would be best to get away from the constant media scrutiny. Even with so much time passing, it wasn't uncommon for him to get stopped in the streets and questioned. I didn't feel comfortable going out without him, and he didn't feel comfortable letting me. We wanted a life together, and we wanted it without having to worry about the press every time we stepped outside.

Last summer we officially moved out of the city. We now live about an hour outside of the Cities, less than twenty minutes from his aunt and uncle, in a house that sits along the Minnesota River. I can sit on our back porch and watch the water flow by, and I often do. Stephan also set up a cozy reading area for me upstairs that has a large picture window where I can look out and see the water when it's too cold for me to go outside. It's perfect, and I love it. I've spent many hours reading and writing in my journal there.

"Brianna?"

I looked up from my journal as Stephan peeked inside the library.

"Ah. There you are. Are you about ready to go?" He lowered his gaze and noticed the journal in my hands. His face softened, and he walked over to give me a kiss. "Finish writing, and then meet me downstairs. I'll text my aunt and let her know we'll be a little late."

"Yes, Sir."

He strolled back out of the room, and I returned to my writing.

I need to wrap this up. It's Sunday, and Stephan and I are making our weekly trip to Diane and Richard's house for dinner. I'm happy to say that Stephan and his uncle have repaired their relationship. Richard has gotten to know me more, and he's seen us together enough to know that Stephan isn't abusing me. Our relationship, the way it is, is what I want—what we both want. Stephan is my husband, but he is also my Dom. There is no separating the two, and I love him just the way he is.

Knowing I needed to hurry but feeling the need to finish, I pressed my lips together and continued.

Once we were settled in our new house, Stephan began encouraging me to start driving again. To get the feel of being behind the wheel of a car once more, he had me driving around an obstacle course he'd set up. We have ten acres surrounding our house, so there was plenty of room in case I messed up. It took over a month of practice before I felt comfortable driving on real roads.

Another thing that's changed is that I am able to go into town by myself. Granted, Le Sueur isn't anything like Minneapolis. It's a small town, not a big city. At first, Stephan went with me, even after I was okay to drive. It wasn't until spring that I ventured out on my own.

I also went back to school. There was a local community college that had a GED program I was able to enroll in over the winter. As of two weeks ago, I have my diploma. Or at least the closest thing I can get to it at this point. It's a good feeling, and Stephan and I have been discussing me taking more courses at the college this fall.

We still have yet to play in the playroom he set up in the attic. I go up there sometimes and walk around, touch things. And we play in our bedroom, and in other parts of the house, but not there. Not yet. Last week, he had me write down a list of goals for the coming year, and one of those had been for us to play, at least once, in the playroom. He'd been surprised but happy, too, I think.

It's hard to believe it's been five years. Sometimes it feels like it was yesterday, and other times it's such a distant memory that it feels as if decades have passed. I'm not frightened of my own shadow anymore. From time to time, a loud noise will still set me off if I'm not expecting it, but Stephan and my new therapist, Dr. Katlin, said that was to be expected. It would take time—a lot of time—but I'm doing it. I'm living my life, and I'm happy.

Closing my journal, I laid it down in my lap and took a minute to look outside at the river. There was a log wedged along the bank, barely hanging on, ready to be swept away by the tide. I was that log. Sometimes I still felt that way—that at any moment something or someone would come along, and I'd be swept away in the uncontrollable current.

There was one thing I had that the log didn't, though. I had Stephan. And I had our friends. I wouldn't get swept away. I wouldn't get lost again in the world. They wouldn't let me.

Smiling and wiping the tears from my cheeks, I stood and went to place my journal on Stephan's desk for him to read later. A lot of things had changed, but one thing hadn't—not since the day he'd walked into my life. Stephan was the most important thing in my world, and he always would be. That would never change.

CPSIA information can be obtained at www.ICGtesting.com
Printed in the USA
LVOW12s0055300514

387712LV00013B/262/P